CAPTURED

Aline thought she could not bear it, that he would continue to kiss her until she melted. Then abruptly, James pulled away.

He stared at her for a moment. His chest was rising and falling and his face was flushed, his eyes shockingly bright. Aline gazed back at him, unable to speak.

"Now," James said. "You will get back on that horse, and we will ride hard and fast. Do you understand?"

Aline realized that the kiss that had just shaken her to her roots had done nothing to James. He hated her, and if there was heat in his lips when they took hers, it was the heat of anger, not desire.

She drew herself up straight. "Yes," she said icily, "I understand perfectly. I am your prisoner, and I must do as you say. I have been aware of that from the moment you seized me. We shall always be enemies."

"That may be, milady," he returned, "but you are my enemy wife."

Books by Candace Camp

Published by HarperPaperbacks

Harper
Monogram

Evensong

⚔ CANDACE CAMP ⚔

HarperPaperbacks
A Division of HarperCollins*Publishers*

This is a work of fiction. The characters, incidents, and dialogues are products of the author's imagination and are not to be construed as real. Any resemblance to actual events or persons, living or dead, is entirely coincidental.

HarperPaperbacks *A Division of* HarperCollins*Publishers*
10 East 53rd Street, New York, N.Y. 10022

Cover illustration by John Ennis

First printing: April 1995

Printed in the United States of America

HarperPaperbacks, HarperMonogram, and colophon are trademarks of HarperCollins*Publishers*

❖ 10 9 8 7 6 5 4 3 2 1

Evensong

Prologue

November, 1162

Aline stopped and looked up at the massive gray castle before them. It loomed ominously, the thick outer wall topped with guarded battlements and unbroken by windows. Here and there along the top were crosses where archers could shoot their arrows down upon anyone approaching the castle. It was a fortress, heavily guarded and almost impregnable.

The cold November wind swept around her, teasing into her hood to touch her cheeks and nose. Aline shivered, as much at the thought of going into the castle as at the wind. But she could not stay out here. If she did, the man she loved would surely die.

She glanced nervously at the men beside her. There were only six of them in their small band, and of those six only two were fighting men—and one of those only a lad of sixteen and not yet knighted. It seemed absurd to think that they could steal into this armed fortress and rescue a man. Yet they must; they were his only hope.

Nor could she forget that, in some way, it was her fault that he was here. It had been over a year now since she had first met Sir James and the duke . . . since her first act of folly had set all the events into motion. And yet, she could not regret it, either, for if she had not taken those wrong steps, she would never have found his love.

Aline drew a breath and started forward. Everything from the moment she had first met him had been leading up to this. Tonight she would succeed in saving him, or else they would die together.

1

October, 1161

The knife sliced into the wood only inches from Aline's head. Several people gasped. Aline's eyes widened in fright, and she tugged in vain against the firm leather straps that bound her wrists and ankles. Another knife thwacked into the board beside her leg and, in quick succession, three more followed, outlining the right side of her body. All around the hall, shouts of encouragement and admiration went up, and the knights began to clap and stamp their feet.

It was a very appreciative audience.

In fact, it seemed to Aline that this audience was all too appreciative. The men had been growing rowdier by the minute. They had hooted and clapped and stomped their feet through the tumbling portions of the show and her father's juggling. When Aline had walked out in her skimpy Saracen costume, her skin darkened with walnut oil so that she appeared mysteriously foreign, the entire great hall had erupted into cheers and whistles. Aline had been grateful for her tinted skin, which had hidden her blushes. Her new Saracen costume was far too revealing—Gyrth's doing, of course.

She glared at Gyrth now as he strolled up to her to retrieve his knives. Behind him Gemma and Beorn, the dwarves, went into a mocking imitation of the knife-thrower's act, in order to fill the dead space while Gyrth set up for the next part.

Gyrth began to pull out his knives, grinning evilly at Aline, unperturbed by her anger. The man was a pig, Aline thought, and she had grown to hate him. Once her father, Harald, had been the leader of their little troupe of entertainers, his skills as master jongleur making him the natural choice. But since Gyrth had joined them, he had been assuming more and more control of the group.

He was a bad-tempered, greedy man, and he had disliked Aline from the first moment. He had thought it his due to have her for his woman, since his formidable skills with a knife made him the most dangerous man in the company, as well as one of the most popular performers. When Aline had haughtily turned him down, backed up by her father's position with the troupe and her own fiery disposition, Gyrth had accepted it with ill favor. Aline suspected that if she had not been so important to his act, he would have forced himself on her or cast her out, as he had an older couple who could no longer perform their acrobatics well. But her dancing garnered as much applause as Gyrth's knife-throwing or Gemma's and Beorn's amusing acrobatics, so all he could do was glower at her and get his revenge in subtle ways— such as this costume.

She was supposed to be dressed like a woman from a Saracen harem, though members of the troupe had only the haziest idea what such a person wore. Aline's flaming red hair was tied back and hidden beneath a headdress and veil. Another veil hung across her face, obscuring everything but her eyes. The rest of her garment, too, was made up primarily of veils. One of them went around her back and up diagonally across her breasts, tying at the neck. Another, of a different color but equally insubstantial material, followed the same pattern but in the opposite direction, winding down from the neck across her breasts and tying in the back. Even the two veils together did not completely hide her firm, full breasts, and she wore two more large scarves wrapped artfully about her torso.

A wide belt of tiny bells, matching the circlets of bells around her ankles and wrists, held the bottom of her costume to her hips. This part of her attire was the bottom half of a thin tunic called a bliaut, which she wore a little loose to enable her to dance and onto which were sewn several more veils. The veils, dangling as they did by one corner, swayed intriguingly as she moved. During the fast parts of her dance, Aline knew, they would whirl out around her, exposing entirely too much of the shape of her legs beneath the bliaut. It was an expensive costume, Aline realized, made almost entirely of silks, and it was also beautiful, the prettiest thing Signy's skillful fingers had ever sewn. But she felt almost naked in it, especially when Gyrth ran his hot, piggy eyes down her body—or when she stepped into the great hall and was met by the immediately lustful stares of several scores of men.

"I will not wear this again!" she hissed at Gyrth as he bent to pull out the knives at her feet.

"Don't be a fool. These lusty knights will be peppering us with gold coins when you dance."

Aline ground her teeth. "That is exactly what I'm talking about. They will be pawing and grabbing at me."

"Oh, I forgot," Gyrth sneered. "You are too good for such things, aren't you? Or is it that you're just too cold?"

"Yes," Aline returned levelly. She refused to let Gyrth intimidate her. "I am too good for that. Anyone is. Being a dancer doesn't make one a whore."

Gyrth shot her a venomous look. "I wouldn't get so puffed up with pride if I were you, wench; I might have to cut you down a bit."

"Are you threatening me?" Aline had a strong will and a ready temper, and she had never knuckled under to any man. She wore a knife strapped to her thigh, just in case she ran into trouble when her father or the others weren't there to help her, and she made sure there was a handy slit in her skirts, even her costumes, so that she could reach in and grab the weapon.

"Nay, I don't threaten. One day you'll push me too far, and you'll find out."

The dwarves had finished their act of buffoonery, and Gyrth strode back to his mark, holding his knives up in the air. The crowd roared and stamped its approval. Aline thought grimly that nothing could get a group of knights so excited as the possibility of bloodshed—especially if there was a barely clad young female involved.

Gyrth turned so that he was facing away from Aline and began the more difficult trick of hurling his knives at her over his shoulder. One or two of his throws came uncomfortably close, but Aline did not flinch. She suspected that he was trying to frighten her, but she had complete faith in his knife-throwing skills—and in his reluctance to mar the beauty that drew gold coins to them.

With each of his throws, the noises from the men grew louder. It made Aline nervous. She glanced toward the dais, wondering if the lord's lady or any other women were there. The presence of women would keep the knights a little tamer. She was relieved to see that Lord Cambrook, the owner of the keep, sat with a lady beside him and that there were two more women at the table. Then her gaze fell on another man at the table, and she could not look away.

He was the most handsome man she had ever seen. His hair was jet black, as were his straight, distinctive eyebrows. Aline could not see the color of his eyes in the dim light of the candles, but they were arresting, accented by the slash of dark brows above them. His cheekbones were high, his nose straight, and his mouth—which was curved up faintly in a smile—mobile and finely etched. Even sitting down as he was, it was obvious that he was tall and slimly built, though with the wide shoulders and muscular arms of a swordsman. He was dressed in soft blue velvet, and a great ruby ring on one finger winked richly in the light of the candles. Aline was certain that he would have looked just as highborn, just as breathtakingly handsome, if he had been dressed in a monk's robe.

Not that anyone could have mistaken this man for a monk, no matter how he was dressed. There was too much sensuality in the mouth, too much virility in the lean body, too much interest in the eyes that were now turned full force on her. He watched her steadily; his eyes never turned toward the man throwing the knives with such consummate skill, and barely flickered when dagger point after dagger point thudded into the board around Aline.

Aline looked away from the man, but her gaze was inexorably drawn back to him. He was still watching her, his eyes glittering. His forefinger rubbed across his mouth slowly, and Aline's stomach was suddenly jittery.

The performance ended, and Gyrth took his bows, then walked over to unfasten her bonds. There was more cheering, and she and Gyrth bowed together. Gyrth moved to the back of the hall, taking his board and knives, and Aline was left in the center by herself. She bowed her head and put her hands together, posing for the dance.

Behind her, Aline's father began to talk about the mysteries of the East, spinning a tale about the Saracen dancing girl who had found her way to their troupe. Slowly, faintly, almost indistinguishable at first, the pipe began to play. Aline walked forward, her movement slow and graceful, until she was right in front of the high table. She saw the lady get up and murmur something to the other two women, and the three of them left the room. Aline was the only woman in the room, except for one or two serving maids. Her stomach clenched.

Aline curtsied low, bending her head down to her knee, her veils billowing around her. She remained that way for a long moment, while the tune of the pipe became louder and more insistent. The tap of the drum sounded. It came again.

Gracefully, Aline flowed up until she was erect, arms held high over her head. She looked down at the floor. She clicked the finger cymbals on her fingers. Her hips swayed, stirring the soft jingle of the bells. She lowered her arms, twisting them so that the bells around her wrists tinkled. Her feet started a steady rhythm, showering the air with the crystal-clear sound. She began her houri dance.

It was slow and sinuous at first, gradually building in speed. Her arms writhed, her feet stamped, her hips swayed. Aline glanced up and met the glittering pale eyes of the handsome lord. There was a young lord on the other side of Cambrook, a merry-looking stripling, probably not as old as Aline herself, with pale blond hair and fair skin. He began to pound his hand down on the table in time to the music. The idea caught on, and soon most of the men were stomping or clapping or banging to the insistent beat. Aline whirled away from the dais. The dark-haired lord's stare unnerved her, taking the breath from her lungs. She swayed faster now, moving seductively to the wail of the pipe. She began to turn, whirling her way around the room. Coins rained down on the floor, and Gemma scurried around, trying unobtrusively to pick them all up. Aline did her best to block out the noise, to not even think of the men, especially not that one at the high table. She concentrated on the music, moving to the beat, as she came full circle around the room and back to the front of the hall.

Suddenly the handsome knight on the dais drew his sword and used it to sweep aside the dishes in front of him. They fell, clattering, to the floor. The man vaulted over the table, startling everyone, and jumped lightly down from the dais to stand in front of Aline, his sword in hand.

Aline froze; the drums missed a beat and the pipes wavered uncertainly. Aline stared at the man, incapable of speech. She could see close-up that his eyes were a light color, blue or gray, very bright even in the dim light, and that he was, if anything, even more handsome than he had appeared from a distance. His teeth were bared slightly—whether in a smile or a snarl, Aline wasn't sure. She hung for a moment in terror, wondering what she could have possibly done to anger this man.

He lifted the heavy sword, pointing it straight at her chest, and slowly moved it toward her. Aline's breath caught. Transfixed by his fiery gaze, she could not move. The sword tip drew closer, closer. It caught a fold of one of the veils she wore over her chest and lifted it off. He pulled back the sword, and the soft, colorful material drifted to the floor.

Aline's knees went wobbly with relief. The men all over the hall broke out into cheers and clapping. The young blond man on the dais burst into laughter and lifted his goblet in a toast toward the dark-haired nobleman, calling, "Sir James, Knight of the Veils!"

It was a cry that was taken up all around the huge room. Aline's fear flamed into fury. *This man had scared her senseless—just to entertain his boorish companions!* It was all she could do not to fly at him, screeching and hitting, but her common sense was strong enough to hold her back. It would be madness for one such as she, a common dancing girl, to attack a knight. At best he would knock her down and she would probably get lashes for her insolence. At worst, he would turn that heavy sword on her and slice her head clean from her shoulders.

Eyes blazing, Aline whirled away from him, starting her dance again. To her surprise, she felt a tug on her skirt, and when she looked back she saw that Sir James had neatly sliced off one of the lower veils. She realized then that he must mean to keep at it until she stood naked before him. His face was slack with desire, and he swayed a little as he stood there, watching her with hot eyes. He was both drunk and full of passion, a dangerous combination in a man—especially a strong, armed man. But Aline was too angry to be scared by him now. She despised this man; he wanted to debase and humiliate her.

Noblemen felt it was their right to take any maiden who was not of their rank, and a woman could not refuse them outright if she valued her life. In the past, Aline had had to cajole, even beg, then seize the first opportunity to slip away.

She backed up from the man and turned her retreat into a dance, swaying and moving her arms in seductive movements even as her feet shuffled slowly backward. The knight followed her, his sword snaking out to slice off another veil, but Aline nimbly moved to the side, and he missed. Howls and laughter broke out among the men, and they called out derisively to Sir James.

Out of the corner of her eye, Aline saw her father hovering worriedly at the edge of the crowd. She looked straight at him and shook her head once, firmly. He would be killed if he tried to interfere with this knight.

Aline knew that her only hope was to get as close as she could to the doors, while lulling the assembled knights into thinking she was dancing. When she was close enough, she would run for the doors and hope that the knights were too drunk and lazy to pursue her. It was a risky plan, but she shuddered to think of what would happen to her if she did not escape.

As she drew closer and closer to the doors, however, two other knights scrambled over their tables, drawing their swords and blocking her way. Grinning, they too began to advance on her.

Aline's heart knocked wildly inside her ribs. *She*

was doomed! Obviously they planned to encircle her and slice her clothes from her, bit by bit. Then, she was certain, they would fall on her like animals of prey. Tears sprang into her eyes as she thought of them forcibly taking the maidenhead she had so long preserved.

She danced frantically away from her new pursuers, back toward Sir James. He cast a hard look at the two men and said coldly, "Stay. She is mine."

He hadn't even raised his voice, but the men backed away immediately. At least she would be spared that, Aline thought, and hope began to rise in her anew. This Sir James seemed possessive of her. Perhaps if she intrigued him enough, he would want to bed her in private, away from this crowd of men. It would be far easier to escape him outside the great hall than it was here.

Her mind busily working, Aline pasted what she hoped was a come-hither smile on her face and danced slowly toward Sir James. He watched her, his sword at the ready, his eyes staring intently into hers. Aline moved sinuously, gazing at him in a way that said she danced only for him, and she was rewarded by the light that flared in his eyes. His mouth widened sensually, and he took a step toward her. Aline advanced and retreated, moving from this side to that, flirting with him in her movements, careful not to move too much for fear that the naked sword edge might graze her skin, yet enough that it hinted of a hunt and capture.

She was hot and tired; she had danced far longer than usual. Sweat glistened on her oil-darkened skin. Sir James's eyes moved lingeringly down her body. With a seemingly careless flick of his wrist, he lifted another veil, and then another. As the music picked up its tempo, veil after veil fell, until at last she was clad in nothing more than the two scarves wrapped diagonally across her breasts and the thin, sweat-dampened bliaut that clung to her legs.

Aline whirled frantically. The pipes wailed. The drums beat frantically. Pulses throbbed with the insistent beat, and everyone leaned forward as the music built.

Her father started toward them with a strangled cry, but a knight seized him and held him, despite his desperate struggles. The noise of the men drowned out his cries.

Abruptly the music crashed to its climax and ended. Aline dropped to the floor, exhausted, and curled over, forehead bowed to the floor and arms flung out wide in a submissive Eastern bow.

For an instant the great hall was utterly still. Then Sir James dropped his sword and took two steps forward, bending down to take Aline's arms in his. He pulled her up. Her head fell back and she looked up at him, trying to read his face for his intentions. He slung Aline over his shoulder and strode out of the room. Behind them the crowd of men burst into wild cheers.

2

Aline closed her eyes, dizzy from a combination of relief and her being carried upside down over Sir James's shoulder. The knight took the stairs two at a time, with an agility that belied his drunken state. Jarred against his hard shoulder, Aline felt every step. She was glad that he had snatched her up and carried her from the hall; it was, after all, what she had hoped and prayed for from the moment the other men had begun to encircle her. At the least, she would not be raped by the whole hallful of men. At best, her wits—and the knife strapped to her thigh—might get her out of this predicament unscathed. While Sir James was obviously superior to her in size, strength, and martial skill, he was only one man and therefore a great deal easier to elude than a whole pack of them. Moreover, he had dropped his sword in the hall below, and, most importantly, he had consumed a great quantity of Cambrook's strong mead.

On the other hand, Aline knew that she was agile

and quick, with great control of her muscles, from the years she had spent dancing and tumbling. She also had the advantage of being clear-witted and desperate. She was certain that it was far more important to her to escape this man than it was to him to take her. There were, after all, plenty of other women around the castle who would be more than willing to grace the inordinately handsome Sir James's bed. Some women, she knew, were proud simply to have caught a nobleman's attention, even knowing how callously, if not contemptuously, they would be dismissed after the lord had been sated.

James strode down a hallway and into a bedroom, kicking the door closed behind him. Aline was glad to notice that he had not dropped down the bar to the door; it would be much easier to get out. James hauled Aline off his shoulder and set her on the floor.

Aline straightened the veil and headdress. She wanted to avoid this man's seeing the color of her hair if she could. She knew instinctively that the less he knew about her the better, and her flaming red hair was distinctive. If she managed to escape and he pursued her, he would be looking for a dark-haired, dark-skinned woman, not the milky-skinned redhead she would be when she scrubbed away the nut oil.

She faced him defiantly, her hand edging to her leg, near the slit in her skirts. Sir James gazed back at her, his eyes moving slowly down her form. They lingered on her breasts, barely covered by the veils. The sweat-damp cloth clung, outlining their full curves and revealing the hard buttons of her nipples. As James studied her, her nipples hardened traitorously, and he smiled.

Aline hated his smile; no doubt he thought the reaction of her nipples was to his passionate gaze, not to the coolness of the air against the damp cloth.

"By the Rood, but you are beautiful," he murmured huskily, his voice slightly slurred by drink. He reached out and brushed his knuckles across the thrusting bud of one nipple.

Aline gasped and took a step backward. It felt as if fire had touched her.

Sir James smiled languorously, his eyelids drooping down over his bright blue eyes. "Come, girl, don't be afraid of me. I won't hurt you." He moved toward her, speaking in a deep, soothing voice. "I just want what you were offering me downstairs."

His hands went to her waist; the feel of his fingers on her bare skin startled Aline, and she shivered. He smiled, his thumbs stroking over her satiny stomach, and he pulled her closer. "That's better. You made me hard as a stone just watching you. I'm afraid you'll keep me awake half the night, the way you affect me."

He lowered his head toward hers, his hand coming up to the veil that covered the lower half of her face and ripping it off. An instant later his lips were on hers, sinking into them, moving them apart to admit his wild, questing tongue. He tasted of the honeyed mead, and his mouth was hot. Aline was rocked with sensations. She had been kissed before; some men she had even allowed to kiss her. But none had ever kissed her quite like this, somehow sweet and fiery all at once, and none had ever left her breathless or made her feel as if sparks were shooting throughout her body.

Sir James's hand came up, sliding over the bare skin of her stomach, and came to rest upon her breast. His thumb circled her nipple, making it stand out against the thin material. Tingles of desire ran along Aline's nerves, startling her, and her abdomen began to grow hot and melting. She trembled with anticipation. His other hand was at her waist, and he slid it down to her buttocks. His fingers dug into the flesh of her hips, pressing her pelvis intimately against him.

Aline gasped. The touch of his manhood hard against her skin jarred Aline from her strange trance. She brought both her arms up against him and shoved with all her might, at the same time jamming her foot down hard on his instep. If he had not been relaxed and unsuspecting, she knew, she would never have moved his much larger frame, but, taken off guard, he stumbled back, letting out a grunt at the pain.

"What in—" He came up against a small trunk as he moved back. It hit him right at the knees, and he lost his balance and fell backward onto the floor.

Aline had to stifle a laugh—he looked so comical, lying there on his back, like an overturned turtle, staring at her with a befuddled expression. He was more drunk than he had appeared, she knew, to have fallen so easily; he had simply been good at concealing it. Still, she wasn't about to take any chances. She whipped out her dagger and held it threateningly in front of her as she backed over to the door.

"Are you mad?" he asked, straight black brows rushing together in anger. "What the hell are you doing?" He rolled to the side and rose to his feet, staggering only slightly as he did so.

Aline's heart pounded harder; he was a much more menacing foe on his feet. But she had reached the door by now, and she groped behind herself for the latch and jerked it open.

"Only protecting myself!" she lashed out, then jumped into the hall and slammed the door shut.

She fled down the hall, expecting any moment to hear the door open behind her and his footsteps in pursuit. She ran as fast as she could, not knowing where she was going. She passed the broad staircase up which Sir James had carried her, but she dared not take it, since it went down into the great hall. She prayed there were smaller staircases that led down, so that she could escape without being seen by any of Lord Cambrook's guests.

Another hallway crossed the one she was in, and she turned into it. She knew that she had to get out of the castle immediately. It wasn't enough to have evaded Sir James this once. He would probably be roaring for her head after the way she had just insulted him. He would call out all his men and search the castle for her. She had to find her parents and tell them what happened, then run for her life, hoping that there would be a way out of the castle besides the huge main gates, which were already shut for the night.

At the end of the hallway, there was a small staircase, and Aline started down it gratefully. It was very dim, lit by only a single rush candle at each floor, and she could not move quickly. It was probably just as well, for she was out of breath from racing down the hallways like a madwoman. She followed the winding stairs, dragging in great gulps of breath. When she reached the bottom of the stairs, she was relieved to find a small door leading out into the yard. She glanced around, trying to get her bearings. Then she saw the low wooden building that contained the brew-house and the kitchen, fire hazards that were usually set apart from the main castle, and she hurried toward the building, hoping that the troupe would have returned to it by now. When they were allowed to, they slept in the warmth of the kitchen, and it was there that they had stored their possessions.

As Aline eased open the door, she heard the rumble

of angry voices. She peered into the large room and saw the company of performers knotted together in one corner, while the servants went unconcernedly about their work, cleaning the remainder of the dishes.

Aline's mother, Bera, was seated on a stool and leaning against a wall, sobbing, her face in her hands. Gemma and Signy were bending over her, trying to comfort her. The men were gathered around Aline's father, Harald, who stood facing Gyrth. Harald's face was red with anger and he was shouting. Gyrth stood with his arms crossed over his chest, looking back stolidly at the older man.

"You should have taken her off with you after your act!" Harald was raging. "She shouldn't have done that dance in front of a crowd of drunken knights!"

Gyrth grimaced. "She'll be all right. It was only one man."

"Only!"

"It'll probably do her good," Gyrth went on insolently.

Harald roared unintelligibly and leaped at the man. Quickly, Beorn, the dwarf, and Wulfram, the other male acrobat of their troupe, grabbed Harald and held him back. Wulfram jerked his head toward Gyrth.

"Go on, man," he ordered tersely. "Get out and let him cool off."

"You think I'm scared of that old man?" Gyrth asked scornfully.

"No. No one thinks that. But if you think it'll do any good for this troupe to have our master jongleur beaten senseless, then Harald was right and you have run mad."

It was a bold speech for Wulfram, a normally silent and diffident man who let his tumbling skills speak for him. Gyrth looked insulted, and he glanced from

Harald to Wulfrum and back as if he weren't sure whom he should swing at. Hastily Aline stepped into the room.

"No, wait. Papa, it's all right. Mama, please, stop weeping. I'm fine."

Everyone in the troupe swung around to stare at her in amazement. Gemma was the first to come to her senses. She left Bera's side and hurried over to Aline.

"What happened, child?"

"Nothing. That is—well, I got away."

Bera let out a high, thin cry, and ran to her daughter and threw her arms around her.

Harald rose slowly. "You mean, you're not . . ."

"No, I'm fine. But we needs must hurry. I—I hit him and he stumbled and fell. And I threatened him with a knife. That's how I escaped."

Gemma's jaw dropped and she stared at Aline in amazement. "You refused him? You hit him?"

Aline nodded.

"Why, he's the handsomest man I ever seen!" Gemma exclaimed. "Do you know who he is?"

"Sir James, that's all I know."

"He's James of Norwen, the Earl of Norwen's bastard brother, that's who!" Gyrth burst out wrathfully. "He's a friend of the king and one of the most powerful men in the country! And now, thanks to you, he is our enemy."

"You have to get out of here," Harald told Aline. "He'll be after you."

"Nay!" Gyrth contradicted. "We have to send her straight back to him. She's ruined us all! They'll punish every one of us if they can't find her."

"I'm not turning my daughter over to any man!" Harald flared.

"And I won't be sent back," Aline added firmly. "I'm leaving." Aline picked up the bundle which contained her personal belongings from the troupe's pile in the corner of the kitchen and slung it over her back. "You can tell those beasts that you haven't seen me."

"You think that will stop them from spitting us on their swords, just in case we're lying?" Gyrth retorted sarcastically. "Or to make an example of what happens to a lowly jongleur who defies a lord?"

"That's what they will do to my daughter," Harald snapped. "Do you think I would allow that? Come along, Bera, we shall leave as well." He pulled their bundles from the pile of belongings, handing one to his wife and hanging two heavier ones over his back.

"We should all go," Wulfram said quickly. "What good will it do you to give her over to the lord, Gyrth? He'll kill her or, at best, beat her for defying him. And you'll lose the dancer who brought in that bagful of silver tonight that's hanging around your waist."

The others were already leaping to their packs and tying them up. Gyrth cast a baleful glance at Aline, and she knew that he would take great pleasure in turning her over to Sir James to be punished for her insolence. But she also knew he realized that Wulfram was right, and that he was too greedy to give up the money Aline brought to the troupe.

"God's bones!" he swore, and clomped over to grab his own things. "All right—we will flee. But, by Mary, you better not play any more of your tricks, wench!"

"I was not playing any tricks," Aline retorted heatedly. "I am not a whore, and I will not be treated like one."

"Come, come, no time to be arguing now," Beorn entreated. "We've no time to lose."

"Where do we go?" Gyrth asked, leading them to the door. "The gates are closed for the night."

Though the times were relatively peaceful, now that Henry was king instead of Stephen, no one was foolish enough to leave his castle vulnerable to attack.

The kitchen servants had finished with their jobs and were now curling up to sleep in front of the fire, ranked in order of their importance, with the lowliest potscrubber the farthest away from the blaze. One or two of them glanced up in curiosity as the entertainers slipped out the door, but the rest were indifferent. Everyone knew that the people who performed were a world apart, strange beings without any place in the world. Their actions were incomprehensible to most of these serfs, whose short lives began and ended within the radius of a few miles, often within the same castle.

"The guard's gate will be open," Beorn said as they stepped outside. "His lordship isn't expecting attack, and they keep a loose guard. I always check our escape routes, just in case." The tiny man was accustomed to using his wits to compensate for what he lacked in size, and he had more than once learned the wisdom of being able to flee danger. "Follow me."

He led them through the courtyard into the outer ward and across to the massive main gates, closed and barred for the night. Beside them was a small wooden door, also barred, but far easier to open. Next to it stood a bored guard, leaning against his pike.

Beorn stopped and motioned the others into the shadows. He whispered, "I'll entertain the guard whilst the rest of you slip out."

"But how will you get out?" Aline asked, worried.

"Ah, you'll see, he'll let me go. That's what I'll be entertaining him for." He walked across toward the guard, exaggerating his odd bowlegged gait. "Good sir!" he called as he drew close. "I've come to beg a boon from you."

"Have you now?" The guard's voice was surly, but, welcoming the break in his monotonous routine, he turned to look at the little man. "And why should I grant you a favor?"

Beorn swept off his hat, a silly peaked thing with a moth-eaten feather adorning it, and swept him a deep bow. "Because, my good man, I can make you laugh."

"A jackass can make me laugh."

"Indeed?" Beorn began to bray, throwing himself forward onto his hands and kicking up his feet behind him in imitation of a donkey.

The soldier grinned and shifted to a more comfortable position, turning his back to the small door. The troupe slipped along the wall in single file, keeping well in the shadows. When they reached the door, Gyrth pushed the heavy bar up and off, then eased the door open. The hinges squeaked, but Beorn, who was keeping an eye on the other troupe members, set up a series of brays to cover the noise and flipped backward several times, keeping the soldier's eyes riveted to him.

One by one Aline and the others edged through the door, while Beorn kept up a comical patter about his desire to visit a wench in the neighboring village without his shrewish wife finding out. People usually assumed that he and Gemma were married, though they were not, in fact. He demonstrated how Gemma would leap and scream, bouncing high in the air, then landing in a roll and bounding up again, punctuating the performance with high-pitched shrieks. The soldier was roaring with laughter and holding his sides by the time the last of them had escaped. The troupe members crept across the drawbridge, usually kept lowered in these safer times, and scampered across the flat, open land to the cover of the copse of trees beyond.

Sure enough, a few minutes later Beorn came bounding across the bridge and ran for the copse, too. As quickly as they could, they slipped through the trees and made off to the east, where the woods lay. It was difficult going in the dark, for though the moon was full that night, the farther they went into the forest, the less and less they could see of the moon. Finally they stopped in the first clearing they found and curled up on the ground. Aline snuggled close to her mother, sharing a blanket with her. For the first time that night, she felt safe. Letting out a sigh, she fell asleep.

Aline was awakened the next morning by the twittering of birds and the rustling of small animals. She sat up slowly and looked around, yawning and stretching. The trees were thick around them. The others were gradually coming awake, too. Aline slipped off with her mother and the other women, careful not to go too far away. She washed away most of her walnut oil stain in a stream and dressed in a bliaut and a *sayon*, a shoulder cape and hood of the sort usually worn by peasants, leaving enough of her red hair visible that no one would mistake her for a Saracen dancing girl.

Gemma came over to Aline as she was drying her hair and squatted down beside her. "Why did you refuse that handsome lord? I would have thought that one was a man who could make you forget your nunnish ways."

"I have told you: I shall not be some baron's leman," Aline said flatly.

Aline had acquired a healthy dislike of the nobility and their arrogant ways over the years, and last night's experience had only deepened that contempt.

She looked challengingly at Gemma, expecting her to say that Aline had too much pride. It was something that had been pointed out to her more than once. However, Gemma merely shrugged.

"Well, perhaps you don't want to be a mistress, but you don't want to be married, either," she pointed out in a reasonable voice. "Remember that nice goldsmith who was so smitten by you? He offered you marriage."

"But I didn't love him."

Gemma looked at Aline as if she'd lost her mind. What did love matter when one had an offer of a stable, comfortable life instead of spending one's days traveling around the countryside, never sure where the next meal was coming from?

"Do you like the dancing that much?" Gemma asked, puzzled.

"No." Aline wasn't one of those people, like her father and mother, who loved the life of the traveling performer too much to settle down. She thought she could give up performing easily enough—she could certainly live without the vagaries of weather or the uncertainties of living by one's wits or having to elude the groping hands that reached for her as she danced. And she thought it might be quite pleasant to stay in one place for a long time, maybe even the rest of her life. But only if there were a man she loved beside her.

The nobility might marry for considerations of wealth, power, and family; even the members of the merchant and craftsman classes looked to alliances and dowries when they married. But Aline had grown up with the example of her parents' marriage, and to her the only reason to marry was for love. Her mother,

Bera, had been the illegitimate daughter of a knight and a serving girl, and because of her connection to the lord of the manor, she had been raised to be one of the higher servants in the castle, doing sewing and such easier tasks. Bera had seen Harald performing at the keep where she lived, and he had seen her. He had performed at his best and received an invitation from the master of the keep to spend the winter there and while away the cold, boring hours for them. Harald had agreed, though he normally didn't stay in any one place for long. But he had been caught by Bera's golden eyes and bright red hair, and he had stayed.

When spring came, Harald left—and Bera went with him, throwing aside the security and comfort she had known in her father's keep for the uncertainty of the road and an entertainer's life. She had loved Harald too much to live without him.

Aline had grown up with that love; to her it seemed the only way to live one's life. She would not settle for less. However, Gemma could not understand her scruples, and she usually attributed Aline's reluctance to a coldness in her disposition. It was hopeless, Aline knew, to try to explain it to her.

Satisfied that she once again looked like a peasant girl, not some exotic Saracen dancing maiden, Aline balled up the dancing costume and walked with the other women back to the camp. Beorn had already managed to get a small fire going, and Gyrth was skinning a squirrel he had killed for their breakfast. Aline went to the fire and dropped her dancing costume in it, watching with satisfaction as the flames quickly caught it. She looked up to find Gyrth glowering at her.

"What do you think you're doing?" he said.

"That's the end of the Saracen dancer," she replied

calmly. "You must see that we can't possibly use her anymore, or Sir James will find out and track us down. I understand he's a very powerful man."

"Aye, that's right." Wulfram nodded sagely. "I hear he's well loved by his brother the Earl, bastard or no."

Gyrth grimaced, but subsided, seeing the force of their arguments. He finished gutting and skinning the squirrel and spitted it, putting it over the fire. As Gyrth turned aside and began to clean off his knife, Harald cleared his throat and spoke up.

"That's something we need to talk about—avoiding Sir James's wrath," he said gravely. "We have to break up, or they'll find us immediately. The lot of us would be too noticeable. But they won't be looking for one or two people on their own."

The members of the troupe eyed each other uneasily. They were used to traveling together, to having the security of numbers against the dangers of the road, as well as the familiarity of all the members of the troupe. It would almost be like breaking up a family.

Only Gyrth betrayed no doubt. He simply turned and said flatly, "Nay. We're not dividing up. We'll stay together."

"But that's madness, surely," Harald argued. "They'll know instantly it's us."

"Not if they don't see us. We'll stick here to the woods for a time. The lords will lose interest."

"But what if they come in after us?" Gemma piped up, her eyes widening with fear. "Or what if there are robbers hiding in here, too? And how will we eat if we can't ply our trade anywhere?"

"She's right," Signy added. "The birds and foxes won't pay to see us tumble."

"I can take care of us." Gyrth pointed his knife toward the squirrel roasting on the spit. "I was raised in the woods in Lincolnshire. We'll live. And why should any robber attack us? It is clear we've nothing to offer them. We can run and hide from the soldiers if they come into the woods. Their horses are slowed down by the trees."

"Gyrth is right," Beorn said. "None of us are enough of an act by ourselves. We've never made so much money as the past few months."

"What good is making gold in the future," Gemma asked sarcastically, "if we lose our heads now?"

Beorn opened his mouth to argue, but Harald raised his hand. "If you want to stay with Gyrth, Beorn, that is fine. But I intend to take my wife and daughter and go on our own. I'm not risking any of our lives on Gyrth's word. Besides . . ." He faced Gyrth squarely. "I don't intend to travel with you again, ever. I should have left you long ago, but, like the others, I was dazzled by the extra money we've earned since you came to us. But after what you let happen to Aline, I can't stomach even the sight of you. I'll not let you turn my daughter into a whore. I'd rather sing and tell stories and get nothing but our supper and a place to sleep than to remain with you and get sackfuls of gold."

Aline cast a proud glance at her father and smiled. She walked over to stand beside him. "I'm of the same mind. Give us our share of the money, and my parents and I will be gone."

"No." Gyrth's mouth curled into a sneer. "'Twas you who said I wouldn't risk losing you, and you were right. You're part of my act, and your dancing is a favorite of the men. I'm not giving up those coins just because you've decided to act like a frightened virgin."

"You cannot hold us!" Aline retorted heatedly. "You have no authority over us!"

"No?" Gyrth grinned evilly and held up his dagger. "This is my authority. There's no man alive who wouldn't recognize it."

"You're threatening me?" Harald's deep, rich voice rolled out in all its power. It was the voice he used to spellbind his audience, a voice that spoke as if with firsthand knowledge of kings and wizards and dragons. "How dare you?"

But his voice appeared to have no effect on Gyrth. "Aye," he said cheerfully. "That I am. You won't be getting even food for your stories with your throat slit. Or perhaps I'll just slice right across our little nun's ankles and we'll see how well she dances then."

Aline's face paled. The idea of being crippled was a performer's worst nightmare. It meant being reduced from a skilled craftsman, free and independent, to a poor beggar tied to the gates of a castle or town and dependent on some lord's or merchant's goodwill. Aline thought she would rather be killed.

"You wouldn't!" She could not disguise the tremor of fear in her voice.

"You want to try me?" He grinned again and twirled his knife up in the air, catching it deftly as it fell.

Aline did not. If Gyrth were faced with losing the revenue they brought in, she knew, he wouldn't have any qualms about crippling her or her father, or even murdering them.

"Mary, but you're a monster!" Harald burst out. "You've the soul of a devil!"

Gyrth shrugged, obviously indifferent to anyone's opinion of his character. Aline turned toward her father. She saw in his face the same impotence and frustration that she felt. Neither he nor Aline could win in an open confrontation with Gyrth; he was stronger than they and deadly skillful with a knife.

Humiliation flickered in Harald's eyes, and Aline knew that he fiercely regretted the lack of strength and youth that made him able to challenge Gyrth. But he said only, "Then I presume that we must agree to do as you say." He paused and looked levelly at the other man. "Just remember that the road runs both ways—should you harm my daughter in any way, you will have lost the value of your threats, and we will be gone."

Gyrth snorted contemptuously. "You think I lust that much after any one woman? They're all the same in the dark."

Aline whirled around and stalked off, hatred for Gyrth burning in her heart. She wasn't sure whom she despised more: Gyrth or the nobleman who had landed her in this predicament. She had never done anything to harm either one of them, and yet, because she had refused to serve Sir James's lust, here she was, forced to hide out in the woods from his men, putting her family and all the others in danger, and, worst of all, trapped in this situation with Gyrth.

Well, she might not be able to defy Gyrth openly, but a woman had her wiles, after all, and there were many ways to defeat him ultimately. She would have to be patient and look for her opportunities. If they managed to elude Sir James, eventually they would go to London to perform again, where it would be easy to get lost in the crowds of people. And there, somehow, she would come up with a way to escape Gyrth. But for now, all she could do was wait—and pray that Sir James would not hunt them down and slaughter them for her defiance.

3

James *was aware of a pain* centered in his head. He opened one eye cautiously and looked around. The movement was a mistake; the rather localized pain exploded into a vast throbbing all through his brain. He groaned and closed his eye, letting his head sink back into the softness of the bed. God's bones, but he felt wretched!

Whatever had possessed him to join Cambrook in that local mead last night? And then to consume so much of it!

A knock sounded at the door, and James realized that it was that noise that had awakened him. "Go away!" he said.

The door eased open a few inches, and a blond lad stuck his head inside. He grinned across the room at Sir James. "I am relieved to see that you are still alive. They are beginning to wager on it in the great hall."

James let out a sigh of disgust and slowly sat up in the bed, grumbling, "I thought I told you to stay out."

"So you did," the young man admitted cheerfully,

and came all the way into the room, closing the door behind him. "However, your squire begged me to be the one to awaken you. I think he was rather afraid of having a boot thrown at his head again."

Stephen, Lord of Beaufort, leaned back against the door, crossing his arms over his chest in a casual pose.

"Did I do that last night?"

Stephen nodded. "So I understand. He said you roared at him to help you undress—which I found rather odd, considering the manner in which you departed the hall yesterday evening." The white grin flashed again on his handsome young face. "But then Everard told me that when he came into your room there was no woman in it, which certainly explains your ill temper."

"Be quiet, you insolent pup," Sir James ordered without heat, rubbing his hands over his face. "No doubt you will have ample merriment over this."

"Nay, dear brother, how can you say so?" Stephen asked with mock hurt.

He was, in fact, not Sir James's brother, even by marriage; Stephen's sister was the wife of the Earl of Norwen, Sir James's half brother. However, that was a close enough kinship among the Norwens, notorious for their tightly knit family ties, to warrant a brotherly relationship. Moreover, Sir James had taken Stephen under his wing when the spindly, frail-looking boy had first come to Norcastle three years earlier. Until Stephen and his sister, Lady Elizabeth, had come under the Earl's protection, they had lived with their uncle, an evil man who would not have hesitated to murder Stephen if he had thought him any threat to him. So Elizabeth and Stephen had lived a lie, pretending that Stephen was as physically frail as his pale blond coloring and the natural slenderness of a rapidly growing boy made him appear to be.

When Norwen had married Lady Elizabeth, he had put Stephen into James's care, giving James the responsibility of correcting Stephen's military deficiencies as well as of commanding the army Norwen had supplied to win back Stephen's lands from his uncle. Though many believed James to be a cold-hearted man—usually with good reason—he had always had a soft spot for children, and Stephen was still young and innocent enough to fit into that category. He had been kind to the boy, and Stephen had returned the kindness, which he was unaccustomed to receiving, with an undemanding outpouring of affection. Over the years, James and Stephen had developed a close bond.

Stephen pushed away from the door and strolled over toward James now, his blue eyes dancing with amusement. "Of course," he drawled, "I can't promise that Norwen will be as silent as I about the wench."

"Christ's bones!" James grumbled, swinging his legs out of bed and slowly standing up. "Of course you would tell him. Richard will never let me forget."

He swayed and grabbed for the bedpost. This was not the first time James had experienced the consequences of overindulgence, and he knew that eventually the pain in his head would subside. Unfortunately, right now he had difficulty believing that. His eyes felt swollen to twice their normal size, and his stomach lurched with every move he made. His throat was dry, and his mouth tasted like straw from the stables. And his head! That was the worst part of it—his brain felt inflamed, throbbing with each pulse beat.

"James!" Stephen leaped forward to grab his arm. All trace of amusement had fled from his voice. "Are you all right?"

"Yes," James answered irritably. "I'll be fine once I

eat something." He paled a trifle at his own words, and his stomach turned rebelliously. But he knew it was true. Once he had forced down a little food, his stomach, at least, would begin to settle.

He rubbed absently at his hip, which felt sore. Then he remembered falling backward over the trunk last night. His scabbard must have bruised his hip when he fell. He thought about how absurd he must have looked lying there. No wonder the wench had fled. He couldn't keep from smiling ruefully at the foolish picture he must have presented.

"Is it true?" Stephen asked conversationally, now that he was assured that James was all right, and sat down on the high bed. "What Everard said about the girl? Did she put you in a vile temper? Was she gone?"

"Yes," James said. He walked to the washbasin and dumped an entire pitcher of water over his head, shuddering as it soaked him. Then he picked up a linen cloth and wiped his face dry. His brain felt a trifle clearer.

"Why?" Stephen asked bluntly. "I would have imagined she would still be here this morning, the way you looked last night."

James shot him a dark look. "What do you mean? That I made a fool of myself over the wench?"

"No, no more than most men are fools over women. You, however, rarely seem so . . . shall we say, uncontrolled?"

James grimaced. "She did heat my blood." He thought back, remembering the way the girl's hips had swayed, enticing him to discover their pleasures. He had been certain that she'd danced for him alone, that she had advanced and retreated seductively to excite only him. After all, that little game they had played, with her coming back to him, daring him to lop off another veil with his sword, had been ripe with sexual innuendo. It had been dark, but he had been positive that those eyes above that wisp of a veil had called to him, begged him.

To his amazement, he felt himself hardening just thinking about it. *Damn!* He turned away, starting to peel out of the clothes he had been too angry and clumsy with drink to remove before he fell into bed. Stephen was right: she affected him more than most women.

"Tell me, Stephen," James asked abruptly, "would you consider me a raptor?"

"A raptor?" Stephen repeated in astonishment. "You? Why, usually you have to beat the women off. Everyone knows that."

It was true. Women had always succumbed to him, smitten by his charming smile and his piercing blue eyes. James had never been particularly vain about it. His good looks were not something he could take credit for; he had inherited them from his father, along with his heartbreaking smile and his charm. James had not really thought much about it; he had merely accepted it—and, truthfully, taken advantage of it. But why, last night, had that woman been so different?

"Then why did that wench last night pull a dagger on me?" he asked.

"What!" Stephen came off the bed in a leap. "Are you jesting? She tried to stab you? Where is she? Why didn't you hold her here?"

James shook his head, gesturing at the younger man to calm down. "Nay, don't go storming out to defend me. She didn't try to hurt me—although I will admit that when she first pulled the knife out from beneath her skirt, I thought she had been sent to murder me."

"By Tanford, of course." Stephen's face was set and flushed with anger.

James nodded. "But that wasn't it. She didn't make a move toward me. She just ran for the door. The truth is, I think she was scared."

"Of you? But why?"

"I—I'm not sure. I think she ran to save her virtue."

"Her virtue!" Stephen hooted. "A dancing whore? Now I *know* that drink of Cambrook's curdled your brain."

"'Tis strange, I know, but 'tis how it seemed. She did not try to rob me or murder me or do anything except get out of my bedchamber as fast as she could. She did not even ask for payment."

James didn't understand it. It had been apparent that her purpose in dancing had been to arouse every man in the room to fever pitch. Why else would she have worn such a a costume? Why else would she have danced so seductively? Surely she had been a whore, advertising her wares in an uncommonly exciting way. She must have expected to give her favors to at least one man, perhaps several. And once he had revealed his desire for her, she had obviously gravitated toward him, danced *for* him. But why then had she run?

"I wish you hadn't let her go. Don't you think it would be good to get some answers out of her?"

James thought of dragging the girl down to the dungeons to be questioned, of her lovely body being tortured to make her tell her secrets, and his stomach twisted.

"She's no danger, I tell you," he replied gruffly. "Perhaps I hurt her and didn't realize it; I had had a great deal to drink. Anyway, it doesn't matter. Nothing happened. She was no spy sent from the Duke, or she would have jumped at the opportunity to get in my bed. And obviously she didn't harm me." He gave a careless wave of his hand. "I am tired of thinking about the wench. We have more important things to do. Now that I've gotten the king's approval of the marriage contract, we need to move. You know the Duke won't give up his niece tamely."

"That's true." Stephen's eyes lit up at the prospect of a battle. "Perhaps at last I'll get my chance to earn my spurs."

James grinned and clapped his arm around the younger man's shoulders, steering him toward the door. "You think I'll let you in the midst of a battle? Why, Elizabeth would have my ears!"

As James had known he would, Stephen rose hotly to those words. "You would hold me back? Do you think I am a weakling, after all this time?"

James burst into laughter, and Stephen grimaced.

"Oh. You're making game of me. You wretch! I don't know how Norwen ever put up with you."

"Fortunately my brother has a high sense of family obligation."

So, laughing and talking, the two of them left the room, the peculiar actions of the dark dancing girl forgotten in the more interesting speculations about battle.

It took the troupe over a month to get to London. They hid in the forest for a week, moving to the southern edge, but before long sheer boredom drove them out. They were used to the life of the road, busy and spiced with people; they liked the laughter and the applause and the sights along the way. The woods, deep and silent, made some of them nervous and others gloomy, and they all had too much time on their hands.

When they ventured out, they found to their surprise that no one had been searching for the troupe or for a dark-skinned dancing girl. They did not understand why Sir James had not pursued Aline, and Gyrth cast her a glowering look signifying that it was all her fault that they had lost a week's worth of earnings hiding in the woods.

Aline suspected that some of her companions had begun to wonder if her tale had even been true. But she knew that she had not lied, and she could not comprehend why Sir James had not come after her. She would have thought that his pride demanded that he punish a dancing girl who had had the temerity to refuse his advances, especially since she had threatened him with a knife.

Then it dawned on her that it was precisely because of his pride that the brother of an earl would not come after her; he would not want to blazon it about that he had been outmaneuvered by a lowly peasant girl.

Aline decided to stop worrying about Sir James, though she could not keep her mind from returning to the disturbing way he'd made her feel when his lips had touched hers. The problem she had to deal with now was Gyrth.

He had not made her do the houri dance again as the troupe traveled toward London, for even he realized how dangerous for them that could be if word got back to Sir James. But aside from that, Gyrth grew more demanding all the time. He reveled in his role as their leader, and he snapped out commands and changed their routines to suit himself. Resentment grew among the entertainers, but they said nothing to Gyrth, too afraid of his strength and his knife to cross him.

Aline could hardly endure his overbearing attitude, and even worse were the heavy-handed advances he kept making toward her. She managed to fend him off by threatening not to dance, and though he argued and blustered, he did not push the matter. But Aline knew that she could not continue this way, and she could also see that her father was growing closer and closer to a confrontaion with Gyrth, out of which he was bound to emerge the loser.

Aline plotted their escape. Her first priority, she decided, was money. Gyrth kept all the money now, as he had after the performance at Cambrook's, and Aline knew shc had no hope of getting any of it. However, every time she danced, she made sure to gather up the coins that were thrown to her and to hide away at least a portion of them for herself and her parents.

One night, as she pulled a few copper coins out of her pocket and stuffed thcm in a knotted handker-chief, she glanced up and saw Gemma watching her with interest. Aline flushed, irritatcd with herself for getting caught. She didn't think Gcmma would give her away, but there was no telling what she might do if Gyrth threatened to hurt her.

Gemma plopped down beside Aline, leaned close to her, and whispered in her ear, "You're planning to run away, aren't you?"

Aline started to deny it, but she could see by Gemma's expression that it would be uscless. Aline turned her head away and said nothing.

"Don't worry," Gemma whispered. "You can trust me. Come." She crooked a finger at Aline and started away.

Aline got up to follow her. From the other side of the camp Gyrth raised his head and regarded them suspiciously. "Where're you two going?"

Gemma cackled and returned a rude answer about bodily functions. Gyrth grimaced and said, "But you've already been. Both of you."

"Just where else do you think we would be going in the dark?" Aline countered irritably.

"It's those apples we ate at supper," Gemma went on. "I think Aline and I ate too many."

"Well, you better be back soon, or I'll come looking for you."

Gemma nodded and waddled off, Aline on her heels. When they were out of earshot, Gemma grumbled, "I'll be glad when we finally get to London." She twisted her head to look up at Aline. "That's where you're thinking about running away, isn't it?"

"Gemma! Gyrth would kill us if he heard us talking about this."

"Aye, but he can't hear us, now, can he?" Gemma squatted behind a bush, tugging Aline down with her, and began to fumble under her skirts, at last pulling out a small leather pouch. "Look at this." She opened it, revealing a small pile of coins. "I've been saving longer than you. He often gets me to pick up the coins—like that night when you got carried off—but what he doesn't know is how many of the little beauties I keep for myself."

Aline looked at the small woman with respect. It took courage to hide even part of the earnings from Gyrth. If he ever found out about it, he would hurt Gemma, and Aline knew how afraid Gemma was of him.

"I noticed quite a while ago how he wasn't doling out our share after every performance like your father always did," Gemma went on. "Harald is a fair man; this one isn't. But I'm scared to go out on my own. I need the protection of a company. When you and your parents go, I want to come with you. I'll share my money with you—by the Rood, most 'tis earned by your dancing, anyway—but I want to go with you."

"Of course you can, Gemma," Aline assured her. "Even if you didn't have the money, you'd be welcome. You've always been a part of our family." The woman had performed with them for as long as Aline could remember.

"Bless you, child, I knew you'd say that. But there's them that don't think one like me is worth anything, no matter how long I've worked with them. Last time, before I met your father and mother, the jongleur I traveled with took up a position at a lord's castle, and he just cast me off with scarce a penny to my name."

"Well, 'tis not the case with us," Aline told her stoutly. "You are welcome to come. I do not know exactly where and when we will leave, though. It will be London, I am sure, for there will be ample place for us to hide there amongst so many people. We will simply have to wait for the right opportunity once we get there."

Gemma nodded. "I shall be ready, whenever it is."

They arrived in London two weeks later. King Henry was in residence, which meant that the city was stuffed to the gills with the members of his court and those who made a living in one way or another from them. Rooms were hard to find, and the small band of performers wound up spending the first few nights in a stable. But Aline didn't really mind. It was wonderful just to be back in London. She enjoyed the bustle of activity, the noises and people, even the smells. She liked traveling about the country, but she was always eager to return to London. The great city was never boring, even if it was at times dangerous or aggravating or ugly.

There was ample work. They could simply set up on a street corner, and soon they would have an audience gathered around them, ready to toss a few coins their way. Before long, they were invited to a baron's house to give a show. After that, they had several more performances at various noblemen's houses around town.

One evening they played in a big house before a particularly large and elegant group. Aline had no idea who the people were, but she was sure from the glitter of jewels and the sheen of fine materials that they were important and wealthy. One of them, a portly, middle-aged man seated beside the host in the place of honor, watched Aline intently all through her sword dance and her tumbling act.

When they were through, the troupe retreated to the back of a hall while a troubadour performed. After that, the portly guest who had been watching Aline got up to leave, and as he and his entourage made their way to the door, he glanced over at Aline and motioned to her to come forward.

Startled, Aline obeyed, nervously wondering if she had done something to offend this obviously important man. She saw his eyes flicker to her head as she drew closer. She wondered if he had been appalled at her lack of any sort of covering on her hair. It was considered immodest for a woman to appear without a coif or head-dress of some sort, but Aline usually abandoned any such headgear when she did her tumbling act. It was was simply too much of a nuisance. Instead, she tied her thick red-gold hair back in a braid so that it was neat and out of her way, crisscrossing ribbons or leather strips over it in a decorative way.

But the man said nothing of her hair, though his eyes went to it again as she rose from her curtsy. He merely smiled down at her pleasantly and said, "I admired your dance very much."

"Thank you, milord," Aline said softly.

"Your Grace," a man standing behind the portly man corrected her.

Aline blushed. He was a duke! She hoped he would think her merely naive and not rude. "Forgive me, Your Grace."

His eyebrows went up and he looked surprised. "You speak French well, child."

"Oh." Aline hadn't realized that she had responded to the other man's Norman tongue by speaking Norman as well, rather than the rough Saxon language she usually spoke. "Thank you, Your Grace. I learned it from my mother. She was a servant in a noble household."

"I see." His eyes narrowed, but then he smiled in a kindly way and reached into a silk pouch at his belt. He withdrew a gold coin and extended it to her. "You speak as well as you dance, my child, and that is well indeed. I am Ian, Duke of Tanford, and I would like for you and your company to visit my house one of these evenings."

"We would be greatly honored," Aline replied, palming the coin and curtsying low to him again.

Then the man and his entourage swept onward, leaving a buzz of interest behind them. Aline tucked the coin away in her pocket, pleased both by the man's words of praise and by the generous gift he had given her. Even Gyrth's growled warning later that she "better not ruin it with *this* lord" could not dampen her spirits. The next day a messenger arrived from the Duke requesting them to appear at his house the following evening.

When they arrived at the side door at the appointed time, a little before supper, a servant let them in and showed them where to wait. But, to Aline's surprise, he turned to her and told her that the Duke had asked him to bring her to the Hall when she arrived.

Nervously she followed the servant into the great

hall and over to the vast fireplace. The Duke was seated in a large chair, facing the fire, staring into the flames. He glanced up as she stopped in from him and made a deep curtsy.

"Ah, yes, the dancing girl," he said lightly, and smiled at her. "But you've hidden almost all your hair this evening. A pity."

Aline smiled faintly, not sure what to say.

"Red is a lovely shade, you know. A special color, I think. I have a niece who has red hair—rather darker than yours."

"Thank you, Your Grace." She waited, trying to hide her nervousness.

"Here, sit down here on this stool beside me."

Aline obeyed him, sitting almost at his knee on a low stool. She clasped her hands on her lap and looked up at him. He smiled at her in a kindly way.

"I have a proposal to make to you," he began.

Aline's heart sank. He was going to ask her to come to his bed. How could she manage to refuse without offending him? It was not wise to offend a duke.

He went on, leaving her speechless. "I would like for you to pretend to be my niece."

4

Aline stared at at the Duke, too stunned by his words to speak—almost too stunned to think. Impersonate a duke's niece! Why, the idea was unthinkable. She suspected that it was probably unlawful as well.

The Duke smiled faintly at her. "I understand your astonishment. I would never have considered it myself except for the, ah, circumstances. And I am not proposing that you do it for any length of time. It would be for only a few days. Just long enough for me to play a little jest on someone."

"A jest?" Aline asked skeptically. It seemed a strange thing to do for the sake of a little jest.

The Duke smiled and replied without heat. "I can see that I cannot fool you. I am afraid that I was never much of a liar."

Aline relaxed a little. Tanford spoke to her without arrogance, as if they were on equal footing, and he seemed to be without guile.

"You are quite right," he went on companionably. "It is not a mere jest. I have enemies. One does, always, and the higher one sits, the more one has. In particular I have one enemy, one family of enemies. In that family there is a very cunning fellow, a low-born knave." His upper lip curled in contempt, and suddenly he looked much colder than he had before. "There is no point in going into it." He shrugged as though thrusting off the bad memories and attempted to smile. "The fact of the matter is that I was foolish, and a few years ago I trusted this man. We had an arrangement, and in return for his performing his part of it, my brother Simon signed a betrothal contract giving him my niece's hand in marriage. The man broke his side of the bargain. Yet ever since, he has held that he has a valid claim to my niece and her dowry."

"But how, if he did not do what he contracted for?"

The man's jaw clenched, and Aline suspected that she must have hit upon a sore spot. "It was not part of the written contract. His agreement with me was verbal. It was too complex for a document. And I was naive enough to trust him. I had not dealt with him before. I did not know his character." He sighed. "The worst of it is, he is a friend to His Highness."

"King Henry?" Aline's voice rose in a squeak. This was lofty stuff indeed, to casually speak of kings and their friends.

Tanford nodded again. "Our ruler likes to grant favors to his friends"—his mouth twisted in a humorless smile—"particularly when they cost the king nothing. So King Henry acknowledged the validity of the bethrothal contract."

Aline was amazed that he would speak so freely about the king, but then she realized that a duke would not fear exposure by her. No one would take the word of a dancing girl over a duke's. Talking to her must be to him like talking to a chair or the wall.

"So now Sir James heads north to seize my niece and marry her, and the king says he has the right to."

"Sir James?"

The Duke glanced at her sharply.

"I met one man named that. A few weeks ago. I do not know if it is the same one."

"Black-haired like his brother, the Earl, but handsome as the devil."

"The Earl of Norwen?"

"Sir James is bastard half brother to the Earl of Norwen. Do you know him? What is he to you?"

"He's nothing to me," Aline flared, and there was no mistaking the anger that lit her eyes. "He was a guest at a house where we were playing, that is all."

"And he did not charm you? I have heard he casts a spell over all women."

"He most certainly did not," Aline retorted indignantly. "He was drunk and rude and not at all charming. I found him detestable. He tried—" She stopped abruptly, thinking that it was not safe to speak ill of one nobleman to another, even if the two were enemies.

"He tried what?" Tanford prodded gently.

"To force me," Aline went on in a low voice.

"It does not surprise me," Tanford said. "I doubt that Sir James has any liking for women. He will take my niece against her will to suit his own selfish desire to get her lands and a connection with a duke. His bastardy burns in him, so I've heard, and he wants to buttress himself with a family of good lineage. It would dilute the taint in his children's blood."

Aline thought of the Duke's niece and felt sorry for her, something she had never thought she would feel for a pampered lady in a castle. It would be horrible to be forced to marry, especially to a man who was an enemy of your family. And especially to a man such as Sir James! She remembered the strength in his arms as he picked her up and tossed her over his shoulder, the dark, disturbing fire in his eyes as he looked at her. He was obviously used to getting what he wanted, and she doubted that he cared what method he used to get it. It would be horrible to be shackled to that man for life.

Fear suddenly seared through her as she remembered what Tanford had originally asked her. "And that is why you wanted me to pretend to be your niece?" she asked, her voice rising. "To be forced into marriage with *him*?" She jumped up from her seat, ready to flee, visions of this portly man seizing her and carrying her off to marry the dark knight.

"No, no, no," the Duke murmured soothingly, motioning her back down. "Do not take fright. I would ask no woman to sacrifice herself in that way. But it will not come to that. It is true that I want you to pretend to be my niece, but only for a while, so that I can get her out of the country and across the sea to my lands in Normandy. There I will marry her to another man, a better one who will not harm her for being my relative."

"Then I don't understand. Why do you need me to take her place?"

"To buy us time. Do you not see? My niece, Clarissa, is a delicate child. She cannot travel swiftly, especially across the sea. Moreover, her nerves are quite overset with fear right now."

Aline would have thought that with the devil riding at her heels, she'd be able to travel rather swiftly, but she said nothing, only listened.

"If we could gain a few more weeks, even days, it would be much easier to get Clarissa away to Normandy and marry her. All I want you to do is pretend to be she, to stay in one of her dower castles while she escapes to Normandy. Sir James will waste a lot of time storming the castle where you are, and Clarissa will get away. Then, when you yield the keep, and he weds you—"

"But, no! I told you—I cannot marry him!" Aline exclaimed, aghast. "No, Your Grace, I beg of you, don't ask that of me. I could not."

"No?" The Duke quirked his eyebrow. "It's a chance I would think most girls would leap at—to marry a wealthy knight, the brother of an earl. Even if he is a knave and a bastard, being a lady would seem a better life than that of dancing for others' entertainment."

"I may not have great wealth or power," Aline retorted, looking him in the eye, refusing to be intimidated even by a duke. "But I have my freedom. I go where I want and do as I please. And I do not have to be ruled by a man I despise. I will not be that man's wife."

Tanford gazed at her with interest, as if she were some new specimen of creature that he had never seen before, but he only said, "And so you won't be. I do not ask it of you. At least, not for more than a few hours. The marriage will not be valid, because it will not be consummated."

"Oh." Aline blushed. "I see."

"I want you to wed him in the eyes of all his witnesses. Then my messengers will interrupt the wedding feast with the news that you are not Clarissa, but only a dancing girl. Sir James will be humiliated before everyone."

"He will kill me!"

"Nay—in front of all the wedding guests? He will cast you aside, perhaps he will rant and rave, but that is all. And my men will be there to take you away, to protect you from his fury."

"How? I will be in the midst of his family and friends. Will a few men fight them all?"

"There will be no fight. No doubt there will be others in attendance besides close friends. He will want neutral people there, too, to validate his marriage, thinking that I will try to deny it in some way. He will not start killing in front of them. That is why you, too, will be safe. I give you my assurance. You will be protected. If it is necessary for your peace of mind, then you will sneak out of the wedding feast, and my men will meet you and see you safely away before it is announced that you are not my niece."

"But, it seems . . . Surely there must be some other way."

"Ah, you are thinking perhaps of his hurt? His embarrassment? Do not let your heart grow tender over that one. The man is a snake, cruel and cold. There are no feelings in him. He has no honor, or he would not have betrayed me as he did. His pride is false, all vainglory. Yes, he will suffer humiliation, but he deserves it. Think of how he wants to capture my niece, a girl your age, and force her to marry him. All for the sake of her dowry—and to wound me." He paused, his face stern and unsmiling. "Yes, I would like to have some measure of revenge on Sir James. Wouldn't you? Have you no desire to make him pay for the way he mistreated you?"

"Yes!" She remembered the indignity of being swung up onto Sir James's shoulder and carried out of the room like a sack of meal. She remembered the fear that had clawed at her gut when he first drew his

sword and began his little game of cutting her veils
from her, the humiliation of having all those lusting
eyes on her body as he revealed it bit by bit. It would
indeed be sweet to take that arrogant man down, to
teach him that a woman wasn't entirely powerless.
"Yes, I should like to get my vengeance on him."

"Good." The Duke nodded approvingly. "I thought
there was hot blood flowing through your veins."

Aline clasped her hands together tightly and turned
her head away, her mind racing. There was something
exciting about the idea of impersonating the Duke's
niece. She had always wondered what it would be like
to be a lady, to have servants at her disposal, to be able
to give commands, to dress in rich silks and velvets, to
be treated with deference and respect. This would be
her chance to find out, her opportunity to eat at the
head of the table and drink from a golden goblet, to
sleep in a soft bed with heavy curtains pulled all around
it to keep out the drafts or the shafts of sunlight.

She thought about facing Sir James again and felt
the familiar tingles of fear and excitement that always
gripped her when she was about to begin a show. It
would be a challenge to fool the man into thinking
she was the niece of a duke. Could she make him
believe her, if only for a few days or weeks?

Of course she could! She had always been excellent at mimicry. She had many times aped the airs of
a great lady for the amusement of the servants of a
household or a group of craftsmen. She had observed
ladies of high standing, just as she observed all people; her curiosity had often gotten her into trouble,
but it had also made her clever. She knew just how to
move her hand or carry her head; she had studied and
practiced it. It would be difficult, but Aline never
shied away from a challenge.

But there were dangers, no matter what the Duke so reassuringly said. It was not he who would be facing Sir James when the brute discovered how he had been deceived. Nor was she foolish enough to believe that a duke would worry overmuch about what happened to a dancing girl if there were other, more personal concerns to worry him.

Tanford, seeing her hesitation, said, "Of course, I am not asking you to do this for nothing. I am prepared to pay you handsomely for it." He took a small leather pouch from his belt and held it out, cupped in his palm. He jiggled it a little, causing the coins inside to clink.

Aline's head came up at his words, and she gazed at the pouch in his hand. If that was gold inside, it would be a goodly amount; even if it was silver, it would be far more than she and Gemma had managed to save.

"Gold, my dear," he said, smiling, as if reading her thoughts. "You should think about the future, you know. What lies ahead for a dancer when he or she grows old? It's many years yet for you, but it will come."

He was right. She had worried about it many times, not so much for herself, but for her parents. This purse could help them immeasurably. It could mean that they would not have to travel if they got sick in the winter when it was cold. It would enable them to live on the reduced funds they would receive when Gyrth and the others were no longer with them. It would allow her parents to live when Harald could no longer do his juggling tricks.

"And there's more than the matter of money," Tanford pointed out. "'Tis helpful to have a friend in me. I can aid you in other ways."

Aline straightened, an idea dawning. This man was infinitely more powerful than Gyrth. If he would give his protection to her parents, then Gyrth would not dare to harm them! "I—my parents are with the troupe, Your Grace. I worry about them. I could not leave them alone."

"Your father was the singer and storyteller?" he ventured.

"Yes, Your Grace."

"An able man. I enjoyed his performance, as well. I think I would like to have him for my personal troubadour." It was common for a noble household to have an entertainer in residence, especially through the winter.

Aline's eyes lit up. That would be the perfect solution for them. Even Gyrth would be afraid to cross a duke; he would have to let them go if Tanford asked for them. "Your Grace"—she could not hide the joyous trembling in her voice—"you are most kind. I would feel much better knowing that my parents are safe and free from worry."

"Of course. I wouldn't have it any other way. They are most welcome."

"There—there is another. A dwarf woman. She is practically one of the family."

"They may bring her, as well." He nodded a little impatiently. "Is there anything else?"

"No—I—it is only that I am not sure I can do it."

"Of course you can. 'Twill not be so hard. I shall arrange for you and Clarissa to spend a day or two together before we hide her away. She can give you any instruction you might need. But worry not. Sir James does not know her. He has never met her. All he knows about her is that she has the family's hair color." He patted his own thinning locks, an orangish red. "Hers is a darker red than yours, but he won't know that. Everyone will call you Lady Clarissa, and he will see the red hair and assume that you are. There's no reason for him to think otherwise."

"But what—what if I do something terribly wrong, something no lady would do?"

"You shall simply have to be quite careful not to, won't you? Clarissa and my daughter will help you there. Just imitate them, and if you are uncertain, try to say as little as possible. Watch any other lady present and follow her example."

He made it sound easy, but Aline was sure that it would not be as simple as he seemed to think. She had been a performer too long not to know that; that was where the craft lay—making something hard appear easy.

"I see only one possible problem," Tanford went on. "You say that you have met the man. Will he recognize you?"

Aline didn't think so. It had been dark, and she had been disguised. There had been that moment when he had torn the veil from her face and kissed her, but the glimpse he had had was brief, and it was even dimmer in the bedchamber than it had been in the hall below. The biggest problems were her eyes and voice. He had heard her speak, but she had used her native Saxon tongue, not the Norman French she would use as Lady Clarissa, and she had been so frightened that her voice had been high and fast, trembling with fear. As for her eyes, they were an odd color, so light a brown they were almost gold, but in the dim light surely they would have appeared merely brown, her pupils so wide there would have been only a small rim of color around them. Also, they would have been heavily shadowed by her lashes, which she had lined and darkened with charcoal, as she had her eyebrows to make them go with her darker skin tones.

"No," she said decisively. "He would not recognize me. I'm positive of that." She explained the artifices she had employed to appear a Saracen dancing girl, and Tanford nodded.

"No, he won't know you. He will be expecting Clarissa, and it will never occur to him to look for any likenesses in her to a dancing girl he met several weeks earlier."

He waited for an answer. Aline thought of her parents and Gemma, safe from Gyrth and warm in a duke's castle for the winter; she thought of the gold and their future; she thought of the challenge of fooling Sir James, who was responsible for most of her problems now. And excitement welled in her.

She lifted her chin and looked the Duke of Tanford in the eye. "Yes," she said boldly. "I will do it."

The risk was almost worth it, Aline thought, just to have seen the look of rage on Gyrth's face when the Duke announced after their performance that Harald, his family, and Gemma would be residing with them now as his private entertainers. Gyrth shot a glance of pure hatred toward Aline, who was standing with her parents and Gemma in front of the Duke's table. But Gyrth could do nothing except bow low with the others and leave, while one of the Duke's servants escorted Aline and her family to a small room on the top floor.

As soon as they were alone, Aline's parents besieged her with questions, as she had known they would. Despite all the benefits they would receive from it, they were reluctant for her to impersonate

Clarissa because of the dangers involved, but Aline was adamant about following through on her plan. She had promised the Duke, and she did not think that such a noble personage would look kindly on her reneging on the bargain. Besides, seeing how easily Gyrth had been vanquished had made her certain that she was doing the right thing. A duke's friendship could make hers and her parents' lives easier for years.

There was little her parents could do except argue against the scheme, and when Gemma stepped in and said that she would go with Aline, pretending to be her servant, in order to keep an eye on her, Bera and Harald grudgingly gave in.

The following day, a maidservant brought Aline several tunics, one of blue wool embroidered with a silver thread called *orsay*, and another of light brown velvet, banded with gold cloth. Still another was of green silk, embroidered with brightly colored thread around the sleeves and neck. The undertunics were of tan and white cloth, as well as one of gold cloth that matched the banding of the brown tunic. There was also a pair of cloth slippers and one of red leather, finer than anything Aline had ever possessed, and a belt of silver links.

Aline was amazed at the riches, and she tried on all her costumes, parading before Gemma and twisting and turning to see as much as she could of herself in a silver tray, which was all she had to show her reflection.

Later, the Duke's daughter, a haughty woman named Lady Agnes, began Aline's education in the ways of a lady—and of a Tanford, who were, Aline gathered, somewhat more elegant and wonderful than any other mere aristocrats. Aline watched the woman carefully, for she quickly decided that this lady was the epitome of hauteur. Lady Agnes affected a nasal tone and, though she was not tall, managed to look down her nose at everyone and everything, keeping her head tilted back. The tilt was accentuated, Aline decided, by a stiff coif that thrust her jaw up and hid the extra folds of flesh beneath it. Sparked by mischief, Aline copied her faithfully. It would be fun, she thought, to impersonate Lady Agnes, especially with Sir James. She could imagine the look on his face as she commanded him or gave him a disdainful look.

After several weeks of lessons, Lady Agnes announced in a rather surprised tone that she thought Aline was ready, and the following day they set out on their journey to Wendmere Abbey, where they were to meet the Lady Clarissa. Lady Agnes's husband, Lord Baldric, and another knight, Sir Hugo, accompanied them, along with a small band of men-at-arms.

Aline was mounted on a gentle lady's palfrey. Since Aline had never ridden before, Lady Agnes had taught her the correct way to ride. However, she was not accustomed to riding for hours at a time. Even though they moved slowly, in accordance with Lady Agnes's wishes, Aline was weary each night when they stopped. Her muscles ached, but she gritted her teeth and bore the pain, not about to give the disdainful Lady Agnes any excuse to comment on her obviously common nature.

At the abbey they met Lady Clarissa, a girl slightly younger than Aline, and possessed of auburn hair and the unfortunate complexion that often accompanied it. Freckles splotched her forehead and cheeks despite the veil that she wore against the sun, and her skin was so white and thin that it seemed almost transparent. Though she was fully as haughty as her cousin Agnes, Clarissa had little of the other woman's intelligence,

and she had a tendency to giggle and utter silly state-
ments with an air that indicated that she thought her
affectations charming. Aline quickly incorporated
several of her mannerisms into the character she was
creating for herself.

As she was thoroughly tired of the two Tanford
women, Aline was relieved when at last Lady Agnes
and Lady Clarissa left the abbey with their entourage,
and Aline headed toward Hickley Keep, where she
would await Sir James's expected attack. Sir Hugo
and his men escorted her. As Lady Clarissa had done,
Aline wore a veil to combat the sun and dust of the
road, and she was grateful for the warm cloak Lady
Agnes had forced the selfish Clarissa to give her,
along with a few more tunics and a pair of earrings.

The November day was chilly and damp, but huddled in her cloak on the back of her gentle mare,
Aline was more comfortable than she could ever
remember being on a winter journey. Riding might
make her muscles ache, but it was far better than
slogging through the mud of the road with the cold
wind biting through her thin blanket. This pretense
was dangerous, perhaps, but at least she was warm
and well fed.

They were two hours from the abbey, and the road
had just started to edge the woods, when suddenly
several horses and riders bolted out of the trees and
straight at them.

"Run, milady, run!" Sir Hugo cried, drawing his
sword and spurring forward to meet the marauders.

Aline, frozen for an instant, recovered her senses
and wheeled her mare around. It was possible that
the attackers were robbers, but the chain mail the
men wore and the fine horses they rode strongly suggested that these were knights—and not ones reduced

to preying on travelers, either, for their horses' coats were glossy and their chain mail gleamed as if it had been polished. She knew, with cold dread at the pit of her stomach, that their plan had failed and Sir James had found her far too early.

Breathless with fear, Aline dug her heels into her mare, and the gentle animal took off running away from the clash of steel and into the meadow that lay on the other side of the road. Behind them, the largest of the attackers, with a single stroke of his sword, finished off the man he was fighting.

Then he turned to thunder after Aline.

5

Aline urged her horse forward, even though she knew the race was futile. The knight was mounted on a superb black stallion, a fierce, fast steed, whereas hers was an old, slow mare chosen more for her easygoing temperament than for her speed. Aline could hear the hoofbeats gaining on her, and she dug her heels into the palfrey's side, bending lower over her.

Then the black horse was beside her and a strong, mailed arm lashed out. To Aline's surprise, the rider did not seize the bridle and pull her mare to a stop, but wrapped his arm around Aline's waist instead and plucked her out of the saddle. Aline screamed and fought, twisting, kicking, and swinging her fists. But her blows fell harmlessly on the mail, and he hauled her easily onto the crupper of his saddle before him.

Aline glared up at the knight holding her. Even though his helmet hid half of his face, she knew who he was. The blue eyes, shadowed as they were by his helmet, were vivid, and there was no mistaking that firm jaw and clean-cut mouth. Sir James had captured her.

"Good morrow, milady," he said equably, unwinded by both the brief battle and the chase in which he'd just engaged.

Panic seized Aline. Sir James had ruined the Duke's plan. He wasn't supposed to seize her on the road, but to gain Hickley Keep after several weeks of siege. What would the Duke do? She had gained hardly any time for Lady Clarissa's escape. And how would the Duke's men know where and when to rescue her?

Aline struggled to collect herself. Losing her head was the worst thing she could do. She drew a shaky breath and tried to fix her features into a look of haughty disdain.

"Who, prithee, are you?" The Lady Clarissa had never met Sir James, so that seemed the most logical question.

A grin lifted the corners of his mobile mouth, and the blue eyes twinkled. "Why, I am your husband, milady." He reached up and drew off his helmet, setting it in her lap. "Sir James of Norwen, at your service."

"If you are at my service, sir, then you will set me down at once and allow me to be on my way," Aline retorted.

"Ah, you are a bold one, aren't you?" He reached out and grasped her veil, lifted it from her face and said, "I would see what my bride looks like."

He drew in his breath sharply when her face was revealed. "God's wounds! I never realized one of Tanford's kin could be so lovely." He gazed at her for a long moment, and Aline feared that he would recognize her.

His eyes suddenly narrowed, and Aline's heart

began to hammer in her chest; she was certain he had discovered her deception. He reached up and grabbed her coif, pulling it roughly from her head.

"Ow!" Aline let out a cry at the jerk of the pins in her hair and raised her hands to her head to protect it.

Sir James stared at the bright red of her hair. Touched by the sun, it had glowing golden-red highlights, and sparkled like fire itself, alive and thick and rich, rippling over her shoulders and down her back.

"In faith," he said softly, "you have the Tanford hair, but who would have thought it could be so beautiful?"

His gaze lingered on her hair, then moved slowly down her face and onto her body, noting the curve of breast and hip. "Jesu, but I have got myself a prize," he murmured. He smiled at her, his wide mouth parting over strong white teeth in a way that set Aline's heart to beating faster. "You were but a child when Tanford betrothed you to me. He must not have been able to see then what you would grow into. He could have sought far more for you than a bastard's treachery."

Boldly his hand glided down over her breast and stomach onto her hip. Aline gasped at the intimacy of his touch. It sent a wild shiver through her. His eyes were glowing with desire, and his mouth had softened. He wanted her. And if he lusted after her, then he might take her before their wedding; it would not be uncommon for a betrothed couple. Or he might insist on marrying her immediately instead of waiting for a proper wedding.

She had to quell his lust. The only way she could think of was to act so much like Lady Agnes that she gave him a thorough disgust of her. So Aline put up her chin and glared at him down her nose in the annoying way Lady Agnes had.

"How dare you, knave! I am your prisoner. Is that not enough? Must you insult me as well?"

The flicker of light in James's eyes vanished, and his mouth hardened. His hand fell away from her. "How could I have doubted that you were a Tanford?" he retorted sarcastically.

"I cannot imagine. I can only assume that someone of your birth has difficulty in recognizing noble blood."

Sir James's face turned even colder, his eyes suddenly chips of ice. Aline felt a small flicker of triumph. She had successfully blunted his ardor, as well as killing whatever doubts about her identity that had made him check the color of her hair.

"When one is dealing with one of Tanford's kin, 'tis wisest to mistrust everything they say or do," he said.

"My father and uncle will have your liver and lights for this!" she retorted. Aline was shaken by the strange sensations that had darted through her at his touch, and she wanted to lash out, as if that would make them disappear.

He grinned again. "They've tried before, milady, many times, but they've never been successful yet. Besides, I claim only the rights of a husband."

"You are not my husband!"

"I am your betrothed. There's little difference. We are bound by contract to wed, in the eyes of both state and church."

"I will not wed you!"

"Aye, you will," he answered flatly, the smile disappearing. "You swore."

"I never did!"

"By proxy you did, and so did I, and it is binding. The bishop has said so, and so has the king."

"I care not! I never swore!" Aline countered frantically. She could not marry this man until her protector had had time to adjust to this new development and send his men to her aid. When she had mentioned Sir James's birth, she saw that she had touched him on the raw. His illegitimacy rankled. It would not be at all unlikely for the proud Lady Clarissa to disdain him for his birth. And if she was adequately condescending and disdainful in her words to him, annoying enough in her airs and silliness, Sir James might turn away from her in disgust and be willing to delay their wedding night.

They rode back to the others. Two bodies lay on the ground, bloody and still, and the rest of Lady Clarissa's men stood or knelt in a circle, their weapons piled in a heap before them. Around them stood several men wearing Sir James's colors, their swords drawn, watching the prisoners. A young blond man, helmet tucked beneath his arm, turned as James and Aline drew close and smiled broadly at James. He was the man she had seen at the table with Sir James the fateful night of her dance.

"We had no men lost," he told James cheerfully, "and only one wounded."

"Who was that?"

"Edmund. 'Tis a cut on the leg. 'Twill be fine once Sir Alfred's lady sews him up. I bound it tight, and the bleeding's stopped."

Aline turned her head away. She heartily disliked the sight of blood, and the still corpses of Sir Hugo's two men made her stomach turn. What a terrible waste their deaths were! The fight had been merely for show, though they had not known that; the Duke had intended for Sir James to capture her, though not this quickly.

"What shall we do with Tanford's men?" the young man went on. "And there's a dwarf here. A woman. Says she's a servant to Lady Clarissa."

Aline straightened. *Gemma!* "Yes!" she cried, looking around for a sign of her friend. "She is my maid. Don't harm her, pray."

The blond man smiled. "I would not, milady." He bowed toward her. "I am Stephen, Lord Beaufort, Lady Clarissa."

Aline nodded to him. He looked like a friendly, pleasant young man, but she would have to keep up her act in front of him as well.

"What shall I do with the lady's men, sir?" The question came again, this time from another man who stood guard over the prisoners.

James sighed. "That's a problem. I have little wish to drag them along with me as prisoners."

Aline gasped. "You would not *kill* them!"

"Of cou—" he began irritably, then stopped and looked down at her consideringly. He had not meant to kill the men, but the lady's horrified protest had given him an idea of how the men could be used to his advantage. "You wish me not to?"

"Certainly not! You cannot kill them in cold blood! They have done no wrong to you. They only fought to save their mistress, and that is precisely what they are supposed to do."

"Yes, loyalty is a good thing, and certainly I would wish for my *wife* to have loyal men to protect her. If you were married to me, then I would be their master as well, and their loyalty would lie to both of us. But I cannot let loose armed soldiers whose duty it would be to stick a dagger in my back and release you." He cocked his head, waiting for her response.

Aline's eyes widened. "You mean, you are holding their lives over my head? You are saying that if I marry you, you will spare them? You—you monster!"

"Monster?" Sir James repeated mildly. "Nay, I

would say it is a kind and generous thing in me to free the men who were fighting me only minutes ago."

"They were fighting only because you attacked them! Besides, that is nothing to the point. You are a monster to force me to wed you by threatening to kill my men."

"I did not threaten or force you, either one," he replied in the tone of one dealing with a madwoman. "You are honor-bound to marry me in any case. I merely pointed out that if you do not do your duty and say your vows willingly to the priest, then these men will still be my enemies, and I am hardly so good-natured as to set them free to try to harm me."

"It matters not how you couch it, sir, it comes down to the same thing. In plain language, my men will die if I do not sacrifice myself by marrying you!"

He shrugged and looked away.

"All right!" Aline exclaimed bitterly. "Aye, I will marry you."

James glanced down at her, somewhat surprised. He hadn't really expected her to fall for that ploy. She might not want her men killed, but he would have thought that when it came down to it, she would be too proud to give in to him for the sake of a few men-at-arms. She had surprised him twice this day: she was both beautiful and caring of her people. His arms tightened briefly around her.

"Milady, perhaps we shall not serve each other so badly after all. I never thought of mercy as a Tanford trait."

"Obviously 'tis not a Norwen one," Aline returned bitingly. She hated this man. He was cruel and inhuman to make such a threat in order to force her to marry him.

To her dismay, Sir James merely grinned at her sharp words and turned back to the knight in charge of the prisoners. "Bring them along to the keep. We'll free them after the ceremony."

Then he kneed his horse and it started off, Lord Beaufort falling in behind them. Aline glanced around her in astonishment. "What are you doing?"

"Taking you back to Redmere," he replied. "Did you think we were going to wed by the side of the road? I'm afraid I didn't bring a priest along."

"I should hope not, since you were abducting someone. What I meant was, why are you still carrying me? Put me down and let me mount my own horse."

"Nay, I find this a much surer way to keep you. You're a slippery lass. I thought I had you back at Kenworth Keep, and then I found that I had only your parents and you had been spirited away. When I finally found your trail to the abbey, I guessed you were heading toward Hickley Keep. But I was beginning to think I'd lost you again. We spent a fruitless day yesterday waiting for you."

"Oh, pray forgive me for inconveniencing you." Sarcasm colored Aline's voice. "However, I do not think I will be able to escape on my palfrey, especially with all your armed guards around and my men your prisoners. It will be easier traveling if I ride my own horse."

"My horse is fine. Your weight is slight. And it's only a few miles to Stephen's keep." He looked down at her, and a devilish grin creased his face. "'Tis a pleasant way to ride, I think."

"For you perhaps!" Aline retorted, trying to ignore the way her heart sped up at his smile. This man was used to charming women; she could see it in his smile and in the way his eyes danced. He expected her to fall under his spell, given time; Aline felt sure every other woman he'd ever come into contact with had.

Sir James chuckled. "You're a bold one." He shifted Aline in the saddle, bringing her hip flush up against his body. She could feel little through his mail, but she was acutely aware of the fact that her flesh was pressed against the very seat of his manhood, and she blushed. "There. Is that more comfortable for you, sweeting? I find it quite pleasurable myself."

"Stop it," Aline said in a stifled voice.

"Stop what?"

"What you were doing."

"Trying to make you more comfortable?" Sir James's voice veritably dripped with innocence, and his eyes danced merrily.

"You know what I mean. Handling me. You were—you were taking advantage of me, because you have me trapped here where I can do nothing to get away from you."

"Handling you? Nay, this is handling you." He pulled off his gauntlet and ran his hand lazily up over her thigh and onto her stomach, ignoring her gasp of outrage.

"Stop it!" Aline blushed furiously and turned her face into his shoulder to hide it. She prayed that Lord Beaufort and the other men were not watching him fondle her so outrageously. She wished that when he did so, it didn't send such wild, strange tingles throughout her.

"And this," he went on, his voice growing husky, "this is taking advantage of you." He plunged his fingers into her hair and tilted her face up, holding it still as his mouth came down and claimed hers.

His kiss was hot and hard, his lips pressing deeply into her, forcing her lips open. His tongue swept in and explored her mouth, possessing it. Aline had never experienced such a kiss, and she stiffened, her hands going up to his chest in a futile attempt to push him away. But he was as immovable as a rock, and his strong hand, splayed across her head, held her firmly in place. He was proving to her how utterly vulnerable she was to him, she knew, but her helplessness was not as humiliating as the melting feeling that ran through her body as he kissed her. He not only could possess her as he chose, but he also obviously could control her response to him, her desires.

She felt herself softening, leaning into him, her lips pressing back against his. When at last he broke their kiss and raised his head, she lay weakly against him, unable to move or speak, her eyes still closed. She did not see the fire that lit James's eyes or the flush of desire in his cheeks.

He gazed down at her, amazed at the lust she aroused in him. Just the sight of her eyes closed in the afterwash of pleasure, so tender and vulnerable, sparked a fire in him. She was beautiful, far more beautiful than any of Tanford's family had a right to be, and her body was as firm and womanly as her face was lovely. He had never expected to look forward to his wedding night, had not dreamed that passion or pleasure would play any part in his marriage to Tanford's niece. But desire poured through him now. He wanted her in his bed, would have wanted her there whether she had been Lady Clarissa or some tavern wench. Desire pulsed in him, heavy and demanding, pressing against the contraint of his chain mail, seeking the release only her lithe body could provide.

She would be a virgin, he was certain of that; a noblewoman of her standing would have been heavily guarded all her life against any male's advances. He thought of pushing into her tight, hot channel, of feeling her close around him, her legs twining around his back.

Her body would be his and his alone; no other man would ever touch her. She would bear his seed, and the thought of that, of his life growing within her, suddenly made him hot and hard. James had never before in his life valued claiming any woman. They came to him easily, and he took his pleasure with them, but he cared not whether they belonged to him or another or no one at all. But this one . . . ah, this one was different. He wanted to possess her. There was a special excitement in knowing that she would be his wife.

Aline opened her eyes and saw him gazing down at her, the desire burning like a blue flame in his eyes, and suddenly fear swept her. She could not let him do this to her. She could not succumb to him, could not let him charm and seduce her, or she would be lost. He was her enemy, and that of the man who protected her and her parents.

James brought his hand up and gently traced his forefinger across her lower lip, then her upper, his eyes intent upon the movement of his finger. His skin was faintly rough upon the delicate flesh of her lips. Aline knew a crazy desire to run her tongue over her lips to taste his skin there, but she restrained herself, steeling herself against his allure.

"I look forward to our wedding night, milady."

"I do not!" she managed to get out.

"I think you lie, milady." A faint smile touched his lips, wide and sensuously soft. "I think 'twill be a most enjoyable night for you, whether you know it now or discover it then."

His thumb slid down over her chin and along her throat, incredibly gentle. Aline swallowed. She could feel herself trembling all over. She hated the effect this man had on her body. No doubt he was very skilled in the arts of love; he would have had plenty of practice.

"Please, sir," she said shakily as his fingers slid down to the neck of her tunic, "there are other people here. They will see."

He smiled. "All right. I will wait, though I cannot say I am content to do so."

For the rest of the ride, he continued to hold her in front of him, but he did not caress or kiss her again. Aline thought she should sit stiffly in his arms, making it clear that she was not there by her own choice, but she could not make herself do it. It was too warm, with his arms curving around her and his chest blocking the wind from her. He adjusted his mantle so that it covered his chain mail and she could rest her cheek against its softness. Warm and lulled by the smooth rhythm of the horse's gait, she soon dozed, curled up trustingly against him.

James liked the warm weight of her against him, the sweet smell of her hair wafting up to his nostrils. He wished that women did not wear those infernal coifs. Lady Clarissa's hair was too glorious to keep hidden. But then, it occurred to him, because of that headdress he alone would see the mass of her fiery hair in bed at night. During the day it would be hidden from all other men. He smiled a little to himself, thinking that there were indeed advantages to marriage. Who would have thought that he would be looking forward like this to his wedding with the Duke of Tanford's niece?

As James had said, it was not far to their destination, and they arrived at Redmere Keep a little less than an hour later. Aline woke up when they came to a halt in the bailey, and she sat up, blushing, when she realized how easily and trustingly she had fallen asleep in Sir James's arms. Sir James handed her down, then dismounted after her. The castellan of the keep came out to greet them, wreathed in smiles and talking without seeming to take a breath. After Aline had been in his company for five minutes, she was vastly relieved when the castellan's lady, a woman as calm and quiet as her husband was talkative, suggested that she show Aline up to the solar, the room on the floor above where the ladies of the castle gathered. Aline followed the lady up the stairs, Gemma by her side.

Pleading tiredness, Aline did not go down to supper in the great hall, but had her meal brought to her room. The servant had just delivered her meal when there was a thunderous knock on the door, and Sir James entered without waiting for her permission. He wore a black scowl.

"God's wounds, woman, what do you think you're doing?" he thundered. He noticed the servant and jerked his head in a quick gesture indicating that she should leave. She bobbed a curtsy and scurried out of the room, looking relieved.

Aline rose and faced him, mentally bracing herself. Gemma came around the bed to stand by Aline. Sir James glanced down at her and said, "Go. I would speak with your mistress alone."

Gemma's voice was shaky, but she looked him square in the eye and said, "I go when my mistress tells me."

Sir James's eyes widened at the small woman's effrontery. Quickly, before he could say or do anything, Aline said, "Do as he says, Gemma."

Gemma cast a worried look up at her. "Are you sure?"

Aline nodded. "Yes. Go. I will be fine."

Sir James watched the small woman leave the room, her lips pressed tightly together, then turned back to Aline. "I asked you a question."

"Since I have no idea what you're talking about, I hardly know how to answer you."

"You're eating your meal here."

"Is that a crime?" Aline retorted. "Am I not allowed to have had enough of your company for one day? Am I to be at your beck and call every minute?"

"I do not care where you eat. It is not I whom you have insulted with your proud airs! It is the castellan and his lady, and by that, Lord Beaufort."

"Insulted!" She braced her hands on her hips. "I have insulted no one. I've hardly spoken to them."

"Aye, and there's the insult. You're the niece of a duke, and it is a rare event in their lives to have such a highborn visitor. They were doubtless thrilled at your presence and looking forward to boasting to their relatives that they had supped with Tanford's niece. The lady has run herself and her servants ragged getting this chamber in order and a meal she deemed fit for one such as you on the table. The least you could do is come down and share it with them."

"Oh." It had never occurred to Aline that her presence would be a special event for anyone. It was not, as Sir James thought, because of her high birth that she had insulted them, but because she had not realized what was expected from a duke's niece.

She started to apologize, but then remembered that she planned to play the proud lady so obnoxiously that Sir James would not want to wed and bed her. So she tossed her head and said, "He's only the castellan of a wretched little keep. What will you have me do next, dine with Lord Beaufort's serfs?"

Sir James's eyes flashed. "Jesu, but you're a haughty little—Sir Alfred may be only a castellan of this keep, but he is of good birth, and he is a loyal knight as well. That's more than can be said of Tanford."

"What!" Aline flared up, warming to the argument when she saw that Sir James wasn't going to beat her for her insolence. "What do you mean? Our lineage is of the best in Normandy or England. We were barons when William was just a weaver's brat."

"I was referring to Tanford's treachery, not his bloodlines."

"How dare you!"

"All know that there's no truth in the man. You could search the breadth of England and not find a man who would trust him."

"Indeed?" Aline retorted scornfully. "This from a man who obtained my betrothal by lies and treachery?"

"Nay, I would not count it treachery. 'Twas loyalty to my brother, something which only a snake such as Tanford would expect to be for sale." He paused, visibly gathering his control about him again. "But we stray from the subject, which is supper. I am here to take you down. I will not have you insulting Lord Beaufort's vassals."

"And if I refuse?"

"Well, then, madam, I shall simply carry you there myself and set you down at the table."

Aline remembered very well the time that he had thrown her over his shoulder and borne her from the hall in Stratford's castle. From the look in his eyes, she had little doubt that he was quite willing to do that now, even to a duke's niece. So she said icily, "Very well. I know that I am not equal to your strength. I must bend my knee to the tyrant."

She swept past him, her head up. Sir James cast a sardonic look after her, muttering, "Oh, aye, I can see that you are thoroughly abject."

He followed her, his long strides allowing him to catch up to her just outside the door. Politely, he offered her his arm, and she took it, shooting him a look that would have frozen a lesser man. They descended the stairs into the great hall.

"Milady, you honor us with your presence," Sir Alfred exclaimed when they entered the hall, rising from his chair to greet her.

"Yes. I apologize for my tardiness." Aline could not bring herself to be rude to this man, who was, after all, not a high and mighty nobleman like Sir James. But she could not resist adding acidly, "I was rather tired after my abduction today."

Sir Alfred blinked at her, silenced by her statement. At the table, Lord Beaufort let out a snort of laughter, which he quickly smothered. Sir James's lips twitched, but he said only, "Yes, my dear, I'm sure it was a tiring experience. Why don't you sit down?"

Aline gave him a regal nod and swept over to the stool he indicated beside Lord Beaufort. As the highest-ranking woman present, she would share a wooden trencher of meat and a goblet with him. He rose and bowed to her, pulling out the stool for her to sit. He was a handsome lad with pale blond hair and merry blue eyes. Aline guessed him to be a few years younger than she was, perhaps fifteen; it was obvious that he had not yet reached his full strength and size.

Lord Beaufort talked to her as they ate, politely carving off slices of meat for her from the array of roast goose, pheasant, and fish before them. Aline listened to him with only half an ear, surreptitiously glancing around as she ate. It was an odd experience to be here, in the most honored place on the dais.

It was neither a grand keep nor a grand meal. Aline had been in many halls that were larger and better lit, and she had seen meals that included far more platters of different kinds of meats—venison, wild fowl, roast suckling pig, with side dishes of vegetables, sweetmeats, and puddings. But never before had she eaten from the first cuts . . . or sat in this position of honor, looking out over the rest of the hall . . . or had servants behind her, ready to pour more wine into her goblet or to bring her another bowl of water or a cloth to wipe her fingertips. It was a rather heady experience, though she did her best to keep her face schooled into an expression of proud indifference, as if she were used to far better things.

Stephen was a pleasant companion, and she found herself unbending with him, even chuckling at his jests. But he was almost her undoing when he reached out and grasped her wrist, saying, "Lady Clarissa, in faith, this is the plainest eating dagger I've ever seen a woman carry. Do you favor plain adornments, like a nun? Or is it that Lord Simon keeps you on short purse strings? James, your bride has need of a gift. Look."

He held up Aline's hand so that all could see the plain metal eating dagger in it. Aline's heart dropped sickeningly. She had not even thought about such a little detail, and obviously neither had Tanford. He had given her no fancy dagger to carry at her waist, no doubt not wanting to spend money on baubles for an impostor. But Aline thought now of the chased or jeweled dagger hilts she had seen on ladies' belts, and she knew that no wealthy noblewoman would be carrying such a plain, utilitarian dagger.

Aline's tongue froze, and she stared blankly at Stephen, but in a moment she realized that there was no suspicion in Stephen's face, only a teasing curiosity. Her breath came back, and she managed a chuckle.

"Oh. That. Indeed, 'tis plain, is it not? I—I had to borrow it from my maid. I lost mine this morning when I was running away. I drew it and it fell from my hand."

"You should have spoken up," Stephen said, "so we could look for it. I know my sister Elizabeth is most attached to hers."

"And well she might be," James interjected dryly. "'Tis encrusted with gems."

"Nay, that's not the reason," Stephen said wisely. "'Tis because Richard gave it to her."

"Well, milady, since it seems that I am at fault," Sir James said, rising and coming around to stand beside her, "let me give you this to replace your lost one."

He plucked the plain dagger from her hands and set in her fingers the chased gold one which he had been using himself. An emerald winked in the hilt.

Aline drew in a sharp breath. The elegant little knife was warm from his hand. "Nay, sir, I could not take this. 'Tis yours. Besides, it is far too expensive."

"You are my betrothed. Whatever I have will be yours."

His words did something strange to her. She knew that probably the dagger meant little to him, that he gave it as easily as she might give away a stick she had picked up beside the road. And yet, there was something warm and intimate in the idea of a gift from one's husband that had little to do with its value. It was more that it joined them in some tangible way. She stroked her thumb over the hilt, feeling the delicate cuts of the engraving. She wanted to keep it, to slide the knife into the sheath at her waist.

But she gritted her teeth and handed it back to James, saying stonily, "Nay, I have no need for a Norwen knife."

She felt James stiffen beside her and saw the castellan's lady widen her eyes in surprise. No doubt she thought Aline insane to refuse such a gift—and from such a man. But Aline knew that she could not let herself soften to Sir James. She had to remain his enemy; she had to make him want to stay away from her.

Sir James bowed slightly to her and took the dagger back, replacing it with her old one. "All right, milady."

For the rest of the meal he ignored her. Aline was glad of it; that was what she had hoped to accomplish. Yet she couldn't help but feel a stab of regret. She told herself that it was because the dagger had been so beautifully crafted.

6

Gemma was braiding Aline's hair the next morning when the pounding came at the door. Aline shot a disgusted look at Gemma. There was no need to guess who stood outside. She had put the bar across the door last night purposely, to keep Sir James from opening it and striding in as he had done yesterday evening.

Aline waited while Gemma finished the braid and tied it with a ribbon before she stood up, pulled a robe on over her nightgown, and went to open the door. Sure enough, Sir James stood outside, waiting with a look of impatience.

"Why do you bar the door?" he asked, walking into the room past her. "There is no one in this keep to harm you."

"Forgive me," Aline replied dryly. "I am not used to sleeping in a houseful of my enemies."

"Your list of enemies has changed," he pointed out. "You'll grow accustomed to it."

He turned and looked at her, his eyes going to the bright flame of her hair, which hung in its thick braid down her back, then sliding slowly down her body. Unconsciously Aline clutched the robe together in the front. His eyes made her feel as if somehow James could see her body naked beneath her gown.

She forced herself to face him squarely and demanded, "Why are you here?" Her voice sounded unnaturally high; she hoped he didn't hear that.

"Because the priest is below in the great hall. You must get dressed and come down."

"The priest?" Aline repeated blankly.

"Yes. We are to be married. I trust you haven't forgotten."

"Today?" Aline squeaked.

"Yes. Today. Now."

"No!" Panic seized her.

"Are you going back on your promise to me?" he asked, his voice silky smooth, but cold.

"Nay. Nay, of course not. But I—not today. You did not say it would be so soon."

"Why delay it?"

"But your family . . . uh, the witnesses . . ."

"We have witnesses. Stephen, Sir Alfred and his wife, my knights."

"I mean someone not your own. I thought you would want to have an outside witness, someone whom my uncle could not accuse of lying about it."

He looked at her oddly. "All my witnesses are quite trustworthy. If they swear to it, 'tis enough for any reasonable man. As for my family, we will go to visit them as soon as we leave here, so that they may meet you."

"But I—why cannot we wait? I have promised to marry you. Why can we not wait?"

"I have found it wisest not to trust in the promise

of one of your family. I would have you safely bound
to me."

Sir James reached out, curled his hand around her
wrist, and pulled her closer to him. His eyes, bright
and compelling, gazed down into hers. Aline looked
up at him, suddenly breathless and unable to move.

His thumb rubbed gently over her wrist, moving in
slow, seductive circles. "Besides, I find I have no wish
to wait for our wedding night."

James's low voice sent a warmth coursing through
Aline's veins. It was difficult to think when he
touched her, even in such a small, restrained way,
and the heat in his eyes seemed to sizzle straight
down through her. She felt herself weakening; she
wanted to lean toward him, to have him step closer to
her. His eyes still holding hers, James raised her wrist
to his lips. Aline stared up at him, entranced.

"You wish it, too, do you not?" he went on. "To discover what the marriage bed holds?" He kissed her
wrist again, his lips moving gradually up to her hand,
where he laid a kiss in the center of her palm. Aline
trembled. "I can feel it in you." A smile touched his lips.
"You want to know. It will be sweet, I promise you."

His voice was as arousing as his touch, and Aline
felt herself melting, yearning. But his lips, wide and
mobile, curved up in a smile that carried a hint of triumph. Aline stiffened. Suddenly she knew: he was
trying to seduce her. He was using his voice and fingers and lips to bring her under his spell, to make her
want to do what he wanted her to.

Aline snatched her hand out of his and stepped
back, heat blazing in her cheeks. "Do not think to dis-
tract me thus. I am no lovesick girl to be blinded by
your smile. You cannot lead me from my purpose
with your blandishments and kisses. I will not fall at

your feet simply because you have skills you have honed with whores and loose women of the court!"

James blinked at her, and Aline was gratified to see the astonishment in his eyes. Let him learn that she was not so easy to maneuver.

"This is too soon," Aline went on firmly. "I have not had time to prepare. I must make a new tunic, and there should be a feast."

"I am sorry that you will not have a grand wedding, befitting your exalted station," James snapped back. "I am sure you expected hundreds of guests and a sumptuous feast and a tunic embroidered with gold and set with jewels."

"Yes, I did. What of it? Lord Simon would not send his daughter to her husband with any less."

James's face softened a trifle. "I know 'tis a proud moment in a woman's life."

"A proud moment?" Aline scoffed. "Marrying you? I think not. The truth is I would rather have it done in secrecy, without hundreds of witnesses to my humiliation."

His brows shot up. "Your humiliation?" His voice was not loud, but it was laced with a fury so great Aline wanted to retreat.

She made herself stand firm, kept her head up proudly. "Aye, humiliation. What else could it be for me, the granddaughter and niece of dukes, to have to wed a bastard? The thought of being wedded to you sickens me. That one of my line should be forced to lie down with the son of a whore!"

His face went white. For a moment Aline was certain that he would strike her, and her anger at his attempt to seduce and manipulate her drained away. She felt suddenly cold and scared and guilty for her cruel words.

"You need not worry about being forced to lie with me," Sir James bit out between bloodless lips. "I have never forced a woman in my life. There are plenty around who are willing enough, tainted blood or no. Besides, I have as much desire to bed you as I would to crawl into bed with a snake. It's obvious that you are truly Tanford's niece. I don't have to take you. All I have to do is marry you, and that I will do in a few minutes."

He whipped around and strode to the door. There he paused and turned back, fixing her with his gaze. "I am going to tell you this only once, my lady, and you are wise to pay heed. Do not ever speak that way of my mother again. Do you understand? Perhaps you have heard that the Norwens are easy on women, and it is true that we were raised to respect our aunt and not to lift our hand to one smaller than ourselves. But do not mistake such an attitude for weakness. If you continue to disparage my name, my birth, or my mother, you will pay dearly. I swear it on my father's grave."

Aline swallowed hard, but she managed to say, "I am not afraid of you."

"Then you are a greater fool than I thought. You are mine. *I* am your protector now, not your uncle— both by law and in the eyes of God. Your lands, your wealth, the clothes on your back will be mine, and whatever you enjoy will be by my mercy. If I choose, I could leave you here, locked in your room, with a guard watching over you."

Aline locked her knees to keep them from shaking and gave him back stare for stare. "Then do so! Lock me up. Starve me to death. I doubt it's a worse fate than marriage to you."

His eyes widened, and Aline braced herself for a blow, certain that she had gone too far. But, to her surprise, he merely grimaced and said sardonically, "Perhaps you're right. In any case, you'll find out, for you *will* marry me. Dress and come downstairs immediately, ready to say your vows."

A half hour later, Aline was there as he had commanded, standing before a priest, Sir James at her side.

She told herself she had done what she had set out to do. Sir James hated her enough now to avoid her bed. Of course, what she had said to him had been cruel. A man was not responsible for the sins of his parents; she did not hold Sir James's bastardy against him. After all, her own mother had been born on the wrong side of the blanket, a nobleman's by-blow. And often the mother of the child was as little to blame as the child. What was a servant or some other powerless woman to do when a noble of the realm decided to take her to his bed?

But Aline could not let herself begin to regret what she had said to him or feel sorry for the man. That way would be disastrous for her. A woman could not afford a tender heart when she was engaged in the kind of dangerous game she was playing. If she tripped herself up, the forfeit might easily be her life.

She stood stiffly, staring straight ahead at the priest, not glancing over at Sir James. Neither did he look at her, nor touch her, even to take her arm. Aline felt terribly alone and afraid, and as the priest mumbled his way through the wedding ceremony, she had to fight to hold back her tears. She wished with all her heart that she had never agreed to this pretense.

It was wrong; deep in her heart, she knew it was wrong to be marrying a man this way. It had been easy enough to accept the idea of wedding Sir James when she'd been standing in the Duke of Tanford's house, listening to his assurance that the marriage would be annulled out-of-hand, but she found now that it was an entirely different matter when she was staring a priest in the eye. She was not as deeply religious as many; entertainers often ran afoul of priests' strictures, and, traveling as they did, she had had no priest instructing her from the time of birth in the ways of God. However, she was not a heathen, either, and she could not help but think uneasily that she would be promising before God to marry this man. What if the Duke proved unable to live up to his side of the bargain, or had lied to her? What if she was binding herself to this man for life?

Her thoughts chilled her. She cast an uncertain glance up at Sir James. He was staring straight ahead, his jaw firmly set. She studied the clean line of his cheek and jaw, the sharp black curve of his eyebrow, the dark lashes that were so thick and long that it seemed an injustice to have them on a man. She wondered if he had any doubts or second thoughts, if he ever allowed himself to be uncertain. Somehow she doubted it.

Sir James stared down at her, and she looked away quickly, embarrassed at his catching her watching him. Then she sensed the impatience in him and realized that he was waiting for her to do something. She had missed her response.

"Oh. I—I'm sorry, Father. I didn't hear you."

Patiently the priest repeated his words, and she said them back to him. "I, Clarissa, daughter of Lord Simon . . ."

The priest instructed James to take her hand, and he did so. His hand was warm and steady, his palm hard, telling her of the years he had spent handling both horses and weapons. He looked down at her impassively. It was time for the kiss that would seal their vows. James tilted up her chin with one hand and bent, pressing his lips briefly against hers. His lips were warm and firm, his kiss as lacking in passion as that offered in an oath of fealty, a true "kiss of peace," without any awareness of her as a woman. Aline was reminded once again of his words that he had no desire to lie with her. His kiss certainly indicated that he'd been telling the truth.

They turned to face the others. Aline stood stiffly, very aware of James beside her. *She was now his wife!* Her stomach clenched nervously. For good or ill, she was now his lady. Sir Alfred and his lady and Lord Beaufort came up to give the married couple their best wishes. Lord Beaufort grinned and planted a kiss on Aline's cheek, perfectly proper, but with a laughing look that made it seem a little mischievous.

"You will be my sister now," he told her merrily. "Or as close as. James is my sister's brother-in-law. So, you see, it's perfectly proper for me to kiss you. My best wishes to you both."

"Thank you, milord." It was easy to smile back at this nobleman and return a lighthearted answer.

"Nay," he protested. "I told you, we are practically related. You must call me Stephen."

"All right . . . Stephen."

He looked at her with an air of patient waiting.

"I'm sorry, have I done aught amiss?"

"No. I am simply hopeful." She looked puzzled, and he continued, "Hopeful that you will say back to me, 'And you must call me Clarissa.'"

"Oh." Aline smiled, relieved. "But of course."

Sir Alfred and Lady Blanche pressed their best wishes upon the couple as well. As always, Sir

Alfred's tongue seemed to wag at both ends, but his wife jumped in when he paused for breath and said, "Milady, Sir James, I hope you will partake of a small wedding feast with us. It isn't much—there wasn't time—but I've had a little celebration prepared. I hope you will enjoy it."

"Yes, of course. How kind of you," Aline said politely, giving the woman a warm smile and squeezing her hand. She felt sorry for the lady. The poor woman had had several important and powerful guests thrust upon her, probably with almost no notice, and from the size of the keep, it was obviously not prepared to sleep and provision Sir James's party. Still, Lady Blanche had done the best she could.

"Yes, thank you." Sir James smiled at the other woman, still ignoring his wife. "You are a jewel among women, Lady Blanche."

Aline noted sourly that the woman, heretofore quite sensible-acting, began to blush and giggle at Sir James's compliments.

"We will not be a charge upon you much longer," he went on. "We return to Norcastle tomorrow."

Aline gasped. "Tomorrow!"

She had not thought about leaving this keep. It would not be too difficult for the Duke to locate her here, once he learned of her party being attacked, and he would send men to rescue her. But if they went to Norcastle, weeks could pass before his men located her. Even worse, once they were in the Norwen stronghold, it would obviously be much more difficult for his men to carry her off.

"Yes, milady." Sir James turned to her and said with sardonic courtesy, "I trust that that will not be a problem for you."

It would, of course, but she could hardly tell him

the truth. She could only seek to delay him. Aline fluttered her hands just as she had seen the real Lady Clarissa do and wailed, "But I cannot possibly be ready by tomorrow."

"And why not, madam? You were traveling when we found you. Your goods are already packed."

"Uh, well, Gemma unpacked quite a few things already. We did not realize our stay would be so short."

"I'm sure your maidservant will be capable of repacking your clothes."

"Of course, but one simply cannot jump up and leave like that. Why, it's rude to Sir Alfred and Lady Blanche, who have been so gracious to us."

"Indeed, I imagine that Sir Alfred and Lady Blanche will consider it a great kindness not to have this great group of guests emptying their larder. I'm sure they never considered our stay to be anything but temporary. And there is no reason to remain here . . . unless you think someone is going to come to your rescue." His voice trailed up questioningly on the end.

"Of course not," Aline replied quickly. She looked at him with disfavor and said, "What good would it do now, anyway? We are already married."

"I'm glad you realize the finality of your situation."

"However, I do not wish to go to Norcastle."

James glanced at her indifferently. "But you shall."

"Indeed?" Aline drawled. "And what makes you think so?"

"Because I have told you to."

Stephen began to glance around. "Ah . . . I'm sure you two have much to discuss. I will . . . uh . . ."

"Yes, why don't you?" James cast him a sardonic look and turned back to his new wife.

Stephen bowed to them both and moved away, taking the waiting priest's arm and pulling the surprised man along with him as he began to engage him in conversation. Sir Alfred and Lady Blanche followed them quickly, leaving Aline and James alone, facing each other.

"I see you have them well trained," Aline commented sarcastically, casting a glance at the group's retreating backs.

"They are kind enough to wish to spare you embarrassment."

"Embarrassment?"

"Yes, at being schooled in front of them."

"I? Schooled by you?" Aline asked disdainfully.

"Yes, milady."

"I think there is little that . . . *you* have to teach me." Though she did not dare to mention his ancestry again, she knew that her manner of speaking would convey contempt as effectively. Whatever doubts she might have about the sham she was engaged in, she could not afford to let down her guard now.

"It would seem that obedience is one thing that you have yet to learn."

"I obey those to whom I owe it."

"Obviously I must remind you that first and foremost of those to whom you owe obedience is your husband. You vowed it to me not ten minutes ago."

"That does not mean that I have to follow you down every unreasonable path you might choose."

"Aye. It does. 'Whither thou goest, I will go,'" he quoted. "You have heard of that, I presume."

"Well, I doubt very seriously if Naomi was forcing Ruth to set out the very next day without a moment's preparation."

"You shall have several moments today after the wedding feast. I am sure it will be ample time to do what you have to. You know, obedience to one's husband is more than simply doing what he says. It is also not making a grand argumentation over every request."

"Request? 'Twas more a command."

"Command, then. Whichever, you should obey it, not dispute it, especially in front of my relatives or their vassals."

Aline grimaced. "I would not, if what you had said were not so unreasonable. I could not help exclaiming over it, I was so surprised."

"There is nothing unreasonable about it," Sir James snapped, obviously at the end of his patience. "Good God, woman, have you never heard of giving up?"

Aline looked disdainful. "It is not in my blood to surrender."

"Sweet Jesu!" he said irritably. "Must everything be a battle with you? Are we to have no peace?"

Aline did not reply, but merely raised her brows disdainfully. Sir James grasped her arm just above the elbow. "Come. Let us attend Lady Blanche's feast, and then you will have the rest of the day to attend to the many terribly important things you have to do before you can leave. Because we *are* going tomorrow, even if I have to pick you up and set you on that horse myself."

7

The wedding feast was as grand as Lady Blanche had been able to make it. Aline sat stiffly beside her new husband and tried to maintain a gracious smile through the several courses. One of the servants had picked up a few tumbling tricks and performed them, followed by the visiting daughter of a neighbor, who warbled several songs. As the girl was singing, Aline glanced around the hall until she found Gemma, perched at the end of the hearth. Gemma looked up and saw Aline watching her, and made a terrible face. The first genuine smile of the morning tilted Aline's lips. She wondered what the other people at the high table would think if she and Gemma jumped up and began to do their tricks. The picture of their blank, stunned faces was enough to make her giggle.

Sir James looked at her, and Aline realized that she had actually giggled out loud. She pulled her face back into an expression of polite interest, her lips pressed firmly together. No doubt he thought she was laughing at the poor girl with the barely passable voice. It didn't matter; he could not possibly think any worse of her than he already did.

Aline picked at her food. She was too worried to enjoy the taste of it, though Lady Blanche's cooks had outdone themselves. Aline could not stop thinking about the vows she had taken this morning and whether she had committed a grave sin. She wondered if the Duke of Tanford's men would be able to find and rescue her and what she would do if they did not. She worried, too, about the night before her, and whether Sir James would indeed avoid her bed as he had said he would.

Just to make sure, she was as haughty and cold as she could be, hardly even speaking to Sir James. After the long meal was finally done and she had climbed the stairs to her room, she made a large, irritating production out of packing her things to leave. She sent maids scurrying up and down the stairs on every pretext she could think of and had them pack and unpack her trunk several times.

She had had only one of her trunks carried up when they arrived, needing no more than a few of her clothes and linens, so most of her possessions were still packed in the cart. Aline decided that she needed her sewing needle and thread, which were tucked away in the baggage in the cart. Soon everything was taken out and stacked around the hall until the sewing basket was found and restored to her. Then it was all put back in. It wasn't until everything had been loaded onto the cart that she remembered an herb lotion that had to be used that evening on her face, and consequently the entire wagon had to be unloaded again.

James walked into the hall with Stephen to find the

floor strewn with baggage and possessions for the second time that afternoon. Aline, Gemma, and two maidservants were madly searching through them, while four male servants waited leaning against the wall, bored resignation stamped upon their faces.

"Good God, woman!" James snapped. "What in the name of all the saints do you think you're doing? One would think you were traveling to the Holy Land for two years instead of going forty miles to a well-furnished and inhabited castle!"

Aline sent him a pained look. "I always carry as many of my things with me as I can. It makes one's stay much more comfortable. Fortunately, I was able to bring my bed. Once I had to leave it, and I hardly slept a wink the whole time."

"Norcastle has everything you could need." It was common to take furniture, especially prized possessions such as a chair or favorite bed, when one moved from one keep to another. But it irritated James to have Lady Clarissa act as if the Norwen seat were no more than a barely furnished, minor possession.

"And," Aline went on, ignoring his interruption, "one never knows what one might find upon a journey. Forty miles is not exactly next door, and innumerable things could happen. There could be robbers or—"

James's face flushed dark red, and Stephen hastily intervened. "There are no robbers on Norwen or Beaufort land, I assure you, milady. James and I made certain of that last year, didn't we, James?"

"Yes, but since they are not Tanford's lands," James pointed out with great sarcasm, "I am sure Lady Clarissa cannot feel entirely safe on them."

"Thank you for telling me, Stephen," Aline said pointedly to the young man. "It will ease my mind greatly." She flashed a look toward James that made it clear that she knew *he* had no interest in easing her fears or her journey in any way. "Now, if you will excuse me, I should return to my room. There is so much left to be done." She turned and waved an airy hand toward the trunks, saying, "Gemma, I can see that we shall simply have to do without the lotion. Perhaps Lady Blanche will be so kind as so lend me some." Then, addressing the servants without looking at them, she said, "You may load the trunks into the cart now."

She swept up the stairs, bemoaning to Gemma the indignity of having to beg necessities from one of Lord Beaufort's vassals.

James and Stephen watched her progress until she disappeared from sight. They turned toward each other. James rolled his eyes. His mouth twitched, then he smiled. Stephen began to chuckle. Soon both men were roaring with laughter.

"Jesu!" James sighed at last, wiping the tears of laughter from his eyes. "What have I bound myself to?" He shook his head and walked over to the sideboard to pour wine into a goblet. "All the men in England should thank me for removing that one from the marital market." He took a long draft of the drink.

"I still can't quite understand why you were so bent on marrying her," Stephen commented. "Surely her lands and her family name could not be important enough to make up for years of being wedlocked to a shrew."

"You are still young and romantic. No doubt you want to marry for love, as my esteemed brother did."

"There are worse fates," Stephen replied quietly. "I have no desire to marry at all right now, but when I am older . . . yes, I would like to come home to a wife who looks at me the way Elizabeth looks at Richard. There is much joy and comfort in their lives."

"Mayhap. There's just as likely to be misery and discord in love. Believe me, I know. 'Love' is a common failing of the Norwen men. My father brought about his downfall with it." He took another sip of his drink, his face hardening, his eyes distant.

"That doesn't always happen."

"No. Sometimes love merely creates bastard children like myself. Love makes a man weak and clouds his judgment. He thinks too much about his bed and not enough of his lands or his vassals."

Stephen smiled faintly. "Yet you do not appear to be entirely averse to women. There was that Saracen dancing girl a few months ago, for instance."

"She was a fetching wench, wasn't she? It's regrettable that my wife does not have some of her attributes. I can't remember exactly what she looked like, though I doubt I'll ever forget the way she moved."

"You see what I mean? And you are not unkind or ungenerous to women."

James waggled a hand. "It's a hard enough life for them, especially the whores who make their living under a man. Why be cruel to what gives one pleasure? But that's a far cry from trusting one of them with one's heart. To do that is foolish." He smiled in that charming, unreadable way he had, throwing up a wall that even a favorite like Stephen could not penetrate. "You know that I have never liked to play the fool."

"I would hardly call it wise to marry a niece of Tanford."

James cast him a sharp glance.

"She hates you, you know, for forcing her to marry."

"I am aware of that, my friend. Believe me, I have no intention of turning my back on her."

"Still, it's like inviting a viper into one's home. Even if you're on the watch for it, the slightest moment's inattention could bring disaster."

James cast an arm around his young companion's shoulders. "You fret too much. Haven't you learned that I like a little danger in my life? I do not worry about the threat Lady Clarissa may pose to me." His grin broadened. "It is more the possibility of her driving me mad with her complaints and her airs that frightens me."

Stephen chuckled. "And well it should."

The two men strolled toward the stairs. As they walked, Stephen said, "Why did you insist on leaving on the morrow? Was it just to antagonize her ladyship?"

"Her ladyship does not need my help in finding things to antagonize her."

"Are you afraid that Tanford is sending aid to her?"

"He is lucky if he has yet heard about our capture of his precious niece; he will know 'tis too late to stop the marriage. But I'm sure this won't be the end of his maneuverings. He's a wily old fox, and there is something peculiar about the ease with which we found Lady Clarissa and overcame her men. Did it seem to you that she traveled well-enough guarded?"

Stephen looked at him consideringly. "If my bitter enemy were searching for one of the women of my family, I would send more men with her. But perhaps her father is more foolish than Tanford. It was he who sent her out. Or perhaps he hoped that if she traveled lightly she would pass unnoticed."

"I think Tanford may have some plot brewing, though I'm damned if I can guess what it is. At any rate, I'll feel better with Lady Clarissa at Norcastle instead of here in a small, weak keep or on the road with us. And the more her ladyship tries to delay us, the more convinced I am that we should leave soon."

"I don't know. She seems so silly it's hard to believe that she could plot anything."

"Any of that family can plot, silly or no. She may merely be engaged on some absurdity of her own making." James sighed. "Still, 'tis better to have her where she can do no mischief."

James wondered if a place where Clarissa could do no mischief actually existed. She was the most infuriating woman he had ever met. Her irritating ways annoyed him, and he despised her for her contemptuous comments about his birth and family. Being around her was about as comfortable as being on the rack, he decided, and he thought that once he had her safely stowed away in a keep on his lands, he would live apart from her. He did not have to be around her, after all; their marriage would give him all he was seeking.

Except heirs, of course—legitimate sons who would carry the bloodlines of two of the oldest and noblest families in Normandy and England. There would be no talk of bastardy with them, no question of inferior birth. They would be able to take their place among the peers of the realm with never a quiver of self-doubt, no long hours of nighttime spent in dark despair. That had been the other thing he wanted from this union with Tanford's kin—not just revenge on one of the men instrumental in murdering his and Richard's father, not just alliance with a high-ranking family or the lands of Lady Clarissa's dowry, but the establishment through his seed of a family of worth. Not simply offshoots of the Norwen family on the wrong side of the blanket, but a noble and proud family in their own right. With an earl on one side and a duke on the other, none would dare discount them as merely a rich bastard's sons.

James thought about the night before him and the angry vow he had made to stay out of Clarissa's bed. The lady was beautiful. He thought of her flamelike hair and her strange, beckoning gold eyes, of her lithe, firm body with its small waist and high breasts. He had not expected her to be desirable.

But the lady had been impervious to his charm as well as to his seductive touch and words. She had looked at him with distaste and contempt and told him she did not want him in her bed.

The thought rankled. It made him want to prove that he could win her over; her very coldness was a challenge.

He thought about going to her bed tonight, as was his husbandly right. He thought about kissing and caressing her until she turned into fire in his hands. He would melt her indifference, destroy her contempt. He would bring her to such a peak of heated desire that she would tremble helplessly in his hands, begging him to satisfy her.

James smiled to himself. That would be a pleasant victory, he thought.

But if he made love to her tonight, who would really be the conqueror? Would it be himself for bringing her to passion, or her, for luring him to her bed when he had sworn he would not enter it? It occurred to him that if he went to her bed, she would think that she had won, that she could control him with the pleasures of her body.

No, he thought, it was far better to stay away from her. Let her begin to taste the life of a wife who did not have her husband's regard or desire. Perhaps then she would soften.

When evening fell, Lady Blanche went upstairs to Clarissa's room to help prepare her for her wedding night. James waited belowstairs with Stephen and Sir Alfred. He would have to go through with this pretense, he thought. He didn't want anyone else to know that he did not sleep with his wife, for nonconsummation of the marriage would give the Duke an excuse to have it annulled. When Lady Blanche came down later, smiling and blushing, to say that Lady Clarissa was ready, he ascended the stairs with the others, enduring Sir Alfred's and Stephen's jovial, ribald remarks.

When he stepped into Clarissa's room, he stopped dead still, his breath catching in his throat. She wore a white gown, soft and thin, that fell straight down her body, touching at breasts and hips, hinting at but not quite revealing the wonders of her body. Her white, slender arms were bare, as were her feet, and somehow even they stirred him. Her hair hung loose, cascading like fire over her shoulders and down her back to her hips.

James's eyes slid over her, and desire began to throb deep in his loins. He looked over at Stephen, who flashed him a grin and said, "Sir Alfred? Lady Blanche? I think it is time we left the couple to themselves."

"Oh, yes," Lady Blanche agreed, casting an arch look at James, then Aline. "I am certain our presence here is no longer required."

James barely nodded good-bye to them as they left the room, closing the heavy door behind themselves. His bride did not do even that much. Her gaze was glued to James. He moved closer, and she stepped to the side, keeping a safe distance between them.

"You are a lovely bride," James said, his voice taut.

Aline swallowed. Her face was pale, and he could see fear in her eyes. It startled him. Could she really be afraid of him?

"Don't look at me like that," James went on. "I will not hurt you."

"I—I'm not afraid of you." Aline drew herself up proudly and gazed back at him. James knew that she would never admit to being afraid, and that touched him.

"I did not come here to bed you," he went on. "I told you last night I had no interest in you that way."

She relaxed a little in relief. "Then why are you here?"

"Form's sake. I would not wish to have anyone doubt that our marriage was consummated." James pulled his small dagger, the one he had tried to give Aline the other night, from his belt and slid its edge over his wrist, drawing blood. He turned to the bed, which had been turned down for them, and smeared his bloody wrist across the center of the bed linens. "There now, 'twill look as if you indeed lost your maidenhead. Lady Blanche will save these for proof."

"What if I deny it? I could reveal what you did and say the blood is false."

She was trying to thwart him, but this time her effort only amused him. James grinned. "Well, if that is the case, then I shall simply have to make the stains real, won't I? Come to bed, wife."

"No!" She backed up hastily. "You are right. I will not dispute the evidence."

"Good. I thought not." James moved away, going to bar the door on the chance that the lady's little maid, who seemed to pop up everywhere by her side, might take it into her head to come in and check on Lady Clarissa. He wanted no one to know that he did not sleep in the lady's bed tonight.

"What are you doing? I thought you were not staying." Her voice trembled a little.

"I can hardly leave five minutes after I walked in here. I think your new husband would stay the night, don't you?"

"Yes. No doubt you are right." She still looked a little nervous at the idea.

"I shall sleep on your maid's cot here." He motioned toward the small wardrobe room which opened off the main room, where a narrow bed had been made up for Gemma. "Your virtue will remain unsullied."

As he had moved, their positions had changed, so that she now stood between him and the fat wax candle that lit the room. Its light shone through the thin gown she wore, illuminating the line of her bare legs and the curves of her torso. Her body was very enticing, and James thought about how sweet it would be to pull the gown from her and gaze at her naked body. He could feel the blood pooling in his abdomen, hot and heavy, and he knew it was dangerous to continue to gaze at her. Yet he could not seem to stop.

The air was chilly, and Aline shivered; her nipples stood out against the cloth of her gown. James's gaze dropped down to the dark circle of her nipples, hard and pointing in the center. James wanted to see them. He wanted to taste her mouth again.

Making a noise deep in his throat, he turned away. He had decided not to make love with her, and he prided himself on always being in control. He refused to let some woman he did not even *like* make him lose his usual calm. She was a beauty, granted, but so were many other women, and none of them had ever been able to make him forget his plans or change a decision. He thought with his brains, not his stones.

"Good night," he said gruffly, and stalked off into the wardrobe room, not turning back to look at her.

*   *   *

Aline was late coming down to the courtyard the next morning, though James had shaken her awake when he'd gotten up and left their room. The entourage waited in the bailey for her for half an hour before James finally sent a servant up to fetch her. She came down and mounted her palfrey, complaining at length about the earliness of the hour, as well as the cold November wind.

"Pull your hood up," James told her unfeelingly, and nudged his horse with his heels, taking his place at the front of the group.

An hour later, Aline pulled her palfrey to a halt. "I can go no farther without a rest," she declared in a carrying voice.

Jaw clenched to hold back the angry words that rose immediately to his lips, James rode back to where she sat, servants, guards, and carts all stopped behind her.

"What in the name of all that's holy are you doing?" he asked, with effort keeping his voice from climbing into a roar.

"I cannot ride farther," Aline replied, looking at him in a way that suggested he was crude and baseborn not to have realized that fact himself. "I am not used to being rocked about like this. When we travel, my mother and I go in a litter. Father does not rush us about."

James grimaced, but called to his men to dismount and pull off the road to rest. He helped Aline down, then strode away from her as if he could not trust himself to be any closer to her. Aline hid a smile as she walked away from the others.

Sourly James watched her make her way through the other members of the entourage until she had passed them all. When she continued walking into the unoccupied meadow, he let out a curse and started after her.

"Are you mad?" he inquired scathingly, grabbing her by the elbow and whirling her around.

Aline looked up at him blankly. "What?" She glanced around, honestly puzzled this time about the source of James's wrath.

"What do you think you are doing, wandering off like that? Are you so foolish that you think you can escape me?"

Aline blinked. In truth, she hadn't thought anything, except that she wanted to be by herself. She was not used to being around so many people all the time, and over the past few days she had felt hemmed in by the walls of the keep. However, she had obviously stumbled upon another way to anger James.

"Or are you simply so stupid that you don't realize you could get lost or attacked?" James went on.

"Attacked?" Aline repeated with wide-eyed innocence. "But I thought you said there were no robbers along this road."

"I said not on Norwen or Beaufort lands. I have no idea what sort of vermin might prey on travelers along this road. They would not dare attack as large a body of men as I have. But if you wander off from our protection, I'm sure they would be delighted to seize you and hold you for ransom." He paused, then added sarcastically, "A decision they would bitterly regret, I am sure, once they'd spent a few minutes in your company."

"Mm." Aline pursed her lips. "Especially once they found out you would rather have me dead than alive."

James's brows shot up. "What? What are you suggesting?"

"Well, why else would you insist on forcing me to ride like a madwoman cross-country? You're hoping that I will sicken and die, and then you will have my lands and no female to bother you."

James's eyes flamed. "I don't know whether to laugh at your stupidity or be enraged at your suggestion that I would cause the death of a woman under my protection. I have no idea what you learned in Tanford's family, but the Norwens do not prey on the weak or helpless, and once a person or a place is *theirs,* they will protect it to the death."

A strange sensation rippled through Aline as he said "theirs." She was now *his.* Somehow the thought stirred her. Looking up into the fierce light of his eyes, she found it hard to look away. What would it be like to truly belong to this man? To be folded in his strength and protection, held by his arms? The idea made her a trifle breathless.

He turned away from her, obviously expecting her to follow him. She did so, too amazed by the reaction of her body to worry about appearing docile. It was foolish, she told herself, to be warmed by his protectiveness, or to think that there was anything special about his saying she was his. The Norwens were simply possessive people; he had said so himself. They would take care of anyone or anything they believed belonged to them, not because of the intrinsic worth of the person or object, but simply because it or she or he belonged to them. That was how he viewed her—as an object, a possession. He said she was his in the same way he would have claimed ownership of a shoe or a horse or a ring. It certainly betokened no affection for her; in fact, she could not imagine him being any *less* affectionate.

Not, of course, she reminded herself, that she

wanted him to feel affection for her. That would be disastrous. He would begin to treat her as a wife; he would expect to take her to his bed; he would kiss her as he had the other evening. It was best that he remain angry at her.

James stalked across to his men, calling to the others to mount and ride. He glanced toward Stephen and said gruffly, "Grant me a boon and help that woman onto her horse, will you? If I do it, I may strangle her."

The young man grinned and went over to help Aline mount. James gestured to his men-at-arms, and the large entourage started forward. He did not glance backward to see if Lady Clarissa was mounted and following. After all, he thought grimly, he was sure he would hear her if she were not.

8

James thought that he could not grow any more irritated with his new bride, but he found to his dismay that he was wrong. After only another hour, Clarissa was once again wailing and moaning that she needed a drink of water, and after that, their stops came regularly, every hour or so. She was hungry. She was feeling queasy from the constant rocking of the horse. She had a headache from the sharp wind. Her legs had grown numb.

James thought that he had never covered a distance so slowly, even the time a Saracen's blade had torn open Richard's leg and he had had to be carried on a litter as they fell back, fighting bitterly all the way. They would travel little more than half as far as he had planned to the first day. More than ever, he was convinced that Lady Clarissa was pursuing some sly plan of her own, and it worried him that he could see no advantage for her in delaying him. He wondered if he was somehow falling into a trap of Tanford's making.

Or perhaps the silly woman was not planning anything or aiding a scheme of her uncle's at all. Perhaps she was simply as foolish and as selfish as she seemed, caring only about the slightest discomfort of her body and not at all about the large entourage that rode with them. Perhaps he had merely been cursed with the most annoying female in the land for a wife. There were those, he knew, who would think it was only fitting justice.

"James!" he heard Stephen call once again, and he stiffened, pulling his horse to a halt. He glared back over his shoulder.

There was Stephen, seated on his horse in the middle of the group, talking earnestly to Lady Clarissa, who was staring back at him with a perfectly blank face. Stephen was gesturing with his hands, and James could see his conciliatory expression. He was trying to stop her from doing something stupid, James was certain.

Then Lady Clarissa tossed her head and said something in return and slid off her palfrey on her own, landing lightly on the ground. She cast a challenging look back up at Stephen, who sighed and began to dismount.

James's lips twitched with irritation, and all the annoyance and worry that had been occupying his mind the past few hours surged up in him full force. He let out an oath and swung down from his horse, marching back to where Lady Clarissa stood beside her mount.

"Damn your soul to hell!" he roared as he grew close, uncaring about the score of interested ears around them. "I would ask if you have taken leave of your senses, except that I know that you have none to begin with!"

Aline looked up, inwardly flinching when she saw the icy blue of James's eyes. He was almost beside himself with fury. Had she pushed him too far?

She forced herself to stand her ground. Lady Clarissa was not the sort of woman who would give up, she reminded herself. She would have no thought except that her wishes were not being attended to.

"Are you speaking in that tone to me?" she asked frostily.

"Jesu! Yes, I am speaking to you, and I'll use any tone I please. What do you think you are doing?"

Aline strived for a look that blended puzzlement and a lack of fear of him. "I need to stop for a rest. I am a lady, not a fighting man. I am not used to riding without pause across the countryside."

"Without pause!" he bellowed. "Without pause? You have stopped to rest six times!"

"Only because I compelled you to. You have showed no concern or consideration for me."

James's hand lashed out and gripped her arm so tightly that it hurt, and he jerked her forward, so that she was standing only inches away from him, forced to look up to meet his face.

In a low voice as cold and deadly as the blade of his sword, he said, "Let us get one thing clear right now, milady. *You* do not *compel* me to do anything. Any stopping we have done has been because I chose to do it. I was trying to be courteous to my bride. But I tell you now, such coddling is over. I will not stand for these childish attempts of yours to gain time or attention or whatever it is you hope to do. You are going to Norcastle, will you, nill you, and all you accomplish by this behavior is insuring that the rest of your married life will be a miserable one with a husband who hates you."

"Then that will make two of us."

"Take care, milady," he said, bending his head closer to hers. "Or you will find yourself with a husband in your bed every night. Or had you forgotten?"

His free hand came up to curl around her breast.

Aline felt her nipple hardening against his palm, and her body was suddenly tingling and alive, eager against her will. She glared at James, furious with both him and herself, for the way he could make her feel.

A small smile touched his lips. "Ah, I see you remember now. I don't have to avoid your bed. I choose to do it. And if I should choose not to, as I just might if you continue to cross me . . ." His hand circled suggestively over the soft mound of her flesh, his thumb stroking the hard button of her nipple.

"You pig!" Aline said, ignoring the warmth that was spreading through her at his touch. "You churl, to use such a threat with me! I would not have expected even you to be so low, so—"

Her words were cut off as his hand left her breast and seized her chin, then held her face still as his mouth came down and took hers. His lips were ravaging and hard; his tongue swept in to conquer her mouth. Aline's heart pumped wildly, and she thought her knees might buckle beneath her. She made a whimpering sound deep in her throat, and her hands came up to his chest, but whether to clutch at him or to push him away, she was not sure. She thought she could not bear it, that he would continue to kiss her and she would melt into a puddle on the ground, until finally, abruptly, he pulled away from her.

He stood for a moment, staring down into her face. His chest was rising and falling in harsh pants, and his face was flushed, his eyes shockingly bright. Aline gazed back at him, unable to speak. It was all she could do to force herself to stand upright.

"Now," he rasped. "You will get back on that horse, and we will ride hard and fast. And you will cease your complaints! Do you understand?"

Aline realized then that the kiss that had just shaken her to her roots had done nothing to James. He hated her, and if there was heat in his lips when they took hers, it was the heat of anger, not desire. With an effort, she drew herself up straight and returned his gaze steadily, saying icily, "Yes, I understand perfectly. I am your prisoner, and I must do as you say. I have been aware of that from the moment that you seized me. You are of Norwen, and I of Tanford, and we shall always be enemies."

"That may be, milady," he ground out, "but you are my enemy *wife.*"

With those words, he lifted her up off her feet. She gasped with surprise as he crossed the few feet to her horse and set her firmly into the saddle. "There! Stay there, and not another word out of you."

With that, he turned on his heel and strode back to his own horse.

Aline rode in silence, staring at Sir James's back, far ahead of her. Tears of fury glistened in her eyes. James had not hurt her when he had picked her up and thrown her into the saddle, but he had lacerated her pride. He had kissed her calculatedly and cruelly, simply to prove to her that he was her master. He had touched her breast with all those others around them, watching, as if she were nothing, not a human who could be shamed, but merely an object that he owned. She vowed that she would never forgive him.

Nor was she going to stop again. She would ride until her joints locked up rather than ask him for a favor. She was so angry she refused even to talk to Stephen.

The pace they set was hard, and it was close to dark before they stopped to camp for the night. Aline was stiff and sore when she dismounted. The days she had spent riding from London had helped her grow accustomed to sitting in the saddle, but it was still difficult for her to ride this long.

She pointedly did not glance toward James, just stalked away with Gemma to the stream to wash up. When she returned, her tent had been thrown up, and she retired to it and did not come out again, even when the tantalizing smells of roasting meat drifted into her tent.

Stephen came to the flap of her tent and tried to coax her out to eat, but she replied flatly, "I am not hungry."

"I'm sure James regrets whatever he said to you this afternoon. If you will only come out to eat, perhaps you can ease the situation between the two of you."

Aline pulled aside the flap and glared out at Stephen. "I have no desire to 'ease the situation' between us. Sir James is a fool and a bully, and the less I see of him the better."

She whipped the flap shut and returned to the bedding rolled out on the ground. Taking off her coif, she began to brush her hair, ignoring the rumbling of her stomach. Sometime later, when she had disrobed and crawled in between her blankets, the flap opened a little and Gemma crept in, a wooden bowl of food in her hand.

"Oh, Gemma, you're a savior," Aline said fervently, taking the bowl and beginning to wolf down the meat.

"You didn't think I was going to let you sit in here and starve, did you?"

"I don't know. I thought perhaps *he* might have stopped you."

Gemma made a face. "Now, Aline, he's not trying to starve you. He knows I brought you the food. He was there when I dished it up."

"I suppose you're right: he will let me eat." Aline swallowed the last of the meat and licked her fingers. "He thinks he can break me merely with the hard riding." She gave a brittle smile to Gemma. "But he'll find out that it takes more than that to bring me to heel."

Gemma sighed. "Sometimes I think you *should* have been a lord's daughter, you're so everlasting proud and stubborn."

Aline merely raised her eyebrows and continued to eat. Afterward, she blew out the low tallow candle and slid between the covers of her makeshift bed. She lay, tired and sore, but still too full of churning emotions to sleep. Outside, she could hear the clink of metal now and then and the low murmur of male voices, growing more and more intermittent. Then, backlit by the low glow of the banked campfire, a male figure came up to her tent. He was tall, and Aline was immediately certain that it was Sir James. Breathless and tense, Aline waited, watching.

He stood for a moment, then walked to the corner of the tent and back to its central flap. He paused again, and then, with a muffled noise of disgust, strode away. Aline relaxed her muscles, letting out the breath she had been holding. Then, overcome by the tension of the day, she supposed, she began to cry. She turned onto her side, buried her face in her arms, and let her tears flow.

James and Aline continued their silent war the next day. They rode for hours without stopping, James at the front of the cortege and Aline in the middle. The jarring pace wore at her, for they rode faster and with fewer stops than she had done with

Lady Agnes and Tanford's men. But Aline gritted her teeth and endured it, refusing to admit that she was either tired or sore. Moreover, her head began to ache during the afternoon, and her throat grew raw from the dust of the road. By the time she dismounted that evening, she was exhausted, and she swayed as she stood. But she walked away, looping an arm around Gemma's shoulders and leaning on her more than she cared to admit, ignoring the slightly worried glance that Stephen sent her. As soon as her tent was prepared, she went inside and lay down, not even bothering to take off her tunic or comb out her hair. She fell asleep immediately. When Gemma brought in her food later, she found Aline deep in slumber, and she hated to awaken her, so she merely set the food aside.

When Aline awoke, she found that the night's sleep had not driven away either her headache or the rawness in her throat. Every muscle cried out as she rose and began to move about the tent. She could not remember the last time she had felt so sore. Her life had always been very active, and her muscles were toned, but she was used to moving, not to sitting in one position for hours at a stretch. The thought of getting back on the palfrey made tears start in her eyes. Then she heard James's voice, calling to one of his men, and she straightened, squaring her shoulders. She would be damned in hell before she gave that man the satisfaction of defeating her.

She left her tent and took the hard piece of bread that Gemma offered her for breakfast, but her stomach lurched sickly when she began to eat it, and she wound up throwing the remainder of it away. When the tents were struck, she mounted her horse. She was not going to be the first to give in.

*   *   *

"James." Stephen sounded troubled as he rode up beside James. "Might we stop to rest midmorning today?"

James cast him an amused look. "Why? Are you getting soft, Stephen?"

Stephen grimaced. "Nay. 'Tis the Lady Clarissa I think of. Some women are not used to riding hard. Not everyone is like Aunt Marguerite, you know."

James grinned at the thought of his aunt, Norwentall and tough through and through. She had saved James and his brother Richard years ago when Norcastle had fallen, and she had raised them after that. She had always ridden hard; she was fond of saying that she could keep up with any man, and James suspected that it was no idle boast.

"Did my good wife send you up here to plead her cause?" James asked lightly.

"No. And if I had asked her, I think she would have said she'd rather I ran her through."

James chuckled. "Ah. So that's what those two holes are burnt in my back. I *thought* I felt her staring at me."

Stephen's lips twitched into a smile. "She is nourishing some anger toward you."

"Some?" James asked, his eyes lighting with an unholy humor. "I would have said that her entire body is filled with anger toward me."

Stephen chuckled. "Perhaps you're closer to the mark." He sobered. "But, James, mayhap you are pushing her too hard. She is pale and—I don't know—somehow she seems in pain."

"Her ladyship is not shy. If she needs to stop, she will inform us all of it." James's mouth turned down grimly. There was a determined set to his face, almost as if he were waiting something out.

"Are you pushing this hard to make her cry surrender?"

"What?" James looked at him blankly. "What are you talking about?"

"I think you're trying to force her to ask you to stop."

"Don't be absurd. That's precisely what I told her *not* to do the other day." James gave him a long, cool look.

"I know, but . . ." Stephen stopped to think as he considered the other man's composed face. "Since you lost your temper with her, there has been a battle between you. She will not come out of her tent to eat with us. She refuses to look at you or speak to you. She never says a word about stopping or resting. And you say nothing to her and simply ride harder. I think you are trying to make her submit to you somehow."

Heat snaked through James as he thought of that proud redhead submitting to him. He could imagine her kneeling before him, her pale face turned up to him, those haunting golden eyes beseeching him. He thought about her reaching out her hands to him in supplication. And when he took her hands, she would tug him down with her, offering up her lips for a kiss. . . .

James moved uncomfortably in his saddle and shot Stephen a black look. "You talk nonsense. I hurry because that witch has been trying to slow us down for some purpose. I want to make up the lost time. I'll be damned if I'll let her spring some Tanford trap on us."

"But we are on Norwen lands now," Stephen protested. "And yesterday we were on mine. Who would dare attack us? Why, we could have easily gone to Blackford and spent the night with Sir Osmund last night, been on beds inside the keep walls, yet you insisted on sleeping out in tents on the ground."

"It would have been out of the way. I told you, I want to reach Norcastle on schedule." He glowered at Stephen. "Stop looking at me like that. Jesu, you'd think I was a wife-beater, the way you're acting."

Stephen smiled. "No. You do not even realize what you do, that's what I think. I also think that Lady Clarissa has gotten under your skin more than you care to admit, or you would not react so to her."

James grunted. "Are you sure you do not speak for yourself? You are the one who has dangled after her half the trip."

Devilish glee lit up Stephen's eyes. "God's bones! You're jealous!"

"Don't be any more foolish than you have to. I am hardly likely to be jealous about a shrew like her. I want her in my bed as much as I'd want a hedgehog."

"A hedgehog doesn't have ivory skin and eyes the color of the dawn."

"How poetical she's turned you."

Stephen chuckled. "I am not the one who has been turned anything by her. You are the one acting in a way I have never seen before. When else have you been so callous to a lady's comfort?"

James's eyes flickered toward his companion and away. "Don't let that one seduce you, lad. She may look sweet and rosy and white, like a flower blooming in the sun. But she will betray you as soon as it is of benefit to her. Never forget that she is of Tanford's line."

"I am not fooled by her, James," Stephen answered seriously. "I have heard her temper and seen her silliness, just as you have. But I have talked with her as well, and there's more to her than those things."

"Aye, on that we're agreed. She is hiding something."

"I didn't mean that. I meant—well, I think she is

pleasanter than she appears. Sometimes she seems to forget about putting on her airs or how much she hates us, and then she is nice, even humorous."

"Lady Clarissa?" James affected amazement.

"Yes. I think that if you gave her a little time, and talked to her, you would find that she is much nicer than you thought." He hesitated, then finished in a rush, "Anyway, 'tis unkind of you to push her like this, when you know her pride will not let her ask you for help."

James let out an exaggerated sigh. "Very well. I will ride back and check on her condition. Will that satisfy your gentle nature?"

Stephen grimaced. "Yes."

James wheeled his horse about and cantered back to where Aline rode. He saw her eyes dart toward him, but after that she kept them looking steadfastly ahead, not even glancing at him. If possible, her back grew even straighter, her shoulders higher. James hid a smile. There was no denying this one's spirit, whatever else he might feel about her.

"Milady," he began, drawing up beside her.

Aline turned her head and gave him a cool, inquiring glance. She did not look pale or sick, he thought. In fact, her cheeks were bright with color. He wondered if she had been playing Stephen for a fool, and the pangs of conscience he had been feeling weakened.

"Are you ill?" he asked stiffly.

"I am perfectly well." Her voice was laced with sarcasm as she went on, "It is so *kind* of you to inquire."

The familiar flicker of irritation stirred in James, but he pressed on. "If you are tired, we can stop."

Her eyes widened in mocking horror. "Oh, no, we must not do that. I am sure it is far too fearsome a prospect to be out here alone, instead of behind Norcastle's walls. Why, who knows, there might be thieves lurking around, or perhaps some stray mercenaries, looking for something to do. I think we should run for Norcastle as fast as we can."

Without precisely saying so, she was calling him a coward, and even though James knew why she did it, he could not keep his ire from rising. "We do not *run* for Norcastle," he retorted in a clipped voice.

"Indeed? I thought that was why we were moving in such haste—to get back under the Earl's protection."

His eyes widened at her audacity, and a hot retort rose to his tongue. But he clenched his teeth against the words. She wanted to get a rise out of him, and he had almost obliged her. Usually he wasn't that easily tricked into anger—or any other emotion. But this woman had put her finger on one of his weakest points, for there still lurked in him, as there did in any younger brother, a fierce shame for the times when he was a child and an older, stronger brother had fought and won his battles for him. It was absurd in a knight of his age and experience, of course, and James was surprised to find that the feeling still ran deep within him. It was even more surprising that Lady Clarissa had managed to ferret out that weak point.

She had done the same with Stephen, of course, except that there she had exploited his kind heart and generous nature. She had acted weak and sickly, and Stephen had felt sorry for her. He would not recognize her lies, for he was not used to the manipulations of women. His sister Elizabeth, who had raised him, was an honest woman, true and faithful, and in the past few years Stephen had been primarily in the company of James and his brother. James suspected that Lady Clarissa was suffering from nothing other than a desire to bend James to her will.

He smiled grimly to himself. It would be a cold day in hell before she managed to do that. "I take it, then," he said frigidly, as if she had not just insulted him, "that you are feeling well?"

"Of course." She cast him a haughty glance that implied he was a fool to think otherwise.

"Good. We shall continue to ride."

He spurred his horse forward and rejoined Stephen.

Aline, watching him go, bit back a groan. She would have given anything for a chance to stop and stretch her sore, cramped muscles. She was beginning to wonder if she could make it to Norcastle without giving way to tears and begging James to let her rest. His sneering presence had given her a momentary strength, so that she had been able to pretend that nothing was wrong, to even spit defiance back in his face. But now that he was gone, she felt like crying, and she wished that she had admitted that her entire body ached from the unaccustomed riding, that her head pounded fiercely and her throat was swollen.

She hung on desperately. She was beginning to wonder if they would ever reach their destination. Sometimes she suspected that Norcastle was merely a figment of Sir James's imagination and she would never get there. She was sick, she knew now, aside from the ache of riding. She wanted only to get off her horse and lie down, and it took all her willpower even to cling to her horse.

They passed through a small village, where the residents came out to stare at them. It had happened in towns and villages before, but these people smiled and waved at the company of men and shouted greetings to them. Aline was surprised that they seemed so happy to see James and his men. True, they must be the people of Norwen, but she would not have thought that even Norwen's own people could love this cold man so well.

When they were past the village, she saw Norcastle ahead of them and to the left. It sat up on a rise, dominating the countryside around it. Their pace picked up, and as they drew near, she saw that it was a vast castle, far bigger even than Cambrook's keep. It was a massive bulk of whitewashed stone, with tall blank walls cornered by large towers. The huge drawbridge was down, the portcullis up, and shouts of greeting came down to them from the towers. As they rode closer, the walls loomed high above them, and Aline's heart pounded harder and harder. This was an obviously well-fortified place, and it seemed to her more a prison than the home it obviously was to James and Stephen. What would these people do if they discovered what she was about? She could imagine being thrown down into the deepest dungeons beneath this pile of stone and being left there for years, until she died or went mad.

Their horses trotted across the drawbridge, hooves clattering on the wooden walkway, and into the outer courtyard. Here most of the men stopped and dismounted. But Stephen and James fell back and joined her. James barely flickered a glance toward her, but Stephen gazed at her with a frown and started to speak, then subsided. They rode across the courtyard and through a heavy wooden gate, standing open now, into the inner bailey.

Here the sheer walls of the inner keep rose up, dotted with narrow windows to let in light and air. To Aline it seemed as if the very walls were closing in on her. Her heart pounded, and her breath came fast in her throat. She felt sick and cold.

One of the two heavy wooden doors to the keep flew open, and a huge man strode out. He was darker than

James, with the same black hair, but black eyes and a swarthier skin, and he was slightly taller, his shoulders far broader, his chest and arms heavy with muscles. There was something about him that reminded Aline of James, though he was not as handsome. She was sure that this was James's brother, the Earl of Norwen.

"James!" he cried, trotting down the steps to where James had dismounted from his horse. The two men hugged and clapped each other on the back in masculine affection, grinning and talking. Then the Earl turned as Stephen dismounted and joined them, and he crushed the young man in a bear hug as well, jesting about how many inches Stephen had grown since he had last seen him.

A fair woman hurried out of the door behind the man. She was carrying a toddler in her arms, and her face was wreathed in smiles. "Stephen! James! Oh, welcome home!"

She flew down the steps and was caught in Stephen's arms and lifted up. "Elizabeth! Mary!"

The child shrieked with joy and held out her arms to Stephen. Stephen kissed the woman and the child, then took the little dark-haired girl in his arms and hugged her, nuzzling her neck until she squealed with laughter.

"Elizabeth." James came up to the woman and embraced her, too, his greeting more restrained than Stephen's.

"James. Welcome home. It is wonderful to see the two of you again. Your messenger arrived three days ago, and we have been waiting anxiously."

The little girl cried, "Unca, Unca!" and launched herself straight at James.

James laughed and deftly caught her, giving her a resounding buss on each cheek. His face was alight with laughter and love, and he lifted the child high above his head while she giggled.

Aline stared at the scene before her. She would never have imagined that James could look like this, so loose and easy, his face shining with love and joy.

"Now, where is your bride?" Elizabeth asked, stepping back and turning to look at Aline, who was still sitting on her palfrey.

James set down the child and started toward her. "Elizabeth. Richard. I would like for you to meet my wife, the Lady Clarissa."

Aline quickly slid down out of the saddle herself to keep James from touching her. Her knees threatened to buckle when her feet touched the ground, but she grabbed at the saddle to steady herself. Oddly, the world began to tilt around her. Heat swept her, and she could hardly breathe. Her hold loosened on the saddle, and Aline crumpled to the ground in a faint.

9

Elizabeth gasped. James let out an oath and crossed the last few steps to Aline. He knelt beside her. She looked deathly pale.

"Jesu," he whispered. "What have I done?"

Elizabeth came up behind him, exclaiming, "James, what happened? What is amiss? Is she ill?"

The others crowded around them. James lifted Aline in his arms and stood up. Her body felt very soft and fragile, and he realized that she was burning hot. "Oh, God, yes, she's ill, and I—" He cast a tortured glance at Stephen. "You were right, and I did not believe you. She made me so damned furious that—sweet Jesus, if I have killed her—"

"Killed her!" Elizabeth repeated, stunned. "James! What are you talking about? Stephen!"

"'Tis not your fault she took sick," Stephen retorted staunchly. "She told me she was not ill."

James started into the keep, carrying Aline, and Elizabeth ran ahead of him, calling for her maid.

Behind them, Gemma, forgotten, scurried after James and his burden.

James carried Aline through the hall and up the stairs to the bedchamber Elizabeth indicated. Elizabeth and one of the maids, who had come running at her command, pulled back the heavy covers of the bed, and James laid Aline carefully down on it. He straightened and looked worriedly at Aline's still, white form.

Elizabeth edged past him with a damp, cool rag and began to bathe Aline's face. "You are right. She is burning with fever."

Gemma walked past the others and reached out to take the rag from Elizabeth's hand. Elizabeth jumped and stared at the small woman. "Who—who are you?"

"I am her ladyship's maid." Gemma gazed boldly, almost defiantly, at Elizabeth. "I am the one who cares for her." She turned her gaze accusingly toward James, aware of the double meaning of her words.

James looked down at her for a long moment, then said, "That's true. Let her be, Elizabeth."

The countess handed over the rag to Gemma and stepped back. She led James away from the bed, murmuring, "An unusual sort of maidservant."

James made a face. "For an unusual sort of lady."

"I see." Elizabeth looked over her shoulder at Aline. "When did this start?"

"I know not. I—we did not speak much," James admitted, color rising in his cheeks. "Stephen thought that she was weary from the fast pace, but I did not realize she was ill." He looked away. "'Twas my fault. I pushed her. She was too proud to ask for rest."

"She should have told you," Elizabeth pointed out pragmatically. "Pride is of little use to one when she's dead."

James glanced up sharply. "Is it that bad?"

"No. I'm sorry. I did not mean that she would die."
Elizabeth laid a hand on his arm. "Probably she
merely has a fever that will pass."

There was a moan from the bed, and both of them
turned. Aline's eyes fluttered open, and she stared
blankly up at Gemma, who was sitting on the bed and
leaning over her, wiping her brow. "Gemma?"

"Yes, milady," Gemma said, staring meaningfully
down into Aline's eyes.

Aline blinked, trying to recall what had happened
and where she was. She turned her head at the sound
of footsteps on the rush-covered floor and saw
Elizabeth and James approaching the bed.

They stood gazing down at her. James's brow was
creased with worry. Aline looked at him, her brain
turning slowly. She had never seen that expression on
his face. She remembered now what had happened,
how she had been standing beside her horse and suddenly the world had gone black. They had reached
Norcastle, and this woman beside Sir James was the
Countess of Norwen.

Elizabeth looked down at Aline with concern.
"How are you feeling, my dear?"

Aline stirred. "I'm not sure. My head hurts." She
raised one hand to her head. "And my throat. I ache
all over."

James flinched at her words, then burst out,
"God's blood, milady, why did you not tell me you
were ill?"

Aline locked her eyes with his, a spark of the familiar
antagonism shining through the fog of her fever. "I
would not ask you to stop."

"You're as stubborn as—as—"

"You?" Elizabeth suggested calmly, the ghost of a
smile playing about her lips.

James cast her an irritated look, but he subsided. "All right. I am sorry."

"James, I know that you are concerned about your wife," Elizabeth went on, "but it would be best if you were to go back downstairs with the other men and let me look after Lady Clarissa. Gemma and Olwen will help me."

James hesitated, then sighed and said, "All right. I know better than to stay here and get in the women's way." He smiled at his sister-in-law and laid his hand lightly on her arm. "Do your best, Elizabeth."

"Yes," Aline spoke up from the bed, her voice faint but sharp. "It would not look good if he were to inherit my lands so soon after we were wed."

James's eyes flashed and he started to retort, but Elizabeth gave his arm an admonitory squeeze, and he subsided. "Good day, milady. I hope your health improves." He nodded toward Elizabeth and strode out of the room.

Elizabeth looked over at her patient. Aline's eyes were following James as he walked out the door. Elizabeth watched her thoughtfully for a moment, then smiled and said briskly, "Well, now, let's see about getting you well, shall we? Gemma, you stay here and try to keep her ladyship as cool and comfortable as possible. Olwen and I shall go to my herb kitchen and get something to help that fever."

Aline nodded and closed her eyes. Her head felt too heavy to lift from the pillow. Even the brief exchange with Sir James had exhausted her. The pillow and bed were so soft and smelled so sweet, and it was easy just to drift into a feverish slumber.

*   *   *

James stalked down the stairs and into the great hall, where his brother and Stephen were standing, talking. Richard was holding his daughter, Mary, and the two-year-old girl looked ludicrously small against Richard's bulk. Both men turned to him when he entered the room, and little Mary held out her hands to him.

She immediately began to wriggle, and Richard set her down. She ran across the floor to James, who bent and whisked her up in his arms. He buried his face in her neck, breathing in the sweet scent of child, and Mary wrapped her arms lovingly around his neck. With Mary, there was no pain, no doubt, no suspicion, none of the emotions such as envy or anger which sometimes tainted even his deep love for his brother or his aunt. Mary's love came as freely as sunshine, and James loved her back with the same lack of reserve.

"How is Lady Clarissa?" Stephen asked in concern. "What is wrong with her?"

James looked weary. "She has a fever." He shook his head. "I left her with Elizabeth. Clarissa awoke. She hates me. Even sick as she is, she tried to blacken my character." He let out a gusty sigh. "God knows, she has reason enough to hate me."

His brother poured him a cup of mulled wine, warming it with a heated poker, then walked over to James and handed him the drink. "Here. This will make you feel better. Mary, 'tis time for you to go to your nurse."

He motioned to the nurse, who was standing patiently waiting, and she came forward to take the child. Mary was reluctant to leave, but finally she unwound her arms from James's neck and gave him a resounding buss on the cheek, then allowed her nurse to take her.

James quaffed his drink and moved with Richard and Stephen over to the large stone fireplace. Richard regarded his brother for a moment, then said, "You know, James, you cannot blame yourself for her illness."

James shot him a derisive glance. "No? Ask Stephen how much concern and consideration I showed for the lady on our ride here. She was ill, burning up with fever, and I would not even stop to let her rest."

"Think you that she would have done better lying in a tent beside the road than she will do here under Elizabeth's care? If you had not traveled as fast as you did, you would have been forced to pitch camp and try to fight the fever yourself, outdoors in November. Mayhap you were not kind to her, but you did not give her the illness, and your fast march got her here in time for Elizabeth to do her some good. There is none better at healing than my wife. Everyone in the castle and the village comes to her when they have an illness."

James looked at his brother and smiled wryly. "You always have a way of making it appear that I have not sinned."

Richard chuckled. "And you always have a way of viewing yourself in the worst light."

"I suspect there are those who would tell you that my view of myself is more accurate than yours."

"Then they do not know you well enough. Is that not true, Stephen?"

"Of course. I, of all people, know how kind you are at heart. Who else would have had the patience to put up with an unknowledgeable lad like me for the past three years?"

"You are a quick learner. And, besides, 'twas not your fault that you were unschooled in warfare."

"That may be, but it doesn't make it any less annoying to have a thirteen-year-old boy following you everywhere you go, asking questions."

James smiled and reached out to ruffle Stephen's

hair. He leaned back in his chair and sipped his wine, soaking up the warmth of the fire. "I hated seeing her so pale and still," he said softly. "Irritating as she is, I think I would rather have her up and sniping at me than lying there like that."

"I shall remind you of that when she is well and ringing a peal over your head about something," Stephen laughed.

James smiled faintly. The truth was, he hated seeing anyone ill, and somehow with a woman or a child, it seemed even worse. They looked so small and fragile. He remembered how it had torn at his heart last year when little Mary had been abed with a racking cough, her cheeks flushed and the rest of her paler than the sheets she lay upon.

"'Twill be worse when she takes to her bed in childbirth," Richard said heavily, his face dark with remembered agony.

James tightened. He did not like to even think of such a thing.

He could still remember that narrow, dark hallway where he had sat when he was only three, huddled against Richard, listening to their aunt scream in the pain of childbirth. His mother, Gwendolyn, had been in the chamber with Aunt Marguerite, and there had been no one to hold him and comfort him in the way that only Marguerite or Gwendolyn could. The fear in Richard's and Uncle Philip's eyes had not reassured him in the slightest. He had been positive that Aunt Marguerite was about to die.

Ever since, the thought of childbirth had filled him with a deep and primitive fear. Two years ago, when Mary was born, he had sat with his brother while Elizabeth was in labor upstairs. Only his love and loyalty for his brother had made him stay there.

They had not been able to hear the cries from the bedchamber, as he had that other time, and he had not then felt the deep affection for Elizabeth that he had for his aunt, but it was still horrible to wait, knowing what was happening to Richard's wife upstairs. The pain on Richard's face had been unbearable—the torture of a man who loved his wife and knew she was in pain, yet could do nothing to ease it. He remembered Richard's frustration at his helplessness and his fear of her death.

Thank God, James thought, taking another sip of his wine, thank God he did not love Clarissa.

Aline slept for hours, a hot, restless sleep punctuated by odd, unsettling dreams. Then Lady Elizabeth returned to the room, and she and her maid Olwen lifted Aline up and made her drink a bitter-tasting potion. Aline wondered vaguely if they were trying to poison her, but she was too weak and hazy to worry about it. She simply swallowed the drink as they urged her to, then lay back down. She floated on the edge of consciousness, aware that Gemma and another woman were undressing her, and she was grateful for the touch of the cool air on her flesh. They bathed her all over to combat her fever.

"Poor thing," she heard a northern-accented voice say at one point.

After that she slept, coming awake only when someone shook her and forced her to sit up to take another drink of the vile liquid. Aline made a noise of disgust, but she drank it anyway, too weak to resist. Then she drifted back into the same light sleep, aware of movement and voices, but too exhausted to open her eyes. She grew hot and then cold; sometimes she shivered and other times she turned the linens damp with her sweat.

She had no idea of the passage of time, only of the presence of Gemma and another woman servant. Frequently Lady Elizabeth was there, smelling sweetly of summer roses even here in winter, laying her hand gently on Aline's forehead and murmuring words of comfort.

Gradually Aline began to drift closer and closer to consciousness for longer periods of time. Once, when she was almost awake, she heard the tread of heavy feet across the floor, and then there was a large presence beside her bed. She found it too tiresome to open her eyes, but Aline sensed that it was a man.

A hand reached down and stroked her hair, which was unfastened and tumbled across the pillow. "You are beautiful," James murmured, so softly Aline barely heard him. "Who would have thought you could look this fragile?"

Aline thought that she ought to open her eyes and let him know she was awake, but it seemed too great an effort. Besides, his hand felt nice upon her hair.

His weight settled on the bed, and James leaned over her. "I am sorry." His hand smoothed her hair gently back from her forehead, and his fingertips lightly traced her features. Then he cupped her face on either side and leaned down to speak right to her.

"You will not die," he commanded. "Do you hear me? I will not let you die!"

Surprise at his words brought her eyes open finally, and she stared up into his bright blue gaze. His eyes bored into hers. Aline stared back at him, determination shining in her eyes despite her weakness.

"I will not die," she replied, her voice faint but firm.

James smiled. "Good."

To her surprise, he bent over and brushed his lips

against her forehead. "I will leave you to Elizabeth's care. If anyone can make you well, it is she."

Then he was gone. Later, Aline wondered if it had merely been one of her odd, fevered dreams. But she could still remember how his lips had felt against her skin, velvety yet firm, and she was certain she could not have imagined that.

Aline woke sometime after Sir James left, and realized that she was no longer fiercely hot. Elizabeth confirmed the fact later when she came in to check on her. "Your fever's down," she said, smiling.

Aline returned Elizabeth's smile faintly. "I feel better."

After that, being young and healthy, Aline improved quickly. She was able to drink a little broth that evening, and by the next morning, she was asking for something more filling. Later that day, she insisted that Gemma help her out of bed and over to a chair by the narrow window, where she basked in the warm strip of sunshine, a blanket wrapped around her.

When Elizabeth came in, she was surprised to find Aline in a chair. "I can see that you are improving apace. I will tell James. He will be so happy."

Aline suspected that James would not be nearly as joyous as Elizabeth seemed to think, but she held back the words. She did not want to make an enemy of this woman who had worked so hard to make her well.

"Are you feeling up to looking at cloth?" Elizabeth went on. "I thought it might interest you, if you aren't feeling too tired."

"No, I'm not tired yet. Cloth for what?"

Elizabeth chuckled. "Why, for tunics, silly. James was sure that you were lacking in clothes, since you left your father's keep so hastily."

Aline refrained from pointing out that Lady

Clarissa had fled with few clothes because Sir James was trying to abduct her. She liked Elizabeth, and James wasn't worth getting into an argument with her.

Lady Elizabeth turned toward her maidservant, who had entered the room behind her and stood quietly waiting by the door. "Olwen, go tell the men to bring in those bolts of cloth I laid out in the solar."

"Oh, no," Aline demurred, stabbed with guilt at Elizabeth's generosity. "You are very kind, but, really, you must not. 'Tis too much trouble, and, besides, I couldn't take any of your materials."

"Whyever not?" Elizabeth responded. "We are sisters now."

What could she say? That she couldn't take it because she was deceiving them all? That she wasn't the real Lady Clarissa and had no intention of being a real wife to Sir James? Aline hated to think what would happen if she did reveal the truth.

"I—well, you must know that I am not a—a willing bride."

Elizabeth turned troubled eyes on her. "Are you very much against it? I know that your uncle and our family are enemies, but that does not mean that you cannot be happy married to James. You know, my own uncle was the Earl's enemy, one of those who brought about his father's downfall. But, still, Richard and I married, and we fell very much in love." She smiled reminiscently, her eyes growing misty with fond memories.

"I do not think that will be the case with Sir James and me," Aline responded stiffly. "I—'tis different."

"Because of his birth?" Elizabeth asked a trifle sadly. "My brother told me that you disdained James's birth. I know you are the niece of a duke, but is James's birth really such an impediment? Why, King

William himself was a bastard. His mother was only a weaver's daughter. The Norwens are as pure and noble a line as any in England, and James's mother was no slut. I—well, when I first came here, I, too, thought that Gwendolyn was beneath me, that it was an insult to have her managing the household, as she was then. But I have come to see that she was a loving, passionate woman who could not marry the man she loved. I have found out these past few years just how powerful a force love is. I think sometimes—if I were in the same situation, if my Richard was already married to another woman, would I be any stronger than Gwendolyn was?"

"It is not only that." Aline could not summon up the energy to put on her act; besides, it didn't seem at all amusing to make this woman think she was a shrew. "There are other things. He is my uncle's enemy. And he—well, he is not the sort of man I wish to marry."

"But you are married to him," Elizabeth pointed out. "Would it not be better to have a loving marriage?"

"Perhaps. But it is somewhat difficult, is it not, to love a man who forced you to marry him."

"Your uncle and father arranged your marriage to him."

"They regretted it. Besides, would you have wanted to marry as your uncle arranged?"

Elizabeth shuddered. "No. I am sure that would have been a horrible choice. But James is not. I assure you he will be a kind husband. He is a fair and courteous man, and quite attractive. You could go the length and breadth of the land and not find one as handsome as James. Many women—" She stopped abruptly and cast a quick glance at Aline.

"Many women what?" Aline asked, feeling a curious little spurt of dislike for these unknown women.

"'Tis nothing."

"No, 'tis something, I believe. You were about to say that many women find him handsome? Or that many women have graced his bed?"

Elizabeth's cheeks flamed. "Oh, no, milady! I didn't—that is—oh, dear." Lady Elizabeth ground to a halt. "I have made matters worse. Please, forgive me. Sometimes my tongue leads me into such trouble."

"Because you are too honest?"

Aline didn't know why it annoyed her to hear that Sir James had had many lovers. She had guessed that fact; it was obvious simply from looking at him that women must have fallen at his feet. It was not a surprise, and, anyway, it was no business of hers. After all, what was James to her other than an irritation? A danger to be avoided? An arrogant man who had mistreated her from the moment that they met?

"Lady Clarissa, I beg you to accept my apology," Elizabeth said earnestly. "I can see that I have not helped James's cause. He has every right to be furious with me. I was only trying to point out to you that there would be benefits to marrying him."

"Certain pleasures which he could provide? Indeed, I am sure he is quite experienced at them."

"Any man of his age who isn't a monk is bound to have known other women," Elizabeth pointed out. "Perhaps it is difficult to overlook, but I'm afraid a woman must accept her husband's past."

"And what if a wife had had that sort of past?" Aline flared, color coming into her pale cheeks. "What husband do you think would be forbearing about it?"

"None, I fear. But it is different for them, I think. Futtering has little meaning to them. I know that James has never loved a woman."

"I am sure that is true," Aline agreed. "He is much too arrogant and selfish to be able to love anyone."

"Oh, no! You and he have made a bad start. He is not a bad man. He wants very much to have the place and pride that marrying into Tanford's family would give him. He feels it sorely that all he has of Norwen property is what Richard has given him. No matter how much he loves Richard or how much help he has given Richard in the past, James still feels that he lives on his brother's largesse, that he has nothing of his own. You know about his birth. I think he feels it keenly. He wants his children to have no such blot on them. He wants them to have good, solid family on both sides—Norwen and Tanford. But that is not bad, is it? All men marry for position or family or profit, don't they? All women, too. That is the way of the world—at least for one of *us*. Perhaps a merchant may marry for love, or a silversmith, but not a duke's niece nor an earl's brother."

"I know. Love is something that comes in few marriages. But when it does, it is rare and wondrous. I saw it with my parents, and it is what I want for myself."

"Really?" Elizabeth looked surprised.

Aline nearly groaned at her own mistake. She had spoken of her parents, who were supposed to be Lord Simon and his wife, Lady Pamela. It was possible Lady Elizabeth knew the couple, and it very well might be absurd to say that they loved each other. Aline leaned forward, and said, to divert the other woman's attention, "Do you not think that love is worth striving for?"

"Oh, yes!" Impulsively Elizabeth clasped Aline's hands. "I do. That is why I hope for you and James to find that love with each other, as Richard and I did."

"I do not think that is possible."

Aline looked away from Elizabeth's shining eyes.

She hated deceiving this kind woman. Why, Elizabeth was hoping for her happiness, and yet she was preparing the way for her family to suffer humiliation. What would Elizabeth think when she found out that the "Lady Clarissa" to whom she had spoken her heart was only a traveling entertainer, the daughter of a jongleur and a bastard? Aline could imagine the revulsion in her eyes, and the resentment.

"I am sorry." Elizabeth patted her hand and drew back. "I will not press you. It will come in time."

Olwen knocked at the door and came in, two stocky men following her, carrying several bolts of cloth in jewel tones. Aline sucked in her breath when she saw them, then blurted out, "How lovely!"

Elizabeth smiled. "I hoped you would like them." She turned to the men. "Here, bring them to her ladyship."

Aline smiled as she reached out to touch the sheen of velvet, the shimmer of silk, the glow of wool. "Such beautiful colors."

"Thank you. I chose the ones I thought would suit you best. Something pale is not right for you. I thought this gold velvet or this blue wool. I have some tippets of fur to trim the sleeves and hem."

Aline started to protest again that this was too much for Lady Elizabeth to do for her, that the fur and cloth were far too precious, but she stopped herself. She was, after all, supposed to be the wife of this woman's brother by marriage; Lady Clarissa would accept such gifts from a family member.

So Aline forced herself to smile and say nothing but "Thank you," and they settled down happily to discuss styles, materials, and trims. Aline could not help but feel excitement over the new tunics, lovely things that were being made for her alone, not hand-me-downs from Clarissa and Lady Agnes. However, at the same time she wanted to run away from Elizabeth's happy, trusting eyes.

Over the next few days, as Aline continued to recuperate, several of the women servants busily cut and sewed the clothes. Elizabeth and Aline would do the more delicate work of hems and necklines, as well as the elegant embroidery that would embellish the sleeves and fronts of the tunics. Aline was thankful that she was an adequate seamstress; she'd always helped her mother sew their costumes before Signy had joined their troupe. All noblewomen were raised to do elegant needlework, and it would have looked distinctly odd if Lady Clarissa had been clumsy with a needle.

Aline recovered her health quickly. Within a few days she was up and walking around again, even able to go downstairs to eat in the great hall with the rest of the family. She was nervous when she entered and walked across to the dais where the family and their guests ate. She had grown accustomed to being only with Elizabeth and the maidservants, and she had made little effort to continue her pretense of being a spoiled lady with a tongue of vinegar. At first she had been too weak to make the effort, and later she could not bring herself to be mean to Elizabeth, who was so kind to her.

But now she was facing James again, as well as the Earl and Stephen. Stephen and James would never believe the change in her; she had to be shrewish again, yet she hated the thought. This role was becoming harder and harder to play.

"Good evening, Lady Clarissa," Elizabeth said, sweeping across the floor to her, her arms outheld. She took Aline's arms and looked her up and down. "You look much, much better. I am so glad. I was just telling the others that you were venturing down this evening. Come here. I suspect that you scarcely remember seeing my husband when you arrived. Richard, this is Lady Clarissa, and this, milady, is my husband, the Earl of Norwen."

Aline swept him a curtsy, then turned and offered her hand to Stephen. "Lord Beaufort," she murmured. She looked past him to James and raised her chin in a stubborn gesture. "Sir James." Her voice came out dry and flat.

"Milady."

Aline looked away from him. He was gazing at her too searchingly with those bright blue eyes, and she felt uneasily as if he could see beneath her act. She warned herself to be careful around him.

Elizabeth's eyes flickered from Aline to James and back, and she began to make pleasant, meaningless conversation while they seated themselves at the table. Aline shared a trencher with James, and he politely carved bits of meat for her and laid them on the wide, crusty piece of bread, saying little except to ask a bland question about which cut of meat she preferred. He poured wine into the goblet and offered her the first sip. With equal politeness, Aline ate what he gave her, not looking at him.

"I am pleased to see you looking well, milady," he said at last.

Aline cast him a flashing glance. "Indeed? I would not have thought so. You did not visit me during my convalescence."

He gave her a sardonic look. "To tell the truth, milady, I did not think you would welcome my presence. I had no desire to set back your recovery. Elizabeth thought it better if you were not excited."

Certainly, being around Sir James was never a calming experience for her. Still, it seemed to Aline that by his not having come to see her except for that one barely remembered time, Sir James had demonstrated a clear lack of concern for her. She merely raised her eyebrows in polite disbelief and turned her attention back to her food.

When the meal was over, Lady Elizabeth smiled down the table at her and asked, "Lady Clarissa, would you do us the honor of singing for us?" Lady Elizabeth glanced around at the others. "I heard her ladyship yesterday. She was singing to pass the time as we sewed, and her voice is lovely."

"Indeed?" James turned to look at her; Aline could feel herself coloring under his regard. "I was not aware of your talent, milady."

"You did not ask, sir,' Aline replied tartly, and stood up. "If I might have a lute, milady?"

"Of course."

A lute tied with colorful ribbons was brought for her, as well as a stool, which a servant placed in front of the table so all could hear well. Aline sat down, and her nimble fingers began to play. She soon felt more comfortable than she had in days. She began to sing, her voice soft and melodious. She was very conscious of James, and she glanced up to find him gazing steadily at her. He was watching her thoughtfully—no, it was something warmer than that. He was watching her with interest—an interest she had prayed that she had thoroughly squelched.

Her fingers stumbled over the chords, and she bowed her head over the lute, concentrating on the song. But it was difficult, remembering the light that she had just seen flare in James's eyes. *She could not let him want her!* It would be disastrous.

Elizabeth and Stephen persuaded Aline to sing two more ballads, but then she begged off, saying she was tired, and left them. As she started up the stairs toward her room, James came after her and put his hand on her wrist. "I will walk with you."

Aline glanced up at him, suddenly afraid that he meant to lie with her tonight as her husband. He saw the fear flicker across her face, and shook his head.

"Nay, I did not mean to go any farther than the door."

"All right."

He held out his arm. She took it, and they began to climb the stairs. Aline hoped he didn't feel the trembling of her hand. They said nothing at first.

Then he began softly, "I wanted to talk to you, to tell you . . . I did not come to see you while you were getting better because I was ashamed."

Aline looked up at him in astonishment, almost stumbling on the steps. "What? You?"

He glanced down at her and smiled slightly at her expression. "I know what you think of me, that I feel no shame, that my soul is too black for that. Is that not true?"

Aline glanced away. "No—well, I—"

"Do not bother to lie. I have seen it in your face. You are certain that I am a wicked man. There is little surprise in that, since you were raised in Tanford's family. You would have heard no good of me." He paused. They reached the top of the stairs and turned down the hall. "But I am not such a devil as to make a woman ride until she falls sick. I was ashamed of myself when I understood what I had done, and I could not bring myself to face you. You had every right to hate me, to berate me."

"And you were afraid to face my anger?" Aline asked skeptically.

"No. I was afraid to look at you and see you so pale and weak and know that I had done it to you. I was afraid to look in your eyes and see there the disgust you must feel for me. I was raised never to hurt a woman, least of all one of my own. We had been married only a few days, and already I had broken my vow to protect you. If I had realized that you were ill, I would never have—oh, damnation! I must be honest. I let my temper get the best of me. I rarely do it." He cast her a thin smile. "You have a great effect on me, milady."

"You mean I turn you into a beast?"

Aline was surprised when he laughed at her wry remark.

"Yes, milady, you do. My only excuse can be that your beauty drives me mad."

That remark made Aline chuckle. "Nay, sir, I think it is not my beauty which does that."

"Not entirely," he admitted. "'Tis that combined with your tongue, which cuts like a knife."

"So I have heard. Yet you seem to have little fear of it."

He looked down at her and smiled. "I do not fear you. You make me furious, yet at the same time you are so lovely that you stir my loins."

His words made Aline's skin strangely hot and sensitive, as if he had physically touched her. They had reached the doorway to her room, and they stopped. James slid his forefinger down her cheek. Aline felt as if he had touched her with fire.

"Sir James, please," she whispered turning her head aside.

He turned her gently back to him. She stood gazing at him mutely as he stroked his finger up her cheek, then down again, slowly, lightly, all the while his eyes gazing deeply into hers. Though he did not hold her physically, she could not move, not even when he bent down and kissed her.

10

Aline remembered the last time James had kissed her, in a fury on the road. This time was entirely different from that fierce, hot possession; now his lips wooed her, coaxed and enticed her, gentle and lingering and sweet. But there was little difference in the way the kiss affected her. Her knees felt as if they might buckle, and she unconsciously leaned into James, her hands going up to his chest. Her fingers curled into his tunic, and at her movement, his arms went around her tightly, pulling her against him. His kiss deepened, his tongue luring her mouth open and slipping inside. Aline trembled at the intimate invasion, and timidly her tongue caressed his.

She could feel the shudder that ran through his body, and she thought she might have done the wrong thing, but his mouth dug into hers even more passionately, one hand going up to her hair, impatiently knocking aside the coif that blocked him and sinking into its silken depths. His other hand slid down her back to her hips and curved over them caressingly. He pressed her hips hard against him, and she could feel the hard ridge of his desire against her flesh, even through both their heavy winter clothes. He lifted his mouth from hers only to change the angle of his head and kiss her again, hungrily. He backed her up against the door of her room, his larger body pressing into her, curving around her. Aline's arms were around his neck, and she clung to him as the world seemed to tilt. She could not think, could barely breathe; she felt consumed by James, surrounded by him, and yet it was not a frightening sensation, but something delightful and exciting.

James braced himself with one arm against the door; his other hand was at her hip, and he slid it down onto her leg, then back up. He caressed her waist, and his hand roamed higher, until he reached the soft orb of a breast. His long fingers curled around it, and a little whimper escaped Aline. Her nipple tightened, and he dragged his thumb across it, feeling it thrust against the cloth of her tunic in response. His breathing turned harsh and ragged, and he mumbled her name.

But it wasn't her name at all; it was that of the woman he believed her to be, and the sound of it pulled Aline out of the sensual storm into which he had propelled her. She realized what was happening and how dangerous it was. Quickly she turned her head away, breaking their kiss. James merely used the opportunity to kiss her throat, his lips nuzzling down the tender white flesh in a way that sent shivers of desire all through her.

"Nay," she murmured weakly, then with more strength, bringing her hands up to his shoulders in an attempt to push him away. "Nay! Stop!"

He was heavy and strong, and she knew, suddenly panicked, that she could never budge him. "James, please!" She tried to wriggle away from him, frantic with her helplessness.

But, then, suddenly, he released her. She slid to the side, fumbling for the latch of the door. He simply stared down at her in stupefaction, his features heavy with passion. "What?" he asked her, his chest rising and falling rapidly. "What is amiss?"

"I cannot!" she responded, on the verge of tears.

Her entire body was on fire, aching for him; there was nothing in the world she wanted as much at this moment as to have his hands on her body again. Yet she dared not. She was not the woman he thought she was, the "Clarissa" whose name he had whispered in his passion, and when he found out who she really was, he would despise her. There could be nothing between them. She could not give in to this desire she felt.

"Nay, please, dearling." He stretched out a hand to smooth it over her hair, and his voice was soft and gentling. "Do not be afraid. I shan't hurt you. Do you fear the pain of the first time? I shall go slowly. I promise."

His hand continued to stroke her hair as he talked, and Aline realized suddenly that he was soothing her the way he would soothe a nervous horse.

"Come," he said, smiling at her, his eyes caressing her, and he brushed his knuckles across her cheek. "I shall not harm you."

Aline's eyes narrowed. She was quite sure that he had used these words, this manner, on nervous or reluctant women before. He was used to seducing them, overcoming their fears and their arguments with his winning smile and astonishing blue eyes. Anger gave her the strength to jerk away from his hand.

"Stop! Stay away from me. I am not a fool who

will fall so easily for your honeyed words." She jerked
the door open and whisked nimbly inside, then closed
it and slammed down the bar.

"Clarissa!"

"No! Go away."

He let out an oath, and his fist slammed into the
door, making it shudder. "God's bones, woman, you
are my wife!"

"Not in my heart!" she shouted back.

"Perhaps not," he responded roughly, "but in your
body, there's a different answer." He paused, then
added grimly, "And before long, I am going to make
you admit it."

She heard his steps as he strode off down the hall.
Aline turned and leaned weakly against the door. She
saw Gemma standing beside the bed, taut as a bowstring. Aline gave her a halfhearted smile.

"Well, you managed to avoid him this night,"
Gemma commented. "But I do not think you will be
able to do it long."

"You are right," Aline agreed. She brought her
hands up to her head, pushing against it as if to bring
order to her tumbling thoughts. Finally she said in a
low voice, "I must get away from him."

Gemma's face lit up. "Oh, Aline! Really? But what
about the Duke?"

Aline sighed. "I know not. I promised him to wait
until his men came, but who's to say when that will
be? Sir James destroyed the Duke's plans when he
seized me on the road. I don't know when he will
come. It could be weeks. What else can I do? I have
accomplished what he wanted me to. I married Sir
James, and I have given them an extra two weeks for
Lady Clarissa to escape. And I—oh, Gemma, I do not
like doing this anymore!"

"Neither do I."

"Lady Elizabeth has been good to me, and when I think how this is going to hurt her family, I feel terrible. I can't bear to keep up that proud-lady act in front of her. And Sir James—I'm afraid that I will— well, you know."

Gemma nodded sagely. "Give in. I know. It would be nothing to wonder at, with that one."

"Very well. We must do it." Aline felt scared, but relieved. "We will go to the Duke and explain. I am sure he will understand. He will see that I did everything I could." She gave a short, decisive nod. "There is no sense in waiting. We will leave first thing tomorrow morning."

The castle gates opened early. Aline dressed in the most sober of her old bliauts, which she had hidden in one of her trunks, and she and Gemma left with a group of pilgrims who had sought the castle's protection for the night, as many travelers did. Aline had considered taking her horse, with Gemma riding behind her, for she would be able to move much more quickly. But after a moment's thought, she had discarded that plan. The guards would recognize her when she rode out, and though she doubted that they would stop her, they would doubtless tell Sir James, and he would come after her. She would never be able to outdistance Sir James's steed, and since with a horse she would more or less have to stay to the roads, he would find her easily.

But if they mingled with some of the lowly people leaving the castle, the guard might not notice her, and they would have several hours' head start before anyone realized they were gone. Also, they could cut across fields and hide in the woods, rather than having to stick to the roads. So Gemma crept down to the kitchen early the next morning and picked up as much food as she dared, and they bundled it up in the blankets they would carry. Aline put on her old clothes and pulled the hood of her shabby cloak far forward so that it hid her face. They went downstairs and waited until the pilgrims left the great hall, then followed them out to the gate.

The greatest danger of being recognized, they knew, lay in Gemma's diminutive size. For that reason, they had done their best to make her look like a child. Aline had wrapped cloth around Gemma's torso under her bliaut, binding her breasts and adding inches to her middle until she had the straight figure of a plump child. Then Aline had braided Gemma's hair and let it hang out beneath her _sayon,_ the hood of which they pulled over Gemma's head to help hide her face. As they passed by the guard, Gemma kept her face turned down shyly, and Aline held her hand as a mother would a child's.

Once outside the gates, they lagged behind the pilgrims until the others were far ahead of them. Then they turned from the road and cut across the fields, scrambling over the low stone walls that edged them. They came upon a track and hurried along it, heading in a generally southern direction. Aline wasn't sure where to go; her only thought was to get back to London, where she had left the Duke and her parents, and she knew that it lay south. But the most important thing now was to make it difficult for Sir James to follow her.

Aline was grateful when they found a small woods. It was colder and damper under the trees, but Aline and Gemma felt safer within their shelter—it would be difficult for Sir James, on his horse, to traverse it. But eventually they came out on the other side; it hadn't been a large enough stretch of woods for them to hide in, really, and once again they cut across a meadow, until they found what looked like a sheep track leading south. The going was easier here, so they followed the track.

After a few minutes Aline became aware of a faint jingling noise. She glanced around, and her heart sank. A man on a horse was crossing a field, another rider behind him. She knew, with a fatalistic certainty, that it was Sir James. She glanced around. There was no shelter in which to hide. Even if she ran back toward the woods, he would intercept her easily. There was no escaping him. With a sigh, she dropped her bundle, and she and Gemma sat down on a nearby rock to await his arrival.

Sir James trotted up beside them and pulled his horse to a halt. He sat for a moment looking down at Aline. Aline suspected he was furious, but nothing showed on his face.

"Milady," he began, his tone ironic, "are you weary from your morning walk?"

"How did you find me so quickly?" Aline asked crossly.

"For some reason the guard found it odd that my wife and her maid were leaving Norcastle at the crack of dawn with a party of pilgrims." His eyes swept down her, and he added, "And in such attire, as well." Unexpectedly, his mouth quirked up into a grin. "Where in the name of all the saints did you get that costume?"

"From a maid," Aline answered pettishly. He was making her feel foolish as well as thwarted, and at that moment she could have cheerfully hit him.

He frowned. "At Norcastle?"

"No. One of my own maids at home. I carried it with me because I thought I might need it." It occurred to her that this excuse sounded rather feeble, but she didn't know what else to say. She could not admit that it was her own nor did she want to get any of the servants at Norcastle in trouble with Sir James.

"Indeed? Then you must have been planning to run away for some time." He swung down from his horse and came over to stand in front of her.

Aline shrugged and did not answer.

"Pray tell me, what did you hope to accomplish by it? Did you really think that I would not pursue you?"

"No, of course not. You're not about to let a bride and her dowry escape you," Aline retorted. She stood, disliking the disadvantage that of having to look up at him. She still had to tilt her head, of course, but at least she did not feel like a child or a supplicant in front of him.

"Of course not," he repeated blandly.

The other man joined them. He wore the livery of the Norwen huntsman, and he looked uncomfortable upon a horse. Beside his horse loped two of the Norcastle hunting dogs. When he stopped, they flopped down on the ground, panting, beside the horse and looked at Aline with wide, doggy smiles. Aline cast them a glance of disfavor; obviously they had followed her scent, and that was how James had followed their path so easily.

"How like you," she commented crisply, "to hunt your wife down like a boar or a stag."

"Boorish behavior, I am sure," James agreed mockingly. "But what else is one to do when his wife takes to her heels like a frightened doe? 'Tis a good thing the Norwen dogs are among the best in the kingdom, is it not?"

Aline merely gave him a sour look, and James turned to the huntsman. "Take milady's maid back to the keep. The lady and I will follow you shortly."

"Yes, Sir James." The huntsman got down and started toward Gemma. Gemma put down her head and ran straight into him, hitting the startled man in his most vulnerable place. He fell back, howling and clutching the offended parts.

"Ride!" Gemma shrieked to Aline as the little woman took off at a run.

Aline sidestepped James, who had turned to stare at Gemma in amazement, and ran to the huntsman's horse. She could never hope to control Sir James's stallion, she knew, but perhaps she could get away on this one. Using the strength and muscle control that years of dancing and tumbling had given her, she grabbed the saddle and sprang up into it. Then she took the horse's reins, dug in her heels, and thundered off.

James let out an oath and ran to his own horse, and within seconds Aline heard him pounding after her. She headed for the woods, for she knew she could not outrun him. She ducked low over the horse's neck to avoid the branches as the horse crashed through the trees, but even so a low-hanging branch caught her coif and snatched it off. As they approached a sturdy tree with high branches, she reined the horse in beneath it, stood up, balanced on the saddle, and grabbed one of the tree's limbs. Nimbly she pulled herself up and over the branch. Then she clapped loudly at the horse, and it lumbered off deeper into the woods. Aline hiked up her skirts and tucked them into her belt, then began to climb the tree.

It was only a moment before Sir James was below her, riding more cautiously than she had, pushing branches out of the way and looking around carefully. Aline went perfectly still, huddling against the trunk of the tree. He rode on past, and hope flickered through her. He had missed her.

But that hope was dashed a moment later when he returned, leading her horse, which was munching contentedly on a small branch. Aline grimaced, looking down at them; obviously the animal hadn't had enough sense to go more than a few steps before it decided to stop and eat. James would know that she was around here somewhere. She watched as James glanced around, then looked up into the trees. Aline waited, motionless, her heart pounding so loud she was surprised he didn't hear it clear down there.

Suddenly a grin split James's face, and Aline knew that he had spotted her. "Milady! Now it seems that you have become more bird than deer. I must confess, your abilities astound me. How did you get up there?"

Aline didn't answer. She was stuck, as high as she could go. She knew that it would be disastrous to climb back down to Sir James. Although he might have been grinning a moment ago, he would be furious about this last escapade once he'd had a chance to dwell on it. He had said he did not mistreat women, but she suspected that beating a wife who had tried to escape him twice in the same morning would not be something he would label "mistreatment."

After a moment of silence, James went on, "Well, dear wife, what do you plan to do now? Are you hoping to roost in that tree the rest of your life?"

She glared down at him. Her choices were exceedingly limited. She could not escape, but neither could she stay here, for she would eventually grow too tired or sleepy to continue to hold on. Yet she hated to think of what he would do when she climbed back down.

James swung off his horse and tied both animals to the trunk of a small tree. Then he returned to his post beneath Aline's tree and gazed up at her, crossing his arms over his chest. He waited. She waited.

Finally Aline sighed and began to descend, branch by branch. When she reached the lowest branch, she swung down and dropped lightly to her feet. James was immediately by her side. Aline closed her eyes and braced herself for his blow.

None came. Finally, she opened her eyes and looked up into James's face. He was grinning down at her. Her eyes widened with astonishment, and she gaped at him. He burst out laughing.

"By the Rood," he said cheerfully, "I've never seen a lady like you! What possessed you to climb that tree? And how in the devil did you do it?"

Aline shifted uncomfortably. She knew that there was no lady who would know the kind of leaps and rolls and other tricks that she did, and that few of them would have the agility to climb a tree. She retreated into the haughty pose she had used so often with James, raising her chin and giving him a freezing look. "I learned to climb as a child. I see nothing so remarkable about that. Even a lady can be resourceful."

"You are certainly that," James agreed, laughter still sparkling in his eyes. He looked her over from head to toe. "You know, I rather like you in this wood-nymph pose."

Aline's lips tightened. She knew that she looked a mess. Her coif had come off and her hair had come loose in the mad run, and bits of leaves and twigs clung to her hair and clothes. "Make game of me if you choose."

"Oh, I'm not making game of you, milady. I mean it. You are profoundly intriguing."

She realized that his gaze had fallen to her legs, and she glanced down. Red flushed her face as she saw that the front of her skirt was still tucked up in her belt, revealing the length of her legs clad in nothing but stockings. Annoyed, she reached down and jerked the skirts of her bliaut back into place.

"Oh, nay, do not do that!" James protested, chuckling. "It is recompense for the trouble of chasing my errant wife. You cannot deny me a little something for that."

Aline turned away stonily, but James reached out and took her shoulders and pulled her back against him. His arms went around her from behind, crossing at her waist, and he nuzzled into her hair.

"Ah, milady, the sight of you stirs me almost beyond measure," he murmured against her ear, his hot breath sending shivers through her. "You look as if you'd just been romping in the leaves with a man. I should like to do that with you, believe me."

He buried his face in her hair, groaning a little, and his hands slid down over her body, then back up, cupping and softly squeezing her breasts.

"You are beautiful." His breath came unevenly, and his voice was ragged. "I would like to lay you down right here and take you."

His lips nuzzled her neck as his fingers caressed her breasts, sliding over her nipples and arousing them to hardness. The fleshy nubs thrust out eagerly in response to his touch. Aline thought with a sense of angry betrayal that she might as well have begged him to continue. Her foolish body was eager for him.

She disliked herself for responding to him, but she could not seem to help it—*she was so weak!* One of his hands left her breasts and slid down onto her thigh. He bunched up the material of her bliaut in his hand, gathering it until he reached the hem. Then his hand slipped under her skirts, letting them fall down again to cover his questing fingers.

Aline stiffened with the shock of feeling his hand on her thigh, but as his fingers moved sensually over her leg, gradually working ever higher, she began to relax. He moved up and onto her abdomen, caressing its smooth flatness, then delved down into the tangle of curls at the juncture of her legs. Aline let out a stifled gasp and arched back against him.

Gently James seized her earlobe between his lips and began to tease it, gently scraping it with his teeth, laving it with his tongue. At the same time, his fingers combed through her nether curls, exploring her most secret flesh. Aline shivered involuntarily, dazzled by the sensations he was creating in her.

His tongue traced the whorls of her ear and crept inside. His fingers separated the tender folds of flesh and stroked them, finding an odd little nubbin of flesh that Aline had never even noticed before and caressing it until she felt as if she were on fire.

James groaned. "So sweet . . . so hot . . . Can you feel how hard you make me?"

His palm pressed against her abdomen, pushing her hips back into his body. Aline felt the hard length of his passion swelling and pushing against her. She felt dazed, bombarded by hot, sensual sensations from every direction. Without even thinking, she moved her hips against him, rubbing up and down. James made a choked noise, and his hand tightened on her breast.

He pulled his hands away and grabbed Aline's shoulders, whirling her around to face him. His face lowered toward hers, and she lifted her face, meeting his kiss. Their lips clung. His fingers dug into her buttocks, lifting her up into his burgeoning desire. He began to pull her down to the ground.

Just then the huntsman's voice sounded through the trees. "Master? Sir James? Are you in here? I have the little wench."

James pulled back, cursing softly. He closed his eyes, obviously struggling to regain control of himself. Aline, panting, began to return, too, from the hazy realm of desire into which James had catapulted her. Embarrassment gripped her as she realized how she must look, her clothes twisted and pulled all awry as well as littered with twigs and leaves. Her face felt flushed, and she was sure her mouth must look red and swollen from James's kisses. The Norwen servant would be bound to guess what they had been about when he saw her—and James, too, for his manhood was pushing at his loose tunic in an unmistakable way.

Aline made a strangled noise and turned aside, blushing hotly. She struggled to arrange her hair and clothing.

"Oh, there you are, sir!" the huntsman exclaimed, spotting them. He came toward them, dragging Gemma reluctantly along with him. "Here she is. I got the little one."

"I see."

"Aye, she's a rare feisty one, that one," the man went on, shoving Gemma forward so that she fell at Sir James's feet. "I would look forward to being the one to give her a lesson or two in treating her betters, if you would let me, sir."

Aline looked anxiously toward her friend and saw that Gemma's face was reddened and beginning to swell on one side. No doubt the huntsman had already taken a little revenge for the pain Gemma had inflicted on him. But Aline knew that the blow he had dealt her was nothing compared with what Sir James might decide to have done to her now. Gemma had, after all, committed a very grave offense—abetting his wife in her escape.

"No!" Aline cried, flinging herself to her knees in front of James and taking his hand in hers. "Please, Sir James, don't punish her. It was all my fault. I am to blame. Punish me instead. Truly, she tried to argue me out of it, but once I'd set my mind on it, she could not but come with me. She wanted only to protect me!"

"By damaging one of my men?" he asked sarcastically, but Aline could see that his face was still heavy with unfulfilled desire for her, and she hoped that his passion had softened him toward her.

"She meant only to help me. To protect me. She was afraid that you were going to beat me for running away, and so she tried to help me. That is all. She loves me."

"I cannot let servants defy me in such a manner," James pointed out.

"I beg of you. She has been with me since I was a child. I love her as one of my family." Her eyes filled with tears as she pleaded with him. "Please, sir, grant this as a boon to me."

James gazed down into Aline's face. God, but she was lovely, with those great golden eyes swimming with tears, looking up at him beseechingly. A man would be likely to do almost anything this woman requested, he thought. There was a great deal more to Lady Clarissa than he had ever dreamed, and he found himself wanting to know her, to unfold each petal one by one until he had reached the soft, secret core of her.

"Arise." He drew her up with his hand. Suddenly he hated the thought of her kneeling before anyone, including him. She was his, but she was his in all her fierceness and her pride, not abjectly. He looked down at Gemma and said curtly, "Get up, woman."

Gemma stood up with some trepidation, but she faced James bravely. He leaned down to put his hands on her shoulders, and his fierce blue eyes bored into her as he spoke. "It looks as though the huntsman has already punished you somewhat. As for me, I will forgive you this once. But only this once. It is good that you would protect your mistress, even to your life. That is what I would have in my wife's maidservant. But remember this: you need protect her only against others, never against me. She is mine, and I intend her no harm. If you ever cross me again, you will pay for that mistake with your life. Do you understand?"

"Yes, Sir James." Relief swept through Gemma, and she would have fallen if Aline had not grabbed her and helped her to remain on her feet. "You are a kind and gracious knight."

A smile touched Sir James's mouth. "There are a few who would dispute that." He looked up at the huntsman. "Take her back to the keep and let her go about her duties. Do not harm her any further, or it will go ill with you. Now begone. I promise you you will be rewarded for your pains today."

"Yes, master." The huntsman nodded and took Gemma's arm grimly, leading her over to his horse. After some effort, he had both of them in the saddle and they rode off, the hounds trotting along behind them.

James turned to Aline and crossed his arms over his chest. "Now, milady, you and I, I believe, have a few matters to discuss."

11

Aline waited warily. She realized what the huntsman's interruption had saved her from, and she was grateful for it. The time had given her ardor a chance to cool, and she was determined not to let herself make the same mistake again. However, she wasn't sure about Sir James—he might be intending to resume what they'd been doing when the huntsman had arrived. Then, again, he might be about to take out on her his rage over her running away.

Aline wasn't sure which prospect scared her more. At least she had encountered blows before, and eventually their pain would subside. But she had never experienced anything like what she had felt earlier, and she suspected that it was something from which she could not recover.

James's eyes drifted down over her. "Lord, but you are a tempting wench."

Aline took a cautious step backward and struggled to assume her haughty mask. "I am not a *wench*, sir."

A grin lightened his face. "I know. You are a very grand lady. Except, of course, when you are racing through the forest or climbing trees. 'Tis a behavior quite common among ladies, I've heard."

Aline's hands clenched in her skirts. *Had he realized that she was an impostor?* Obviously no real lady would have done the things she did. It had been foolish to flee from him that second time; she had acted impulsively, without thinking.

"I would love to stay here in the woods and dally with you, wife, but I think it is best we return home." He paused, then said huskily, "'Tis not meet for your first loving to be on the cold, hard ground."

He cupped her cheek with his hand. His hand was warm and roughened by calluses, and the feel of it upon her skin made her shiver. How was she to hold out against him, when everything he did—every look, every touch—made her burn with desire?

He smiled, a promise in his eyes, and Aline had to look away, breathless. He chuckled softly. "So eager, and yet so afraid. You are a puzzle to me, milady."

James untied his horse and led him out of the trees. He gave Aline a hand up onto the steed, warning sternly, "Do not think to try to dash away on this horse, milady. You are likely to find yourself thrown, even trampled. He does not take kindly to strangers."

"I am not a fool," Aline told him crisply. "That is why I took the other horse."

"Of course. How stupid of me." He swung up in the saddle behind her.

James settled her between his legs, as he had ridden with her on the day he had captured her, so that she was cradled against him, his arm around her back, her hips snugly nestled between his rock-hard thighs. But that other time there had been chain mail covering his body, and they had not kissed and caressed until they were on fire only minutes before. Nor had he rested his other hand on her thigh, as he did today. She could feel him against her hip, hardening, as the rocking of the horse moved her subtly, intimately, against him.

"You know what I would like to do one day?" he murmured into her ear, his voice low and husky in a way that stirred her.

Aline shook her head mutely, and he went on, "I should like to take you riding, where none are about, as here, and you would sit facing me."

Aline sucked in her breath sharply, and her startled eyes flew to his face. She could imagine herself sitting in that way, flush against his body, her legs wrapped around him. She saw in his eyes acknowledgment of the picture she conjured up, and she blushed to her hairline and ducked her head.

His dry chuckle held less humor than sexual appetite. "Yes, like that," he whispered. "And you would ride me as we rode together."

Aline's face flamed even higher. She thought that she must be a shallow, wicked person to turn so hot and hungry at the image his words evoked, to pulse with desire for a man she did not like, a man for whom, in fact, she should feel only distrust and fear.

James's arm went around her more tightly, and his other hand slid restlessly up and down her leg. "Ah, Clarissa, I am a fool to torture myself." He nuzzled her hair. "'Tis like heaven and hell to hold you this way."

"I—I'm sorry," Aline ventured in a muffled voice.

He laughed. "Nay, there is nothing you need to be sorry for. 'Tis the way the Lord created you, the most desirable armful of woman I ever met. And as you are my wife, I can only rejoice in that fact, and wonder why He saw fit to torment me so."

James released a sigh and reluctantly loosened his hold on her. "Come. Let us talk of something else, or I fear I shall forget myself."

"All right." Aline was happy to retreat from this topic; it bothered her far too much, in ways that she could barely comprehend.

They rode for a moment or two in silence, then James asked quietly, "Why do you fear me?"

Aline sat up straight and turned her head to stare at him with astonishment. "You can ask that? When you have just chased me down like a hound after a hare?"

"Well, you are my wife, milady. Did you think that I would pay no attention to the fact that you sneaked out of the keep at dawn? And on foot? What would any husband do?"

"That may be, but 'twas not the only thing you have done. What about your abducting me? Forcing me to marry you? Making me ride for hours on end and make camp in the open, until I fell ill?"

His jaw tightened. "I have told you, I am sorry for that. I would have stopped if I had realized that you were falling sick. Certainly I did not do it in order to make you ill. Besides, that was not what I meant—I meant why do you fear my lovemaking?"

Aline looked away, blushing. "I know not what you mean."

"Ah, but I think you do. It is natural for a woman to be uneasy about her first time, I suppose, but it seems to me that it is more than that with you. Last night you drew back from me and looked at me with a kind of terror, and this morning you ran away. I cannot think but that the cause of your flight was the fear that I would insist on coming to your bed. Why are you scared?"

"I'm not sure," Aline said lamely. She could not

tell him that her fear was not of lovemaking as much as the possibility that her desire would lead her to make a dreadful mistake—that she was afraid not of him, but of her own feelings.

"I thought back last night, and I realized how many times when I began to desire you, you blunted my passion with your haughty air or some snide comment about my birth. You have been working me to your purpose, have you not? Making me dislike you so I will not desire you, will not insist on bedding my wife?"

Aline was stunned. She could not look at him. She was certain that he must be furious with her now. How could she answer him? She sneaked a peek at him. To her surprise he did not appear angry; he was merely staring at her in an intent, faintly puzzled way.

"Yes," she admitted softly. Perhaps if she told a little of the truth, it would make the rest of what she said more believable. "I did not want to lie with you."

"Why? It is a natural thing between a husband and wife."

"I do not know you."

"'Tis the case with many husbands and wives."

"Perhaps, but what makes you think that any of those brides go happily to their wedding beds? It is something they have to do, and perhaps they cannot think of any way to avoid it."

James smiled slightly. "Not being as clever as you?"

Aline squirmed uncomfortably.

"Or perhaps they are not as desperate to avoid it as you, even if they do not wish it," he suggested.

"Perhaps. I know not. I only know what I did."

"Some women fear the unknown, but I think that is not the way it is with you. You, I think, are more likely to rush to meet it." He paused, and his hand came up to touch her hair lightly. "I would be gentle with you. I would bring you pleasure. You have felt it when I touched you."

"No. Please." She felt weak as he stroked his hand down her hair.

"I think perhaps you fear the pleasure of the marriage bed."

Aline drew in her breath sharply and glanced up at him, amazed. He smiled at her silent admission. "I am right."

"I cannot belong to my enemy," Aline said, seizing on the only excuse she could think of.

"What?"

"If I give in to you, if I truly become your wife, then I will be . . . a part of you."

James's mouth widened sensually. "That is true," he said, his voice ripe with satisfaction.

"I cannot be. Do you not understand? I would be betraying my family, my very flesh and blood. Would you wish to betray the Norwens thus?"

"It is no betrayal."

"Not for you!" she flashed. She knew this much was true, and her eyes shone with that truth. "For you can take me and not care. I cannot do that!"

"Then what you fear is loving me?"

"No!" Aline exclaimed, then realized that she had trapped herself with her explanation. For what else did her words mean? Was it true? Was what she feared so much falling in love with Sir James?

"No," she repeated softly, but she turned her head so that he could not see whatever her eyes might be revealing.

"I am no enemy to you, milady," James told her gently. "If you give me your heart, I will protect it, just as I will protect your body."

Aline noticed that he said nothing about being

willing to give his own heart in return—and noticed, to her amazement, that the observation hurt.

"I cannot!" she cried. "I cannot trust you. You have been an enemy to my family for years."

James stiffened. "Your family deserved every loss it suffered. Tanford destroyed my family."

"You lie!" Aline responded heatedly, grateful to be away from the confusing, upsetting subject of desire and love. She would have had to defend the Duke in any case, because he was supposed to be her uncle, but she had personally liked the man. He had been kind to her, had given her a way out of her problems.

"No. I am sure that it was he who came up with the plan to infiltrate Norcastle." He glanced down at her then. "Have you been told the story of my family? Of how the Norwens were betrayed and killed?"

"No," Aline admitted, her brow knitting.

James's jaw was clenched, and his eyes burned with a pale blue fire. "Twenty-three years ago, when I was a small boy, my father's wife, the Lady Mary, opened the castle to a group of men, enemies of the Norwens. My father, you see, had turned her bitter and angry because he had brought my mother Gwendolyn, his mistress, into the castle. My parents were very much in love, but, as you might guess, his wife was furious over the matter. She feared that my father, Lord Henry, would disavow her son, Richard, and try to make me his successor. It was a foolish fear; he would never have done it. Lord Henry loved Richard greatly, and so did our grandfather, the Earl. But some people put that idea into her head. They preyed on her jealousy and her bitterness, and they persuaded her to betray her husband.

"They came in at night through the door she had opened, and took the guards by surprise. Then they opened the gates, and within minutes the yard was flooded with enemies. Aunt Marguerite and Uncle Philip saved Richard and my mother and me. But all the others perished. The old Earl died with two of his knights at the bottom of the stairs. My father and his remaining men made their stand on the small twisting staircase that leads up to the turret. My father died there, hacked to pieces by William of York. Richard's mother and our sisters were slaughtered."

Aline stared at him him horror. "Oh, James," she whispered, "I did not know. How terrible it must have been for you!"

"I don't remember it. Richard does, but I was only three at the time, and I remember none of it, though the others tell me that I had nightmares for years after that."

Without thinking, Aline reached up and laid a comforting hand against his cheek. "I am sorry," she said.

He glanced down at her, surprised by her action. Then his face hardened, and he said flatly, "It was your uncle who planned it."

She dropped her hand, and her eyes widened. "No!"

"Aye. It was he, I am sure of it."

"No. I can't believe that," Aline protested, shaking her head, shocked. The Duke involved in murdering Sir James's father? It was ridiculous. He was too quiet and thoughtful, not the sort of man to plot to kill another in cold blood. "You're mistaken. You must be. My uncle would never do such a thing."

"Oh, Tanford *seemed* the least involved, I'll give him that. He took only a small keep and some strategic land, and even our sovereign pled his case with us, saying he was involved in only a minor way. It was Sir Godfrey's and William of York's troops who actually entered Norcastle. But I know William, and he hadn't the brains to think of such a plan. It could have been Sir Godfrey—he was crafty and sly. But I don't think it was. The whole idea has the stamp of Tanford—to work on one's jealousies and fears, to prey on a mind already halfway to madness until it snaps completely. 'Tis too subtle for Sir Godfrey. But 'tis very much the way Tanford works."

"Nay! It isn't true!" She thought of Tanford and the kindly way he had treated her. He had spoken to her perhaps not as an equal, but at least as if she was a person. Surely he could not have been party to the dreadful attack Sir James had just described.

"You will believe as you want. But it is the truth."

Aline thought about all the things that the Duke and his daughter had told her about Sir James: his treachery and his lies, the way he had tricked Tanford into betrothing his niece to him. She sneaked a glance up at him. They had warned her, too, of how charming and convincing he could be, how he was known to be a seducer of women. That much was true, she was sure; look at how easily he had almost succeeded in seducing her this day before the huntsman's timely arrival. But she was not sure that it followed that he was lying now. There had been the ring of truth in his voice; he had looked so fierce and bitter.

"They say it is you who are the deceiver," she said. "That you tricked my uncle into betrothing me to you, that you promised him something and then did not do what you had said you would." Hesitantly, she asked, "Is it true?"

"Have you seen the betrothal contract? Does it state anything there that I did not perform?"

Aline stared at him. "How could I know? I cannot read the document."

"Oh. I'm sorry. I did not think. The women in my family read."

"Lady Elizabeth?" she asked with interest.

"Yes. And my aunt, Marguerite."

"Truly? They must be very intelligent."

Her voice was filled with awe, and James smiled. "They are quick-minded," he admitted. "But, in truth, Richard's cousin, the Lady Gertrude, can read as well, and she is as dull as a cow."

"No!" Aline mulled this over. Very few women could read, even among the nobility; indeed, not many men could, either. Reading and writing were generally matters left to the clergy. "Then I assume that you must read also."

"Of course. I know many think that it is a waste of time. All a man needs to know is how to wield a sword and lance and ride a destrier. But there is much to know in this world besides war. How can you be certain if your bailiff is cheating you if you cannot tot up figures yourself? How can you know whether what someone tells you is written in a letter is truly there?"

"Do you think—could I learn to read?"

"Certainly," he said carelessly. "I will teach you."

A smile lit up her face. "Would you?"

He nodded, smiling back down at her.

Aline was so pleased and excited at the prospect that it wasn't until later that she realized that James had never actually answered her question about his betrothal promise.

James and Richard's aunt, the Lady Marguerite, arrived the next day with her husband, Sir Philip. She was a tall, vigorous woman with the dark good looks of the Norwen clan. She seemed the opposite of the dainty, soft-spoken Elizabeth, but the two women got on well, and they readily admitted Aline into their sessions of work and conversation. Aline could not help but like Lady Marguerite, just as she liked Elizabeth, and the knowledge of that made her increasingly uneasy. She compared their quick wit and open, down-to-earth manner with the silliness of Lady Clarissa and the airs of her cousin. Frankly, Aline was finding that she liked the Norwen clan better than Tanford's, and she could not help but wonder if the Duke had told her the truth about Sir James and his family. Or had it been James who had spoken the truth when he said that the Duke of Tanford was a wicked, treacherous man who had plotted to destroy the Norwens?

Aline worried about what she should do. Obviously, running away was impossible; James would capture her as easily as last time, and she could not subject Gemma to his punishment even if she were willing to incur his fury herself.

However, with every passing day she had less stomach for this game she was playing. She was no longer certain who was right or wrong in the matter of the betrothal, but she knew that she did not enjoy deceiving these people who were so kind to her.

Her tangled feelings for Sir James only made matters worse. She tried to hold on to the dislike she had felt for him. She reminded herself of how arrogantly he had carried her out of Cambrook's great hall and up the stairs to his room, of how he would have raped her had she not drawn her knife on him. And yet . . . would he really have done so? She was no longer certain. He had not forced himself on her all these weeks of her marriage, even though he had every right to take her. Was it not possible that he would have let her go that other time if he had known that she did not wish to be his leman?

In fact, she wondered, was that not exactly what he had done? Having been around Sir James for several weeks now, she doubted that she had frightened him when she'd pulled the dagger from its scabbard. Even drunk, she felt sure, he could have disarmed her. And he had not pursued her.

He could be arrogant, that was true. He could be cold, calculating, and difficult. His head ruled his heart. But he could also be charming and witty, even mischievous, especially when he and Stephen were hatching some joke. And where he did love, he loved completely. His loyalty to his brother seemed unshakable, and Aline knew from Lady Elizabeth's comments that there was no one whom the Earl trusted and relied upon as much as he did James.

She no longer knew how to feel about James, or what she should do. So she waited in a state of uncertainty as the winter slowly passed.

James began to teach her to read, and he was patient with her mistakes, though they were many. When he looked at her with desire in his eyes or took her hand and raised it to his lips or kissed her good night, she melted inside.

James spent the winter wooing her. From the time of her attempted escape, he'd been patient and gentle, never demanding that she sleep with him. He strolled with her in the garden, where the walls sheltered them from the winter winds. He sat with her in the embrasure of a window in the great hall and talked, holding her hand and stroking his other forefinger across the palm and down each finger until, tingling, she silently wished he would caress more than just her hand. He laughed; he cajoled; he told entertaining stories of his adventures in the Holy Land on the Crusades. He often walked her to the door of her room at night, and there he would kiss her until she was breathless and yearning. But then he would leave, not pressing her to let him enter the bedchamber.

She found herself thinking about him when he was not around, daydreaming about what it would be like to really be married to him. She knew that he was biding his time, seducing her with great skill and patience, and yet she could not dislike him for that. It showed that he honored her, she thought, that he wanted her enough to wait, enough to use all his best efforts to win her.

Aline could not deny that she wanted him in return. He was the most handsome man she had ever seen, and it seemed as if each day he grew more handsome to her. She knew immodest urges to see what his chest looked like beneath his tunic or to feel his mouth upon hers again.

Often he and Stephen or he and Richard would practice their skills with the sword outside in the courtyard, and sometimes Aline would go to one of the narrow windows and watch. She found herself drawn to the play of muscles in his legs as he moved and the intent expression on his face, even to the way his hair dampened with sweat from his exertions. There was something wonderfully, primitively male about him at those moments.

November ended, and the excitement of Christmas activities started, first with Advent, then Christmas Day and then Boxing Day. Aline joined in the festivities with a divided heart, enjoying the pleasure of the rich food and beautiful gifts and the warmth of being included in the Norwen family, but feeling guilty the whole time for being there under false pretenses. She made James a wide cloth belt heavily embroidered with *orsay,* and he thanked her with as pleased a smile as if she had given him something truly valuable.

In return, he gave her a belt made of golden links, broken here and there with strips of gold set with garnets. Aline's eyes widened at the valuable gift, and her heart swelled with feeling. She smiled at him tremulously, tears misting her eyes, and quickly wrapped the belt around her slim waist, discarding the cloth sash she had been wearing. She smoothed her hands down the cool gold links.

"'Tis beautiful," she murmured. She had never had anything so precious or so lovely.

"Nay. 'Tis *you* who are beautiful." He took her hand and gravely kissed it. "I have another gift for you."

She looked up, surprised.

"'Tis really my bride gift to you, but it only just arrived. I ordered it from a goldsmith in York."

He handed her a cloth, and she unfolded it to reveal a gold necklace and earrings, both set with yellow topazes. She sucked in her breath in astonishment. "James! Nay, this is too much."

James chuckled. "This from the mouth of Lady Clarissa? Do my ears deceive me?"

Aline grimaced at him. "I am not a greedy sort. That is one sin of which you cannot blame me."

"That is true. You never ask for anything. But I choose to give this to you. They match your eyes, see? 'Tis why I ordered them. I knew as soon as I saw you what I would give you."

Aline almost burst into tears. Her heart swelled within her chest. She loved the jewels he had given her; she wanted them more than she had ever wanted anything before. But she felt even more wretched than usual about deceiving him.

Impulsively she threw herself against him, hugging him tightly, and his arms went around her. He chuckled, and she could feel the rumble of it deep in his chest. "Dear wife, had I but known how this would affect you, I would have done it weeks ago."

Aline gulped back her tears and stepped away from him, grimacing at him. "Jest if you like, but I shall treasure them always. They are beautiful."

"Might they earn me a kiss?" he asked teasingly.

"They might." She leaned forward and gave him a peck on the lips, but his arms went around her, holding her to him, and he deepened the kiss until Aline felt dizzy and weak from it.

He released her and stood looking down at her for a moment, and Aline could see the fires of passion burning deep in his eyes. Then he regained control of himself. His eyes shuttered the desire that had shown there for an instant, and he stepped back from her, giving her a stiff smile. Aline swallowed hard. She wished, deep inside, that he had not drawn back.

It snowed, then turned bitterly cold for several days, and everyone was landlocked into the keep. The men grew restless in their enforced inactivity. One afternoon, as Aline, Elizabeth, and Marguerite were sitting and sewing in the solar, they were disturbed by the ringing of steel on steel. The three women looked at each other in horror, certain that the restlessness had driven the men into some dangerous argument. They ran down the staircase, then stopped as they rounded a curve and saw what was going on below.

It was, indeed, men fighting, but it was equally obvious that they were merely practicing, not fighting in earnest. Apparently they had decided to alleviate their boredom by turning the great hall into a practice field.

The women relaxed, chuckling, and before long both Elizabeth and Marguerite moved back to the solar. Aline stayed, unable to pull her eyes away from James. Their exertions and the fire in the huge fireplace had made the men hot, and most of them had stripped off their long tunics, leaving them in braies and undertunics. James's undertunic was damp with sweat and clung to his chest, and it was unlaced partway down, revealing the skin beneath. His sleeves were rolled up, and sweat glistened on the bulging muscles of his arms. Aline was fascinated. She could not pull her eyes away from the ripple of muscle beneath his taut skin. She wished that she could touch it, that she could peel away the clinging cloth and reveal the full expanse of his chest. Her thoughts were wickedly lascivious, she knew, but she could not stop them.

Finally, she forced herself to turn away, and as she did so she saw a man standing in the hall below, close against the wall, his arms folded, watching the mock battle before him. Almost as if he had felt her gaze on him, he raised his face, and their eyes met. Aline felt a chill, though she was not sure why. She turned away hastily and hurried back toward the solar, where the other women were.

That night at supper, however, she felt the distinct sensation that someone was watching her, and when she glanced discreetly around, she saw the same man, gazing at her. She turned her eyes back down to her plate, vaguely uneasy. After the meal was over, James joined his brother and several of their knights in front of the fire, while Elizabeth and Marguerite both went upstairs. Aline followed them, feeling a bit cross that James had preferred the men's company to her own.

As she walked down the hallway toward her room, suddenly a man stepped out of the shadows. Aline stopped with a gasp, and the man quickly reached out and took her arm with one hand while he clapped the other one over her mouth.

"Shhh!" he hissed. "Do not scream. I must talk to you. I come to you from His Grace, the Duke of Tanford."

12

Aline stared at the man, wide-eyed. She knew that she should have felt relief at his words. Instead, she was filled with dismay.

He took his hand from her mouth. "We must talk."

"Not here." Aline glanced nervously up and down the corridor. Someone might come out of one of the chambers at any time, and it would look very odd for her to be standing here talking to a stranger.

"Then where?"

Aline thought quickly. "The spinning room."

There were never servants at the looms or spinning wheels after dark, and the way to it led away from the family bedrooms. She turned and walked quickly down the corridor in the opposite direction, her candle flickering. The man followed her silently. They went down a small staircase and emerged on the floor below, some distance from the noise and activity of the men in the great hall. Aline slipped quietly along the hallway and into the large room where cloth for the castle was prepared and sewed.

When the man followed her in, Aline carefully closed the door and turned to face him. It made her nervous to be here in a large, dark room with this stranger. Her candle barely lit where she stood, and most of the room lay in deep shadows. It was unnerving, and she stayed close to the door, ready to throw it open and run, should he prove to be dangerous.

"Who are you?" she demanded.

"My name is not important," he responded. "You may call me Fingal. I work for the Duke of Tanford."

"Then he knows where I am and what happened to me?"

"Aye. He is well pleased. It was not exactly as he planned it, but it worked out well."

"For him perhaps!" Aline retorted sharply. "But it hasn't been easy for me."

The man shrugged, irritating Aline further. She was about to lecture him on his insolence, when it struck her that she was beginning to think and act as if she truly were a lady. She had forgotten that her concerns and problems were of little importance to someone of a higher rank.

She grimaced and said, "Have you come to take me out of here?"

"I?" He appeared amused. "Nay, not I."

"Then who will? And when?"

His eyebrows lifted derisively. "What? Do you think that His Grace is going to storm Norcastle to bring out a jongleur's daughter?"

Aline glared at him. "No, of course I do not think he will lay siege to the castle. But he said that he would get me away before—" The words stuck in her throat. She thought of what James would think, how he would feel, when he found out that he had married a dancer, not the niece of a duke. She swallowed hard and continued, "—before he reveals who I am."

"How would you suggest he do it? Should I put you on a horse and ride off with you? Norwen's men would be after us in a moment, and, believe me, wench, I have no desire to be captured and tortured to death just to make your life easier."

"But His Grace told me he would . . ." Aline persisted stubbornly, panic beginning to rise in her. "He said that I need have no fear."

"A man like the Duke has other things to think about than some dancing girl," the emissary told her bluntly. "Besides, why do you care? I would think you'd be happy to live here like a lady, eating at the high table, prancing about in all your finery. 'Tis better than dancing half-naked for scraps from the table."

"But why wait any longer? Sir James and I are married now."

"His Grace likes to let his plans ripen. His Grace sent me to tell you that he wishes to wait to reveal who you are until the bastard comes to Court again, so that he will have a large and appreciative audience."

"No!" Aline cried. Sir James would not go back to London for months, at least until this spring or summer.

"He said I would not have to keep up this pretense long. He said it would be over before the marriage was consummated!"

The man released a short bark of laughter. "You mean to tell me that he hasn't got beneath your skirts yet? Sir James of Norwen, the man women swoon for? That's a rich one. His Grace will laugh when he hears it." He chuckled again, then sobered. "But I do not think that is what His Grace intends."

"But yes, it is! That way it can be annulled, if it is not consummated."

"Why would His Grace want it annulled? The longer the marriage goes on, the more humiliation for the bastard."

Aline sucked in a breath, staring at him. "Are you saying, then, that it was all a lie? Everything His Grace told me? Everything he promised me? Did he lie about Sir James? Is what James told me true, that the Duke of Tanford is a lying, deceitful man who set out to destroy the Norwens? Am I carrying out the wishes of a monster?"

Fingal jumped forward, grabbed Aline's arm, and twisted it up behind her back, clamping his other hand over her mouth. He slammed her back against the door so hard tears came to her eyes.

"Hush, you stupid little whore! You'll bring the bastard down on us with this caterwauling."

"He will kill you!" Aline said.

"That may be," the man replied, his eyes cold as death. "But you will die with me. What do you think he will do when I tell him who you really are? When I reveal that you are a henchwoman of the Duke of Tanford? Oh, Sir James would love to discover that his wife is a peasant, a *dancer*. Do you think he will show mercy to the woman who betrayed him? You'll be lucky if your death is swift. More like it will take you days to die."

Aline's blood ran cold. The horrible man was right. Sir James would be livid; he would hate her for betraying and humiliating him. Knowing James as she did now, she saw that Tanford's plan to destroy James was perfect: his weakest spot was his illegitimacy, and to discover that he was married to someone of low birth would devastate him. He would feel doubly shamed to have his humiliation witnessed by all his peers, and it would destroy his hope of founding a family whose heritage from his wife's side would wipe out any stain of his own birth. Aline did not even notice that she dreaded James's certain pain and hatred for her more than she did the fact that he might very well kill her for her betrayal of him.

"Ah," the man said with an amused satisfaction, "you had not thought of that, had you?"

Aline lifted her chin, trying to imbue her expression with confidence. "My husband would believe *me*, not you. He loves me."

The Duke's man let out a harsh cackle of laughter. "You think so? Then you're a greater fool than I thought. That one loves no one and never will. If he finds out you've betrayed him, he will squash you like a bug." He shoved her away from him. "You'd do best to forget your silly notions and do what His Grace tells you. The Duke wants you to live with the man a while longer. Consummate the marriage. What does it matter if he futters you? You made a living spreading your legs."

"I am no whore!"

He shrugged, disbelieving. "A dancer who looks like you? Find a better tale. I am no fool—the only reason you're avoiding bedding him is because he'll be furious you are not a virgin."

Aline's hand lashed out to slap him, but he caught her wrist, and for an instant, his eyes flashed. "Oh, but you're a fiery one, aren't you? I am tempted to take you down a notch." Then he sighed and released her hand. "But His Grace would not like it if I marked you. It would make your husband most suspicious. So I will wait." A smile curved his mouth. "When this is over, I will make it a point to find you."

"What do your threats matter? You just told me I'm as good as dead when Sir James finds out the truth."

"Tanford will get you out if he can. His Grace looks after his own. And you are a beauty. He can use you again."

Aline shot him a look of pure loathing, and he chuckled. "I must leave you now. If the Duke has further instructions, I will bring them to you. Until then, play your part well." He strolled to the door, where he turned and added slyly, "It isn't only *your* welfare at stake, you know."

"I don't know what you're talking about," Aline snapped.

"Why, my *lady*,"—he stressed the word mockingly—"have you risen so high that you've forgotten your parents?"

Aline froze. "What do you mean?"

"Only that your parents are living on His Grace's largesse at the moment. You would not want them turned out into the cold—or worse."

Aline's stomach rolled sickly, and she had to lock her knees to keep them from buckling. He was threatening her parents. It was clear from his tone and the smug, malicious expression on his face what would happen to them if she disobeyed the Duke.

"You're a monster! Both of you!" she said. "Get out of my sight. I hate you."

He merely smiled, a thin, tight smile that made Aline shiver, and then he was gone.

Aline sat down on a stool, unable to stand any longer. She dropped her head into her hands. What was she to do?

She was living in luxury, wearing materials finer than she had ever dreamed of and being waited upon by servants. Her stomach was never empty. She was learning to read and write like the finest of ladies. She was honored and protected. Yet never had her life appeared more bleak.

"Lady Marguerite?"

The woman in the solar looked up, and her face creased with a smile. "Clarissa! How nice to see you. Come sit with me."

Lady Marguerite put aside her sewing and stretched out her hands toward Aline. She had become genuinely fond of Sir James's bride. She had expected the worst from a niece of Tanford's, but Lady Clarissa had been a pleasant surprise. The girl had wit and spark and a strength of will that Lady Marguerite could not help but admire, possessing those qualities in full measure herself.

"You look troubled, my dear," she said as Aline took both her hands and squeezed them tightly in greeting, then pulled up a stool to sit at her feet.

"I am," Aline admitted. She had spent most of the night worrying and wondering. She could see no way out of her mess, and, worse, there was no one, other than Gemma, in whom she could confide. It was obvious that she had been a fool to believe the Duke. But she knew that just because Tanford had turned out to be wicked, it didn't mean that the opposite was necessarily true, that Sir James was a good man. There was nothing to say that he was not as treacherous as the Duke. After all, he had not answered her question about the betrothal contract. She felt caught in a web of lies and deceit, and she felt that somehow she must find out the truth. Then, she thought, perhaps the way out of this situation would become clearer.

They sat in silence for a moment. Lady Marguerite regarded her with interest, but did not press her. Finally Aline began, "Was Tanford—was it my uncle who planned the attack on Sir James's father?"

Sadness touched Lady Marguerite's elegant features, as it always did whenever she was reminded of her brother's death. "I do not know for certain," she said carefully.

"Please, do not try to spare me. I want to know the truth."

"I believe he was," Lady Marguerite responded. "I have no proof, but it showed his touch. William of York was not clever enough. He was simply a greedy bull of a man. It's possible it could have been Sir Godfrey, but I think more likely it was Tanford working discreetly. 'Tis certain that he played some part in it, for he received two Norwen holdings. There are those who say that he simply took advantage of the chaos to grab a few things close to him, and that may be true. But I have long suspected that he played a larger part. He simply was clever enough to conceal it."

Aline nodded. She had already more or less accepted that James's account of the attack was true. "Did Sir James deceive my uncle? Did he make a promise to get the betrothal contract, and then betray the Duke?"

Lady Marguerite frowned, looking at Aline thoughtfully. Finally she said, "I know not." She raised her hand when Aline grimaced. "Nay, I am not prevaricating. Truly. I do not know the details of what happened between James and your uncle. James can be . . . a hard man, and he is very skilled in the slippery ways of the court. He is not straightforward like the Earl."

A reminiscent smile touched her face. "Richard is blunt. He says what he thinks, and few are willing to dispute him. I remember when he was child, he would always own up to anything he did wrong. He would tell you right out and take his punishment. Whereas James—" She chuckled a little to herself. "James did not lie, precisely, but he always had a host of reasons why he had done what he had, and they always sounded perfectly reasonable. He could argue you into the ground, and if that didn't work, he would make you laugh and forget why you were angry with him in the first place."

Aline smiled. "Indeed, milady, he still can do that."

Lady Marguerite smiled back. "Are you coming to love my boy? Is that why you are asking these questions?"

Aline blushed to her hairline and began to stammer, "Nay, milady . . . I . . . I do not love him." She turned her head away, adding beneath her breath, "I dare not."

"He is a difficult man *not* to love," Lady Marguerite said. "But sometimes I think he is just as difficult a man *to* love." She leaned forward earnestly. "Talk to James, my dear. Ask him your questions about the betrothal contract. It is not my place to tell you, and even if I would tell you, I haven't the facts. But, whatever he tells you, whatever happened between him and your uncle, I want you to remember something. Two things, really. One is: you are married to James, and he is your family now, not Tanford."

"I know, milady." Aline blinked away tears from her eyes. Guilt seared her at the woman's words. If only Marguerite knew how little the Duke was her family! "And the second thing?"

"Only this. Do not judge James too harshly or too quickly. He has had a difficult life—he was only three when he was torn from his home, his father killed.

Our life was hard and uncertain. He learned to fight, and he learned not to trust anyone, man or woman. He and Richard became King Henry's men. He was our only hope of regaining our lands here. But any court is a thing full of deceit and deviousness. It was harsh training for a young man. Still, James managed to retain Henry's favor through the years. He made Richard's way smooth when Richard would have run aground with his bluntness any number of times. He did what he had to do for his brother and his family. Perhaps it has left him . . . armored in his emotions. Sometimes he may have used methods that were not the most honest. But he never acted maliciously or did anything with a low purpose. And if he can be brought to love, he loves with all his heart."

"I have seen that. He loves Richard very much. And Mary and Stephen."

"There is room in his heart for more—though a wife might have to battle her way in." Marguerite gave Aline a significant look. "'Tis a battle that would be well worth it."

"Not every husband and wife are meant to love as you and Sir Philip or the Earl and Lady Elizabeth."

"That is true. But you might also say that loving that way is a trait of the Norwens. We are a fierce and possessive lot." Lady Marguerite paused, then added, "I will tell you another thing. If you do capture my nephew's heart, then you had better be worthy of it. For he is dear to me and the Earl, and the Norwens are equally as fierce in their vengeance."

Aline glanced up at her, startled.

"I like you, my dear. I do not mean otherwise. But if you hurt James, I am your enemy."

"I know, milady." Aline looked back down at her hands. "I have no wish to hurt him. And I do not count myself kin to Tanford any longer." Her eyes came back up to meet Marguerite's, and tears swam in them. "I have come to think he is an evil man. I— think I misjudged him."

"It is hard to see one's own relatives clearly," Lady Marguerite said carefully. "Sometimes one feels loyalty to them even when they are not worthy of it."

"No," Aline said decidedly. "I have no loyalty to him. But I do not think James would believe that. I do not think he will forgive me."

"Forgive you?" Marguerite looked puzzled. "For what?"

Aline realized how close she was coming to revealing her secret, and she bit her lip. No matter how warm and welcoming James's aunt was, it would be disastrous to tell her the truth. "For being who I am," she finished lamely.

"Give him time. That is my advice. Give him time, and give him love. It will all work out."

"I wish it could, Lady Marguerite. You don't know how much I wish it could."

Aline got to her feet and gave the older woman a watery smile, then fled the room before tears could overcome her.

Aline avoided James as much as she could after her meeting with the Duke's man. It was more important than ever now that she not give in to the desire James could arouse in her. Tanford wanted their marriage to be consummated. He was hoping that it would bind James forever into a marriage with a peasant, so that James would always be reminded of the humiliation he had suffered at Tanford's hands. However, being married for the rest of her life to a man who hated her was not a prospect that pleased Aline. If she stayed out of James's bed, both of them could be free after he found out about her—provided, of course, that he was not so angry that he killed her on the spot. James could get an annulment of their marriage, and he would be free to marry the sort of woman he wanted, one of proud lineage who could bear him heirs that no one would scorn.

A cold, hard knot formed in Aline's chest at the thought of James marrying another woman, but she tried to ignore it. It was the only thing that could protect James in any way from Tanford's plan. She would like to thwart Tanford if she could, and, moreover, she hoped that it would ease her guilt over what she had done to James.

What a fool she had been to accept Tanford's offer! She had grabbed at the opportunity it had offered to free her and her parents from Gyrth, careless of the hurt it might inflict on other people. She had not stopped to think the thing through, to realize what could happen to her. Worst of all, she had foolishly trusted a man who was not trustworthy. She had accepted everything he had told her without question, simply because his manner seemed open and kind. But he had been wicked, as was his plan, and she had participated in the wickedness!

Aline's guilt was so overwhelming that she could hardly bear to look at James or be close to him. Every time he smiled at her or leaned close at the dinner table to whisper something to her, she stiffened uncomfortably, swept by shame and remorse.

She saw puzzlement flash through his eyes at first when she tightened up into the cold, remote woman she had been when he first met her. After a day or two, he intercepted her on her way down to dinner, and drew her into the quiet seclusion of the wardrobe.

"Clarissa, what is the matter?" he asked. "Why do you avoid me?"

"Avoid you?" Aline assumed an innocent expression, but as soon as she gazed into his eyes, she had to look away. "Nay, sir, I do not."

"I have eyes. I have ears, milady. It is obvious that you do." He crooked his forefinger under her chin and tilted her face up. "Have I done aught to offend you?"

He stroked his thumb slowly over her lower lip, watching her. Aline turned her head away. "No."

James frowned. "Clarissa! What is amiss?"

"Nothing."

"Christ's wounds, Lady! Why do you lie to me? Why do you suddenly spend every waking minute at that blasted needlework or chatting with my aunt or Elizabeth, as if you could not breathe away from them!"

"It offends you that I enjoy the company of your relatives?" Aline retorted coolly.

"You know it is not that. I want to know why you despise *my* company so much suddenly."

"It is not sudden, sir." Aline still could not meet his gaze, but out of the corner of her eye she saw him stiffen.

"I see. So now we are at swords' points again. Is that it?"

"We do not suit. I would think it would be as obvious to you as it is to me." Aline moved away from him.

"Do we not? And here I had come to think that we suited quite well, like a glove to a hand, or a sword to its sheath."

There was a heavy sexual connotation to his words, and a flush rose up into Aline's face. "You are wrong, sir." She hoped James did not hear the faint tremor in her voice.

"I think not." James reached out to take her arm, but Aline flinched away from him. As if he had been turned to stone, he stopped in midmotion. Then his arm dropped back to his side.

"I am sorry." His voice was grim. Aline sneaked a sideways glance at his face and saw that his expression was thunderous. "Obviously I have been mistaken."

He turned and strode out of the room. After a few minutes, Aline followed him down. Throughout the meal, James barely glanced at her, and he addressed no more to her than was absolutely necessary. His coldness hurt, Aline found, but she told herself that she had done the right thing.

The next few days proved her right, she thought. Sir James stayed away from her almost as assiduously as she avoided him. He spoke to her only when they met at the meal table, and then their words were brief and formal, as if they were strangers. Things would be fine now, Aline told herself at night when she had a strong urge to cry into her pillow. James had seen that pursuing her was hopeless.

A few days later, James strode into her room without knocking and announced, "Best see to your packing, milady. We leave tomorrow."

"What?" Aline jumped to her feet. "Where? What are you talking about?"

"I have decided we should make a wedding tour of our estates. First we shall go to one of my keeps. Afterward, we should present ourselves to your vassals for their homage."

"No," Aline stammered, her heart racing in her chest.

He quirked an eyebrow. "You refuse?"

"It's foolish to travel now. It's the middle of winter."

"My keep is not far, and we shall bide the winter there."

"But why? Norcastle is so comfortable, and your family is here."

"That is precisely the problem. There are far too many people here. I think it's time that I was alone with my wife.

"Be ready to travel tomorrow," he went on, then turned on his heel and strode out of the room as abruptly as he had entered.

Aline stood staring after him, her heart somewhere in the region of her knees. Holy Mary! How was she to avoid James now?

13

James glanced over at his wife. She was staring straight ahead with a set expression on her face. They had ridden the better part of the day now, and she had yet to say more than a brief word or two to him, and then only when it was impossible to avoid. Since he had told her that they would be leaving for his keep this morning, she had been decidedly cool with him. However, he felt sure that he could bear that attitude as well as he had the nervous, stiff way she had been around him for the last week.

At first he had been hurt by the change in her demeanor toward him, and that had been followed by fury, both at Clarissa and at the fact that he would allow himself to be so bothered by anything she did. The ability to wound him gave her a certain amount of power over him, and he hated that. He had withdrawn from her, deciding that if she had no need of him, he had none of her, either. So he had spent several days glowering at her from a distance, until it had occurred to him that he was spending more of his time brooding about his wife than he had spent in her company before, that she was controlling him as surely as if she were leading him around by a rope. It was also obvious to him that Clarissa was relieved, rather than hurt, by his absence.

It was then that he'd realized that absenting himself from the lady was not the answer. The reason she avoided him was that he had been successful in making her want him. He remembered the way she had kissed him that day in the forest, the searing heat of her skin when he touched her. He thought of the way she had smiled when he was wooing her, as if she could not help herself, and the way she would lean a little closer to him on the bench. Her desire scared her or made her feel guilty, and so she had withdrawn from him. What he had to do, he'd decided, was make Lady Clarissa want him so much that she would abandon whatever scruples or fears she had.

If he got her away from the people who surrounded them, she would no longer be able to avoid him. As soon as he'd had that thought, a primitive desire had hit him deep in the gut. He wanted to have Clarissa all to himself. He would take her away to where there would be just the two of them, no other companions except their servants, and there he would start to woo her again. He would flirt and laugh and talk with her, kiss and caress her until she was on fire with a passion so great it would burn away all her doubts.

At first he had been unable to think of such a place. Norcastle was full of his family, and his mother was the chatelaine at Stephen's seat, Beaufort Place, where James had lived much of the time while managing Stephen's education. James had two small properties of his own, but one had only an old tower fort on it, hardly fit for a lady to live in, and the other was managed by a castellan. It was the same with all the other Norwen or Beaufort properties: they were occupied by vassals or castellans. He and Clarissa could not be alone in any of them.

Then he thought of Chaswyck. It was a small keep which the king had given James not long ago, one of the lesser possessions of a ward of the king who had died. King Henry was fond of rewarding his loyal men with gifts which cost him nothing. And, as Henry had pointed out, though it was not a large keep and had only a little land, it was strategic, for it lay close to Norcastle.

James had not visited Chaswyck yet, for he had spent the months since he'd left Henry's court in pursuing Lady Clarissa. Now would be a good time to go, he thought. Though he had never much cared where he slept before, he found that he liked the idea of taking his bride to a place that was his alone. Its small size would be all to the good. There wouldn't be many servants, and better yet, there would be no one around for his wife to talk to, thereby avoiding being with him.

He glanced over at her again. Clarissa had a lovely profile, he thought, and it was sheer pleasure to look at her skin, creamy white yet glowing with color along her cheekbones. When she was angry, her cheeks flamed red. James smiled to himself; he enjoyed watching her when she was furious, even though her fury was usually directed at him. She looked so beautiful that way—her cheeks pink, her eyes blazing gold.

Just the thought of her was turning him hard. He wanted to take her in his arms, to pull her right off her horse as he had the first time he saw her and cradle her softness in his arms. He remembered the feel of her hips flush against his manhood, and he thought about kissing her, his tongue sinking deep into her warm, honeyed mouth.

He was sunk in such thoughts as the road they followed curved into Norwood Forest. He did not glance back to discover that he and Clarissa and the two knights who rode with them had far outdistanced their baggage train, with their servants and the rest of his men. Nor did he notice the flicker of movement among the trees until it was almost too late.

Suddenly, with a cry, two men on horseback charged out of the trees toward them, and three more dropped straight down out of the branches above them. Aline shrieked with surprise, and turned toward James. He drew his sword and was laying about him with it, edging his horse closer to Aline so that none of the men could slip around him to reach her.

"*À moi!*" James bellowed to his men. "For Norwen!"

For an instant Aline thought that perhaps these were Tanford's men come to rescue her, and she froze, half-frightened, half-relieved, but then she realized that they were only common thieves, of the sort that often hid out in the safety of forests and preyed on innocent travelers. No doubt they had thought that this small group of well-dressed travelers were easy victims, for James and his men had not bothered with full armor for the ride to Chaswyck. They wore hauberks of mail beneath their surcoats, but no mail leggings or protective helmets. Aline quickly drew her dagger out of her belt and held it ready.

One of the men who dropped out of the trees landed on Sir Brian, who, along with Sir Guy, was riding behind Aline and James, and the thief and the knight tumbled from the horse. They rolled in the dirt, grappling. Sir Guy, like James, drew his sword and began to swing it. There was little contest between knights on horses, trained to fight and armed with a sword, and men on foot, armed primarily with cudgels and long daggers. But there were so many of the attackers!

They swarmed out of the woods and all around them. Though James protected Aline on her right side, her left side was exposed. Sir Guy was trying to make his way forward to her, but the attackers swarmed over him, pulling him from his saddle. One of the ruffians grabbed for Aline's bridle, and she kicked him in the chest, knocking him backward, but already another man was reaching for her saddle on the other side and trying to swing up behind her. She turned, slashing down with her dagger, and ripped open his arm. He dropped back with a howl, but the man she had kicked was back up and grappling with her legs, pulling her from the saddle. She kicked wildly, twisting around to use her dagger on him, but her palfrey, unused to the noise of battle, reared in panic. She toppled off her horse and onto her attacker.

"James!" Aline screamed, trying to scramble to her feet, but another man grabbed her by the arms and began to drag her away.

James turned at the sound of her cry. "Clarissa!"

He wheeled his horse and started toward Aline, but her frightened mare, now bucking and lashing out with her hooves, was in his way, and his own horse, not his destrier but merely a riding horse, shied away from the palfrey. The ruffians massed around him, reaching up to drag him from his mount.

Aline cried out at the sight of James surrounded. Neither Sir Brian nor Sir Guy could get through their attackers to aid him. Aline frantically thrust up and back with her dagger. Blood spurted over her as her attacker grabbed at his abdomen with both hands, astonishment writ clear on his face.

Aline shrieked again, more with horror at the blood than with fear, and jumped to her feet. She whirled and started to run toward James, who was swinging his sword about him, fighting his way through the crowd to get to her. But a man grabbed her hair from behind, pulling her abruptly to a halt. She kicked and struggled in an attempt to pry his hands from her hair. He struck her with his fist, and Aline's head snapped back. She went limp. The man threw her over his shoulder and began to run.

James let out a roar and spurred his horse hard, charging through the men remaining between him and Aline. Red-hot rage filled him, and he swung his sword with devastating effect on either side. The thieves fell back with screams of pain. Several of James's men from the baggage train arrived on the run, having heard his call, and the robbers scattered, taking to their heels into the trees. But James was interested in only one: the squat, strong man who carried Aline slung over his shoulder.

The man was into the trees before James could catch up with him. James quickly realized that his horse was useless in the dense trees and underbrush, and he swung off his stallion and left it standing while he ran after the man. He left his sword behind too; he could not swing at the man without endangering his wife. As he jerked out his dagger from his belt, the man cast a panicked look over his shoulder and dropped his burden.

But it was too late. James was on him in three quick strides. They tumbled to the ground. The thief was strong, but no match for James, who was both skilled and filled with a deadly rage. He locked his arm around the man's neck, pulling his head back, and plunged the dagger deep into the attacker's abdomen, then ripped it upward.

James dropped him, jumped to his feet, ran back to where Aline lay, and dropped to his knees beside her. "Clarissa!"

She lay still, and her face was pale except for the red mark on her cheek where the churl had struck her. Rage surged through James anew at the sight, and he wished he had the man back to kill all over again. Then he saw the red stains spattered over her gown, and his blood ran cold.

"Clarissa! Sweet Jesu, where are you hurt?" He moved his hands frantically over her still body, searching for the wound. "Oh, God, why was I such a fool? Why didn't I pay more attention? If you die, I'll—" His voice broke. Why couldn't he find the wound? Where was she bleeding?

"James?" Aline's eyes opened, and she saw him kneeling over her, his face tortured.

She threw herself up at him, her arms clenching tightly around his neck. "Oh, James! Thank God! I was so scared!"

His arms went around her thankfully, and he buried his face in her neck to hide the tears that sprang into his eyes. For a moment he could not speak, could only hold her hard against him.

Aline trembled with relief. It felt wonderfully safe in James's arms. She breathed in the scent of him, clung to his warmth. She heard him murmur something into her hair, but she could not understand what he said.

He pulled back abruptly and looked down into her face. "Where are you hurt?"

Aline's hand went gingerly to her cheek, and she moved her jaw experimentally. "I don't think anything is broken."

"I mean the blood. You've bled all over your tunic. Where are you cut?"

Aline glanced down blankly at her front. Then she remembered, her face darkening. "Oh. I stabbed a man with my dagger, and his blood went all over me."

"You stabbed a man." He stared at her.

"Yes. I believe I may have killed him. I—I kicked the other one who tried to grab me, and I cut another's arm. I tried, I really did, but they unseated me. There were so many of them."

James threw back his head and laughed. "You killed one, and doubtless disabled two others. I should have known." He pulled her to him and kissed her soundly. "I married a warrioress." He chuckled.

"No. I was horribly scared," Aline confessed. "I thought they would kill me before you could get to me."

He smiled and smoothed his hand over her uninjured cheek. "But you did not doubt, did you, that I would reach you?"

Aline shook her head. "No," she replied simply. She had not. She had known instinctively that James would save her.

James kissed her cheek and forehead tenderly, then pressed his lips against hers softly. "God fashioned a bride especially for me, I think. There could not be another woman in this kingdom who would suit me as well."

Aline looked up at him in amazement. Tears filled her eyes and spilled over, and she buried her face in James's chest.

"Dearling, what is it?" he asked, puzzled. "What's the matter?"

Aline shook her head and tried to swallow her tears. She could not tell him of the melancholy sweetness that filled her to hear his praise of her and to know at the same time how he would despise her if he learned the truth.

"I am sorry. It's just that . . ." She shuddered. "That man—"

"He is dead," James said flatly. "And so shall the rest of them be, as soon as my men and I root them out. We will scour the woods and rid them of these vermin. No doubt they felt themselves safe at this distance from Norcastle and with Lord Broke a minor and Chaswyck ruled from London." He smiled grimly. "They shall not be safe much longer."

James put his arm around Aline and lifted her to her feet. Then he picked her up in his arms and started back toward the road.

"I can walk."

"I will carry you." His voice brooked no protest, and Aline contentedly subsided. It felt good to be carried by James, to lean against his strength and let her fear seep out of her. The awkwardness she had felt around him recently was gone, obliterated in the heat of the battle. When they were attacked, her only thought had been of him, and now he was her comfort. It seemed natural and right to snuggle against him, his arms tight around her.

Several of James's men had come running up while James and Aline were talking, but they had stayed well back, not wishing to incur Sir James's notice and possible wrath. Sir James was generally a good master to fight for, but as close as he and his lady had come to death, it was quite possible that he would deliver a severe tongue-lashing to them for having fallen behind his party.

Hesitantly, one of them stepped forward. "What would you have us do with the bodies, sir?"

"Hang them from the trees," James replied promptly. "Let them serve as notice of how Norwens handle thieves on their land. And that one back there"—he nodded toward the man he had slain—"geld him, and let it be known that that is the fate of any who lays a hand on my lady."

"Yes, sir."

James carried Aline to her horse and set her down. He would have liked to carry her on his horse with him the rest of the way to Chaswyck, but he knew that he could not. They might encounter more of these thieves farther along the road, and he must be able to draw his sword and fight.

Their baggage train and the servants had arrived by this time, and Gemma jumped down from one of the carts and came running over to Aline. "Milady! Are you hurt?"

"Nay, I am fine, as you can see. Sir James saved me."

Gemma fussed over her, clucking and insisting that she sit down and rest.

"You might as well," James agreed. "Sir Brian looks to be injured. I must see to him."

"I will get out my basket of herbs," Aline said, looking over at the wounded knight, "and tend to him."

For the first time she glanced down at Sir James's leg. "Sir! You are hurt, too!"

"What?" He glanced down as well, and made a dismissive gesture as he saw the slashed braies and the caked blood. "Oh, that. 'Tis nothing but a scratch. One of the churls managed to get in close enough to take a slice at me. It will wait till we reach Chaswyck."

"Sir James," Aline said sternly, putting her hands on her hips.

He grimaced. "Oh, all right. You may look at it as soon as we see to Sir Brian."

The knight had a deep cut in his arm that had bled copiously before finally stopping. Aline wet a cloth with water from one of the waterskins they carried, then carefully cut away his sleeve and washed the wound. The man sucked in his breath and tried not to curse.

"'Tis all right, Sir Brian," Aline said soothingly. "Go ahead and say what you will. I will not be shocked. I have heard worse, I daresay. And a man in pain is not held accountable for his language."

He smiled back at her weakly. "Will it have to be sewn?"

"I think not." Aline's stomach turned at the thought. Though she had helped her mother with administering to most of the ills and injuries that befell the people of their troupe, she was not accustomed to the cuts of swords and knives, and she had never sewn up a wound before. "'Tis not long, and I believe it will heal on its own. I shall put a poultice on it."

Gemma brought her basket, and Aline pressed a moss poultice to the wound, then wrapped it with a strip of cloth to keep it in place. Next she turned to James, who pulled apart the rip in his braies to expose a shallow cut on his thigh. It was crusted with dried blood and bits of wool from the leggings. Aline knelt beside him and gently washed away the blood and cloth. It was very different from tending to Sir Brian. Being this close to James, touching the skin of his thigh, even with a cloth, made her heart speed up its beat and her breath come more quickly in her throat.

She glanced up at James's face. His eyes were

heavy-lidded as he watched her, his mouth sensual, and she knew that her touch was affecting him just as it was her. Hastily she put on the poultice, her finger pressing it to his hair-roughened skin as she wrapped the bandage around it. She was aware of a desire to slide her fingers up James's thigh beneath the braies, to explore the hard muscle of his leg, but she controlled herself. To do so would be the action of a slut, she reminded herself sternly.

Aline finished and sat back on her heels. "There. 'Tis done now."

"What about your face?" he asked.

"There's little that can be done." Aline drenched another cloth in the icy water from the skins in the cart. She started to press it to her cheek, but James reached out and took it, then held it gently to her cheek. She looked up at him, and their gazes locked and held.

James said, "I am sorry. You must think that I am worthless at protecting you. First I push you too hard on the road to Norcastle and you fall ill, and now this."

"Nay. You must not say that," Aline protested quickly. Without thinking, she took his hand and brought it to her mouth. Gently she pressed her lips into his palm.

James drew in his breath at the velvet touch of her lips. He was already warm and restless from feeling her exquisitely gentle fingers on the skin of his thigh. Now a hot quiver of desire speared through him.

"You saved my life," Aline told him, gazing up earnestly into his face, "and I thank you. Am I to blame you because thieves exist?"

"Milady." James leaned forward, so close to her that only a breath lay between them. He wanted to kiss her, but he knew he must not with all his men around. "I want to be your husband," he murmured.

"You *are* my husband."

"I want to be your husband in truth. It would be heaven to lie with you."

"You should not blaspheme," Aline countered weakly. His words stirred her. She knew she should push him away, should reestablish the cold hauteur she had of late been employing against him, but she was unable to. The attack and its aftermath had made it impossible for her. In that moment when she had faced death and her only thought had been to go to James, she had known what she had been trying to ignore for some time now: she loved him.

Whatever his faults, however foolish it might be of her, she loved him, and nothing could change that. All she wanted at this moment was to melt into him and have him hold her. She wanted him to stroke her and caress her and let her pretend for a time that she was his wife and that he loved her, too. Of course, she could not do that, not here on the road in front of his men and the servants.

"'Tis not blasphemy. 'Tis truth." His fingers curled around hers, and his thumb rubbed sensually over the back of her hand. "Will you continue to deny me, milady? You will kill me with your coldness."

Aline made a noise of protest, her eyes flying up to his face. His eyes glowed with passion, a bright and beckoning blue. Just the way he looked at her made her feel weak in the knees.

"Chaswyck Keep is small," he went on. "There may be only one bedchamber for the master and his lady."

"James, please," she whispered, looking away. "You take advantage of my weakness. I am confused."

"You have no need to think. 'Tis something you feel, milady. Do you have no desire for me?"

"You must know that I do," Aline choked out.

"Sometimes I think it. Others, I am not so sure. I will not take advantage of you, Clarissa. I will treasure you. No other woman has ever stirred me as you do."

Aline leaned back against her sturdy palfrey, closing her eyes. "Please, I cannot think when you look at me thusly."

"I do not want you to think. I want you to say yes to me."

"You will not even want me in your bed tonight, sir," Aline said, striving for a light tone. She brushed her injured cheek with her fingertips. "I shall be all colors of the rainbow and doubtless puffed up."

"Think you that I cannot wait? You could not be less than beautiful to me, but I know that you will be in pain. 'Tis no time to teach a maiden to love. I do not ask to take you tonight. I want only to lie beside you. To hold you in my arms all night long."

Aline trembled at his words. They awoke such a longing in her that she wanted to throw herself into his arms and beg him to make love to her. "Oh, Sir James."

"Nay. Say only my name. I want to hear no title from you."

"James," she responded obligingly, her voice shaking on the word.

The tremor in her voice affected James as much as if she had stroked her hand over his skin, for it betokened a desire that overwhelmed her.

"Now," he said, his voice husky with passion, "say, 'Yes, James.'"

"Yes, James."

It took all his restraint not to pull her into his arms and kiss her. But he said only, "Good. Now, let me help you onto your horse."

She mounted, and soon they started forward again. This time James rode alertly, forcing himself not to think about his wife or what she had just promised him: that they would lie together tonight. They rode through the forest at a fast pace. Once out of the woods, James did not slow down. He was eager to reach the keep.

They would seek their bed early tonight, he thought with a smile. He would not try to make love to her tonight, for he had promised. But he would hold her, gentling her as one would a skittish horse, until she became accustomed to his scent and touch. And then, gently, slowly, he would introduce her to the joys of lovemaking.

They topped a rise and saw the keep before them. It was small and built of gray stone, sitting in the middle of a moat. They spurred their horses and rode forward, eager to reach safety and a place to rest. The drawbridge was down, and they thundered across the moat. The planks of the bridge rattled beneath them, and one of the heavy carts lumbering behind them broke a wheel through the bridge. Cursing, several men gathered around and pulled the wheel out, and the cart rumbled on over the bridge into the courtyard. They pulled to a stop in the bailey.

The air was filled with silence. One of their horses nickered, and the sound was abnormally loud in the quiet courtyard. The silence made Aline uneasy, and she noticed that several of the men glanced around as if they, too, were anxious. James dismounted and pounded at the heavy iron ring on the door of the keep. Nothing happened. He pounded again.

"Open up!" he roared. "'Tis Sir James of Norwen, and I have come to inspect my new property. I have here the royal writ granting Chaswyck Keep to me. Open up, I tell you."

There was more silence, and finally the massive

door creaked open a few inches, and a wizened face peered through the crack.

"Who are you?" James asked impatiently. "Open up the door, man!"

"I am Cuthbert," the old man responded, his voice as creaking as the door. "I mean you no harm, sir. Won't you go away? This keep belongs to the king himself."

"His Majesty did indeed inherit it when his ward died early this year. But he has granted it to me for services I have rendered to him. If you have not received word of this, I have the royal grant here to prove it."

"It means naught to me, milord—I cannot read." The old man stepped back, opening the door wider. "We received a message, but we could not read it, my woman and I, and neither could the priest. He said to wait and he would take it to Beldon Abbey one day. The abbess can read."

"I will read it to you," James assured him, turning to his party and motioning them to dismount. He went to help Aline down, and together they climbed the steps and walked into the great hall of the keep.

They stopped. Their mouths dropped open.

The keep was dimly lit, having few narrow windows and no candles of even tallow to brighten it. But, even so, it was easy to see that the floor was thick with dirty, matted reeds, and the heavy wooden table listing to one side had lost a leg, as had several of the stools lying scattered about. No tapestry or curtain warmed the walls and pleased the eye. A dog slunk up behind the old man, then took off madly across the room. Aline looked and saw that it was chasing a large rat, which was squealing and racing off through the filthy reeds.

"Sweet Jesu!" James said. His new home, the keep to which he had brought his bride, was a rotting heap!

14

James turned warily toward Aline. There had been times in his life when he had lived in as bad conditions or worse, but he was sure that his wife never had. He remembered her proud and haughty behavior, and he cringed inwardly at the thought of what she would do or say about his having brought her to this place.

She was looking all around, her eyes growing larger and larger. She pressed her lips tightly together and put her hands up to her mouth.

"Milady," he began, "I beg your pardon. I did not know . . ."

To his surprise, she laughed. She tried to hold them back, but her giggles burst forth. "Oh, James, thank God I packed a bed!"

How could she laugh at such a moment? But her merry laughter was catching, and he could not help but grin, then chuckle. "Yes, at least we shall have one piece of furniture unbroken."

The knights, and then the servants entered the hall to find James and Aline wiping tears of mirth away from their eyes.

"Holy Mary!" Sir Guy exclaimed, and the few servants they had brought with them groaned.

Their comments set Aline off laughing again, but finally she drew a breath and collected herself. "I'm sorry. I could not help it. It is just so startling."

"Indeed it is." James turned to the old man. "What happened here? Where are the men to guard the keep? Where are the servants?"

"There's no one here but my woman and me," the old fellow told him. "The captain died, and then most of the men decided to leave. They were a lazy, discontented lot anyway, sir. After that the servants began to drift away. There wasn't much reason to keep things up, you see, and they'd gotten lazy. Some of them went back to the village." He pointed vaguely.

"But Ida and me," he continued, "we're too old. We had no place to go, and no wanting to, anyway."

"But surely you and Ida did not do this," James exclaimed, gesturing toward the broken furniture.

Cuthbert looked frightened. "Oh, no!"

"Then what happened?"

"'Twas the men from the forest, sir." His voice dropped and he glanced about uneasily.

"The men from—you mean, the reivers? The thieves?"

The old man nodded. "Yes, sir. They came once to take things, but there was not much here to take. Then, for a time, they lived here. They were idle, you see, sir, because there's not much travel on the road in the winter. They would drink their mead, and sometimes they would get angry about this or that, and they'd fight. Or they would get to laughing and shouting and throwing things around."

"So I have them to thank for *this,* too," James murmured, his eyes narrowing coldly. The old man took a step back at the look on James's face. James turned to Sir Guy. "We'll send tomorrow to Norcastle for more men." He smiled slightly. "If I know my brother, we'll probably have both him and Stephen on our doorstep, too." He sighed, then said, "I suppose I'd better see the abovestairs as well."

He strode through the filthy reeds to the staircase and turned, surprised, to find Aline following him, her skirts held up to keep them out of the muck. "You need not come," he told her. "'Tis not a pretty sight, I'll warrant."

"Nay, I did not expect it to be." Aline smiled at him wryly. "But cleaning it will be the women's work, while you men are out chasing down robbers. So I need to see what it's like more than you." She gave him a saucy look. "Perhaps it is I who should say, 'You need not come.'"

He wanted to grab her to him and kiss her right there, she looked so delectable when she grinned that way. He wondered if there had ever been a woman like this one, who waded through a battle, and then a ruined keep, with a merry spirit. He remembered how she had carped and complained when they had first traveled to Norcastle after their marriage, whining that the food was too rough for her or that she could not possibly get her belongings packed in time to leave, or griping about any of a hundred other things. She seemed a different woman now; that seemed a different time.

Aline took his arm, and they mounted the steps together. They made their way carefully down the corridor and looked into each bedchamber, and even ventured up to the third floor to view the ladies' solar.

"I do not think I can bear to look at any more," Aline said with a sigh. "May we save the storerooms for the morrow?"

James groaned. "I don't want to even think about them."

"Well, we must," Aline returned practically. "And before you send to Norcastle, too, for we may need a great deal more supplies than we brought if the storerooms are anything like the rest of the keep."

"You are right." James turned and started back down the stairs. "We shall have to make camp in the bailey tonight."

"Yes. The bedchambers are unusable."

"I do not like the thought of even being in the courtyard. I'm sure it stinks of the moat. But there's little other choice. If we throw up tents beyond the keep, there's the possibility of an attack from the thieves."

"I am sure it will be fine," Aline said blithely. But inwardly she cringed. She had slept in courtyards more than once. And while no keep they'd entertained in had been in the state of this one, the bailey was invariably a dusty, noisy, foul-smelling place.

She grinned up at him as they went down the stairs. "There is one good thing."

James cocked a brow at her sardonically. "And that is?"

"Why, that the keep is a small one. 'Twill be fewer rooms to rake out and clean."

He had to smile at her words. Then he said, "I think that you should go back to Norcastle tomorrow. I shall leave a small group here in case the thieves decide to attack, but the remainder can escort you to Norcastle amd return with supplies and more men. You can stay with Elizabeth and

Marguerite until we have the keep secured and in order."

Aline looked at him with surprise. "Your men will clean the keep?"

"We shall bring back ample servants from Norcastle, including one capable of directing them."

"But why? I see no sense in it."

"So that you will not have to endure the keep in this state. If I had known what it was like, I would not have brought you. It will take days, even weeks, to get this place cleaned, and in the meantime we will be living roughly. It is not the place for a lady."

Aline knew that this was her perfect excuse. She knew she should not spend these weeks in close contact with James. She loved him, and she was teetering perilously on the edge of falling into bed with him. She knew she should run, and James was offering her the chance to do so. She knew she should seize the opportunity.

"Nay," she said, "it is precisely the place for the lady of the keep. Where else would she be? Besides, it would be a waste of time and men to send me back to Norcastle. You would have to go as well, or at least send more men in order to protect me, and that would delay your getting to work here. You and your men would be better employed rebuilding walls or hunting down the thieves than escorting me back to Norcastle." She did not say what was in her heart, her major reason for staying—that she did not wish to be parted from James.

James looked at her for a long moment, and then he smiled and raised her hand to his lips and kissed it. And Aline knew that she had pleased him in some very deep way.

*   *   *

The men set up a makeshift tent for Aline in the courtyard. They had not brought such equipment with them, for the journey from Norcastle to Chaswyck was but a day's ride. Therefore, her tent was made of hastily-laced-together blankets and several branches. There was no cot as there had been on her original trip to Norcastle. She and Gemma spread out her blankets. She hummed as they worked, and Gemma glanced at her from time to time in a worried way.

Finally Gemma said, "Aline, I fear you are making trouble for yourself."

Aline glanced at her in surprise. "Why? What do you mean?"

"That one"—Gemma jerked her thumb in the direction of where James stood in the courtyard—"won't like being made a fool of."

"I know." Aline looked down at her hands. "But what else can I do? I told you what that horrid man said."

"I know." Aline had poured out the entire story of Fingal's visit to Gemma later that night in her bedchamber. "There's naught you can do except go along with their plan if you want to save your parents. But you will make it harder for yourself—and him—if the two of you fall in love."

"I won't let it happen."

"You think you can stop something like that?" Gemma asked skeptically.

"He won't fall in love with me."

"Then you are willing to break your heart for a man who you know will never love you?"

"I don't know. I don't know what else to do. I can't leave him. Tanford will punish me through my parents if I do, and, besides, I—" She turned and looked at her friend with wide, unhappy eyes. "I do not think I *could* leave him, anyway. Not until he sends me away. Oh, Gemma, I think it is too late. I love him already."

Tears welled in her eyes and spilled over. Gemma hurried over to her and put her arm around Aline's shoulders. "There, there, child, don't take on so. Perhaps 'twill all work out."

"How can it?" Aline sobbed. "If I tell James, I betray my parents, the same as if I leave. Yet if I stay and do not reveal the plan to him, he will eventually suffer a shame worse than any he's ever felt. I hate myself whenever I think of what will happen to him. And he will hate me, too. I cannot bear to think of how he will look at me, what he will say."

"It will be worse, child, if you continue in this way."

"What way?" Aline pulled back, sniffling and wiping her tears away.

"You know what I am talking about. You are sharing a tent with him tonight. If he takes you—"

"No! He said he would not make love to me tonight. He said he would only lie with me."

Gemma snorted. "I've heard of more than one maiden who was told that story and woke up no longer a maiden."

"He was not tricking me!" Aline flared. "I trust him."

"When it comes to the treasure between her legs, no woman can trust a man. He doesn't even mean to lie. But you let a man in your bed, and he stops thinking with his head up here." Gemma tapped her forehead, then gestured crudely downward. "He thinks only with the head between his legs."

"Gemma!"

"'Tis the truth, and well you should know it. More than one man has tried to have his way with you, including this one. Or have you forgotten the way he carried you up to his bedchamber that night, and how you barely got away? You would not have if he had not been full of mead."

"James has never hurt me," Aline said, "even when I have given him much provocation. He would not force me."

"He will not need to force you. Only persuade you. Mayhap not even that—I think you've more than half persuaded yourself already."

"No. I know it would be a mistake."

"It would be worse than that. You will be deeper in love with him than you are now. You'll be tied to him. And he to you. You say he will not love you, but you cannot be sure of that. What if he gives you his heart? How much worse will he feel then when he finds out how you've tricked him?"

"Stop!" Aline clapped her hands over her ears.

Gemma pried one hand away. "I know you do not want to hear it, but you must. If he has come to care for you in any way, it will make the blow harder. He will feel more betrayed. And how can he sleep in your bed every night, take pleasure from your body time after time, and care for you not at all? He would have to be a man without a heart."

"Nay. He is not that." Aline sighed deeply and stared down at the ground.

"That is not even the worse of it. What if you get with child?"

Aline's head snapped up, and she stared at her friend.

"Aye. You must know that it can happen if you bed with him. And what will happen to you and the babe?"

"I know not," Aline whispered, dazed.

"You have to think, Aline."

"I know. I was fine. I kept apart from him, and he was angry and stayed away from me. But today when those men attacked us, it all changed. I don't think I can go back to being as I was. How can I bear to be cold to him when I love him?"

Gemma sighed. "I know not, child. But you must do something."

She left Aline pondering her words and went out to help start their supper.

James walked to the steps of the keep and turned to look back at their makeshift campsite. The fire burned brightly in the center, and the men and servants were making their beds in a semicircle around the north side of it. To the south lay Lady Clarissa's small tent. The light of the fire shone through even the dark wool blankets that made up her tent, and James could see her dark form as she moved about. The tent was too small to allow much movement, and her shape was only a shadowy image, but still the sight made him intensely aware of her presence there. He wondered if she was waiting for him to join her.

He wondered if he would.

It was hardly the soft, warm bed he had imagined this afternoon when he had made his plans for lying with her. The ground would be cold and hard, with but a blanket or two between it and them, and they would be lying only a few feet away from his men and the servants. Still, the thought of lying curled up beside Clarissa, even under such circumstances, made him shiver with anticipation. But was he capable of holding her, of feeling her warmth and softness nestled against his body, without taking her?

He thought Clarissa would soon yield to him. But he wanted her to give herself to him freely, not because he seduced and argued her into it; he wanted her to have no doubts and no regrets. He wanted her first time to be as perfect as it could possibly be, and a muffled coupling on a blanket on the ground, with people only a few feet away from them, would not be perfect.

James drew a deep breath of the cold night air and tilted his head back. The stars glittered brightly overhead. He reminded himself that a whole lifetime with this woman stretched before him. Within a few days they would be in their own bed inside; her face would no longer give her pain. She would be accustomed to his presence in her bed, relaxed and no longer in any fear or anxiety around him. She would give herself to him then, and their lovemaking would be better for the wait.

He just wished that the wait were not so difficult.

James walked over to the tent and bent and crawled inside, pulling the flap down after him. His wife was lying between the rough blankets, her loose hair spread out behind her head, and she sat up when he entered. The blankets slid down, revealing the pale woolen undergown in which she slept. It covered her chest and arms fully; there was no glimpse of her flesh below her throat, and the material was too thick to see through. But somehow the sight of her in her sleeping gown struck him hard in the gut. Merely the thought that nothing else lay over her bare skin was enough to excite his already heightened senses.

"You came," was all she said.

"Yes. Did you expect me not to?"

"I knew not. Since we were here in this crude tent, surrounded by others, I was not certain if you would still wish to . . ." Her voice trailed off.

"I would always wish to lie with you, here or in a castle or anywhere else you could name," James said in a matter-of-fact voice. Then he began to pull off his shoes.

Aline watched him undress in the dim light that

filtered through the blanket walls. He removed boots and braies and outer tunic, leaving him in only the thigh-length undertunic. His legs were powerful and masculine, roughened by dark, curling hairs. She wondered what his chest and shoulders looked like bare, then told herself that it was as well that she did not know.

He crawled beneath the blanket and settled down beside her. Cautiously, Aline lay back down. Their arms were separated by less than an inch. She turned her head to look at him. James was gazing back at her. Her breath caught in her throat at the expression of desire on his face. Quickly she looked away.

"James," she began in a small voice. "I would ask you a question. Will you answer it honestly?"

"Aye."

"Will you tell me about the betrothal contract? Did you deceive my uncle, as he says?"

"Yes."

Aline went tight, startled at his words, and a lump formed in her throat. She realized that she wanted to cry. She had grown so sure that James had done no wrong to Tanford, that it had been the other way around.

"He offered you in marriage to me," James went on, "in return for my betraying my brother."

"What!" Aline stared. Now she remembered his saying something like that when he'd first seized her.

"Yes. He wanted me to turn against Richard, to help him kill Richard and Elizabeth and then take over the Norwen estates as guardian to the infant Mary. I pretended that I would do it, in order to keep Richard informed of his plans. In the end, of course, I did not follow through with my promise. I went to Richard's aid. That is why Tanford hates me so. I bested him in a game of treachery."

"Oh. Thank you." It was horrible to think of what Tanford had asked James to do, but his words wiped away her last doubts about James. He had been cunning and perhaps not exactly honest, but she could not fault him for what he had done. He had done what he had to to keep his brother safe.

She turned over on her side, facing away from him, and said in a muffled voice, "Good night.

"Good night."

James scooted up behind her and curved one arm beneath her head and the other over her stomach. His body was warm and hard against her back; his legs fitted neatly into hers. She could feel the faint scratch of his hair on her calves, for her own gown had ridden up to her knees as she had lain, restlessly tossing and turning, waiting for him to come to her.

She wasn't sure how she could sleep like this. She could barely think or breathe.

He rubbed his cheek against her hair. Aline could hear the faint sound it made. "Your hair makes a sweet pillow," he murmured huskily.

Aline released a little sigh. Her entire body was tinglingly alive, aware of the faintest sensation, from the scratch of the blanket upon her arm to the warmth of James's hand against her stomach. His breath moved over her ear and cheek, making goose bumps pop up along her arms and a warm, itching sensation start up between her legs.

It was unfair of him to do this to her, she thought. He probably was not affected by such small, insignificant things. After all, he had doubtless slept with many women. But then she felt something hard insistently pressing against her hips, and she knew that he was as affected as she by their closeness.

"I want so much to learn your body," James

whispered into her ear, and his hand came up to stroke her hair. "Your hair is like silken fire. I'm glad that no man can see it but I."

He covered his neck and face with her hair, burying his mouth in its lush softness. "I want to feel you bathe me with your hair. I would like to have you rub it over every inch of my body."

Heat quivered through Aline at the image he created. "Oh, James."

His hand slid down over her hair and onto her chest. He traced the hard lines of her collarbone beneath the material of her gown, then moved downward to cup a breast in his long fingers.

"Ah." He sighed as her nipple hardened, pressing against the cloth. "Your body is more ready for me than your mind." Teasingly, he circled the bud through the gown, making it harden and elongate. "You see? I think you are ready for me."

His fingers moved to the other breast, kneading and caressing it, too, until Aline's breasts felt swollen, almost to bursting, with need for him. "I wish I could see you naked right now. I want to taste you."

"No." She moaned. "Oh, James, please, no."

"You are right. The sight would drive me mad with longing. I may go mad anyway."

He moved his hand downward over the plane of her stomach, down to the apex of her legs. Aline flinched when his fingers touched that private, sensitive spot, but she did not pull away. She had neither the strength nor the will. James nudged his knee between her legs from behind, moving his leg in between hers and opening her a little. His fingers moved farther down, between her legs, rubbing gently against her softness. Suddenly she was flooded with moisture and searingly hot. James made a small sound of satisfaction as he rubbed the cloth upon her flesh and felt it dampen.

"Mmm. You do want me."

"Yes." Her voice shook.

Passion burst within him, pooling like liquid fire deep in his abdomen. "Not tonight," he murmured. "It must not be tonight. But soon."

His hand slid down her leg and came up under her gown, moving slowly, caressingly upward until it found the soft, damp heat. Gently his fingers caressed the tender folds of flesh there, separating and exploring. Aline gasped and writhed, biting her lip to hold back the moans that threatened to burst out of her.

"Please, no, you must not," she begged, the heavy passion in her voice belying her words.

"I am your husband. Who has a better right? I am the only man whose touch you will ever feel. I shall know every inch of you. Just as you will know me."

Aline whimpered at the pleasure his fingers were creating in her. She had never dreamed anything like this existed. She squeezed her legs against him and released them rhythmically, yearning for more, though she was not certain what exactly she ached for.

Then he showed her, slipping a finger into her. She let out a noise of surprise at his invasion of the most intimate part of her. James buried his face in her neck, his breath rasping in and out of his throat, as he slid his finger in and out of her hot, tight femininity. Aline moaned, moving her hips. He slipped another finger inside, widening her.

"Ah, sweet heaven, you are so tight," he whispered. His face was damp with sweat from the strain of holding back. His body surged with the need to be inside her, to push deep into that tightness. James swallowed convulsively, exercising every bit of control he possessed to keep from rolling her over onto her back and taking her.

He pulled his hand from her at last, and Aline gasped at the loss. "No," she pleaded. "Please. I want . . ."

"What?" He pulled his hand out from under her gown and pressed it against the fleshy mound at the base of her abdomen.

It was pleasurable, but not nearly enough. Aline pushed upward with her hips against his hand, circling and thrusting with an instinct as old as time.

"I want more," she said.

"I know. I do too." James forced his body to lie still. "I know what you want, and you shall have it in full measure. But not tonight. Not like this."

Aline pulled back from him, turning so that she lay flat on her back, and gazed up at him with eyes dark and huge with hunger. The blanket had fallen away from her heated chest. Her throat glistened with a sheen of sweat, and her gown had dampened and clung to her breasts, the nipples standing out proudly. She was the picture of all that was desirable, and James's fingers itched to grab that gown and rip it away from her body, exposing her luscious breasts to his gaze, his touch.

"Tomorrow," he promised, his eyes lingering on her breasts, "tomorrow we will have further lessons. We will make your body more ready for me."

"I do not think I could *be* more ready," Aline panted. "I feel on fire."

James's eyes closed as a fresh wave of desire washed over him at her words. "I promise, you will burn even more, with a flame that is ten times hotter and that will never be consumed." He skimmed his palm over her breasts, watching the push of her nipples against the gown. "Tomorrow I will undress you and touch you. I will taste your skin."

Aline's breath shuddered out. "Now."

"No." Reluctantly he pulled the blanket up, covering them both, and took Aline into his arms, pressing her back against his throbbing manhood. "We must wait. And it will be all the sweeter for it."

15

Aline grew cold. Gradually she opened her eyes and glanced around sleepily. The warmth of James's large body was gone. She huddled more deeply within her blankets, hugging to her James's scent, which still clung to the covers. She thought about the night before and blushed rosily. She had never even thought of some of the things James had done. And he promised further delights tonight!

She shivered a little in anticipation. It seemed an achingly long time until bedtime.

No! She must not think about it! Aline sat up, shoving her hands into her hair and clenching her fingers, as though the pain would drive her wayward thoughts from her head.

She dressed quickly, still half-wrapped in her covers, and crawled out of her tent. It was chilly outside, and she went quickly to the fire, where James was standing. He turned as she approached. As his eyes swept down her body, Aline blushed, knowing what he must be recalling.

"Good morrow, sir," she said in a muffled voice, looking away.

"Good morrow, milady." His voice was laced with amusement.

He reached out, took her hand, and kissed it. Aline looked up to find him gazing down into her face, his blue eyes dancing merrily.

"You appear in good health," he murmured, and kissed her hand a second time. "I trust you look forward to this evening with pleasure."

Aline's blush deepened to a fiery red, and she jerked her hand away from him and turned aside. But she could not rid herself of the heat that had slammed through her body like a bolt of lightning at his last words, turning her insides to molten wax. She stalked away, very aware of the wetness that was suddenly between her legs. Behind her James chuckled. Even his laugh, Aline discovered, made her pulse with yearning.

The only way to drive out her wayward desires, she decided, was to throw herself into work. There was certainly an ample amount of it to be done. After they had broken their fast, she put on one of her old tunics and undergowns and led the small group of servants into the castle.

James had most of his men working around the outer wall, gates, and moat, shoring up the run-down defenses, but he gave Aline several of the men to help with the heavy work inside the keep. There was so much to be done, it was almost impossible to know where to begin. Aline sighed, feeling inadequate. She had no idea how to run a keep, especially one as badly in need of care as this one.

But then, she reasoned, was there anyone who would know what to do with a place like this? She decided simply to jump in and get started. First she

had two of the servants scour the bailey and its build-
ings for all the cats and dogs they could find. Then
she directed the men to carry the broken furniture
into another room to await the ministrations of the
woodworker they hoped would arrive from Norcastle.
When the servants brought back two lanky dogs and
three cats, she set them loose in the keep to search
out all the vermin they could. From the frantic sounds
of scurrying, squeals, and barks that soon resounded
through the keep, she knew that the animals were
meeting with success.

She set the servants to raking and shoveling out
the dirty reeds, even hiking up her skirts to her knees
and digging into the mess herself.

In the meantime James had ventured down into the
storeroom and returned with the report that it was
half-empty, with only barrels of rotted fish, rancid oil,
and worm-infested grains remaining. He made his
way to the great hall to find Aline raking out reeds.
He gaped at her in astonishment.

"Clarissa! What are you doing?" He hurried over
to her, and she turned, pausing in her work and leaning against her rake to rest.

"Raking the reeds," she replied reasonably, wondering if he'd taken leave of his senses. "We're piling
them in the bailey to be burned."

"But, my love, you should not be doing this."

Aline smiled, warmed by his words. She wondered
if he knew that he had called her his love and whether
he had meant it, or was it simply an endearment he
used carelessly on any woman he shared a bed with?

"Why not?" Aline responded lightly. "I am young
and strong, and there is so much to be done. The
more I help, the sooner I can sleep in a real bed
instead of on the ground." She stopped, realizing that

he could easily take her words to mean that she was eager for his lovemaking.

He smiled, his eyes lighting up in a way that told her he had chosen to construe her words in precisely that way. "That is true. Perhaps I should turn all my men to cleaning out the keep." His eyes gleamed meaningfully. He took one of her hands and raised it to his lips. "But I would not have you harm your hands. You will get blisters."

"You are right. I shall put on my riding gloves."

He smiled. "Good. I will send Brian to the village to bring back more servants. You must not tax yourself, no matter how eager we are to lie in a bed again." His hands went to her shoulders and kneaded them gently. "I would not have you sore, wife."

Aline let out a sigh of contentment as his supple fingers worked wonders on her muscles. She leaned forward, letting her forehead rest upon his chest. Finally, reluctantly, James stopped what he was doing and set her away from him.

"Nay, I cannot go on, or I will shame us both in front of our servants," he said, his voice low and strained.

Aline looked up into his face. It was drawn taut, the lines of desire etched upon his skin, and his eyes were hard and bright as glass. James drew in a sharp breath as she turned the full force of her luminous gaze upon him.

"You could bring a dead man to life, milady." He took a step backward, clasping his hands behind his back as though to forcibly keep them from reaching out to her. His eyes moved down her body. Then he wrenched himself away and strode out of the keep.

Later in the day, when Aline and her servants stopped for a rest and a bit of food, she caught sight of James, working and sweating alongside his men on the wall, and she thought that he, like she, was trying to work off his desire in physical labor.

Sir Brian returned in the afternoon with more servants, and Aline quickly set them to work. He had also, to her relief, brought a rat-catcher from the village, who set out his traps in the storeroom and in every nook and cranny through the keep where the vermin might run to hide.

By the time night fell, Aline was exhausted and covered with dirt, but at least the offensive reeds had been removed from the keep and burned. The next day they could begin to scrub the floors and walls.

She had to take a bath. It was too cold outside, of course, but she did not want to go into the keep to bathe, for it was echoingly empty and still too dirty and odoriferous for her to feel comfortable there. But she could not bear to go to bed with this grime all over her. Besides, she could not help but remember James's promises about tonight. She had to be clean for him. Finally she hit upon an idea. The detached kitchen in the courtyard, where the old couple had continued to cook their meals, had been kept somewhat cleaner than the rest of the keep; at least no mice and rats ran free in it. And it was blessedly warm from the day's cooking.

So after they ate, Aline and Gemma set up a large tub in the kitchen and filled it with water that had been warmed over the fire. Aline bathed while Gemma kept watch at the door. The tub was not large enough or the water quite warm enough, so Aline made short work of her bath. But at least she was able to wash away the dirt. She was grateful that her hair had been protected beneath her coif while she cleaned and that she did not have to wash it.

She dressed in a clean shift and wrapped her warm mantle around her, then she and Aline dumped out the dirty water. Finally she hurried back to her tent through the crisp January air. She slid immediately between her blankets and pillowed her head on her arm. She waited.

Time crawled by. She listened to the rumble of male voices around the fire and the men's occasional laughter. She decided that it would be better if she turned with her back to the tent opening; otherwise, it might look too much as if she were waiting for James. Aline flopped over to her other side and waited some more.

She couldn't stop thinking about the things James had promised to do to her tonight, and the idea of them made her jittery. Her breasts felt full and aching, and her nipples tightened even as she thought about James.

She wondered if he had forgotten about her. Or perhaps he had decided he would rather cast dice with his men or tell ribald stories. Perhaps he was too tired after working on the wall all day and preferred merely to sleep.

Aline was far too jumpy to sleep.

There was the soft scrape of a shoe outside, and Aline jumped and whirled around as the tent flap was pulled up and James crawled inside. She let out a sigh of relief.

"James."

"Good evening, milady." He smiled, his teeth flashing white in the dimness, and pulled off his shoes. He pushed back his cloak, and Aline saw that, like her, he had been dressed in only his nightclothes beneath it.

He climbed under the covers with her, giving an exaggerated shiver. His hands and face were cool, and as he drew her close to him, Aline realized that his hair was damp. She smiled to herself with satisfaction. James was late in coming because he, too, had found a way to bathe first. He had wanted to come to her clean and sweet-smelling.

She turned to smile up at him, and he kissed her on

the forehead. His eyes moved down over her cheek, which earlier today had appeared swollen and bruised.

"How is your face?" he asked.

"It hurts a little," Aline admitted. "But the work was good. It took my mind off it."

"And are you sore now from the work?"

"Some." Her muscles had lost some strength during her weeks as a lady, and she had been surprised to find her legs and back aching.

"I hate to see you cleaning like a servant."

"I want it done quickly."

"I do too." He was silent for a moment, and his eyes moved over her face and down her throat to where the blanket covered her breasts. "Do you remember what I told you I would teach you today?"

Aline nodded. Her chest was suddenly squeezed tight, and she could hardly breathe.

James took hold of the top of the blanket and peeled it down to her waist. But Aline did not feel the cold. All she felt was his eyes on her.

"Ah, you came prepared." He smiled in almost a smug way and traced his forefinger along the scoop neck of her shift.

For the first time, Aline noticed that instead of the long-sleeved, high-necked undergown she had customarily worn this winter, she had put on a sleeveless shift with a low scooped neck, easy to put on and take off. She blushed as she realized the implications of her action.

Aline turned her head away, embarrassed to meet James's eyes, but he only chuckled and smoothed his knuckles down her uninjured cheek. "Do not be ashamed, my love. 'Tis only right and natural. It makes me proud that you are eager for me."

"I should not . . ." Aline began in a stifled voice.

"Forget what you should," he told her soothingly. "Forget your father and your uncle. Forget what the priests have told you. There is no sin, no wrong, in a husband's touch."

"But I—"

James raised his finger to her lips in a shushing motion and shook his head. "Do not worry. You have nothing to fear. I will not claim my marital rights tonight. I promise that I will not take you now, even if you should ask me to. Tonight I want only to come to know you."

He took the straps of her shift in his hands and pulled them down over her arms. Slowly the material moved downward, scraping over her nipples and exposing the lush white globes of her breasts. James drew in his breath. Even in the dim light of the tent, Aline's beauty was obvious. No blemish marred her creamy skin, and her breasts were firm and full, faintly uptilted. Her nipples stood out proudly, dark and engorged. Below her breasts, her body narrowed down into a small waist, as smoothly perfect as her breasts.

James left her gown at her waist, the straps still hanging loosely at her wrists. He lay on his side, propped up on his elbow, and gazed at her, drinking in every detail of her exposed flesh.

Aline was flooded with warmth. She felt embarrassed under his lingering, hot gaze, yet strangely proud and even eager.

"You are fair, milady," he murmured. "Exceedingly fair."

He covered one of her breasts with his hand. It spread out over her fair skin in sharp contrast: hard and brown. He squeezed gently, then stroked her with his fingers, lingering over the dark ruby tip. Her nipple tightened in response to his touch, hardening and elongating as he rolled it between his forefinger and thumb. Then his hand moved to the other breast, teasing and playing with its nipple, too, until Aline was throbbing with desire.

"James, oh, James." Her head lolled back, and her chest arched up.

He bent over her, gazing into her eyes. "Do you remember what else I said I wanted tonight?"

"Yes."

"What was that?"

Aline blushed. "You know."

"Yes, but I want to hear you say it."

"You said—you said you wanted to taste me."

His mouth widened in a sensual smile. "And do you want me to do that?"

She wet her lips nervously. Her mouth felt too dry to speak. Finally, she whispered, "Yes."

"Good. Because I want to, very much."

He lowered his head and brushed his lips across one nipple. Aline gasped, arching, and the small bud tightened even more. Again he moved his lips across her in the barest movement, a mere feathering of a touch, and it struck her with such intense pleasure that it was almost pain.

James cupped the breast in his palm, holding the quivering, soft flesh still as his mouth moved slowly across it, kissing and nuzzling, sending wild sensations of pleasure showering through Aline. She gasped and moaned at each new sensation. James rolled over on top of her, supporting himself on his elbows, and took her other breast in his other hand, holding and kneading both mounds while his mouth trailed from one to the other.

He stopped, his mouth poised over one breast, and to Aline's shock, his tongue came out and made a slow, wet circle around her nipple. Aline bucked against him, whimpering.

"Is that pleasurable to you?" he asked.

"Yes, oh, yes."

"It only grows more so," he assured her, and his tongue flickered across the hot, hard bud. Aline dug her fingers into the blanket beneath her, clenching her teeth to hold back the groans that threatened to burst from her throat. They were only a few feet from the fire and the people who sat there, and Aline was determined not to let them hear anything.

James moved to her other breast, and his tongue worked the same miraculous pleasures there. Aline moved her legs restlessly, a fire burning deep in her loins. She put her hands on James's arms and dug her fingers into him with each new spurt of pleasure. Then, astonishing and delighting her, he lowered his mouth fully over her nipple and began to suck. Desire speared down through her, and she could not hold back a groan. Slowly he pulled and suckled, and Aline felt hot wetness flooding between her legs.

He rolled off her body, and she gasped at the loss. His weight upon her had been exciting somehow. But she soon understood why he had moved, as he pushed aside the blanket and tugged her loose gown down over her hips and off her legs. She lay completely naked, the air cool upon her fevered skin.

James slid his hand up and down her leg, with each stroke reaching closer and closer to the hot center of her passion. At last his fingers touched the curls between her legs. He smiled against her skin as he felt the dampness. His fingers slid over the slick folds of her femininity, exploring and arousing. Aline bent her knees, planting her heels on the blanket and thrusting her pelvis upward, blindly seeking release. But he did not satisfy her, only teased and caressed. Then, finally, he slid a finger inside her, simulating the motion of lovemaking.

He raised his head and lay watching Aline as he slid two fingers inside her and stroked. She gasped and whimpered, her head rolling against the ground. He stretched her with his fingers, inserting a third. There was a slight sensation of pain, but Aline barely noticed it in the white-hot maelstrom of pleasure that swirled inside her. She ached for fulfillment, and her fingers scratched at his arms, urging him to complete the act.

"Please," she said softly. "Please, James."

"No." His voice was hoarse, and it took every ounce of self-control he had to refuse her. But he had sworn not to take her tonight, had eased her doubts and fears with the ultimate promise that he'd hold back even if she wanted to finish the act. Her trust was more important than this one moment of pleasure, and there would be many, many times to come when he could satisfy them both.

He pulled away from her, taking one last look at her luscious body. Aline sat up, reaching for him, and he took her hands and held them tightly, kissing them both.

"No, my love. I gave you my word I would not. I will not break it. I will never break my word to you."

"But I do not want you to keep it!" Aline said in frustration. However, deep inside, she knew that she valued his restraint, his steadfastness.

James picked up Aline's gown, lowered it over her head, and pulled it down to cover her from his sight. With a growl of frustration, Aline flopped back onto the ground and turned away from him, huddling into herself. James lay down beside her and drew her into his arms. She felt his throbbing staff, rock hard, against her bottom, and she knew that the frustration was as bad for him as for her, if not even worse. Still, it irritated her that he would not give in to his passion, that he could remain calm when she was too wild with desire to be reasonable. So she wiggled her hips back into the cup formed by his pelvis and thighs, and was rewarded by the groan that escaped his lips.

"Oh," she said waspishly. "So you aren't entirely indifferent?"

"No, Lady, I am not indifferent," James said, and his hand went to her hips, pressing her hard against him. "Do not tease me, or you shall find exactly how interested I am."

"Is that a promise?" Aline asked slyly.

He chuckled against her hair. "You little vixen. Hush now, and go to sleep. Soon we will couple."

"When?"

"When your face no longer pains you. When neither of us can any longer stand these teasing games. When you look at me clearheaded in the morning and say, 'Husband, I want you inside me tonight.'"

Aline thought that that would be very soon indeed. Right now her body was humming so with desire that she thought that she would have shouted the words from the rooftops in the middle of the night if that was what he wanted.

However, when she awoke the next morning, after only a few hours' sleep that were plagued by hot, disturbing dreams, cool reason had returned in some measure, and Aline knew that it was better to hold off the event rushing down on her. If she could wait, perhaps some miracle would occur, and her way would become clear. It would take a miracle, she knew, to unknot the tangle she had gotten herself into.

James and his men returned to working on the wall, and Aline sent Gemma and some of the other servants to gather fresh reeds. Aline and the majority

of the servants attacked the inside of the keep with soap
and water. Beginning at the top level, they scrubbed the
floor and walls of the solar, then moved down to the
bedchambers. By the time night fell, they still had not
reached the ground floor. It was a long, hard task, and
Aline's already sore muscles ached as she worked.

Late in the afternoon, a group of armed riders
approached. They moved slowly, for behind them
rolled several carts. Norwen's coat of arms flashed on
their pennants and on the surcoat and shield of the
large man leading the procession. James's brother had
decided to bring James aid in person. As they rode into
the courtyard and dismounted, Aline saw that Stephen
had come along with him. Both the men seemed elated
at the prospect of cleaning out the nest of thieves.

Aline saw James greet them, then watched as the
three men stood talking and laughing. She shook her
head. Only men, she thought disgustedly, could be so
happy about riding out the next morning to shed
blood and risk getting killed themselves. She thought
about James riding with them, and fear welled up in
her. Knights fought; that was what they did with their
lives. She had always accepted it, as she accepted the
rest of the order of the world. But now, the knight
was James, and should he not return, she knew, her
heart would shrivel inside her. Suddenly she wished
Stephen and the Earl to hell so that they would not
lead her husband into danger on the morrow.

She tidied herself and went forward to greet their
visitors pleasantly, masking her fear and anger. But
that night when James came into her tent, she pushed
him away and turned her back to him.

"Why don't you go spend the night with your companions?" she asked, fear infusing her voice with a
haughty venom that she had not used in weeks.

"What? What are you talking about, woman?"

"I'm sure you'd have much more fun discussing how you will run some other man through or burn down a hut or two."

He blinked, trying to see her better in the dim light. Her sudden attack left him confused. "Clarissa, you make no sense. Now you are feeling pity for those churls who attacked you?"

"They are merely men. No doubt they have families to feed."

"And so it is all right for them to attack and rob, even murder? Clarissa, you're talking like a fool. Come here to me, and let's forget this—"

"Fool, am I?" Aline flared, whipping back around to glare at him. "Then I suggest you get out of this bed. You should not be sleeping with a *fool.*"

James's brows snapped together. "You dare to toss me out?"

"I dare anything!" Aline retaliated, her eyes shooting sparks, her body rigid.

James stared at her for a moment, then unexpectedly began to chuckle. "Yes. I believe you would. Come, Clarissa." He reached out toward her. "What is amiss with you?"

"There is nothing amiss with me," Aline retorted, treacherous tears springing into her eyes. "It is you who are riding out tomorrow to fight. What if you don't come back? What if you are killed?"

He began to laugh, and Aline picked up the closest thing at hand, her pillow, and threw it at him, hitting him squarely in the head. "Don't laugh at me."

"I am sorry, my love." He tried to stifle his laughter. "It is just the idea of my being killed by that bunch of ruffians! Sweet Mary, what a poor view you have of my fighting skills, that you think that my brother and I and our men cannot defeat a few men afoot, without armor and armed only with cudgels and knives."

"It is possible! You are going to fight, and anytime you fight, something could happen. Something could go wrong. They might have archers, and an arrow could slip between your mail and helmet, or—"

"Yes, yes," he said soothingly, scooting over and enfolding her stiff body in his arms. "Or some morning riding to the village I could slip off my horse and break my neck. Or I might get caught out in the rain one day and die of a chill."

"Don't make game of me!" Aline thrust out her chin pugnaciously.

James smiled and bent to plant a kiss on her chin. "Then, my dear lady, you must not be so silly. I will not be killed tomorrow."

"How can you be so sure?"

"Because if I were, I could not come back to you. I would never get to make love to you, and I refuse to allow that to happen."

"Can you do nothing but jest?"

"Nay, 'tis no jest. I mean it. You can be sure that I will be more than ordinarily careful. I would not want even a knife in the leg to hinder me from making love to you."

His words sent a wave of warmth through Aline, and she relaxed against him, her arms going tightly around his waist. "Oh, James, I do not want you to risk yourself."

"What would you have me do? Send my brother and Stephen out to rid my woods of thieves by themselves, while I hide in my keep? Would you have me tremble with fear at the idea of a few lowly robbers? Be honest, Clarissa. You would not let such a coward *near* your bed."

Aline sighed. "No doubt you are right. It is just that I am afraid of losing you."

James kissed her hair. "I am glad to hear that you hold a tenderness in your heart for me. That you would be sorry to hear that I was killed."

Aline gasped at the thought. "James, do not say such a thing!"

He smiled. "Then you do care for me?"

"I love you."

She went still, her eyes widening, as she realized what she had admitted. James crushed her to him, and he buried his lips in her hair.

"Oh, my love. Sweet Clarissa," he murmured. "I will not be killed by those churls. I swear it to you. 'Tis my sacred vow. I will come back to you, and I will make love to you. And our days will be unendingly sweet."

He lay down, still holding her tightly. Aline clung to him, tears welling in her eyes. *If only his words could come true . . .*

16

James and the men left early the next morning. Aline said good-bye to him in the bailey, pale and dry-eyed, her mantle wrapped around her. She clamped her lips against the pleas that threatened to pour from them, and kept her hands locked in the folds of her mantle so that she could not cling to him.

She would not tell him of her fears, would not beg. James was right: she was foolish to think that anything might happen to him. A ragtag band of robbers hiding out in the woods were no match for James and the Earl and their men. The only problem they would have would be searching out the men, for the woods were large, with many places in which to hide. At its worst, the project would take time.

But love could create terror where the mind merely scoffed, and Aline felt as if she were being ripped open as she watched James mount and ride away. When the men passed through the gates, she ran for the tower in the wall and darted up the stairs, rushed to the parapet, and, her hands digging into the cold stone, watched until the company of men was out of sight. Then she went back down and into her tent, where she threw herself on her blankets and cried until all the tears were drained from her.

With a heavy heart and swollen eyes, Aline went about her tasks that day. She could think of nothing to ease her worry except to drown it in work, so she did. She drove the servants from dawn to dusk, but none dared complain, not even Gemma, for Aline's gold eyes flashed fire.

They finished scrubbing the floors and walls, and Aline set them to cutting fresh reeds. They laid the reeds on the floor, and Aline scattered herbs among them as she had seen Lady Elizabeth do, to make them smell sweet. Finally, the men carried in the bed which they had brought from Norcastle and set it up in the largest bedchamber, and Aline covered the mattress with her finest linen.

She set up another of the chambers on the second floor as a solar and a smaller cubicle as the wardrobe, where she laid away their clothes, folding them with herbs to keep them fresh. The carts from Norcastle had brought a woodworker, Aylwin, and he spent his days repairing the tables, chairs, and stools that the robbers and neglect had laid waste to. The rat-catcher and dogs and cats had done their work, ridding the keep of vermin. Lady Elizabeth had sent over some tapestries, and Aline hung them on the cold stone walls. The keep, Aline thought, surveying it with pride, was now livable. And, after all the effort she had put into it, it seemed dearer and much more her home than the large and formal Norcastle.

She daydreamed about living here the rest of her days, bearing James's children, leading a simple country life. Perhaps if they never went back to London, if they kept to themselves, visiting only at Norcastle or the Beaufort estates, she could keep James from finding out the truth. It was a foolish hope, she knew; Tanford would eventually reveal her origins even if she thwarted him by keeping James away from London. But it was sweet to imagine, and she told herself that it did no harm. Soon enough she would have to suffer for what she had done. In the meantime she could dream and hope.

When they finished with the keep, there was still more than enough to do. The outbuildings—the kitchen, the chapel, and the armory—needed thorough cleanings, too. Aline set up one of the servants, more skilled than the others, as cook, but he still needed much instruction and direction, which Aline often felt inadequate to give him. Also, there seemed always to be some sort of petty squabble going on between one servant and another, or else they came to her with questions about the linens or the spinning, or the delineations of their duties. Such things taxed Aline to the limit, for she had never been in charge of them before. Nor had she held the kind of power and responsibility she did now. At least, she thought, she could be glad that James was away while she was muddling her way through these problems, so that he did not witness her ineptitude. He would certainly expect a lady raised as Clarissa must have been to know how to handle servants and run a small keep.

Every day or two, James sent back a man with a report on his activities. Aline was pleased by his thoughtfulness, for she knew that he kept her so well informed only because he knew that she worried about him. He reported that all was going well, though it was taking time, as expected, to dig out the thieves from their various hiding holes.

Usually the messenger delivered his report orally, but once James scrawled off a hasty note to tell her that he missed her and thought of her often. It was simply enough written that she could read it, and Aline was filled with pride and pleasure at actually being able to read her husband's words. She folded the message and carried it with her, taking it out now and then to read it again. He would be with her soon, she thought, and she would be able to hold him and kiss him, to see for herself that he had come to no harm.

Finally, one day James's messenger appeared slightly after the midday meal. He swept off his cap and bowed before her, saying, "Milady, Sir James bids me tell you that their campaign is successfully finished. They found the last recess where the robbers hid and rooted them out. Their leader is now hanged."

"And my husband?" Aline asked, standing up from her chair, her hands clasped tightly together. "He is well? He is coming home?"

"Yes, milady. Their lordships are riding to Norcastle and Sir James returns here with his men this evening."

"Today?" Aline's voice vaulted upward, ending in an almost noiseless squeak. "He comes today?"

"Yes, milady. I would say by evensong."

He would be here by twilight. That left her only a few hours to do everything she had to do. Aline flew to the kitchen to instruct the cook to make James's favorite foods, as well as to prepare enough food for the company of men that would be returning home with him, far more than they had been accustomed to feeding the last few days. Then she called Gemma to help her select the gown she would wear for his arrival while two maidservants prepared her bath.

When the water was warm and waiting for her,

Aline sprinkled in dried rose petals, which Lady
Elizabeth had given her, to give her skin and hair the
faint scent of summer roses. She bathed with her
finest soap and washed her hair thoroughly, then
stood and let one of the maids pour clean rinse water
over her. Afterward, when she was dry and had
pulled on her undertunic, she sat on a stool before the
fire and combed out her hair, letting it dry in the heat
from the flickering fire.

Gemma braided it loosely, winding a ribbon
through it. The braid hung down, thick as a man's
wrist, to her waist, and around her face it was soft
and full. It was not proper to not wear the coif, but
Aline reasoned that it would be almost bedtime when
James arrived, and, besides, there would be almost no
one there except her husband to see it. She wanted
him to see her at her best tonight, and she knew how
her hair affected him.

Aline wasn't sure when she had decided to make
love with James that night. She had tried her best to
avoid thinking about it, but somehow during the days
of worrying about James and missing him, she had
come to realize that when he returned she would
truly become his wife. Her mind refused to even listen to the arguments against it. She would not think
about the future, which was so uncertain, but would
live for the moment. And for that moment, she
wanted her husband to find her the most beautiful,
desirable woman in the world.

The tunic she chose was a soft gold velvet which Lady
Elizabeth had given to her, banded at the sleeves with
fur and enriched down the front with fine embroidery in
greens and golds. Around her waist she wore the belt of
golden links and garnets which James had given her. At
her ears and throat she hung the golden topazes of her

bridal gift. The color of the gown turned her eyes bright gold, the color reflected again in the topazes.

The afternoon drew to a close. Aline went to the corner tower of the keep, from which she had the best view of the woods. She stood and waited, scanning the landscape. After a time Gemma brought her her cloak, for it was chilly in the tower with the sun going down. Not long after that it grew too dark to see, and reluctantly Aline climbed back down the stairs.

It was time for the evening meal, but Aline was too nervous to eat. Instead, she sat on one of the chairs Aylwin had repaired and waited.

At last she heard a cry from the parapets, and she sprang to her feet. She flew through the hall and flung open the door, then stepped out and peered into the dark. The heavy gates in the wall were being drawn open by the guards, and moments later, men on horseback clattered across the bridge and into the bailey. Aline stood waiting, shivering a little in the cold, unaware of how the torches on either side of the doorway illuminated her, glittering off her golden gown and turning her hair to flame.

James vaulted off his horse at the foot of the stairs and came up them two at a time. He was covered with dust from the road and was still wearing full mail. But he did not move like a weary man. "Clarissa!"

"James!" Aline swallowed, tightening her fists at her side to keep from reaching out to him. She must not embarrass him in front of his men by throwing herself at him and covering his face with kisses. Ladies did not act that way; she supposed it was the common blood in her that made her want to.

His hands came out, and she extended hers to him. To her surprise, however, he did not take her hands, but pulled her into his arms and squeezed her to him. Aline let out a small, surprised noise, then wrapped her arms around James's neck and clung to him. She did not care about the dust which covered him or the interested stares of his men and the servants, who had crowded behind Aline to greet the returning lord of the castle.

James kissed her, a deep, searching kiss that left Aline almost swooning. His tongue swept in and claimed her mouth. She dug her fingers into his surcoat, hanging on to him to steady her world. Finally, reluctantly, he raised his mouth from hers and set her away from him. He stood for a long moment, gazing down at her.

"I dreamed about you every night," he murmured huskily, "and you were always so beautiful it made my heart hurt. But now that I see you—you are ten times more beautiful in reality."

"James! I've missed you so!" Aline wanted to pull him back into her arms and lift her mouth to be kissed again, but she sternly controlled the impulse.

He smiled down into her face. "I've gotten you dirty." He peeled off one of his gauntlets and brushed a smudge from her cheek.

"I don't mind," Aline responded truthfully. "All that matters is that you are here." She took his hand and turned to lead him inside. "Come in and eat. You must be famished."

"I am," James admitted. He stopped and stared around the great hall in amazement, seeing its many improvements. "You are an enchantress. Only magic could have done this to this keep."

"Not magic," Aline said emphatically. "It was plenty of hard work, I can tell you."

"'Tis most handsome." He walked around the room, looking at the floor, the walls, even the fireplace, now clean and boasting a roaring blaze.

"Lady Elizabeth sent us that tapestry. Wasn't it

kind of her? She must have realized what we would need when your man described the place to them."

"I'm sure." James looked a trifle dazed at the changed appearance of the room, but his eyes kept returning to Aline, whom he could see better here in the light of the wax candles.

He thought that he had never seen anyone as beautiful as she. Her hair was like silken fire, and the way in which it was arranged made it appear as though at any moment it might pull loose of its restraints and come tumbling down. Just the thought of that made his loins begin to throb. Of course, almost everything about her, from her odd, leonine eyes to her slender white hands, made him throb with desire. He had been on fire the entire week they'd been separated, and he had cursed the thieves tenfold for keeping him from his wife's bed. Now all he could think about was making up for lost time.

"Come. Sit down and eat." Aline clapped her hands for the servants, and an instant later they came bustling in, bringing wine to pour into James's goblet, followed by trays of his favorite dishes: roasted goose, venison, and meat pie.

James did not really want to waste time eating; he would have preferred to whisk his wife upstairs immediately. But he knew the ribald laughter that would follow such an action, and he did not wish to embarrass Clarissa. Besides, he could hardly refuse her gift to him, the food that she had obviously ordered prepared with him in mind. So he motioned to Everard to remove his hauberk and mail leggings, then sat down to eat.

Aline picked at her food, her stomach too jittery to eat, but James and his men devoured theirs. They talked little; Aline's mind seemed a blank, the only thoughts on it those of the night ahead, and James was too busy eating. But his eyes stayed on her constantly, gazing at her hair, her face, her form, with such heat that a small, sharp ache, unknown to her until recently, blossomed between her legs.

When the meal was over, Aline took James upstairs, showing him the reclamation of the bedchambers. He stood just inside the door of their chamber and looked around. His gaze came back to her.

"You have made it beautiful." He paused, and for a moment Aline thought that he was going to pull her into his arms and kiss her again, for something briefly flamed in his eyes. But then he said, "I would bathe before we retire. I am caked with the dirt of the road."

"All right. I will send the servants to bring up water."

As she turned to go call the servants, James reached out and took her wrist, stopping her. "But after they have brought the water, dismiss them. I would have my wife bathe me tonight."

Aline's breath caught, and she nodded, color rising up her throat. She hurried into the hall and called sharply to the servants.

While they filled the tub with water and laid out clothes for James to wear afterward, Aline waited, her hands loosely clasped in front of her. She dared not look at James, even though she could feel his eyes on her. She was certain that if she looked at him, her face would give away everything she was thinking and feeling, and she was embarrassed to do so.

Finally the servants left, and Aline turned to James. His eyes were on her in the same hot, hungry way they had been all evening. She sucked in her breath. He looked so large and male, was burning with such an intense heat, that it was almost frightening—yet at the same time deliciously exciting.

"Come here," he said, his voice low and husky, and

Aline went to him, pulled by the raw need in his voice. She stopped only inches from him, gazing up into his face. "If you are to bathe me, you must undress me first."

Aline's eyes widened, and he smiled. "What? You thought that I would bathe clothes and all?"

Aline shook her head, giving him a tremulous smile. "No," she said breathlessly, "in truth I hadn't thought anything. I cannot think when I'm close to you."

James groaned. "Ah, wife, you should not say such things, or I may pull you to the floor and take you on the cold stone."

Truthfully, Aline did not think she would mind if he did, but she refrained from saying so, afraid he would think her overly bold and lustful.

"Come," he said softly. "Begin."

She knelt at his feet and removed his soft boots first. Then she stood and reached up timidly to untie the laces at the neck of his tunic. Her fingers trembled so much that she was clumsy with the laces, but James did not seem to mind. He simply stood, his head lowered almost to hers, breathing in her scent. Finally she was done, and James bent so that she could pull his tunic up and over his head.

He stood before her with his chest and shoulders bare, and Aline's eyes moved slowly over him. His shoulders were broad, but he was not thick or heavy. Rather, he was built on long, lean lines, with a narrow waist, his muscles smoothly sculpted. Hair as black as that on his head curled on his chest, tapering down in a V to his stomach. Even though he was streaked with dirt, Aline thought that she had never seen anything as beautiful as his powerful male body.

Unconsciously, she reached out and laid her hand upon his chest. James sucked in his breath sharply, and Aline snatched her hand back, blushing. Though she enjoyed his touch, perhaps it was different for him. She wasn't sure what was expected or desired in a wife. "I'm sorry."

"Nay, do not apologize." He drew her hand back to his chest. "I enjoy your fingers on me. We never finished our lessons. This is one of them. I have discovered much about your body. Now you will discover mine."

"Oh." Aline thought about moving her hand over him the way he had caressed her, and excitement coiled in her abdomen. Slowly she slid her hand across his chest, exploring the prickle of hair, the firm swell of muscle. Her palm slipped over his flat, masculine breast, and she felt the nipple tighten beneath it.

She glanced up at him. His eyes were closed, his face taut, almost as if he were in pain. Then he opened his eyes and looked down at her. His eyes were dark with passion, the lids heavy.

"Why did you stop?" His voice was hoarse.

"I'm not sure. Does it feel the same way when I touch you there? The way it feels for me?"

"I know not. I only know how it feels for me." He laid his hand over hers and moved it over the firm bud. "And that is wonderful. Do not stop."

She circled her finger around the nipple, and his breath grew shorter. She took the fleshy button between her forefinger and thumb and gently rolled it. James clenched his jaw, stifling a groan. Aline smiled. It pleased her to be able to excite him, to know that she could arouse him just as he had aroused her. A woman's body belonged to her husband; she had heard that all her life. It was intriguing to find that her husband's body could be hers, also.

"May I do whatever I want?" she asked softly.

"Yes. Especially if it's that," he whispered.

Aline smiled to herself. She spread her hands out

flat and ran them up his chest and across his shoulders, exploring the different textures of muscle and bone, of hair and skin. She moved down his arms, her fingers pressing in, then releasing. Slowly she walked around him, gliding her hands onto the thick muscles of his back and sliding a finger down the ridge of his backbone. She realized that she would like to run her mouth and tongue over him as he had done to her.

Her eyes slid down his back to his buttocks, still concealed by his braies, and desire curled in her loins. A little surprised by her daring, she slipped her hands down his back and curved over his hips. The muscles of his back twitched, and he tightened his buttocks. Emboldened by his reaction, Aline dug her fingers into the flesh of his buttocks and was rewarded by a groan he could not suppress. James raised his arms and sank his hands into his thick hair, clenching them.

"Jesu, woman, do you wish to kill me?" he murmured.

Made saucy by the knowledge she had been gleaning, Aline chuckled and asked, "Do you wish me to stop, sir?"

"No." He gave a shaky laugh. "By all that's holy, do not stop."

Aline came back in front of him to untie the waist of his braies and roll them down. When she reached for the ties, she saw that his manhood bulged against the soft material, pulsing and eager to escape. She hesitated, suddenly shy. Swallowing hard, she made herself reach out and take the ties. His stomach flinched as she accidentally grazed it with her fingers. She stole a glance up at James and saw that his chest and face were now covered by a faint sheen of sweat.

Carefully she untied the strings, then hooked her thumbs under the cloth at each side and began to slide the braies down. The cloth tugged over his swollen manhood, and Aline turned her head aside, curiosity, trepidation, and excitement mingling within her. She slipped the garment down his legs, her fingertips gliding over his flesh. James stepped out of the leggings, and she tossed them aside, then stood and took a step back. Finally she raised her eyes to look at what she both feared and yearned to see.

Her eyes widened, and she drew in her breath sharply. He was magnificently male, hard and huge and throbbing with desire. Aline knew from gossip what happened in the marriage act, and she could not imagine him putting *that* inside her.

"Nay," she whispered, and she looked up into James's face a little fearfully. "You cannot. 'Twill tear me apart."

"Do not be frightened." James moved forward, reaching out to cup her face between his hands. "'Tis nothing fearsome, only part of me. Do you not know I would not harm you?"

"But how—"

"'Twill fit, my love, I promise you. 'Tis part of the pleasure of it, that you will be tight as a glove around me and that I will fill you." His face softened sensually as he spoke, his own words arousing him. "Trust me. There will be a little pain at first because you are untouched. But I have done what I could to make sure there is as little pain as possible." Aline remembered the way he had slipped his fingers inside her those nights before he left, stretching her. She understood now why he had done so, and it touched her that he had wanted to avoid causing her pain when they made love the first time.

"Whatever pain there is," he went on, stroking his thumb across her cheek, "it will be brief and just that once. I promise you that after that there will be only pleasure in it. For both of us."

Aline cast him an uncertain look, but she had come to trust this man, as well as love him, and she believed that he would be careful and tender with her. She relaxed and gave him a shy smile. "Come. You should get in the bath, or the water will grow cold."

She took his hand and led him to the tub, and he climbed in, settling down with a sigh of satisfaction into the hot water. He leaned forward and dunked his head in the water, wetting it, then leaned back against the tub, his eyes closed in pure sensual pleasure. Aline knelt beside the tub, not sure where to start. Excitement sizzled along her veins.

Dipping the soap into the water, she rubbed it between her hands, then put it aside and sank her hands into James's hair. His hair was thick and soft, and it gave her a visceral thrill to rub her fingers through it. She worked the soap into a thick lather, rubbing his scalp and stroking the soap through his hair.

He enjoyed it. His head lolled back, and his eyes were closed, his face blissfully relaxed. Aline enjoyed it, too. There was something deeply satisfying about taking care of him this way, and she loved the silky feel of his wet hair between her fingers.

Finally she stopped and rinsed his hair with an ewer of warm water. Then she picked up the rag and dipped it into the water and started to soap it.

"Use your hands."

Aline stopped and looked at him. His eyes were closed. "What?"

"I want you to wash me with your hands." James opened his eyes and looked at her. The hunger in his eyes made Aline feel weak.

"All right." She wet her lips nervously. She set the rag aside and began to rub the ball of soap between her hands. She put her hands tentatively on his neck, moving down over his shoulders and onto his arms. She lifted his arm and held it with one hand, washing it down to the fingertips. Her fingers intertwined with his, white against his darker skin. He was so powerful, yet she remembered how gently his fingers had moved over her body.

The familiar dampness came between her legs as she worked over him, holding and washing his arms, then going back to his chest. It was incredibly sensual to slide her soapy hands across his water-slick skin. She watched her hands move over him. A flush of desire mounted up his throat and into his face; a certain slackness touched his mouth. His chest rose and fell more rapidly. She knew that what she was doing stirred him, and that thought aroused her even more. She moved her soapy hands down his chest, finding and teasing his nipples to hardness.

James stood up so that she could soap the lower part of his body. She started at his feet, as he propped first one and then the other on the edge of the tub. Then she moved up one leg, sliding her hands across his flesh, feeling the crinkle of hair beneath her skin, the tightening of a muscle. Her hands grew slower and more cautious as she moved above his knee. His thigh was as hard as a rock. She glided up slowly, softly, until she came to the juncture of his leg. She wanted to touch him intimately, was curious and excited, but she had not the courage yet.

So she started on his other leg, working her hands upward the same way until again she reached the apex of his legs. She could feel the sensitive sac between his legs heavy upon her knuckles. She dared not look at his manhood, so she stared fixedly at his stomach, watching a rivulet of soapy water trickle down and disappear into the well of his navel.

"Go ahead," James whispered, his voice low and hoarse, throbbing with passion. "Please touch me."

Aline could not deny the appeal of his words. She turned her head and gazed at his powerful manhood. It stood out proud and thrusting from the dark hair that ringed it. Tenderly she moved her fingers, cupping the sac that hung between his legs. James released a low moan and he reached out, digging his hands into her hair. Her loose braid came undone at his rough touch, and her hair cascaded down over her shoulders, covering his hands with its sweetly scented silk.

Her hand slid onto the base of his shaft, and she was astonished at the exquisitely smooth texture of his skin. She slid her hand along the length of him, exploring the exciting contrast of the tender, soft skin and the hardness underlying it.

"Ah, Clarissa." The words were a sigh, and his hands clenched in her hair.

Aline stopped, hating to hear that name on his lips, spoken with such longing and affection. At that moment Aline hated Lady Clarissa. She wished that she could hear *her* name in his mouth, have him murmur to *her*.

"Nay, don't stop. 'Tis sweet, so sweet," James told her, misinterpreting her reason for halting her ministrations.

Aline pushed aside her irritation, knowing that she was being unreasonable. It was *she*, after all, that he was addressing, and if the name was not hers, it was no one's fault but her own. It was she, not Clarissa, who had caressed him until he was trembling with passion, and the passion was solely for the woman in front of him.

She wrapped both hands around him and stroked upward slowly, then down again, until finally James groaned aloud. "Nay," he panted, "you must stop. I would take you in our bed, not here. And if you do not stop, I will be unable to wait."

He sat down and rinsed off his soap, then stood to let her pour a final ewerful of water over him. Aline wrapped the bath linen around him as he stepped from the tub, then took another panel of cloth and began to dry his hair. She moved the sheet downward and dried his shoulders and back. He looked so beautiful to her that she could not resist leaning forward and pressing her mouth softly against his back. James shuddered and whirled around, clasping her to him and burying his mouth in hers.

He was still quite wet, and he got her tunic damp, but Aline did not mind. She cared about nothing at this moment but the feel of his mouth on hers. His tongue swept into her mouth, and she met it with her own, stroking and circling in mock swordplay.

Finally he pulled back. His face was flushed, his eyes glittering, and his chest rose and fell in rapid pants. He dropped the bath sheet and swept Aline up in his arms, starting toward the bed.

17

James set Aline down and shoved the door to behind him. He turned to her, reaching out to undo the ribbons that laced up the neck of her tunic. His fingers were clumsy on the ties, and before he got them completely undone, he had to pull her to him and kiss her, his hands running wild over her body. He wanted to taste and touch her and have her all at once; he wanted to sink into her softness and pour out his hot seed, yet at the same time he wanted to savor every pleasure of her body.

He kissed her mouth over and over, until her lips were rosy and swollen, and then his lips moved over the rest of her face, kissing her eyes, her cheeks, her forehead, and, finally, her ears. His teeth worried at the lobe of her ear, sending shivers darting through her, and then he laved it tenderly with his tongue. His tongue traced the whorls and crept inside, and Aline gasped and dug her fingers into his arms. Everything he did sent a new and delightful sensation through her, making her shudder and whimper with pleasure. She was almost wild with the need to feel him on her bare skin.

"Please," she murmured, tugging at her tunic.

He understood what she wanted and released her, grasping her tunic and pulling it up over her head. He knelt to remove her slippers and stockings, but he became distracted by the silken smoothness of her legs beneath his fingers, and when he had removed the stockings, he slid his hands caressingly up and down her legs. He pushed up her undertunic to expose her slim, shapely legs, and pressed his lips against her thigh. His hand caressed the soft inner flesh of her thigh while his mouth traveled over the outer side. Aline dug her fingers into his hair, but he did not notice the slight pain. His entire attention was focused on the wonder of her body.

James's hands slipped to the back of her legs and up until he reached the curve of her buttocks. He buried his head in her stomach as his fingers cupped and caressed her buttocks. Heat roared through him, and his desire was so intense that he trembled. Her undergown irritated him, obstructing his hands and covering far too much of her, and finally, with an oath, he stood up and shoved the garment up and over her head, then hurled it across the room.

Aline stood before him naked, and he looked upon her with wonder. He had seen her body only dimly the nights that they had lain together in her tent, for there had been no light save that of the fire filtering through the blanket walls. It had been beautiful to him then, but now, in the light of the wax candles and the sconces that burned about the room, she was so lovely that she took his breath away. Her body was well formed, shapely and soft, yet also toned and sleek. Her breasts were firm, her nipples a dark rose, pointed with desire. Her body flowed gently into a narrow waist, then flared out again into sweetly rounded hips. His eyes were drawn to the red-gold curls at the apex of her thighs.

"Ah," he said. "You carry your fire everywhere, do you not?" His hands went to her breasts, cupping them. "I would throw myself into your fire most willingly."

Gently he kneaded her breasts, gazing down at his hands on her, watching her nipples pebble at his touch. His thumbs circled the buds, and they stood out even more proudly, as though to meet his fingers. James groaned and lifted her up, bending her back over his arm, and he bent and took one nipple in his mouth. He sucked strong and deeply, and a cord seemed to thrum from her nipple straight down into her abdomen, turning her loins to wax. Aline could feel the moisture flooding between her legs, and she was embarrassed about it, for she thought it must be an indication of wantonness in her. But James did not seem to mind it, for his other hand slipped down over her buttocks and between her legs from the rear, and when he touched the wetness there, he moaned and spread her nether lips, sliding along the slick folds of flesh.

He walked to the bed, carrying her, his mouth and hands busy on her body. He laid her down on the bed and stretched out beside her. His mouth went to her other breast, and his hand delved between her legs, stroking her softly. Aline whimpered and moved her hips, arching up against his hand; her fingers slid restlessly over his shoulders, arms, and back, caressing every part of him that she could touch.

At last James raised his head from her breast and moved between her legs. Aline opened to him gladly, and her hands went eagerly to his chest, available now to her exploration. James made a low sound as she took his nipples between her fingers and began to play with them. He paused, his body rigid, delighting in her touch yet fighting hard to keep his desire from hurtling him beyond all control. Sweat glistened on his body and dampened his hair. Aline thought that she had never seen a sight as glorious as he was at this moment, his face stamped with passion, his muscled body taut as he held that passion back.

She slid her hands down his chest and around to his back, coming down to caress his buttocks. He bucked at her touch and released a groan, and then he thrust into her, shoving past her maidenhead in a single, quick push. Aline let out a soft cry at the sudden pain, for even his tender preparations those two nights had not completely done away with the barrier. She tried to move back away from him, but his hands clamped down on her hips, holding her fast. The pain was brief, and she realized that he filled her in a most pleasurable way, as if she had been empty all her life and only now was whole.

James began to move gently within her, and Aline sucked in a breath, startled, for this sensation was even more pleasurable. He slid almost out of her, and she dug her fingers into his back, trying to hold him to her. To her intense relief, he did not leave. Instead, he thrust slowly, tenderly back in until he was embedded in her the full length of his shaft. Aline arched her head, assaulted by a torrent of sensations she had never before experienced. There was still a frisson of pain when he moved within her, but far overshadowing it was a startling pleasure.

He pulled back and thrust in again, straining to keep his movements slow and gentle despite the desire that raged inside him, aching to pump into her hard and fast until he was gloriously spent. He stroked in and out. Aline instinctively wrapped her legs around him, and it was that movement, innocently seductive, which finally broke his control. He thrust more quickly, his strokes hard and deep, and then he shuddered, releasing a hoarse cry, and collapsed against her.

Aline wrapped her arms around him tightly, savoring the feel of him, slick and heated, vulnerable in the aftermath of his pleasure.

"Oh, love," he murmured so softly she could barely hear it, and he pressed his lips tenderly to her neck where it joined with her shoulder.

Aline held his words to her heart; it made several times now that he had called her his love. Did he truly mean it? He had not told her that he loved her; the words could simply be the meaningless sort of endearments a man said to a maid when he wooed her. Or they could be the words of his heart, the things he could say only indirectly.

He kissed her shoulder and rolled off her. Aline almost cried out in protest at the loss.

"Are you all right?" he murmured, pulling her into the crook of his arm. "Did I hurt you?"

"A little," Aline admitted, snuggling her head into the hollow of his shoulder. It was almost as good to lie this way, cuddled against him. "But I am fine now."

"It will be better next time," James promised. "I will make sure of that. From now on you shall feel only pleasure."

"Indeed, I felt pleasure tonight."

"Did you?" She could hear his smile in his voice, and it warmed her.

"Yes." She threaded her fingers through the hairs on his chest, idly playing with them. "Could you not tell?"

"I had some suspicions. But I was so struck with it

myself that I could hardly trust my senses." He took a strand of her hair and began to curl it around his finger. "You are the most beautiful woman I've ever known."

"Nay." Aline chuckled. "You need not flatter me."

"'Tis no flattery. 'Tis only the truth." He turned his head and kissed the top of her head. "I could think of nothing but you while I was gone. I'm lucky I didn't get myself killed, I paid so little attention to my task."

"James! No! Do not say such a thing!" She shuddered. "I had rather that you never think of me than that you risk your life doing so."

"I exaggerate. 'Tis true I thought of you constantly, but there was little danger." He stroked his hand slowly down the line of her body. "You are so beautiful. I would have no other to wife, milady. You are all that I desire."

Aline kissed him, and it was only when she tasted the salt of her tears mingling with their kiss that she realized she was crying.

"How now, Lady? Why do you cry?" James asked, taking her chin between his thumb and forefinger and lifting her head up. "Do you regret what we have done?"

"Nay. I cry with joy." She threw her arms around his waist and snuggled against his chest. "Only with joy."

Aline opened her eyes and blinked, looking vaguely around. She was lying naked in her bed, and she felt odd, a little sore, and—suddenly the memories of the night before came flooding in on her, and a flush rose in Aline's cheeks.

"And well you might blush," Gemma piped up.

Aline turned her head to find her friend perched on a chest beneath the window. Gemma was sitting cross-legged, her elbow on one knee and her chin in her hand, watching Aline.

"The way you two looked at each other last night, I thought you would not last long enough to make it to the bedchamber. I was sure I would find you this morning asleep on the table or floor."

Aline grinned mischievously. "Too hard. We 'gentle' folk like our comforts, you know."

Gemma snorted. "You are a fool, girl, and you're riding for a hard fall." She shrugged. "But try to tell a woman in love anything. You'll only get slapped for your pains, like as not."

"Hush, don't be so hard on me. Oh, Gemma, right now I am the happiest woman alive."

"I only hope you can remain both—happy and alive."

"Won't you even congratulate me or wish me well?"

"Oh, aye, I wish you well. You know that." Gemma hopped off the trunk and came over to climb up on the bed. "All I want is your happiness."

"I know. But you do not think this will bring me happiness."

"I don't see how."

"Well, I am happy now." Aline sighed and rolled over onto her back. She glanced around. "Where is James?" Even saying his name made her feel giddy, and the fact embarrassed her.

"He went down to break his fast some time ago. He bid me not to wake you, though." Gemma's eyebrows peaked in a lewd leer. "No doubt you were well tired out."

"Sir James is a thoughtful husband," Aline retorted with a grimace, and bounced out of bed.

"Aye, I am sure so. And all of his thoughts are obviously on one thing."

Aline giggled. "'Deed, I fear mine are, also."

She washed and dressed in a deep blue tunic with a white bliaut beneath it, and Gemma helped her arrange her coif and top it with a thin gold circlet.

Gemma sighed. "'Tis no wonder that the master is grinning like a goose this morning. Half the men in England will envy him for having you. You are the fairest woman I've ever seen. You were always beautiful, but dressed up in lady's clothes, you shine like a star."

"Thank you, Gemma," Aline replied, surprised and touched. Impulsively she went to her friend and hugged her. "I am sorry that I act so foolishly. I do not ignore what you say. It is just that—"

"I know—that you are so much in love. It has ruined many a woman before you. But them I did not love like my own sister."

"I love you, too. And I promise, whatever may happen, I will do my best to see that you come to no harm. I will say you did not know of my pretense, that I took you on after I became the Lady Clarissa."

Gemma shook her head. "'Tis not myself I'm worried for, Aline."

"What I have to do is make sure that James does not go to London. 'Tis there that Tanford plans to reveal the trickery. His man told me so. If I can just keep him away, perhaps it will all turn out well."

"I pray you're right," Gemma said, her tone holding out little hope of that possibility.

"I do too."

James was finishing his morning meal when Aline swept into the great hall. There was no one there but James and a few servants. All of his men had already eaten and were about their work. Aline paused at the bottom of the stairs, looking at James, until he felt her gaze on him and glanced up. A smile spread across his face, dazzling her.

"Milady." James rose and went to her, giving her his arm to escort her to the table. "I did not expect you up so early."

"I awakened not long after you left. I must have gotten cold." She blushed.

"Indeed, 'tis no wonder, given the way you were arrayed—in all the glory of your hair."

Her flush deepened, but she could not help but smile back at him. "'Tis your fault," she teased boldly, "for leaving me there alone."

"I stand corrected. I shall not do so again." His eyes ran down her body, and his face turned serious. "But the truth is, I felt I had to leave. Looking at you, I knew that if I did not leave, I would awaken you and take you again."

Aline lowered her eyes, flirting with him. She was heady with love and excitement. "Dear sir, that sounds a pleasant way to awaken."

A light sprang into James's eyes, and she felt his arm tighten beneath her hand. "I thought—" He cleared his throat. "I feared it would be too much for you. I did not know how sore you were."

Aline could not meet his eyes. "A trifle."

"Too much so to go riding with me?"

"Oh, no, I would love to!" She looked up excitedly. "Where do you go?"

"Only to the village. I have some business there. But I thought you had not been there and might like to see it."

"Oh, yes." The chance to spend the day in James's company was irresistible.

"Good. Then eat up, and we shall go."

It was a pleasant ride into town, chilly, but not unbearably so, as Aline's fur-trimmed mantle kept out the cold. Even if it had been freezing cold, Aline did not think she would have minded. It was enough simply to be in James's company. They talked and laughed. She told him about cleaning out the keep, making jests out of the hours of hard work, and he told her about their search for the robbers, who were no match for them in fighting skills, but who were difficult to find in the vast reaches of the forest. Sometimes they said nothing or just looked at one another and smiled, and that was sweet enough.

The village, when they reached it, was little to see. The residents came out of their houses to see them, some simply staring and others calling out and waving to them. Aline smiled and nodded, reminding herself not to be too friendly. A grand lady's greeting was not that of an entertainer.

James paid a visit to the leaders of the village, for he wanted to reassure them that Chaswyck Keep now had a new master and that the depredations of the robbers were over.

"There may be some here who were in league with them," James murmured to Aline before he dismounted to greet the men, "but 'twill be well for them to know, as well, that such days are over and I'll brook no thievery."

Aline watched him as he greeted the men with just the right amount of reserve and graciousness. Her heart swelled with pride as she watched him. He might be illegitimate, she thought, with little more blue blood in his veins than she herself had, but he was truly a nobleman, born and bred to it. He did not have to think how to act; he knew it, had known it all his life.

Aline was sure that even when he and Richard were living near penniless with their aunt in France, having lost their birthright and most of their family, James had still had the carriage and manner of a nobleman.

He introduced the men to Aline, and she gave her hand to each of them, leaning down from her horse and giving each a gracious smile. A peek at James's approving face told her that she was acting precisely as she ought to.

Just at that moment, there was a cry from nearby, and everyone whirled around. As James whisked his sword from its scabbard, a small boy erupted from the doorway of a shop and ran straight toward them. Behind him a large woman came huffing and puffing out, shrieking with rage and shaking her fist at the boy.

"Come here, you little thief!" she shouted. "I'll hang you by your heels!"

The boy dodged the outstretched hand of one of the village men and dived to the ground, rolling under the belly of Aline's horse. Startled, the animal reared, and Aline, sitting casually in the saddle, the reins loose in her hand, lost her balance and went tumbling to the ground.

"Clarissa!"

"Milady!"

There was a chorus of horrified exclamations all around her, and in an instant James was by her side, kneeling in the dusty street. "Are you all right?"

Aline nodded, struggling to breathe. The wind had been knocked out of her, and it hurt terribly, but it had happened to her often enough before when she had done an acrobatic trick wrong, and she knew that it would pass with no lasting effect. It was only painful—and frightening—for a moment.

"Get that boy!" James ordered to the men clustered

around him, never taking his eyes from Aline's face, which was contorted with pain. He held her hand and smoothed the hair back from her forehead. "You will be all right," he murmured soothingly to her. "Your breath will come back to you."

And it did. Aline sucked in great gulps of air as both the pain and the panic receded. "I am fine."

"Thank God." James took her into his arms, cradling her to him. He kissed the top of her head and held her tightly. "Are you sure? No broken bones?"

"No, I don't think so." Aline tentatively moved her arms and legs. "There is no harm done."

James helped her to her feet and turned toward the other men. "Where is that boy? I'll have his head for this."

"No! Oh, James, no, he didn't mean to hurt me." The lad had been quick and agile, and Aline instinctively admired his grace of movement. "I would not have fallen if I had not been careless."

"That is no excuse. He is still to blame for it."

"But he is only a boy."

"A thieving rat, that's what he is," interjected the large, red-faced woman who had chased the boy into the street. "Took a piece of bread right out from under my nose, he did!"

Privately Aline thought that the woman could stand to give up a piece of bread, given her size, especially when compared with the boy's pitiful thinness, but she said nothing.

"Here he is, sir, the lying little beggar." One of the village men was dragging the boy toward them. He did not come easily, but kicked and struggled to tear loose from the man's powerful grip. Casually the man lifted his other hand and slapped him. "Keep still, boy!"

He threw him into the dusty street in front of

James's feet, and the boy scrambled up, glancing around at the circle of faces looming above him. He was dressed in rags and so filthy that one could not tell the color of his hair for all the dirt caked on it. There was a defiant tilt to his chin, though, as he looked around at the impressive number of people arrayed against him, and Aline saw a certain lively intelligence in his dark eyes.

This idea was confirmed when he threw himself at the feet of Aline, the one person in the crowd who held any sympathy in her heart for him.

"Forgive me, lady! I did not mean to affright you! I swear! Please, I will be good. Do not hurt me!"

"I will not hurt you," Aline assured him, bending down to grasp his arm and help him up. "I am sure you did not mean to make my horse rear, and, indeed, I should have been holding him better, shouldn't I?"

He looked up in astonishment at her friendly tone.

"He should be punished for what he did to you," James told Aline firmly. "You are too softhearted, wife."

"That's right, milady," one of the men piped up. "He should be punished. He's a troublemaker, this one. He is that slut Elma's get, and many is the time he has had to be beaten for this sin or that. If Father Jermyn wasn't so soft on him, he would have been missing both hands by now. Last time he just got lashes for his thievery."

Aline drew in a sharp breath. Justice was harsh and swift, and she had seen more than one thief punished by losing a hand or a foot.

"That's right," another voice chimed in. "This time, sir, you best give him what he deserves."

The large woman nodded. "He's a thief. He should lose his hand for it."

The scrawny boy gulped and drew closer to Aline,

his face paling under its dirt. Aline's heart went out to him. "No! You must not do that."

She turned to James, looking at him with pleading eyes. "Husband, please, I ask you. Do not punish him so. I am certain that he is not a bad lad. He looks hungry."

"That is no excuse," the boy's accuser said pugnaciously.

Aline drew herself up and turned a freezing gaze on the woman. "I do not believe I was addressing you."

Even that woman's belligerence quailed under Aline's imperious manner, and she subsided, with a baleful glance at the boy. Emboldened by Aline's championing of him, the boy drew back against her skirts and turned to look up at James.

"Please, sir," he said. "I did not mean to hurt your lady. I ain't had nothing to eat for over a day, and I was very hungry."

James gazed down at the boy. He was pitifully thin, and though he was a dreadful mess, there was something undeniably appealing in his face. James sighed and looked at Aline.

"And, what, I pray, do you think I should do with this miscreant? Just set him loose, after he's stolen this woman's bread?"

"You could pay this woman for the loss of her bread, and the boy could come with us," Aline suggested, thinking quickly. "He could work at the keep. I could use another servant. He is quick and agile. I am sure there are all sorts of things that he could do. He could be a potboy or run with messages—you know, we have no page."

"This one's hardly a page." Pages were always the sons of nobility, given for training to another household, and when they grew older, they became squires, like James's Everard.

"I know, but—please, James." She smiled at him tremulously. "I pray you. Grant me this boon."

"It means this much to you?"

"Oh, yes."

James smiled tenderly at her. "Then how can I refuse you?"

Aline's heart swelled with love. "Thank you," she murmured, wishing that she could kiss him, although, of course, she could not in front of all these people.

"Here, woman." James turned and tossed a coin to the complaining woman. "This should compensate you for your loss." He swept the rest of the villagers with his cool, implacable gaze. "I shall take the boy home and deal with him there."

Aline felt the boy slump back against her skirts in relief, and she put her hand on his shoulder, giving it an encouraging squeeze. James turned back to them and looked down at the boy. "Well, lad, it seems you've acquired a job. What's your name?"

"Malcolm, milord."

"Very well, Malcolm." James sighed and said with resignation, "I see nothing for it but to put you up behind me, dirt, fleas, and all."

"I ain't got no fleas!" the boy retorted indignantly, then looked comically thoughtful. "Leastways, I don't think I have."

James had to laugh. He turned to Aline, his eyes alight. "Lady, you will owe me for this."

Aline smiled back. "Will I?" Her eyes danced; she was well aware of the sexual innuendo in James's words. "Then I will pay, sir. Gladly."

18

When they arrived home, Aline called Gemma and turned Malcolm over to her. "I think this one needs food and a good application of soap and water."

"Ah, the poor little thing," Gemma said, curling an arm around his shoulders. Gemma was softhearted where children were concerned; Aline knew that she regretted the fact that she had never had any children of her own. "You're all skin and bones. Come along with me, and we'll take care of you."

Aline watched the pair leave. She smiled and said, "I think Malcolm may have found a friend for life."

"The wretched little urchin," James commented. "He nearly talked my ear off the whole way back." He fixed a stern look on his wife. "Is this a habit of yours, milady? Are we to pick up stray children whenever we venture out?"

"Not always," Aline responded with an airy shrug.

James smiled at her indulgently as he stripped off

his riding gloves. "Come here, you little vixen. You have a forfeit to pay."

Aline's brows went up in astonishment. "Now?"

He looked amused. "What better time? I expect my debts paid quickly. And for such a sacrifice as having that little jabberer holding on to my back, the debt is very great." His mouth widened sensually, and he started toward her, holding out his hand. "Come, milady, let us go upstairs."

Aline's heart thumped wildly in her chest as she slipped her hand into his. It seemed exceedingly daring and outrageous to be going to their bedchamber to make love in the broad daylight, and that fact made it all the more exciting.

"But everyone will know where we are going and why," Aline protested faintly as they went up the stairs.

"What does it matter? You are my wife. We commit no sin."

Aline wasn't entirely sure about that, but she said nothing. James whisked her into their room, closing and barring the door behind them, then began immediately to undress her.

"Oh, no, sir," Aline said, pulling away, seized by an impish impulse. "'Tis my debt to pay, as you said, and you should not lift a finger." She led him over to the bed and gave him a gentle push backward. "You must sit and rest."

"Indeed?" James grinned and lolled back on his elbows, watching her with hot eyes.

Aline's hands went to her belt and unfastened it, and she let it slide through her fingers onto a low table. James's eyes followed her every movement, his body going utterly still, and she knew that she had captured him. She smiled, a secret, seductive, very feminine smile, one that spoke of ancient knowledge ingrained in every female. She wasn't sure why she had decided to undress before James or where she'd gotten the courage to do it, but the urge was strong and powerful. She wanted to entice and seduce him, to exert her sensual power over him. But at the same time, she was aroused, too, by what she was doing, and by the feel of his smoldering eyes on her as she displayed her body to him.

Her fingers unfastened the side laces of her tunic, drawn in to accentuate her waist, and she slowly wriggled the garment upward and off over her head. She removed her shoes and stockings, moving without haste, showing more and more of her leg, but not quite all. She glanced over at James. His hands were clenched into the bedcover and his eyes were avid, his swollen shaft pressing against his clothes.

Aline smiled and began to remove her loose bliaut. It had a wide scoop neck, and she let it slip down one arm, revealing a soft white shoulder. Then she moved it off the other shoulder and slowly downward. It drifted over the swell of her creamy breasts, catching for an instant on her puckered nipples. As Aline's breasts came free, she heard James's quick intake of breath. She pulled the garment lower, over her flat stomach and down to the swell of her hips, where it hung tantalizingly.

"Where did you learn to do this?" James asked hoarsely, his eyes eating her up.

"I did not learn it," Aline answered honestly, her fingers teasingly slipping beneath the material and inching it downward. "I find my answers as I go, watching you."

"You school yourself well then," he muttered. "God's blood, woman, get on with it, or I may tear that damned thing from you myself."

In that instant, she thrust the bliaut off her hips, and it slid lazily down her legs to the floor. She stood before him naked. For a long moment, James gazed at her, unmoving, drinking in every detail of her lovely body in the full light of day.

"There can be no other woman as beautiful as you," he said softly, and he reached out and grasped her hips, pulling her up to the bed to stand between his legs, flush up against him.

His hands caressed her buttocks, delighting in the firm, smooth flesh. Holding her hips tight against him, he began to feast upon her breasts. Suckling, licking, nuzzling her with his lips, he took possession of the creamy mounds. And all the while, his hands rhythmically stroked her hips and back and thighs. Then his fingers slid between her legs from behind, separating and caressing the slick folds. Aline shook beneath the force of the combined pleasures.

His finger found the little nubbin of flesh that was most sensitive, and gently he worked it. Aline moaned and began to move her hips, urging him on. She felt him smile against her breast, and his tongue began to lash her nipple in time with the flicker of his finger upon the lower nub of flesh. Aline trembled, feeling as if she might fly apart in all different directions, so great was the fiery pleasure. Something was building up inside her, a huge, overwhelming force that grew and grew. She dug her fingers into James's shoulders, moving her hips frantically, sobbing in her need for release. Then, like lightning, it came, bursting upon her and sending waves of pleasure all through her body.

In the aftermath, she sagged limply against James. He smiled and settled her onto the bed. "Oh, no, dearling, you are not through yet. We have just begun."

Aline opened her eyes and looked at him with

wonder. *How could there possibly be any more?* He stood, and she realized that he was still fully clothed, his manhood pulsing against his garment. James must reach fulfillment, too, she knew, but she felt too drained to move.

She watched as he undressed quickly, revealing his powerful body, his aching desire. He slid between her legs, lifting her hips to accept him, and moved slowly inside her. He filled her, and the satisfaction was so great that Aline moaned with pleasure. She felt possessed, owned, and at the same time quite powerful, holding this man inside her. She squeezed against him, and he groaned, pushing as deep into her as he could go. He pulled back, then thrust slowly, deeply in. He was not as driven as he had been the night before, and he took his time, stoking the fires of Aline's passion with his long, powerful strokes, moving in and out in a primal rhythm. Aline was amazed to find that she was on fire for him again, passion spiraling up in her, growing with every thrust of his hips. She tensed, arching upward, and the wild, hot pleasure seized her again. At her movement, James shuddered, vaulting to his own soul-shaking release. He bucked against her, pouring his seed into her, and Aline clung to him, propelled into a joy she had never known existed.

The following weeks were happy. Aline knew that any day the Duke might reveal who she really was, and her life would be shattered, but she pushed the idea to the back of her mind, refusing to think about it. Life was too good at the moment to spoil it with dreadful musings.

She knew that she should tell James the truth, but each time she worked up the courage, she would back down. Tanford would harm her parents if she told James; he might even kill one or both of them. And James would . . . well, she frankly did not know what James would do if he found out. She could imagine several equally disturbing possibilities. She could not bring herself to tell him.

So she lived her life day by day, hoping that something would happen to stave off the disaster, praying each night that God would grant her a miracle and let her keep James's love and save her parents' lives.

Winter passed quickly inside their snug keep. There were still ample things to do about Chaswyck to keep everyone occupied. James took up Aline's reading lessons again, going beyond the simple words she had learned before. And neither James nor Aline had any objection to going to bed early and waking up late the next morning, then lying abed for an extra hour or two. They never tired of exploring each other and the many pleasures they could give one another.

James willingly guided Aline on her discovery of the male body, and he was just as eager to find each sensitive pleasure point in her. Their nights were filled with passion.

Late in the winter, food was scarce, and James went with his brother and Stephen to hunt, not returning for three days. While he was gone, Aline tried to occupy herself with her usual tasks, but her life seemed empty and miserable, and she wondered how she could ever live without James. Somehow, she had to find a way to keep the Duke from telling James the deception she'd practiced.

Then, almost as if she had conjured him up with her thoughts, that night Tanford's man, Fingal, entered their keep, disguised this time as a traveling monk.

Aline saw him as soon as she came down to supper, and she froze, her heart pounding wildly. She knew he wanted to speak to her, and she tried to think of some way that she could avoid him. But she quickly realized that that was foolish; he would find her eventually and would only be angry over her attempts to hide. Besides, she had to know what the Duke planned. It was the only possible way she could help James. So after supper, she sent word to the friar, asking him to join her in her evening prayers. She crossed the courtyard to the chapel, being sure to take Gemma with her. There she lit a candle and knelt to pray earnestly for help in guiding her safely out of this awful coil.

Moments later the Duke's man came in. He stopped short when he saw Gemma kneeling beside Aline. "What is *she* doing here?" he snapped.

Aline rose and turned to cast him a cold look. "Gemma always accompanies me on my trips to the chapel. It would look odd if she did not. The Lady Clarissa would not closet herself alone with a man, even a pious friar." She invested the last words with tremendous irony. "Gemma knows everything," she went on. "So you need not hide what you say from her."

"And if she talks?"

"She could have done that already, and she has not. She has nothing to gain by it now, for Sir James would not be pleased that she had waited this long to say anything. That should be reason enough to satisfy you. As for myself, I know that she is my friend and I trust her. You, of course, would not understand such a thing."

The man grimaced, but made no more objection. He strode forward to the front of the chapel. Aline braced herself, not allowing herself to step back from him, as she wanted to.

"The folk of the keep say you have the bastard in the palm of your hand," he said approvingly. "Very clever of you. His Grace will be pleased."

"You hear wrong," Aline retorted crossly. "My husband is his own man only. No one controls him, least of all me." She tried to look irritated and petulant at the thought, as though she had tried to capture James's heart and failed. She certainly did not want this man to think that she could influence James to do anything. "You told me yourself that he is not one who can love, and 'tis true. He's given me no baubles save this belt." She brushed her hand contemptuously over the precious gold links James had given her.

"A woman might well expect more." Fingal smiled coldly. "But you cannot expect jewelry in such an out-of-the-way place. You must go to a city to find a goldsmith. London, perhaps."

Aline tightened. "What are you suggesting?"

"His Grace is returning to London in a few weeks. Now that travel is possible, there will be many who will return to Court. Since you have never been there, you will be eager to go."

"I have no desire to go to Court, nor to see London. I have been in the city many times."

"His Grace does not ask it of you, wench. He commands it. You will bring Sir James to London this spring or summer."

"I cannot make him go."

"'Twill not be difficult. He would probably go even without your urging. He is a creature of the Court. He likes it there, as does His Grace. It suits their love of secrets and schemes."

"Sir James is not like the Duke."

The man cocked one eyebrow. "He is younger and perhaps not as wily. But he is a planner, that one. He likes to turn and twist things to his own end. In that way he could be kin to my lord."

"You are mistaken."

"Do not tell me you have fallen under that man's spell!" he said, amused. "You will be sorry if you have."

"I have not fallen under his spell," Aline retorted hotly, for she knew that Fingal and the Duke would be quick to use such information against her.

He shrugged. "It doesn't matter—so long as you get no foolish notion about saving the bastard from His Grace's vengeance. Don't try to cross the Duke of Tanford. He will squash you like an insect."

"I am not afraid of your threats."

"Then you are foolish, indeed." He grasped Aline by the arm and jerked her forward, bending down so that his face was only inches from hers. "Hear me well, girl. His Grace has plans. You and Sir James will come to London, or it will go ill with you."

Aline cringed inside as she thought of what it would do to James to have her birth revealed in front of the Court. He would be humiliated before his peers; for a proud man like James, it would be devastating. She could not let that happen!

But how was she to stop it?

"I understand." Aline wrenched herself out of his grasp. "We will come." She turned and strode past him out of the chapel. Gemma jumped up and hurried after her.

"Oh, milady! Wait!"

Aline stopped at the sound of Fingal's voice and whirled around to face him.

"You forgot something." He caught up with her and handed her a small religious medal. Aline recognized it immediately. It belonged to her mother; Bera wore it always, saying that it protected her.

"What are you doing with this?" Cold tendrils of fear wrapped around Aline's heart.

"Why, your mother gave it to me," the man responded. "She wanted me to give it to you, to keep you safe." Aline stared up at him. "Of course, she does not need it now, since she is under His Grace's protection."

"And no doubt that is safer than God's," Aline replied sarcastically.

"Don't be foolish."

"I am not. I understand perfectly well what you mean." Aline's hand closed around the small medal. He had only wanted to remind her of the Duke's power over her parents. "Is she well? Are they all right?"

"Of course. They are welcome guests of the Duke. No harm will come to them as long as he is a friend to them."

"I know." Aline turned and walked away from him, her steps growing faster and faster, her head down, lost in thought.

"Milady!" Gemma called, catching up with her. "Slow down! And don't scowl so. You hardly look like someone who has been in prayer for the past few minutes."

"Perhaps the friar has been lecturing me on my sins," Aline retorted, but she sighed and slowed her steps, assuming a more pleasant expression. "Oh, Gemma, what am I to do? This is all such a coil. I cannot betray James. But how can I stop it?"

"You cannot. Once you set out on something like this, you cannot stop it."

Aline came to a halt and looked down at her friend. "But I cannot bear for James to be hurt. He will be shamed before everyone."

"Then would you forsake your parents?" Gemma returned.

"No!" Aline recoiled from the idea. "Of course I cannot. If only there were some way to keep them safe . . ."

"How would you do that?"

She could not, of course. She had not even been able to protect them from Gyrth without the Duke's help. Gyrth no longer seemed such a terrible danger, compared with Tanford and what he could do.

"Oh, why did I agree to this?" Tears sparkled in Aline's eyes. "Why didn't I leave everything as it was? I should never have meddled."

"Lords are always dangerous," Gemma agreed. "'Tis best not to get caught up in their battles, for 'tis ones like us who get hurt, not them."

"Not always," Aline murmured. James would be hurt. "I must do something. Perhaps if I simply keep James away from London this summer . . ."

"What about what the Duke will do to Harald and Bera?"

"Surely he will not hurt them unless I do something to openly defy him. If I just delay and pretend that I cannot get James to budge, then it is not my fault. The Duke would just continue to threaten me with my parents, wouldn't he? He would not go ahead and hurt them, for then his threat would be gone."

"He could hurt them without killing them," Gemma pointed out grimly. "Or kill only one."

"I know. But if I can convince him that I did not do it willfully, that James is obstinate or suspicious or something, then he would let them be. Don't you think?"

"I don't know." Gemma shook her head. "All I know is, I'm glad it is you and not I who's disguising herself as a lady."

"Oh, Gemma, I have regretted doing it more times than I can count. And yet, I cannot but be glad that I

did, too, for otherwise, I would never have known
James."

"This seems to me too great a price for meeting a
handsome lord."

"Nay." A soft smile curved Aline's lips, and her
eyes turned dreamy. "I do not think there is too great
a price for finding James."

"Fah!" Gemma waved her hand in disgust. "You
are past help or hope."

"Yes. I suppose I am. And the worst of it is, I can't
regret that, either."

Aline raised her head from her needlework. Was
that the blast of a distant horn she heard? She sat
poised, listening, her hands still in her lap. Again the
faint, tinny sound came. With a cry, she stood up and
dumped her embroidery on the stool on which she
had been sitting. She darted out of the room and up
the stairs to the tower, lifting her skirts indecorously
to take the steps at a run. She burst into the small,
round tower, the highest lookout in the keep, and
scanned the forest, her hand up to shield her eyes.

There they were! Even from this distance, she knew
James's black hair and the black horse upon which he
rode. She turned and dashed back down the stairs to
her bedchamber, calling for Gemma. She hadn't the
time to bathe, dress, and do her hair as she had the
other time James had returned, but she hastily took off
her tunic and pulled on a more attractive one over her
bliaut, then adjusted her coif. She flew down the stairs
and through the great hall, then out onto the steps just
as James rode up, followed by Sir Guy and their dogs
and huntsmen.

She paused at the top of the stairs for a moment,

but when James swung off his horse and started up the stairs toward her, taking them two at a time, she could not contain herself. She ran down the stairs that separated them and threw herself into his arms. He picked her up and squeezed her to him, nuzzling into her coif and muttering an oath as the hard metal circlet atop it bit into his cheek.

Then, much to Aline's surprise, instead of setting her back down, James swept her into his arms and continued up the stairs and into the keep. Aline laughed and threw her arms around his neck.

"Sir! You are behaving quite scandalously," she teased, stroking his thick, dark hair with loving fingers.

He flashed her a searing glance and growled, "My behavior would have been more scandalous still had we stayed where we were." He started up the stairs to the upper floor.

Aline giggled and buried her head in his shoulder to hide her blush. "I ordered a bath prepared for you."

"Good. You will doubtless appreciate it even more than I."

The scent of horse and sweat clung to him, and dirt stained his face and clothes. Aline smiled. "I don't mind."

"I knew you were a woman in ten thousand."

"Only ten thousand?" she jested.

"In as high as a man could count."

James strode into the bedchamber, carrying his burden, and the servants filling the tub turned and gaped at them. James jerked his head toward the door.

"Out."

They immediately began to curtsy and bow and scurry around James out of the room. James set Aline down and unbuckled his belt. She watched him, her breath coming fast in her throat, as he laid his belt and sword across the X-shaped chair. Then he came toward her purposefully, ripping his tunic up and over his head. He stopped before her and pulled her into his arms, taking her mouth in a devouring kiss. His hands came up and ripped the coif from her head and flung it away. He sank his fingers into her thick hair, kissing her hungrily, as if he could never get enough of her. As they kissed, James walked her backward until they slammed up against the wall. He braced his forearms on the wall above Aline's head, kissing her over and over, until Aline was so weak in the knees she could hardly stand. James made a noise deep in his throat.

"I cannot wait," he mumbled, reaching down with both his hands to her hips and digging his fingers into her tunic. He began to draw up her tunic and bliaut together, gathering them in his hands until they were at her hips, then her waist, exposing her legs, naked except for her stockings.

Aline drew in a sharp breath. She was aching and hot, wanting him with an urgency that matched his own. She hooked her hands in his braies and tugged downward, and his manhood sprang forth, hard and pulsing, eager. James's eyes were like blue fire as he gazed deeply into hers. He lifted her by the hips and guided her onto his swollen staff, sinking deep inside her.

Aline moaned. She was impaled upon him, filled with him, and nothing had ever felt as good. She wrapped her legs tightly around his back and dug her hands into his shoulders. He braced her against the wall and began to thrust within her. He was dirty and sweaty, but she didn't mind. Somehow that was part of the moment, of the driving urgency that seized them, and Aline would not have had it any other way. He pumped into her, shaking her with every thrust, as though he could drive himself ever deeper inside her, pierce her very soul and heart. Aline clung to him, her fingers digging into his flesh, her desire spiraling upward until she felt as if she would die if she didn't reach that pinnacle.

Then suddenly she was there, and the world was flying apart all around her. She shrieked, scratching at James's bare back, and a hoarse cry rose from deep within him, bursting from him as his seed shot into her womb.

For a moment they stood there, leaning against the wall, Aline still wrapped around him. Then James stepped back, setting Aline down on the floor. He looked at her, concerned.

"Are you all right? Did I hurt you?"

"Nay." Aline smiled, blushing a little at her own wild reaction.

"I'm sorry. I couldn't wait. I—" He gestured toward her clothes. "I got you dirty."

"They will clean. I didn't care."

He pulled her to him and kissed her again. "I love you," he said.

"I have never trusted a woman—or man, for that matter—outside of my own family. And now, here I have given my heart to the niece of my enemy. Am I a fool, do you think?"

Aline drew a shaky breath. "You are no fool. But I—do you mean it? Have you truly given your heart?" She looked up searchingly into his face.

James gazed into her eyes. "Aye. I fear I have. While I was gone, I thought a lot. And I knew. No matter how much I did not wish it, I fell in love with you. I never thought to do so. No woman had ever possessed the wiles to bewitch me, and I believed I would forever remain heart-whole. But you—you hold my heart, my life, in the palm of your hand now."

Aline shivered inside, knowing how little she deserved James's trust. *What would happen to her if he ever found out the truth?*

"And I love you," Aline whispered. "With all my heart and soul and body, I am yours." She prayed he would remember her words and believe her, even when the awful moment of truth finally arrived.

19

When they awoke hours later, they talked of their brief time apart, agreeing that it had felt like ages. Then, idly stroking Aline's hair, James informed her, "Stephen is going back to Beaufort to Beaufort Place soon. He wants us to visit him, and I thought we might. My mother is there, you know, and I wanted you to meet her."

He seemed strangely hesitant, so Aline streched up and gave him a quick peck on the mouth. "Yes. I would like to. It seems strange that I have not met her yet. Why, we have been almost four months married."

"Aye, but, well, I wanted us to be alone when we left Norcastle. Gwendolyn had duties at Beaufort Place, and it was far for her to travel in the winter. She is no Marguerite, you see, to dare the weather to do its worst to her."

"A sensible woman."

Aline sensed him relax, and he smiled, bending down to kiss the top of her head.

"Then, in a few weeks," he went on, "we will set out for London."

Aline stiffened and suddenly turned cold as ice. *London!*

Her first impulse was to cry out "No!" but she stifled it. Such a reaction, she knew, would certainly make James suspicious.

Instead she schooled her face and voice into calm indifference and said only, "London? Why do we go there?"

"Why?" He turned to look at her, his face faintly puzzled. "To go to Court, of course." He paused. "I had thought you would be more excited."

"I don't know. I have no desire to go to Court. I like the country, you see."

"Have you ever been to London?"

"No." She hoped Lady Clarissa had not. It was not a subject they had mentioned, but the Duke had said that James had never seen her because she had lived all her life on her father's properties. It seemed likely that she had never made the long trip to London.

"Ah, then that explains it. Once you have been there, you will understand why one goes to London."

"My cousin, Lady Agnes, always told me it was a dirty, smelly place full of beggars and thieves."

James chuckled. "Aye, it is that. It is also full of all manner of tradesmen and merchants, with wares from all over the world. There are goldsmiths and silversmiths, who would doubtless love to adorn your lovely ears and throat."

He stroked his fingers down Aline's cheek and throat. "You would like that, wouldn't you?" He traced the whorls of her ear with his forefinger.

Aline smiled. "What woman would not? But, indeed, you have already given me the most beautiful necklace and earrings, and I am well content with them."

"Prettily said, my love, but since you may have them and new ones, too, why not?" He paused, gazing intently at her. "Do you not wish to go there?"

Aline was filled with hope. "No. In truth I do not."

"But why?"

"I told you. I love the country. And I am well content here. I have been to York and it did not appeal to me."

"But York is not London. London is a big, perpetual fair. Do not tell me you do not crave a little excitement. There is too much spice in your blood for you to be ever content here." His brows drew together. "There must be another reason."

Now she had aroused his suspicion, Aline thought despairingly. She cast about for some reasonable excuse. "Well, you will think me silly."

"I will not laugh, I promise." He drew his finger over her lips. "Only tell me. I wish to know what is in your head."

"I do not wish to meet the king. He sounds frightening to me. And my father would never let me go there. He said that King Henry was too fond of women."

James grinned. "He is that. And one as beautiful as you would catch his eye. However, he would not try to seduce my wife. He would not offend the Norwens. We have ever been among his most loyal supporters. He is too canny for that. Besides, I promise that I would not let you out of my sight. So rest your mind."

"That is not all." Aline hesitated, then was struck by inspiration. "I do not wish to see my uncle."

"Ah. Now that is quite understandable."

"Do not jest. 'Tis true. He will question me about you and try to worm things out of me."

"What things?"

"I know not. Whatever he wants to know. When you told me what he had done to your family, I did not want to admit it, but deep inside I knew it was true. I have seen other things he has done, heard things he told my father. He *is* a wicked man. And if I go to London, he will try to entice me to spy on you or to join him in some treachery. And when I refuse, he will chastise me and remind me of all I owe my family. He will missay you to me, and if I defend you, he will accuse me of being a traitor to my family. He will turn them all against me—my parents, my cousin, everyone. I do not think I can bear it."

James pulled her close to him, wrapping his arms tightly around her. "My love, I am so sorry. Of course you would fear that. I had not thought. But you must not worry about your uncle. Let me do that. I have had much experience with it." He sat up, pulling her up with him, and looked intently into her eyes. "You need not fear Tanford. I will be with you every moment. I will not allow him near you to threaten or plead with you."

Aline shook her head. "He will find a way. I know it."

"Do you not trust me?"

"Of course I trust you."

Aline felt as if her heart were breaking. It was easy to trust James; what was hard was knowing that James should not trust *her.* She felt wicked and guilty, telling James lie after lie. She hated herself for doing it. She knew that she ought to confess right now. Yet she could not force the words past her lips. If she told James who she really was and the part she had played in the Duke's machinations, James would despise her. He would put her away from him; she would never again know his love, his touch, his smile. And for her revealing his plans, the Duke would kill her parents.

"Then let me take care of the matter."

"Why couldn't we simply stay away from London?" Aline cried, near tears.

"Because I must be at Court, at least for a while. Tanford will try to turn Henry against me. I must be there to plead my side of whatever story he tells the king, to show Henry that I am still his loyal subject, his good friend. And I want to present you to the king, to prove that we are well and happily wed, for God only knows what lies Tanford may tell him."

Aline gazed at him in despair. If only he knew how Tanford planned to turn that presentation against him! She could well imagine the Duke waiting slyly for James to present his wife to the king, then revealing to Henry and his court that James's wife was not Tanford's niece, but a mere dancer. The idea made Aline shudder. *It would be horrible!* She could not let that happen to James.

James pulled her into his arms again, stroking her hair and back soothingly. "Come, let us talk no more of this."

Aline cuddled close to him, loving the feel of his arms tight around her, his murmured, loving reassurances. Somehow she must keep him from going to London, and if she could not . . . then she would have to tell James the truth, no matter what the consequences.

James and Aline left Chaswyck Keep two weeks later, in early April. The roads were still muddy, and their heavy carts got stuck and had to be pulled free. But the trip to Beaufort Place was not a long one, as the Beaufort lands bordered Norwen's to the west, and Chaswyck lay on the southern side of the Earl's property.

It was obvious that James was well known on

Beaufort property, for the serfs in the villages and fields greeted him with eagerness and respect, and when James and Aline neared the gates of Beaufort Place, the guards called a greeting and waved their party through.

Beaufort Place was a lovely, graceful building of whitewashed stone, smaller and more elegant than Norcastle. James would have told her with a snort that it was not half the keep Norcastle was, for it was far less defensible, but Aline saw only that it was beautiful.

Stephen came bounding out and down the steps toward them, his face alight with boyish enthusiasm. "James! Clarissa! Gwendolyn and I have been watching for you by the minute." He helped Aline down from her mount and kissed her soundly on the cheek, then turned to James.

"Good lord, boy," James exclaimed. "I think you've grown another inch since I saw you last. You're nigh as tall as I am now."

"'Tis not true," Stephen retorted with good humor, pride tinging his face. "You simply did not notice it when we were hunting. Your mind was on . . . ah . . . other things."

A woman came out of the castle at a slower pace than Stephen had, though she, too, hurried. She was an older woman, but startlingly beautiful. There were lines in her face, and the skin had begun to sag, but it was still lovely, soft and translucent. Her eyes were large under well-shaped brows and rimmed by thick lashes, very much like James's eyes, except that this lady's were green in hue. When she smiled, as she did now, her whole face seemed to glow, and it was easy to understand why James's father had been so entranced with her years before.

"James!" she cried, and he went to her, then bent down to give her a hug. "It has been ages, and I have been eager to meet your bride. Why did you not come sooner?" She looked up at him and gave him a roguish smile. "As if I didn't know."

To Aline's amazement, James looked embarrassed. He glanced uneasily toward Aline, and suddenly Aline knew: he was afraid that she would snub his mother. It came clear to her now why Gwendolyn had been unable to leave Beaufort Place to visit them at Norcastle, as Marguerite had, and why they had wintered at Chaswyck Keep instead of coming here to meet his mother. Aline had wondered about these things and had begun to think that perhaps James did not like his mother or was ashamed of her. But it was obvious from the way he greeted Gwendolyn that that was not true. He was worried that Clarissa, in her pride, would be unkind to his mother, who had been nothing more than a leman to a nobleman.

Well, Clarissa might have been unkind, Aline conceded, but *she* was not about to be. She moved forward quickly, holding out her hands to her mother-in-law. "I am sorry. I am the one you must fault," she said, smiling. "We had not realized when we went there that Chaswyck Keep had fallen into such disrepair. We had thought to come here earlier, but I could not leave the place in such an awful state."

She could see James relax, and he smiled, saying, "Mother, this is my bride, the Lady Clarissa. Clarissa, this is my mother, Gwendolyn."

Gwendolyn took Aline's outstretched hands in hers and squeezed them, smiling into Aline's eyes. "My dear, it is wonderful to meet you."

"Thank you. I apologize for it taking such a long time for us to come together."

"Nonsense. I understand perfectly."

"Yes," James put in, "and of course, you are right, Mother. Do not let Clarissa fool you. 'Twas not her fault we are so tardy in paying our respects. 'Twas as you thought. I wanted to keep my bride all to myself."

"And no wonder," Gwendolyn said, smiling. "She is such a lovely creature." She turned back to Aline. "Now, come inside. I will take you up to your room, my dear, and we shall have a good chat while we leave Stephen and James to talk about all those dull men things."

She led Aline through the great hall and up the stairs to a bedchamber. It was a bright room, with more windows than any room at either Norcastle or Chaswyck, and furnished luxuriously. Aline drew in a sharp breath of admiration.

"'Tis beautiful!" she said breathlessly, going over to touch a rich tapestry that hung on the wall.

"Yes. James has always liked lovely things. You see this bed covering? He brought it back with him from the Crusades." Gwendolyn went to a chest, and slid her hand over the chased brass casket on which it sat. "He brought back this, too, but I will let James show you what lies inside. No doubt he is eager to."

Aline's curiosity was piqued, but she said nothing, for Gwendolyn continued to talk. "But I will give you this, for it is solely mine to give." She came over to Aline, sliding a large ring off her finger. It was gold and set with a winking ruby, a rich and heavy thing. Gwendolyn held it out to Aline. "Here," she said, smiling, when Aline did not reach for it. "Take it. It is yours. I am giving it to you."

"To me?" Amazed, Aline picked up the ring and turned it over in her hands. "It is lovely. But—"

"Nay." Gwendolyn held up her hand. "Do not deny me this. 'Twas a present to me from James's father.

'Tis fitting that you should have it. I know James had no jewelry with him to give you when you wed."

"He gave me this." Aline lovingly stroked her hand along the gold links of her belt. "And a beautiful necklace and earrings."

"But you should have this as well," Gwendolyn insisted. I am sorry that I could not give you a ring from our betrothal. It is not, perhaps, what a lady like you might expect."

"Oh, no, do not be sorry," Aline said quickly. "I could not ask for anything lovelier. I would be proud to wear it."

"It is a ring of love, and that is what I wish for you. That my son and you are bound together in the kind of love that his father and I knew. The church tells me we were in sin. But I think, how could it have been a sin, when what we felt was so beautiful, so right? That is what should happen between a man and a woman. I think perhaps it is happening with you and James?"

"Yes. I think so." Aline smiled at the woman, but tears glittered in Aline's eyes as Gwendolyn slid the ring onto her finger. Guilt weighed her down at the thought of accepting this woman's gift from the heart. If Gwendolyn realized how she would hurt her son, Aline knew, she would surely scorn her.

"That is good." Tears stood in Gwendolyn's eyes, too. She lifted Aline's hand in hers to look at the ring. "So many times, I have seen the bitterness in James, and I have had to live with the knowledge that it was my fault. That if I had not done what I did, he would not have to live with the shame of his birth."

"You cannot wish that!" Aline exclaimed. "For then James would not have existed—and I, for one, would not wish that."

Gwendolyn smiled. "That is true. You are kind to remind me. I think that James has chosen well. I had my doubts, but now that I see you, talk to you, I realize, you are the wife for him."

Impulsively, Aline reached out and hugged the older woman. "Thank you," she whispered. "I pray that you are right."

That evening, after eating, James and Aline retired to their bedchamber. Gemma helped Aline out of her clothes and into her sleeping gown, then unbraided her hair and brushed it out so that it lay like a fiery cape around her shoulders.

After Gemma left, James, who likewise had undressed in the anteroom with the aid of his squire, wrapped his bedrobe around himself and led Aline over to the heavily embossed and engraved casket. "I have something to give you," he said, arousing Aline's curiosity about the casket even more. He took out a small key and fitted it into the lock.

He turned it and pushed back the lid. Inside lay jewelry, piled high: glittering gems and sinuous gold and silver chains and chunky bracelets set with stones. Aline stared, amazed.

"James! It is lovely!" She stretched a hand out toward the glittering pile, but did not quite dare to touch it. "Did you bring all this back with you from the Crusades, also?"

"I see my mother has been talking," he commented with a wry smile. "Yes, a good deal of it I brought back from the East. The rest of it I have gotten since."

Aline gazed, fascinated, at the gems, linking her hands together in front of her. "But which is it that you wanted to give me?"

James chuckled. "All of them, you goose. You are my wife. Who else should I give them to?"

"Oh." Aline sucked in a breath and looked up at him in wonder. "Really?"

"Of course, really. Here." He took a ring and slid it onto her finger, then another. He picked through the jewels and found chased earrings with dangling fingers of silver, each ending in a little black stone, and he fastened them to her ears.

"And this will match your hair." He took a chain that had a ruby in its center and slipped it around her neck. "Except that even its fire cannot match that of your hair."

James's mouth softened sensually, and his hand slid down under her nightgown to caress her smooth shoulder. With a lazy smile, he pushed the gown off her shoulders and watched it drift over her body to pool on the floor. The pendant hung cool against her naked flesh, nestled between her breasts.

Heat flamed in James's eyes as he looked at her, and he fitted a circlet of chains that dangled with coins onto her head with hands that trembled. He led her to the bed, and she lay down upon it. He carried the casket over and settled beside her on the bed with it.

Slowly, stopping now and again to kiss and caress her, James adorned her naked body with the jewelry. He dropped a single, unattached emerald into her shallow navel and bent to lay a kiss upon the quivering flesh beside it. He draped her breasts with gold and silver chains, and her rosy nipples peeked up saucily through them. He paused to gently kiss the sweet buds, then went on, strewing jewels and gold down the length of her body.

He lay looking at her for a long moment, then said huskily, "You are more beautiful than any of them."

Almost roughly, he swept the jewels aside and pulled her into his arms and made heated, almost frantic love to her, until both of them peaked in a wild tumult of pleasure.

They stayed a month at Beaufort Place. Aline shoved aside the thought of going to London and gave herself up to the joy of the moment. The nights with James were glorious, and during the days Stephen and Gwendolyn were good companions. Stephen was witty and full of enthusiasms, and Aline looked upon him as a younger brother. She liked James's mother more and more with each day that passed. She found that she felt more at ease with her than she had with Marguerite or Elizabeth, no matter how kind and likeable they had been. Gwendolyn, like herself, had only minimal interest in sewing and housekeeping, and she and Aline spent much of their days in thoroughly unnecessary things such as singing or playing the lute or retelling their favorite stories of heroic struggles and loves.

Sometimes Aline sneaked away with Gemma and Malcolm. She had discovered not long after they'd reached Beaufort Place that Gemma had been teaching the boy Aline rescued how to turn flips and cartwheels. Aline had at first been scandalized, afraid that James would find out, but as she'd watched them tumble, she had realized how much she'd missed the fun of it herself. Soon she was joining them.

Malcolm was a quick student, and he picked up whatever they showed him. Their lessons became almost daily events, and Aline regretted the times when she was unable to slip away to the copse of trees above the castle and work with Malcolm and Gemma.

As the days passed, Aline noticed that her monthly

flow was late, and elation seized her as she realized that she might be carrying James's child. She hugged the knowledge happily to herself, wanting to make sure that it was true before she spoke of it to James. She daydreamed about the baby, imagining how it would look and how sweet it would be. It was some days before she realized that this pregnancy might be the very thing to save her. If she told James that she was pregnant and did not want to travel, perhaps he would not ask her to go to London. He would not want to endanger his heir or her, and she suspected that if she had to remain at Beaufort Place until the babe's arrival, James would not go off without her to London, especially if she worked a little at persuading him to stay.

That happiness lasted until one day late in April. As she and Gwendolyn were walking into the great hall to partake of the evening meal, James's mother Gwendolyn chatted merrily. "Isn't it wonderful? We will have entertainment tonight whilst we eat. A troupe of jongleurs came this afternoon. They're terribly good. I watched them out of my window while they were practicing in the courtyard. There is one who throws knives at this poor girl, and you would not believe how close the knife comes to hitting her, and yet never touches a hair on her head."

Aline went freezing cold inside. She turned her head and tried to look inconspicuously down the long hall. A group of people stood beside the large hearth, dressed in the colorful garb of jongleurs. There was a dwarf, whom she recognized instantly as their own Beorn, and another woman and man, as well as the slim, pretty Signy. And there, standing with his broad back to her, was the knife-thrower, Gyrth.

Aline whipped back around. She felt suddenly sick, and she stumbled. Gwendolyn reached out a hand to steady her, and her brows drew together in concern. "What is it, dear? You look so pale."

"'Tis nothing." Aline tried to smile. "I—just felt a trifle odd. It will pass, I am sure."

What was she to do? She went icy with terror. Gyrth would be certain to look at the main table, where the coins would come from, and he would see her. She looked different, no doubt, in her elegant clothes and her white linen coif and golden circlet, but not that different. He would recognize her before his act was over.

There was only one thing to do, she realized. She grabbed at the edge of the table and leaned against it. It didn't take much acting to pretend that she was ill. Her stomach was churning, and the fright had chased the blood from her face.

"Clarissa?" James was there at her side, and she leaned gratefully into him, hiding her face in his chest. "What is amiss? Mother? What happened?"

"I know not. Suddenly she turned pale and weak." Gwendolyn looked worried, and Aline felt guilty for frightening them.

"I am fine, only a little ill, I fear. My stomach . . ." She pressed her palm flat against her belly for emphasis.

"I will take you back to your room." James glanced toward his mother as he lifted Aline easily into his arms. "Send for Gemma."

James carried her across the hall and up the stairs, Aline keeping her face turned into James's chest so that none of the performers could get a glimpse of her face. He took her into their room and laid her tenderly on the bed.

"What happened to make you ill?" he asked, frowning with concern as he smoothed his hand over her forehead.

"I know not. No doubt it will pass." Now, she realized, was the perfect time to tell him that she might be pregnant. It would be a perfect excuse for feeling ill and staying in bed until the troupe left. James had been talking about leaving for London soon, and now he would decide that it was a bad idea because of her pregnancy.

But somehow the words would not pass her lips. She merely lay and looked at him, giving him a reassuring smile.

Gemma came into the room, and she and Aline convinced James to return to the hall below. As soon as he had left, Gemma sat down on the bed beside her and said, "You saw them, then."

"Yes. Why didn't you warn me? I walked into the hall and nearly fainted right there."

"I didn't notice them until a few minutes ago. I've been out with the boy almost the whole afternoon. When I came in, I nearly ran right into them. Thank heaven I saw them before they saw me. I ducked behind a water barrel, but by the time I could get away without being seen and sneak around the keep and come up here, you had already gone down to supper." Gemma drew a deep breath and fanned her face. "Mary save us. I thought for a moment we were ruined."

"I did too."

"Well, I better fetch some herbs, to make it look as if you are really sick."

She went off to the solar to find Aline's basket of herbs and potions, and Aline lay alone, thinking. She could keep Gyrth and the others from seeing her. They would not stay more than a day or two, and Aline would have to do no more than pretend to be sick and miss a few meals. Gemma would be an able conspirator.

But that would suffice only for this one time. She

had involved herself in an enormous lie to her husband, and someday, somehow, he would find out. Some other performer would recognize her, or the Duke or one of his men would spread the tale around. Eventually, she would be exposed. And the longer she lived the lie, the worse it would be, both for herself and for James. She could no longer delay and pretend, no longer put the matter out of her head.

She had to tell James the truth.

It made her feel sick to think of what that would mean for her parents. Tanford would hurt them, maybe even kill them. She could not let that happen! Perhaps she could get her parents out of Tanford's house if she went to London with James. Then she could tell James the truth without risking their lives. She decided that she had to at least try. If she could not rescue them, she would have to tell James the truth and pray that Tanford would not carry out his wicked threats against her beloved parents.

She could not tell James she was pregnant, she realized now. He would refuse to go to London if she told him, and she would have no chance to rescue her parents. So she would have to pretend to get well, and then go with him to London. And there she would tell James the truth.

20

Aline tried to seem excited about witnessing the sights and sounds of London, since it was supposedly her first time there, but she could not. Her head was pounding, and her stomach was queasy, and it was stifling inside the curtained litter. James, worried by the illness she'd feigned while hiding from Gyrth, had suggested that she be carried in comfort to London, rather than riding. Aline knew that it was a great concession on his part, since he heartily disliked moving so slowly. She would have preferred to ride, but she had agreed to go in the conveyance, primarily because she was becoming more and more convinced that she was pregnant and she feared that riding would hurt the baby.

It had been a miserable trip.

Having the pillows to cushion her was nice, as was being able to stretch out and change positions. But the constant swaying of the conveyance made her stomach queasy, and it seemed to trap and keep the heat inside its curtains, which she had to close to keep out the road dust kicked up by the horses. Worst of all, it was boring. She could not chat with James as they rode along together. She could not even look at him because of the closed curtains. Sometimes he would drop back to inquire how she was doing, but it was not the same as being together.

When they reached the outskirts of London, she peeked out, but the noise and smells quickly drove her back inside. It was a vast relief to reach the Norwen town house and climb out of the litter. James was there to help her down and take her arm to lead her inside. It was a lovely place, not as large or grand as Tanford's London house, but elegant and well appointed. Best of all, it was already staffed and in excellent order. She smiled at the servants who lined up to greet them, then gratefully let one of them lead her up to her bedchamber. She lay down for a nap, but not before she sent Gemma off with instructions to try to get inside the Tanford house and find out what she could about her parents.

Gemma came up before supper and helped her dress. Her cheeks were flushed, and Aline suspected that she had just barely returned. Gemma glanced around carefully before she began to speak.

"It's all right," Aline told her. "We are alone."

"I found them," Gemma said, keeping her voice low despite Aline's reassurance.

Aline's heart began to pound. "Are they well?"

Gemma nodded. "Yes, but they are worried and confused—and scared for you."

"Scared for me? But they are the ones who are in danger."

"If you cross the Duke, you will be, too. Or if your husband finds out about what you've been doing."

Aline drew a breath. "He will. I have to tell him."

"What? No! You cannot! He will kill you."

"That is a chance I will have to take. I do not think he will harm me. He has always been gentle with me, even when I was at my worst, and Lady Elizabeth told me that the Norwens are reluctant to hurt a woman."

"Finding out how you've deceived him will drive away all reluctance," Gemma commented dryly.

Aline shook her head. "No. I have to do it. You cannot talk me out of it. I will do my best to protect you, and if I cannot, you will have to run away. He will not bother to chase you down."

"'Tis *you* I am worried about."

"Do not be. Let us not talk of this. I want to hear about my parents. What did you learn about them?"

"They're free enough inside the house, at least during the day. But the last few weeks, since they came back to town from Tanford Hall, they have been locked in their room at night. During the day, the guard at the door of the house will not let them out. They tried once when they first returned to London, saying they needed to buy strings for your father's lute, but he would not let them pass. They have not been ill-treated. But I don't know how we are to get them out."

"We will have to try. Do you think if we bribed a guard? I have the jewels James gave me."

"I know not. We can try, but if we fail, then Tanford will hear of it, and he will have them more closely watched."

"'Tis true. We must think."

But though she thought through supper and the evening, still she could come up with nothing. She knew that she had to think of a plan soon. Her time was running short.

*   *   *

That night, Aline slid across the bed to James and began to caress him. He looked surprised.

"I thought you might still be tired from the journey," he told her, kissing her tenderly. "Are you sure you feel well?"

"Yes. I'm certain." Aline gazed into his eyes, knowing that this was probably the last time that she would see him look at her with love—or, indeed, with anything but contempt.

She leaned forward and kissed him, and they melted together in their usual hot passion. Aline made love fiercely, sweetly, reveling in each pleasure. She kissed and caressed his body as though trying to memorize it for the long nights that lay ahead of her. In the middle of the night, she awoke, and they made love again. When at last that boundless pleasure rocked them both, she began to cry. James held her and kissed her, worriedly asking her why she cried, but she could not tell him, only clung to him until finally she drifted off to sleep.

James was puzzled by her reaction, but then, Clarissa had been acting oddly lately. She had seemed full of fits and starts, ready to flare up into anger or burst into tears. And she had been sickly all through the journey to London, as well as those two days in Beaufort Place.

It occurred to him that she might be breeding. For an instant, the thought pleased him, but then cold fear slammed into his gut. He wanted heirs; that was one reason why he'd married. But he had not expected to fall in love with his wife. Now he felt true at the thought of putting his beloved Clarissa through that ordeal.

His arms tightened around her convulsively, and he held her to him through the rest of the night.

*   *   *

Aline had hoped to have some time to get her parents away from Tanford's clutches, but she awoke to find Gemma laying out her most elegant clothes, and when she questioned her, Gemma replied colorlessly, "The master said for me to lay them out. You're going to Court today."

"What!" Aline sat up, all the blood draining out of her face. She had not expected them to go so soon, had thought she'd have a day or so to plan out what she would say and to steel herself for the ordeal.

She got out of bed. Her legs trembled, and she felt cold all over. She had to tell James now. She could wait no longer.

"Where is he?"

"Downstairs."

"You must go and ask him to come here. No, wait. Help me dress first. I would look my best to face him."

She washed and dressed, putting on the golden tunic that made her eyes blaze with color. Then she sat and let Gemma do her hair in the same long, loose braid she had worn when James had returned from wiping out the reivers in Norwood Forest. The first time they had made love. She was not sure whether the memory would allay some of his anger or infuriate him. But she had to look good for her pride's sake. She could not face him looking as wretched as she felt.

Then she sat down on a backless chair by the window, waiting. She kept thinking, not of what she would say, but of how James had looked one time or the way he had smiled at her another.

When he came into the room, she bounced to her feet. Her heart was in her throat; her pulse was racing. James smiled at her, and she thought her heart would break.

"You are stunning. But don't you think you had best put on your coif? Henry is fond of me, but I'd rather not tempt him beyond a man's power to resist."

"I have to tell you something." Aline spoke through bloodless lips, taking a step closer to him. She was afraid she might faint.

"Now? But we should leave."

"You must hear me first."

"All right." James assumed a posture of indulgent listening, crossing his arms across his chest and resting his weight on one leg, his expression open and waiting.

Aline drew in a breath. She could not speak.

"Well? Clarissa, love, what is amiss?" James straightened and started toward her.

"No!" The word was ripped from her. Aline knew she could not bear it if he touched her, if he stood close, those intense eyes boring into her. She dropped to her knees, her head lowered, in an attitude of submission. She hoped it would soften him toward her, but she also could no longer stand up.

"Clarissa!" He hesitated, confused. "What are you doing? Stand up. What is wrong?"

"I seek your clemency."

"My clemency?" he repeated, dumbfounded, and a faint coldness began to grow around his heart. "What are you talking about? You make no sense."

"I have deceived you."

There was a long pause. James asked in a colorless voice, "In what way have you deceived me?"

His tone was like a knife in her heart. Love had fled, and in its place was that cold, waiting quality that had been there always when she first met him.

"I am not the Lady Clarissa."

There was a stunned silence. Finally Aline looked up and met his gaze. James was staring at her as if she had suddenly sprouted two heads.

She wet her lips and went on, "It was a trick played on you by Tanford. I am not his niece. He picked me out because I had red hair, and he knew that you would identify me by the Tanford hair."

"Have you gone mad?" James growled. "Do you expect me to believe such a story?"

"You must, or else the Duke will shame you in front of the king and Court today. He is waiting for you to come to Court, to present me as your wife. Then he will step forward with the real Lady Clarissa, and he will say, no doubt, that you are trying to pass a peasant girl off as a lady."

James's face was white with shock. He turned away as Aline began to silently cry. "Please, you must believe me."

"I believe that you are treacherous," he said coldly after a long silence. "But which of your lies am I to believe now?"

"I am telling you the truth. Do not go to Court."

"Why are you telling me this?"

"I cannot bear to see it happen to you." Aline looked at him with pleading eyes. "Please, James, believe me. I love you."

"Do not say those words to me!" he roared, spinning back around to face her, his blue eyes blazing like the center of a flame. "You wouldn't even know what love is."

"Forgive me. Please forgive me. I did not know when I began—I believed what he said about you and I—I thought you had acted cruelly to me once. I did not know you."

"I acted cruelly to you! I had never even met you!"

"You did. You just did not know it was I. My name is Aline, and I dance with a band of entertainers."

She looked at him, her golden eyes wide and gleaming with tears. Suddenly a memory snapped into place in his mind: wide golden eyes, made darker by the dim light, gleaming above an Eastern veil.

"God's blood! The Saracen dancing girl!"

Aline nodded. "My skin was darkened with oil, and you could not see my hair or much of my face."

"And I was drunk," he added flatly. "You are a hazy memory, at best. The main thing I recall is lust." His mouth twisted. "I should have known. You are still quite clever at arousing that."

He stalked away to the window and stood, staring out, his hand braced against the wall. Finally he said, "So you hated me, and you cooked up a plan with Tanford to deceive me." He turned to look at her, arms crossed, and his face was remote, his eyes like ice. "Then why are you telling me this now?"

"I cannot let you walk into Tanford's trap. I long ago realized how wrong I was about you—and about the Duke. Neither of you was the man I thought you to be. I found out what a wicked man he was, what he had done to your family and . . . and I fell in love with you."

James's lip curled. "Let us have no more deception. You don't love me. You are a whore hired to betray me, and now, for whatever reason, you have decided to betray your master instead."

"I am not a whore!" Aline flared, rising to her feet, infused with a saving anger.

He quirked an eyebrow. "What else would you call it? You take another woman's place in a man's bed."

"You know that I was a virgin when you took me. You are the only man who has touched me."

"That means only that you were clever enough to

save it for the highest price. An expensive whore, but still a whore."

"I did not agree to sleep with you for him! Tanford said he would get me away before the wedding night. He lied to me. I don't think he ever had any intention of taking me away. He wanted you to bed me, to make me truly your wife."

"If he did not do what you had bargained for, if he left you there exposed to my *lechery*, why did you continue with the play? If you discovered that he was an evil man, why did you not tell me the truth and expose him?"

"Tanford threatened me. He had my parents, and he said he would harm them if I didn't do what he said. And I was afraid of what you would do to me. I knew you would be furious at the deception, and I feared you would kill me. Or torture me, imprison me. I did not know."

"All those things that I might do to you now." He came closer, until he was standing right in front of her.

Aline struggled to hide the shiver that ran through her. "Yes."

"Can you give me any reason why I should not do any of those things?"

"No." Aline's voice was barely above a whisper. She could not look at James's cold eyes. He hated her, despised her, just as she had known he would. She felt bruised and broken, though he had not laid a hand upon her, and never had.

"Perhaps I should kill you," he went on conversationally. "It seems to me that it would be a pleasure right now to put my hands around that lovely white throat of yours and squeeze all the life out of you." He reached out and wrapped one hand around her throat, his thumb lying teasingly at the hollow, caressing, pressing.

Then he released her abruptly and stepped back. "I must think how best to thwart Tanford's plans. And what I should do with you." He started toward the door, then turned. "You will stay in your room. There will be a guard outside to make sure that you do so."

Aline's eyes filled with tears, but she struggled to hold them back. "But, James!"

He whirled, his eyes flashing. "Do not call me that. You have not the right."

"What should I call you?" Aline said. She had been wrong and wicked to do what she had done, but she refused to let any man, even him, trample on her. "Sir? Master? After I have shared your bed for weeks?"

"I care not. Just do not use a wife's familiarity, for you are no wife of mine."

Aline straightened, bringing her chin up. "I do not ask for mercy for myself. But I must ask it for my parents. They are innocent in all this. They have done nothing wrong, and Tanford will hurt them when he realizes that you know about me. Let me go. Let me try to save them. I promise that I will return."

James cast her a sardonic glance. "Really, woman, I am not that much a fool. You will stay here, as I have ordered." He paused. "Who are your parents? Where are they?"

"Their names are Harald and Bera. My father is a jongleur, and they have been staying with Tanford, entertaining. But he will not let them leave the house, and at night he locks them into their rooms."

"How do you know this?"

"Gemma found out for me yesterday." Too late, Aline realized that she had admitted that Gemma knew her secret. She clenched her jaw, hating herself. She had not even managed to save her friend from his wrath.

"Ah, yes, Gemma. Of course. The dwarf. I remember now. There were two dwarves in that company."

"She has done nothing wrong. I swear it. She did not want me to do this. She came along only to keep me safe."

"And has been lying to me through her teeth for months, just like you. I should have realized that you were far too kind to her for her to have really been Clarissa's maid."

"Don't harm her, please. She meant no wrong. I beg of you. Leave your wrath on my head."

He promised nothing, only said, "I will see what I can do for your parents. In the meantime, you will stay in here, as I commanded you." He opened it, then half turned, not looking at her, and said, "Cover your hair. I do not wish to see it."

Then he was gone.

Aline spent the rest of the day in her room, thinking about what had happened and wondering what was going on outside her door. She did not see Gemma or anyone else, except the guard, who carried in her tray of food at noon and in the evening. Later, Everard, James's squire, came in, accompanied by the guard, and scurried around, picking up several of James's things. He did not look at her except in quick, furtive glances, and Aline made no move to speak to him. She had not expected James to return to their bed, but still it made her heart hurt to see the boy remove his possessions.

Finally, when the candles had burned low, and it seemed as if every tear had been drained from her body, Aline went to bed. Sleep did not come easily, but it did come at last. She passed the night in restless, disturbing dreams, and when she awoke the next morning she felt little more rested than she had when she retired.

One of the maidservants came in with her breakfast. She curtsied. "Mistress, the master says I am to help you dress this morning. He said you are going to Court today."

"What?" Aline sat up like a shot, staring at the girl. "Are you sure? What did he say?"

"Only that." The girl looked at her uncertainly. "I know nothing else."

Of course the girl would not, Aline thought. It occurred to her that James was playing a cat-and-mouse game with her, punishing her by keeping her wondering, and the thought stiffened her spine.

So Aline splashed cold water on her face, hoping it would help erase the mark of tears. Then she let the girl help her dress once more in the golden velvet dress and the necklace and earrings of topazes. She donned her coif, setting atop it the circlet of chains and coins that James had given her from his trip to the Holy Land. It gave her a faintly exotic look, adding to the peculiar beauty of her golden eyes. Something stirred in her as she looked at her image in the mirror which the girl held up for her. Let James see her this way, and then see if he could look at her with such ice in the depths of his eyes.

She swept from the room as regally as a queen, and Aline knew that no one, by just looking at her, would have guessed that her blood was any less than noble. She walked down the hall, then the stairs, with measured tread, unwilling to show any haste to James.

He waited for her at the bottom of the stairs, but she hardly glanced at him as she came down. Her eyes swept the room for signs of Gemma or, she wildly hoped, her parents, but there was no one there except

James and his men, waiting to escort her to the palace. James held out his arm formally, and she took it, neither of them looking at or speaking to the other.

It was an odd, silent trip to the White Tower. Aline glanced over at James once. He seemed a cold, hard stranger. She hardly knew him. She looked back ahead, her nerves tightening in her stomach, her mind mulling over what he had planned for her. But she would not unbend to ask him. His gaze was remote and calculating. Aline sensed that he was testing her in some way, but she had no idea how or what he hoped to prove.

They paused outside the palace, and James turned to her, saying in a low voice. "What is your name? Your real name."

"Aline." Aline blinked, surprised. Was he planning to expose her in front of the entire Court? To reveal what she and Tanford had done to him? She would not have guessed that he would do so, for it would also make a laughingstock of himself, but perhaps he had been able to come up with nothing better to thwart Tanford.

Tanford would live it down, of course. He was a duke, and no doubt all the other nobles already knew what a snake he was. They would shrug it off. She would be humiliated, the object of scorn and contempt from a hundred eyes. And none would even feel pity for her, a wench from the streets trying to pass herself off as one of her betters.

They passed through the halls of the castle and toward the audience chamber. The servants at the door recognized Sir James and bowed, opening the door for them. They entered a large room that seemed to Aline to be full of noise and people. Slowly they made their way through the crowd toward the front, where a short, redheaded man sat on a raised throne.

When the king saw them, a smile split his face. He motioned to them. "James! Come here! I've been wondering where you were."

James started forward, taking Aline with him. She saw Tanford's face among the crowd, slyly smiling. Aline's legs were trembling; she was afraid that they might give out at any moment. But she kept walking, holding her head high, until at last they reached the king.

James stopped and swept an elegant bow to Henry. Aline sank down into a deep curtsy. She would have liked to stay there, but the king himself reached down to pull her up. She looked into his twinkling blue eyes. He was little taller than herself and built rather like a barrel set on spindly legs. But there was a compelling energy and charm about him. She had heard that he wore down all the members of his court with his constant traveling and tireless energy.

"Well, James, what have we here?" he asked merrily, flashing a smile at Aline. "Who is this beautiful lady with you?"

James glanced at Aline, then smiled at his sovereign. "Why, this, my liege, is my wife."

21

There was the collectively indrawn breath of interest. Behind them Aline could almost feel Tanford tensing, triumph beginning to pour through him.

"Your wife?" King Henry smiled. "The Lady Clarissa? What a pleasure it is to meet you, my dear."

Aline drew breath, not knowing what she would say, knowing only that she had to stop this folly somehow.

Then James spoke, smiling, "No, Your Highness, not the Lady Clarissa. My bride's name is Aline."

Aline froze and shot him a quick glance.

"Indeed?" King Henry's eyebrows went up, and his eyes took on a new light of interest.

"Yes. I saw what folly I was committing, to ally myself with one I could not trust." James looked pointedly at Tanford, who was staring at them. "One should, after all, choose one's in-laws wisely."

Aline waited, breathless, for Tanford to move, to say something. But he did not. She saw how cleverly James had stifled the Duke. It would have been reasonable for Tanford to have recognized that James's wife was not his niece, but it would appear most odd if he were to know who Aline was and to reveal her background. He could not do so without implicating himself in the scheme to defraud James.

Aline smiled blindingly, filled with happiness at her realization, and the king blinked. He bent down conspiratorially to James and murmured, "And when one could have such beauty, 'twould be folly indeed to choose a woman related to Tanford."

James flashed a smooth grin. "Indeed, Your Majesty, you have the right of it."

King Henry took Aline's hand and raised it to his lips. "It is a pleasure to make your acquaintance, dear lady. My friend James is fortunate indeed to have a wife such as you."

"Thank you, sire," Aline said clearly. She wanted all the court as witnesses to her well-spoken voice. She knew that Tanford would soon enough spread rumors vilifying her background, and she wanted the people to remember that she had spoken like a lady, not a peasant. It would not hurt, either, that the king had favored her. "Indeed, I would say that my husband is fortunate to have a friend such as you."

Henry chuckled. "Well said, my child, well said." He cast a roguish glance at James. "Ah, James, you have chosen wisely—wit as well as beauty. I think she is suited to be a Norwen."

"Thank you, sire."

They backed away from the king, and Aline had to endure well-wishing by the other members of the Court. She turned after a moment and found herself face-to-face with the Duke of Tanford. She stiffened, her stomach knotting. *What would he do to her parents in retaliation?*

His eyes blazed furiously into hers. "A pleasure to make your acquaintance," he said smoothly, his tone belying the fierce hatred in his eyes. "What did you say your name was?"

"Aline, Your Grace," Aline forced out.

"And where are you from, *milady*?" he asked, putting an ironic emphasis on the last word. "Is it possible I know your parents?"

"Yes, Your Grace, I am sure it is possible." She felt sick with fear.

He leaned forward, his mouth close to her ear. "You will pay for this, you slut. You will pay dearly."

Aline stepped back, shaken. Suddenly James was there, stepping in between them, "Hello, Tanford. How kind of you to pay your respects to my bride."

Tanford bared his teeth in what looked more like the rictus of death than a smile. "But I am most grateful to her, for she has saved my niece from that fate. I'm sure this one is more suited to you."

"No doubt." James grinned wolfishly. "I am glad to see you taking it so well that I married another, instead of the Lady Clarissa. After all, some might take that rejection as, well, an insult."

Tanford's smile was bloodless and as sharp as a knife. "Nay, indeed, not if they know you, for 'tis far more rare, I've heard, to be a woman you have *not* had than one you have."

James smiled as if he found the remark amusing, and Tanford drifted away. As soon as he could reasonably do so, James took Aline's hand and led her out of the crowd, then out of the palace. He dropped her hand as soon as they were outside, and they returned to the Norwen house in silence. Aline noticed miserably that he did not utter even a word of praise for the way she had handled herself with king and Court.

When they entered the house, James immediately parted from her without a word, striding swiftly away. Aline gazed after him with a pang, then slowly began to walk toward the stairs.

"Aline!"

She turned, looking across the hall to the large fireplace. By it stood three people—Gemma and a man and woman in the rich but restrained garments of a merchant and his wife. It took a moment to recognize the couple as her parents.

"Mama! Papa!" She flew across the room and flung her arms around them. "How did you get away? What happened?"

"'Twas Sir James's doing," Bera offered.

"He got you free?" Aline's heart soared. Surely he did not completely hate her, or he would not have done this for her. Oh, why hadn't James been kind enough to tell her that her parents were free this morning before they left for Court? She would have felt much more at ease. But, then, she supposed that was more punishment for what she had done to him. Or, perhaps, he was waiting to give her the gift of her parents until he saw whether she behaved correctly before the king.

"Yes. One of Tanford's servants arranged it," Harald added. "Apparently he spies for Sir James. He bribed one of the guards, dressed us in these clothes, and took us with him through the gate this morning."

"We hardly knew what to think when he came to us and told us the plan."

"At first we were afraid it was a ploy of Tanford's— to trick us, you see, into trying to escape, so that he would have an excuse to hurt us."

"I doubt he would need an excuse for it." Aline wrapped her arms around them and hugged them again. "I was so worried. This morning James crossed the Duke, and he knew that I had told James everything. I was afraid for you."

"That's why he couldn't take them out any earlier," Gemma piped up. "He did not want to make Tanford suspicious before he went to Court this morning."

"Of course. That makes sense." A bright smile burst across Aline's face. James hadn't been testing her or punishing her; it had simply been the logical, practical thing to do. Even after the way she had wronged him, he had given her her parents' lives. He had even given up his spy in Tanford's house, for the man obviously could not go back there now. Moreover, he had not repudiated her before the king. He had actually told Henry that she was his wife. Did that not prove that he still loved her?

She gave her parents a quick smile. "I must go, just for a short while. I will be back soon."

She hurried from the great hall, looking for James. She found him in the study, bent over a ledger, frowning in concentration.

"James!"

He glanced up at the sound of her voice. His face looked tired and drawn; his eyes were pools of pain. His expression quickly changed to one of remote indifference.

"Cl—Aline. What do you want?"

She came forward quickly, tears of gratitude shining in her eyes. "I came to thank you. You saved my parents' lives. I am more grateful to you than you can ever know."

He stood up as she drew close, his expression wary. Aline reached out and clasped his hand, raising it to her trembling lips. "Thank you. Thank you. You are so good. So kind."

"I could hardly leave my wife's parents in Tanford's clutches. He would find a way to use it against me."

"Then you still consider me your wife?" Aline asked, raising her liquid eyes to his. Hope surged in her.

"Nay, do not think that I have softened toward you," he told her sharply, jerking his hand from hers. He walked away. "You betrayed me, deceived me. I cannot forgive you that."

"I did not want to!" Aline cried, tears streaming freely down her face. "I love you."

He turned back, his mouth curled up in a sneer. "Oh, easy words! You are afraid of what I will do to you, and you would say anything. I know how well you lie, how effortlessly words of love come to your lips. I am not a fool, woman, to be deceived by you again."

"I am not lying." Aline clasped her hands together tightly as her body grew more and more rigid. She felt as if she might fly apart into a hundred pieces. Every word James said was a new blow to her heart. "It was not easy for me to lie to you. Oh, at first it was. It was fun to act the proud lady. But, later, when I came to know you, to know your family, I hated myself for what I was doing. Every lie I told was torture to me, because I had come to love you. But I feared for my parents. What else was I to do?"

"You could have come to me," he retorted. "You could have told me the truth. Didn't I get your parents out of Tanford's household just now?"

"I knew not that you could save them, or that you would even try. I was afraid of your wrath, of your looking at me the way you do now, as if I were less than a worm beneath your feet."

"I was a fool!" he roared, slamming his hand against the wall. "I was a fool to give away my heart. I have known it all my life. A woman can take a brave man and make him a coward, or a wise man and make him a fool. I swore it would never happen to me. I was sure that I would never let a woman have the power to ruin me."

"I love you," Aline cried desperately. "I never lied about that!"

"I know nothing of you but lies. I did not even know your name. The woman I thought I loved was a myth, a tale. I fell in love with Lady Clarissa—and who is she, where is she now?"

"You fell in love with *me*," Aline retorted, a saving anger rising in her. "I was the only person in your bed. Lady Clarissa was never there. You just don't want to admit that the woman you love is a common dancing girl, not the noblewoman your heart is so set on. *I* cannot take away the stain of your birth. I can only add to it. Therefore I am worthless to you."

"Oh, no, you are not worthless. Your value is that of a very hard lesson. And I have learned it. I would not make it a second time." He turned and walked away. "We will wait a few days. It would seem suspicious to do it immediately, after I have just presented you at Court as my beloved wife. But within the week, I will send Sir Brian and several of my men to escort you and your parents to Beaufort Place. Stephen and Gwendolyn can keep an eye on you there while I decide what I am to do with you. You committed fraud when you married me, you know, pretending that you were Lady Clarissa. That makes our marriage null."

"I see," Aline said. It broke her heart to see James treat her like a stranger, to think that he would send her away from him. She wished that he would rage at her, even strike her. Anything would be better than this coldness.

She had one thing that she could use to persuade him, to win him back. If he knew that she was carrying his child, he might not send her away. He might not annul the marriage, for he would not want to make his child illegitimate, as he had been. It was the one hold she had on him—yet she knew she could not use it. When James decided what he wanted to do, it would have to be based on what he felt for her. Let him weigh his love against her ignoble birth, against her lies. She would not use her child as leverage.

So she said nothing about the life that she now strongly suspected was growing in her womb. Instead, she murmured only, "All right. I will be ready to travel in the morning."

She turned and walked away.

The next few days were such misery for Aline that she was almost glad when it came time for her to leave London. It was hard to be in the house with James, to catch glimpses of him from time to time, yet to have no more contact with him than with a stranger. The only time they were together was at meals, and though they sat close together then, he might as well have been in a different house for all the attention he paid her. He scarcely glanced at her, and he addressed no more words to her than were absolutely necessary. Each time they sat together this way, Aline's heart shriveled in her chest. She could not eat, the nausea from her pregnancy and hurt combining to make the food utterly unpalatable.

She made herself as attractive as she could, hoping to win him back to her bed. She thought if she could but awaken his desire for her, she could bring him to love her again. But he remained coldly indifferent, and she despaired, sure that she had given him such a revulsion of her that he would never again want her.

The night before she was to leave for Beaufort Place, Aline was awakened in the middle of the night by the sound of the door opening. She saw a man's figure come toward the bed, and for one wild moment she froze with fear. Fingal, come to avenge the Duke! Then she recognized the man as James, and hope leaped within her.

She said nothing, just pretended that she was still asleep and peeped up at him through her thick lashes. James stood beside the bed and gazed at her for a long moment. His face was so tortured that Aline almost cried out.

He reached down and touched her hair, smoothing his fingers across it as it lay spread out on the sheets. She thought she heard him murmur her name, but the sound had been too soft for her to be sure. Aline waited, taut as a bowstring inside, praying that he would sit down on the bed beside her or lean over to kiss her—anything that would give her a chance to touch him, to kiss him, to seduce him into her bed again. Perhaps that, too, would be deceptive, but Aline didn't care. She would do anything, she thought, to win James back.

But he stepped back and turned away.

"James!" Aline's eyes flew open and she sat up, reaching a hand out toward him.

He turned. Her bedclothes had fallen down to her waist, and Aline saw his eyes flicker down her body, covered only by her thin summer nightgown. She felt her nipples pucker at the touch of his eyes, and James's mouth took on the heavy look of sensuality it had when he was aroused. Aline waited in an agony of suspense and hope, her hand out to him, her eyes pleading.

"No!" he said thickly, and wrenched away. He strode out of the room.

Aline slumped back onto her bed.

The following morning James did not come to say good-bye to her. Aline went downstairs to find Sir Brian waiting for her with his men in front of the house, and moments later her parents, Gemma, and the boy Malcolm joined them. Aline waited, looking back hopefully at the door of the house, but it did not open. Sir Brian came to her and helped her into her litter, and she knew that James did not intend to give her even a formal farewell.

The trip to Beaufort Place was interminable. Aline was sunk in such misery that her frequently churning stomach seemed a minor nuisance in comparison. She endured it all—the morning sickness, the dust, the heat, the long hours of traveling—with the same grim despair. Her parents and Gemma tried to cheer her up. Her father told her stories and sang songs when they were camped at night, and Gemma did her tricks in the hopes of tricking a laugh out of her. Sir Brian and his men listened intently to Harald's tales, for he was a master storyteller, and they roared with laughter at Gemma's antics, but Aline could manage no more than a wan smile.

They reached Beaufort Place at last, and Stephen and Gwendolyn came out to greet her, puzzlement written on their faces. They glanced with curiosity at Harald and Bera as they ushered them all into the great hall. Sir Brian handed Stephen the letter James had given him to deliver, and Stephen began to read. Aline cringed inside, knowing that now Stephen and Gwendolyn would hate her, too.

Stephen's eyebrows rose and he cast a quick, startled glance at Aline, then returned to the letter. His face was as hard as stone by the time he finished. He handed the letter to Gwendolyn and turned to Aline.

"I will send servants to prepare your room," he said stiffly, all the old affection and warmth wiped from his face.

Gwendolyn gasped as she read the missive, and Aline saw horror spread across her features. Gwendolyn's hand trembled on the parchment, and tears formed in her eyes. She looked up at Aline as though unable to believe what she'd just read.

Aline was swept with guilt and grief, and she turned away from Gwendolyn's horrified eyes. Until this moment, she had not realized how very dear all of the Norwen clan had become to her. She did not know how she would manage to live like this, banished by the man she loved, hated by those who had come to be her family. She thought about leaving, just running away. But she knew she could not. She had to wait until she had heard James's decision. She had to know whether he would set her aside or if, despite everything, he still loved her enough to keep her.

She turned and walked toward the stairs, saying in a choked voice, "I will go to my room."

Richard, Earl of Norwen, entered London just as the sun was setting, followed by a small, weary band of his men. He had pushed them hard all the way from Norcastle. It had been obvious that a demon was riding him; his face was dark and hard, set in grim lines.

He pulled to a stop in front of the Norwen house and swung down from his saddle, tossing the reins of his horse to the nearest of his men. He strode past the guards and into the house. A servant came scurrying to help remove his hauberk, and Richard allowed him to pull the heavy mail tunic off over his head.

"Where is my brother?" he asked, glancing around the great hall.

"In the study, milord."

"What the devil is he doing there?"

"I know not, milord," the servant answered diplomatically.

Richard grunted and made his way to the small room where he conducted his business when he was in the city. The room was dim; there was one wax candle, burning low, on the desk. James was slumped in the chair, a goblet in his hand. His thick hair was mussed, as though he had been running his fingers through it, and his face was stubbled with a few days' growth of beard.

He looked up when Richard strode into the room, and his eyebrows vaulted upward. "Richard!"

He stood up, weaving a little, to greet his brother. Richard hugged him hard, then thrust him back down in the chair.

"Faugh!" Richard exclaimed. "You're drunk."

"Nigh onto it," James agreed amiably, and took another quaff of his drink. He gestured toward the slender silver pitcher on the desk before him. "Would you like a cup?"

"Aye. I'm thirsty from the dust of the road." As James started to rise again, Richard motioned him back down and stuck his head out the door to bellow for a servant to bring him a cup. Then he lit two more candles from the guttering one, brightening the room. James watched him idly.

"I received a letter from Stephen," Richard began.

"Ah, I see. I wondered how you had heard so

quickly. Why, it's been no more than two weeks since
I sent her away. So you have come to rescue your little brother from his folly again?"

"Again?" Richard smiled slightly. "I would have
said it was usually the other way around. You were
ever the coolheaded one."

James snorted. "What a time for me to choose not
to be, eh?"

Richard sighed. A servant brought in a goblet, and
Richard poured wine into it from the pitcher. He took
a long swallow and let out a sigh of satisfaction, then
perched on the edge of the desk and looked down at
his brother.

"What are you going to do with her?"

James turned his face aside. "I have not yet
decided."

"I went to York first and had an audience with the
bishop. He said her common birth would be ground
enough."

"Aye, I know. I spoke to a priest, too. There is her
lie, as well. Either are grounds enough."

"Have you started the process?"

"No."

"Why not? Even with money to grease the way,
you know how slowly the church moves."

"I am not sure yet that I want to do it."

"God's bones, man, why not? How else can you
remarry?"

"Nay." James let out a shaky little laugh. "I think I
have done with marrying."

"But 'tis what you have wanted always; a woman
of good birth, heirs."

"I have already presented her to the king as my
wife; it was the only way I could think of to thwart
Tanford." His mouth lifted slightly. "Who, by the

way, has gone near mad with rage, I understand. 'Tis said that he has openly vowed to kill me."

"Aye, you will have to watch your back. That's one reason I came."

"To protect me. I know." James smiled at him. "You are a good brother. But, in truth, I do not need it. The more open he grows, the less dangerous Tanford is."

"But if he's making threats here, where even the king can hear it, he must have lost all control, all reason. A madman can be dangerous, brother. He has no restraints, no fear of reprisals from the Norwens or fear of Henry's displeasure."

"It doesn't matter. You know I am always careful."

Richard dropped the subject. In truth, he did not worry overmuch about James being harmed by Tanford. Tanford was treacherous, but James would be doubly guarded now against any trickery. He was more concerned with the problem of James's wife. James had been uncustomarily attached to the woman, and Richard had been glad, hoping that James would find the kind of love with her that he had with his own wife. Elizabeth was convinced that James loved Aline. If such was the case, Richard was worried that it would go hard with his brother, who had guarded his emotions so well for so long.

"Perhaps the best thing would be for the woman to meet with an accident," Richard mused. "That would take care of matters without causing the embarrassment an annulment would." Though Richard was generally a softhearted man where women were concerned, he had no qualms about harming this particular one. When he had read the letter from Stephen, his fingers had itched to wrap around Aline's lying throat. Nothing made Richard so furious as hurt done to one he loved.

"No!" James replied sharply. "You will not touch her. Promise me."

"Then tell me this—how will you get the wife you want? The woman of good birth who will give you heirs. 'Tis what you have planned for years."

"I find I no longer care so much for a wife of good birth. And what good are sons if they come from the body of a woman you dislike?"

Richard sighed. "'Tis worse than I thought, then. You are still in love with her, even after her treachery."

James shot to his feet, hurling his cup against the far wall. "Damn her to hell!"

He began to pace the room, words bubbling from his mouth. "I never thought myself to be such a fool. I hate her for what she did—the lying words she spoke, the pretense of love she made. Every look, every touch was a lie. Oh, she was a master at it; she pulled me into her web with great skill. The worst of it is, I cannot get her out of my blood. Even as I despise her, I still love her. I still want her. She is like a fire in my veins! Jesu, I cannot sleep at night for thinking about her, and if I do sleep, I dream of her. I miss her. I keep thinking of something I want to tell her or I imagine a look on her face and yearn to see it. It is like torture to be without her."

James stopped, his last words almost a sob. He shoved his hands into his hair and clenched his fingers, struggling not to lose control. "Sometimes . . . sometimes I think that I could live with her. That I could control the situation—sleep with her, look at her, talk to her, yet not trust her, not give her my heart to trample on again." He shook his head. "But I know that this is fool's reasoning. The night before she left, I went to her room. I told myself, what does it matter if I possess her body? She is my wife, after all. It is my right. I can take her and keep my heart whole. But when I looked down at her, sleeping there, I knew I was deceiving myself. If I were to lie with her, I would be once more under her spell."

"You cannot give your heart to a woman you cannot trust," Richard told him. "It will break you sooner or later."

"I know. So what am I to do?" James turned and gazed at his brother with eyes so tormented it made Richard's heart squeeze with pain. "Stay apart from her forever? Hope that somehow I will lose my love for her? My desire?"

"I know not." Richard's voice was heavy.

"Neither do I. Sometimes I think that I am lost." James sighed and moved back to his chair, flopping down and picking up his cup of wine again. "If only Tanford knew. He truly got his revenge. He has made my life a hell."

22

Over four months had passed since Aline had returned to Beaufort Place. There was no doubt now that she was pregnant, and she was reaching the point where she could no longer disguise the fact. At first it had been easy. She saw Stephen and Gwendolyn rarely except at meals, for she kept to her own room or the garden and most of the time she saw only her parents or Gemma or one of the servants. Stephen and James's mother were not harsh with her. On the contrary, there were times when she wished they would rant and rave. She'd have accepted any behavior from them, anything except the cool, remote courtesy with which they treated her. Having once been on such friendly terms with them, it struck her hard to be treated like a stranger—and a not very well liked one, at that.

Aline often stayed in her room even during meals, for she had little appetite. She grew thin and pale, and often her eyes were red-rimmed with dark circles beneath them. She wore very loose-fitting tunics, so when her stomach began to grow, they easily hid the swelling mound. She told no one but Gemma and her parents about her pregnancy; her mother was her chief adviser, having experienced it five times, though only Aline had survived childhood. When Aline was in the bleak, dark despair of the first few months, Bera held her hand or stroked her brow and convinced her that both the illness and the despair would pass, leaving her with only love and eagerness for the baby's arrival.

It was not precisely as her mother predicted. The nausea did eventually cease, and her mood lifted considerably, also. She began to dream about the coming baby, imagining what it would look like and how it would feel to hold it in her arms. But her spirits remained low. James did not come to her or write her. Every time a courier arrived from him, bringing a missive to his mother or to Stephen and nothing for Aline, it was a fresh wound to her heart. The only cause for hope was that he had sent no word about having their marriage annulled. Surely, she thought, that must indicate that he did not completely hate her, that he still in some part of his heart wanted her as his wife.

As long as there was no annulment, she had hope, and for that reason she did not want Stephen or Gwendolyn to know that she was carrying James's child. They would immediately tell James. If James came back to her, she wanted it to be because he loved her, not because she was carrying his heir.

So wrapped up was she in her own misery that she did not notice that both Stephen and Gwendolyn had begun to soften toward her. Both were naturally kind-hearted people, disposed to like others, and they had had a great deal of affection for Aline before James had informed them of her deception. As they watched her through the weeks, so wan and thin and obviously unhappy, it was hard for them to maintain the cold anger that had filled them at first. Also, Gwendolyn began to suspect that Aline was with child. She herself had borne three children, and she was familiar with many of Aline's symptoms. It had taken her some time to recognize them, for at first her judgment had been clouded by her anger, but when she began to think about it, the pieces of the puzzle quickly fell into place. Gwendolyn could not hold herself aloof from her future grandchild's mother.

Gwendolyn noticed that the few times a courier arrived from James, Aline crept halfway down the stairs and stood there waiting, her face tinged with hope, until it was obvious that James had sent no message for her. Then, crestfallen, she would turn and run back up the stairs. The last time one of James's men came, Aline hurried in from the garden, where she had been watching Gemma and Malcolm practice their tumbling tricks. She stood unobtrusively at the far end of the great hall, but Gwendolyn, bustling out to greet the man, saw her. When the man handed one sealed parchment to Stephen, then went off to get some food and drink from the kitchens, Aline whirled and hurried away.

Gwendolyn also noticed that Aline moved more clumsily and looked heavier. Suddenly James's mother was filled with a determination to end the secrecy. She went after Aline, and found her alone in the garden, sitting on a bench, crying. The sight pierced Gwendolyn's soft heart, and she went over to the unhappy young woman.

"Aline."

Aline looked up, startled. "Gwendolyn!" Hurriedly she stood up, wiping the tears from her cheeks, and Gwendolyn could see that she was about to flee again.

"Wait," Gwendolyn told her firmly, and took her arm. She pulled her gently back down onto the bench. "Sit with me a moment."

Aline swallowed and obeyed her, wondering what Gwendolyn wanted with her. The older woman was looking at her with kindness in her eyes, and suddenly Aline found that harder to bear than the coolness with which Gwendolyn had treated her before. Tears pricked at her eyelids, and it was exceedingly difficult to hold them back.

"I have to know," Gwendolyn said. "Please, you must tell me. Are you carrying my son's child?"

Aline could no longer keep back the tears; they welled up in her eyes and spilled over onto her cheeks. She nodded, biting her lip.

"But, Aline, why didn't you tell me? We must write to James and let him know. This could change everything."

"No! No, please, don't tell him." Aline grabbed the woman's hands pleadingly.

"But why not?" Her face clouded. "Unless—it isn't his babe?"

"No! Oh, no, you must not think that! It is James's. I don't think even James, no matter how much he hates me now, suspects me of unfaithfulness. He knows I came to him untouched, and there could have been no other man."

"Then why wouldn't you want to tell him? He should know," Gwendolyn insisted.

"Because I don't want it to influence him. If he would keep me, I want it to be because he wants to, not because I carry his child. If he chooses to set me aside, I would rather my child be a bastard than to hold James with the baby."

"You must not say that." Gwendolyn frowned.

"James would not allow it. He would be furious. You must not conceal the baby from him."

"Please, I beg of you, do not tell him. I must know whether he loves me still. I must know that he has forgiven me, and is not just tolerating me for his child's sake."

Aline did not mention her secret fear that James might take the child when it was born, keeping her baby but casting her aside. She could not bear that. She was certain that Gwendolyn would not believe that her son would do such a thing, but Aline knew how he felt about an heir, and she had also seen the rage that had blazed in his eyes the last time they were together. And she could not be so sure that James would not seize her child.

Gwendolyn stared at her, puzzled and pained. "You seem to love him."

"I do! Oh, why will no one believe that I love James!"

"But why did you deceive him? Why did you plot with Tanford against him?"

"I did not know him then. To me he was just a nobleman, one who would have ridden over me if I had gotten in his way. When Tanford suggested the plan to me, I did not realize what kind of man the Duke was, either. He seemed to me a kind man, and I believed what he told me about James. I thought James deserved the trick Tanford wanted to play on him. And, God help me, it made my life easier."

She poured out the whole story to Gwendolyn, telling her about Gyrth and the troupe and her parents and how Tanford's plan had seemed the perfect opportunity to her. She told her how her guilt and worry had begun to grow after she met James and the other Norwens, and how she had finally realized that Tanford was a villain.

"But I could not tell James the truth then. I didn't know what he might do. And I was afraid for my parents, for what Tanford would do to them if I betrayed him. Don't you see?"

"Yes, I see," Gwendolyn said sympathetically, putting her arm around Aline's shoulders. "And you were afraid of losing James's love."

"Yes! Oh, yes, you understand." Aline's face glowed.

"Of course I do. Poor thing, it must have been terrible for you."

Undone by the woman's kindness, Aline laid her head upon Gwendolyn's shoulder and gave way to tears. Gwendolyn patted her on the back and murmured soothing words of comfort.

Finally Aline sat up, wiping her eyes. She gazed at Gwendolyn in wonder. "Do you truly forgive me, then?"

"Of course I do. Didn't our good Lord say that only those who are without sin should cast stones? I am scarcely without sin. I, too have committed grave wrongs against other people. Sometimes I think about how my presence in Norcastle must have hurt that poor woman, Richard's mother. What I did to her was terrible, but I did not care. I was too much in love with Lord Henry, too proud of the attention and affection he showed me. Anyway, it is not my place to forgive or not forgive you."

"I know. That is James's place, and I am beginning to fear that he will never understand."

"Oh, no, James will understand," Gwendolyn assured her. "It may take him a little time to get over his hurt and his anger, but eventually he will come to realize that you love him. That you did not want to hurt him. You will see."

"No. I fear not," Aline told the other woman sadly.

"You did not see his face when I told him. He despises me now. I am not the noble wife he wanted. He scorns me for being a mere dancing girl, and he hates me for spoiling his plans. Tanford must be whispering about me, starting rumors about my true birth. James will have that cloud hanging over us always if he does not set me aside, and that would humiliate him. He does not *want* to love me or desire me."

"Perhaps he does not, but sometimes what we feel is far stronger than what we want to feel. I suspect that you did not 'want' to fall in love with James, but still it happened."

"That's true."

"And it would happen more quickly for James now, I think, if James knew about the baby."

"No, please, don't tell him. Give me a little more time. He doesn't have to know just yet, does he? It will be ample time for him to know when the babe is born, and until then, I can hope that he will come to me on his own."

Gwendolyn sighed. "I do not feel it is right. And I fear that James will be angry with me for not telling him. Besides, there is Stephen. He is young, and a man. It may be a few more weeks before he realizes that you are breeding, but eventually he is bound to."

Aline smiled at her winningly. "You could talk him into not telling. I'm sure you could."

"You wretch," Gwendolyn said, chuckling. "Now you will try to flatter me into holding information from my son. What James will say to me, I hate to think."

"He will say nothing. He loves you very much."

Gwendolyn smiled fondly. "Yes. He is a good son. And he will be a good father, a good husband." She waggled her forefinger at Aline. "You wait and see." Gwendolyn sighed. "All right. Against my better judgment, I will agree not to tell him for a while. I will ask Stephen not to, either. But not forever, mind you. I intend for James to be here when my grandchild is born. That is a day I have been looking forward to for a long time."

After that day, Stephen's attitude toward Aline noticeably thawed. By the time another month had passed, the group of people at Beaufort Place were forming into the same sort of close family they had been before. Of course, Aline still ached with loneliness for James. There were nights when she wept, wishing he were with her, and other nights when she burned, unsatisfied, with a flame that only he could put out. But, all in all, life grew more bearable. The old friendship between her and Stephen grew up again, and they once more teased and laughed and chatted like brother and sister. Gwendolyn, who confessed to Aline that she was more at ease with the dancing girl Aline than she had been with the Duke's niece, Lady Clarissa, vied with Aline's mother over who could cosset her and fuss over her the most. Harald, Gemma, and the now-skilled Malcolm kept them entertained through the long evenings with juggling tricks, stories, and tumbling. Stephen, who had a smooth tenor voice, and Aline often joined in the singing, and Stephen was so intrigued with some of Harald's sleight-of-hand tricks that he insisted on learning them.

The only sore spot, the thing which kept Aline's spirits weighed down, was James's continued rejection of her. Stephen sometimes read her his infrequent letters—only because she begged him to—but they were always a disappointment. James never mentioned her in them, only mundane matters or gossip from the

Court or political matters. He remained a trusted
friend of King Henry, while the Duke of Tanford, he
reported, seemed to daily grow wilder in his accusa-
tions and rumors about James, until even many who
had formerly associated with him drew away, made
uneasy by the madness that bubbled just below the sur-
face in him. James was told that one day Tanford had
erupted into a temper tantrum in the king's presence,
ranting about James and his iniquities, until Henry had
ordered him from his presence. After that, Tanford had
left London in a huff, withdrawing to his country seat
in the north. But in that news, amidst the inquiries
about Stephen and James's mother, there was never a
word mentioned or a question asked about Aline.

"He knows that if there were anything wrong, I
would write and tell him," Stephen assured her, trying to ease the hurt that stamped Aline's face. "I am
sure he is too proud to ask about you outright."

"He does not care, you mean," Aline replied bitterly. "Why try to hide it? He does not plan to ever be
with me again."

"He never says anything about annulling the
marriage, you know that. When Elizabeth wrote me
saying Richard had returned from a month of visiting James, she said that James did not intend to
seek an annulment."

"Aye, perhaps he will keep me as his wife, because
he was forced to present me to the king as such in
order to thwart Tanford's plans. But he obviously
intends to live apart from me. He will stay with the
Court and I here, or wherever else he decides to send
me. But he does not wish to see me."

"Nay, I am certain that he wishes to see you. It is
merely his hurt and his pride that keep him from it.
He has always been armored against Cupid's arrows.

Women have swooned over him, and he has remained willing, but indifferent. He finally lost his heart, and when he found out that you had deceived him, he was cut to the quick. It was far worse for him than it would have been for any normal man, I think. He had had no experience of having his love forsaken."

"I did not forsake him!" Aline cried. "I loved him! I still do."

"I know. But he is too hurt and scared to believe it."

"James?" Aline repeated sardonically. "Scared?"

Stephen smiled. "Not physical fear. I am not sure he has ever felt that. He has nerves of steel. I mean fear of what he feels, of what others think of him. There, I think he has great fears. It is because you are so important to him that he feels he must stay away from you. He fears your power over him."

Aline chuckled. "Truly, Stephen, you have a silver tongue. You could make a person believe the sky was orange. You should easily make your way at Court."

He smiled. "I speak only the truth, Aline. James would come home, I think, if he knew about your babe. Let me tell him."

Aline shook her head, moving back. "No. Don't you understand?"

"Yes, I understand. You want a clear admission of his love. But you may have to give in a little if you want him to give in a little. A compromise. You see? He is too stiff-necked to come to you, and you are too stiff-necked to call him home."

"Nay, 'tis not that!" Aline cried indignantly.

"Is it not? Do you not think James has a right to know that he is about to become a father? Should he not have the right to choose whether he will be here for the babe's birth? Even if he does come for the baby, not for you, at least then you will have the chance to woo him, to win him back. After all, given what you did, do you really think it should be so easy to regain his love? Should you not at least have to smile and flutter your eyelashes at him a little?"

"The way I look, I doubt I would be able to seduce him." She swept her hand over her rounded stomach. She was into her eighth month. Her mother and Gwendolyn were estimating that the baby would be here soon. The time was running short, and her hopes of James's coming to her freely were falling to ruin. Besides, Stephen did have some forceful arguments: James had a right to see the birth of his child. And she could hardly expect him to come back to her easily.

"All right," she sighed. "Tell James that I am with child."

Stephen traveled to London to tell James the news in person, feeling it was too important to entrust to a messenger. Besides, he had a few niggling doubts about how James might react, and he thought it would be best if he were there to persuade him.

James was not there when he arrived, so Stephen had time to clean up and change clothes before he spoke to him. By the time James finally strode in the front door, Stephen was seated casually by the fire in the great hall, sipping a cup of mulled wine. James stopped abruptly and stared at him, and his face drained of all color.

"Stephen?" He started forward rapidly. "What is it? Why are you here? Has something happened to—"

"Aline?" Stephen asked, rising to meet him. "Nay, nothing bad. I have come with news that I hope you will find good."

"Indeed?" James looked relieved. He reached out

to hug his young friend, then stepped back. "Has Elizabeth had a baby? Richard told me he thought she was breeding again."

"Nay. Not Elizabeth. The fact is, I am here about Aline."

"Oh." James's face closed down.

"You do not look well," Stephen blurted out.

"How now, what a friend you are," James joked, turning away to call to a servant to bring him a glass of wine. "I am often with the king. You know how he is. One minute you are here, and the next, there. I think I have covered the southern half of the land these last few weeks. You are lucky that you caught me in London."

"It isn't the king, and you know it," Stephen countered, gazing at him seriously. James had lost weight, and there were dark smudges beneath his eyes. But far more than the physical evidence, there was a weariness of spirit that showed in his face. "Aline has looked much the same way for months."

James grimaced and moved away, using the excuse of the servant's entrance to busy himself with the wine. He put the poker in the fire, heating it, then plunged it into the deep mug of wine, all the while avoiding Stephen's eyes. Stephen watched him, waiting patiently for James to set the poker aside and turn back to him.

"But now she is better?" James said at last, his face set in indifferent lines, as he sat down in the chair opposite Stephen's.

"She has gained back much of the weight, but there is still the sadness in her eyes."

"You are too softhearted, Stephen. You are worse than Richard that way. Let a woman look sad, and you are worried. You'll have to learn, or you will be taken advantage of by every trollop who comes along."

"I'm not a fool, James. And Aline is no trollop."

"Perhaps not. She is, however, an expert at deception, so I would watch my step around her, were I you."

"I have. But I cannot ignore the evidence of my eyes and ears, just as you would not have been able to if you had been around. I think that is one reason you have stayed away, so that you would not have to face the truth."

James cocked an eyebrow. "My, such a fierce cockerel you have become. What is this truth that I am avoiding?"

"Aline loves you."

James let out a crack of laughter. "Of course. That is why she played me for a fool for months."

"And you love her," Stephen plowed on, ignoring James's response.

"Indeed?" James took a sip of wine. "There I think you are wrong. For the past few months I have worked hard at rooting out whatever affection I felt for her, and I have been most successful, I'm happy to report."

"And how have you done that? By wenching and drinking? Richard told me how you had taken to becoming besotted every night."

"Nay. I gave that up. And I have little taste for wenching anymore. I have devoted myself to the king and politics. Fortunately, Henry is happy to use up every minute you will give him. It has been a mutually satisfying relationship."

"I believe you not. Oh, not about Henry. I'm sure he has kept you hopping, and you have been grateful for the occupation. I speak about your feelings for Aline."

"I *have* no feelings for Aline!" James roared, slamming the cup down on the arm of his chair so hard that wine splashed out the top.

"Then why does it upset you so to talk about her? You can hardly bring yourself to say her name. That is not the manner of an indifferent man."

"All right, then I am not indifferent," James admitted. "I hate her."

"James, she has explained it to me, and while I cannot like what she did, I can understand how it happened."

"I am sure she has made it sound most reasonable. She has a way of wrapping a man around her finger," James retorted viciously. "Now that *I* am out of her reach, no doubt she has decided to try to lure *you* into her clutches."

"She has done no such thing!" Stephen's cheeks flared with color. "How dare you intimate that I have—why, Aline is like a sister to me. She is your wife. And she loves no one except you! James, if you could have but seen her sadness, the way she cried, how she grew so thin and wan . . ."

James sneered. "She is playing you like a fish, and soon you'll find yourself gasping and flopping like one. I would say take her with my blessing, if I did not love you."

"God's bones, but you're a hard one!" Stephen exclaimed, jumping to his feet. "Aline was right. You will never listen. You don't care about the truth. All you care about is your pride!"

He turned and strode toward the stairs. James stood up, calling, "Stephen! No, wait. Do not walk away in anger."

"I cannot help it." Stephen glared at him. "You act like an ass. I shall take leave of you tomorrow, and I pray that next time I see you, you are more amenable to reason."

"Stephen, nay, do not leave so soon. You should at least rest."

"I will rest when I am back at Beaufort Place," Stephen shot back. "I, for one, intend to make sure I am there for the baby's birth."

"Baby?" James stared at him. "What baby? Elizabeth's?"

"No. Aline's. Your wife. That is the news I came to tell you. Aline carries your babe and will be delivered of it within the next few weeks. But worry not. Stay here and play your games with Henry and his court. Your mother and I will take care of her and the child."

James stood, stunned, as Stephen stalked across the hall and started up the stairs. James turned white, then flushed. Finally, he broke from his paralysis and, dropping his cup, ran after Stephen, bellowing, "Stop! Wait!"

Stephen turned, looking down the stairs at him, his brows raised coolly.

"You cannot drop such news on me, then just calmly leave."

"I was not calm," Stephen reminded him. "I was angry."

"By all the saints, man, come back down here, and tell me."

With a sigh, Stephen walked down the steps to James. "What would you know?"

James looked taken aback. "I am not sure. You have given me a blow that is like to knock me off my feet." He turned away and shoved his fingers through his hair. "Is it true? Does she indeed carry my child?"

"Yes."

"When is she due?"

"Gwendolyn guesses another few weeks, and so does Aline's mother." He paused, then added with boyish frankness, "She looks as if she's about to have it any day now, if you ask me."

James chuckled. He felt like bursting into laughter; he felt like crying. All the careful walls he had been building up around his heart the last few months came crashing down in an instant. He was suddenly as bleeding and raw as he had been when he'd first sent Aline away.

"But is she well? Does she go on all right?"

"Aye, except for melancholy. But only *you* can end that. She was very thin at first. She ate little. Gwendolyn and I began to worry that she might waste away and die."

James closed his eyes as pain ripped through him. "No. No, it is but pretense. She does not miss me."

"Pretense?" Stephen asked. "Do you think I am that stupid? That your mother is? That we cannot tell whether her cheeks are sunken or there are black circles beneath her eyes? Do you think it is pretense that her bones push against her skin? Or do you think she was starving herself apurpose, just to pretend that she loved and missed you? Why should she care to pretend?"

"I know not. But I cannot believe . . ."

"You *won't* believe, you mean. 'S blood, but you are the most thickheaded, stubborn man I have ever met."

"Do you—is it really mine?" James asked, and only the tortured look in his eyes kept Stephen from exploding.

"That is one thing Aline thought you would not doubt. I know not. All I can swear is that she was with child when she came to Beaufort Place; she must have been, oh"—he figured it in his head, his forehead knotting—"two months or so along."

"She would have conceived in March, then." She had gotten pregnant at Chaswyck, during those lazy days when they had done little but explore their capacity for love-making. James had to struggle to keep a sensual, self-satisfied smile from his face.

He turned away, churning with emotion. He thought of his child lying inside Aline, curled up beneath her heart, and he was filled with pride and joy, along with an intensely sexual jolt. But swelling up in him, too, surrounding and seeping through all the rest, was fear: black, basic fear that had been with him since he was a child. Aline might die, as other women had died; at the least, she would be in pain, as his aunt and Elizabeth had been. He ached to see her big with his baby, to hold his child in his arms, and just as fervently, he wished that she were not pregnant.

James turned back to Stephen. "I will ride with you on the morrow."

Stephen smiled. "I knew you would."

23

James opened his eyes. It was dark still, but he knew that he was done with sleep. He glanced across the room, where Stephen lay, curled up on his side on his pallet, sword cautiously within fingers' reach. James sat up, rubbing his face. He wondered how long it would be before light, before they could begin their journey again.

He stood up quietly, straightening his clothes. Then he picked up his sword and mantle, and the blanket he had been wrapped in, and crept from the room, careful not to disturb Stephen. He made his way down the stairs of the inn. In the common room, several men slept on the floor, close to the fire. The winter cold had driven many people inside. He eased out the door and slipped outside, breathing deeply of the chilly air. The blood was pumping through his veins, hot and eager, and the cold air invigorated rather than chilled him.

He would see Aline today.

James could not hold back a smile at the thought. He wasn't sure how he felt or what he would do. His emotions were like a storm within him, pushing him first one way, then another. All he knew was that he was filled with life for the first time in months. He was eager to reach Beaufort Place, and in only a few hours more they would be there.

He had been pushing Stephen and his men unmercifully all the way from London. If he had been alone, he would have gone even farther each day. Yesterday evening, he had wanted to ride on through the night to reach Beaufort Place, but Stephen had dissuaded him, pointing out that no one would have been up by the time they got there and that they would have had to rouse the entire house to get in. Finally, James had agreed to stop for the night, but now he was thrumming with eagerness to go on.

It occurred to him that there was nothing to stop him from doing precisely that. There was little danger from brigands now that they were on Beaufort lands, so there was no need to travel in an armed group. Stephen would understand if he rode ahead of him and the men. He thought of seeing Aline again, of being able to greet her by himself, and the idea of leaving immediately for Beaufort Place grew even more appealing.

Quickly, he broke the ice skimming the bucket and splashed his face with water, then combed his fingers through his hair. It was enough for the moment. Later, when the sun was up, he would stop and scrape the days' growth from his face and put himself into some semblance of order. Right now he simply strapped on his sword and flung his cloak around himself and tied it. Then he strode to the stables, hurriedly rolling up his blanket as he went.

It took a few minutes to wake a sleeping groom and get his horse saddled, but then he was up on the stallion and off. He knew the way well, having traveled it many times, and his mind drifted. He paid little attention to the road or the land around him. His thoughts were on Aline; he wondered what she would say when she saw him, what she would do. He wondered if Stephen had been right, and it had been only his pride holding him back these months. Could it be that Aline really did love him?

He was so deep in thought that he did not notice the gradual lightening of the sky around him. Nor did he pay any attention to the bridge ahead. His horse started onto the bridge, hooves clattering on the wood. Suddenly out of the trees on the other side of the bridge rode two men on horseback. They were heavily armed.

James tightened with suspicion, automatically grabbing for his sword and tossing back his cloak to free his sword arm. The two men reined in at the end of the bridge, drawing their own weapons. James spurred his horse forward, the familiar surge of excitement pouring through him.

Then something thwacked into the muscle of his back, and pain shot through his arm and shoulder. He realized that he had been shot with an arrow. Still, he kept his grip on his sword and charged forward, swinging. There was the sound of hoofbeats behind him, and then there were mounted men all around him. He was struck hard with the flat of a sword across his back, and he swung, his sword connecting solidly with armored flesh.

"Do not kill him!" a man roared. "Remember, His Grace wants him alive!"

Then his head seemed to burst, and everything went black.

*   *   *

Gwendolyn and Aline giggled over their sewing. Aline's mood had been lighter from the moment Stephen left for London. She would see James soon, she hoped, and it no longer seemed to matter why he was coming, only that he would be here. It was difficult to pay attention to her needle, even if what she was sewing was for the baby.

"His Lordship approaches!" came a cry from the battlements, repeated across the yard and carried inside by a servant.

Aline looked up, fear and eagerness mingling on her face. There was no time to run up and change, and besides, she knew that there was little she could do to improve her looks, given the size of her stomach. So she settled for making sure her coif was straight and that her tunic fell smoothly around her.

Gwendolyn hurried to the front door and out into the courtyard, Aline right behind her. Eagerly they looked toward the gate. Stephen rode through it, and behind him came six of his men.

Aline's heart fell to her feet. James was not with them. He had refused to come, she thought, even for the baby. She felt dizzy and sick, and she leaned back against the door, trying to will enough strength into herself to face the situation.

Stephen was grinning from ear to ear, and he jumped off his horse lithely, tossing the reins to a groom who had come running. "Good day to you, ladies!" he called cheerfully, bounding up the steps to kiss Gwendolyn on the cheek. "Where is James?"

He turned to Aline to greet her as well, and he saw the pale cast of her face, the hurt and confusion in her eyes. He went still.

"What is amiss? Why do you stare at me thus?" He looked from Aline to Gwendolyn. She, too, was gazing at him blankly. "Gwendolyn! Aline! What is it? Where is James? Has something happened?"

"What do you mean? We do not know where James is!" Gwendolyn exclaimed. "We thought he would be with you."

"With me?" Stephen took a step backward. "Is he not here? But he left before I awakened."

"He came from London with you?" Aline asked, relief flooding her. But hard on its heels came fear. "Then where is he?"

"The groom said he ordered his horse saddled before dawn. I thought he would have been here a good two hours before I arrived. We dawdled so that he would have time to greet you privately." He looked again from one woman to the other.

"He has not been here," Aline said through bloodless lips. She pressed her hand against her stomach, afraid that she would be sick. The baby began to kick wildly.

"No. Sweet Jesu, no." Stephen turned and ran back down the stairs and across the courtyard, calling to the guard.

"What could have happened?" Gwendolyn asked, turning to Aline, and the two women instinctively reached out to each other in fear and worry. "Do you suppose he met with an accident?"

"Why wouldn't Stephen have come upon him as he traveled?" Aline pointed out, her voice rising with a note of hysteria. "Something worse has happened to him. Brigands have fallen on him, or—or—"

Stephen returned at a run. "We will search for him. I will leave only a few men here. They are lowering the drawbridge. Don't let anyone in except me or

James. I don't know what has happened, but I fear trickery."

Aline and Gwendolyn nodded, and Stephen remounted. Suddenly the courtyard was a hive of activity as men rushed around getting armed and mounted and riding out.

"Come, let us go back inside, child," Gwendolyn told Aline.

"No. I want to go to the battlements. I want to see them coming back."

"Nay, it's too cold," Gwendolyn said soothingly. "You cannot stand there so long. Who knows when they will return? You will harm the babe, and you must not do that."

Finally Aline acceded to the other woman's reasoning, and let Gwendolyn lead her inside.

There they waited in stunned silence. Hours passed. News of the mystery spread through the castle, and soon Gemma and Aline's parents and even Malcolm came and sat with them in the great hall, saying nothing.

It was evening when Stephen at last returned. Malcolm rushed to the front door to peer out, then turned back disappointedly. "It's only His Lordship. The master ain't with him."

Aline clenched the arms of her chair. She had to be strong, she knew; she could not dissolve into fear and worry. James might need her, and she had to be strong for him.

Stephen entered the great hall, his face grim. He walked up to where Aline and Gwendolyn sat. Aline remained in her chair; her knees were too weak to stand.

"We could not find him. At one bridge there were signs of many horses and activity. They obviously left the road and took off through the fields. We followed for a while, but we lost the trail. Then we found some serfs who said that they had seen several riders in armor. It was from a distance, and they recognized none of them. They wore no man's colors or coat of arms. But one of the serfs was sure that one horse carried a man's body tied over its back." He shifted uneasily and looked away from Aline. "The others thought it was only sacks."

"What do you think?"

"I think it was James," Stephen admitted.

"Killed?" Aline could barely get the word out through her closed throat.

"I know not. He could have been dead or wounded or knocked out. It would not have been easy to take James alive, but they could have done it. I do not want to raise your hopes, but I think there is a possibility that they wanted him alive."

"Why?"

"Why take the body with them if they had robbed and killed him? Also, they were headed northwest."

Aline looked at him blankly, then her eyes narrowed. "Toward Tanford Hall? Do you think Tanford has captured him?"

Stephen nodded. "Who else bears such a grudge against James that he would go to such trouble? The only other possibility would be brigands who captured him to hold for ransom. If that is so, we will receive word soon enough of what price they demand."

"Pray God it is that." Aline looked at Stephen bleakly, knowing, as he did, that it was not likely. "But why would Tanford take him and not kill him outright?"

"Perhaps he wants to squeeze the Earl for all he

can in exchange for James." Stephen paused. "More
likely, he wants to do the killing himself."

Gwendolyn let out a moan of distress. Aline did
not glance at her; she kept her eyes on Stephen, fighting to force down her own nausea and fear. "What
are we to do?"

"I sent three of my men to Norcastle. Richard will
respond in force as soon as he hears of it."

"But how long will Tanford keep James alive? Can
the Earl make it in time?"

"I fear not. My men and I can ride at daylight for
Tanford Hall. I could send for my vassals and raise a
larger army, but that will take time. Anyway, Tanford
Hall is a well-guarded keep. It would take an army
months to conquer it by siege. I'm not even sure it
could be done. James would be dead long before then.
In fact, I am afraid they will kill him as soon as
Richard and I appear outside."

"It is hopeless then?" Aline asked, her face as pale
as parchment, her great golden eyes huge and stark in
her face.

Stephen could not meet her eyes. Aline fought
down her sickness. *She had to think.*

Suddenly she raised her head, and her eyes bored
into Stephen's. "All right, if it cannot be taken by
force, what about by trickery?"

"To the best of my knowledge, we have no
informer inside Tanford Hall, such as James had in
Tanford's London house."

"I was not thinking of someone inside the keep. I
was thinking of someone going to Tanford Hall and
getting inside. Someone whom no one would think
anything about—pilgrims going to a holy shrine . . .
or entertainers."

"Yes!" Aline's father jumped up from his seat on

the hearth and came forward. "The Duke loves entertainment. He never turns away a jongleur or a troubadour."

"He is likely to think that he has gotten clean away with capturing James," Aline put in. "If no armed men come to storm the castle, if he sees no sign of an approaching army, he may leave the gates open. In any case, he's likely to let in a few entertainers through the door even if the gate is closed to horsemen."

Stephen perked up. "That is true. A small band of people might be able to find James and get him out."

"But we will have to move fast," Aline said, standing up, energy flowing through her.

"We?" Stephen repeated. "Oh, no, milady. I am the one who will go."

"One man by himself? Do not be silly. You need a whole troupe."

"I will go," Harald offered. "I know the castle. We wintered there. And Gemma, if she will."

"Of course," Gemma agreed.

"Me too," Malcolm piped up, running eagerly into the center of the group. "I can do lots of tricks now."

"And I," Aline put in calmly. Normally she would have protested at the thought of a child like Malcolm going on such a dangerous expedition, but right now all that concerned her was James's safety.

"No," everyone chorused. "You cannot."

"But I will. It is Papa who cannot go. Tanford knows him." She turned toward Harald. "He saw you perform many, many times."

"I will disguise myself."

"Even your voice?" Aline cocked an eyebrow. "He has heard me sing only once, and that was long ago. I will darken my skin as I used to, and my hair as well.

I will wear huge clothes and wrap cloth around me so that I look fat all over, not heavy with child. I can sing, even if I cannot dance or tumble—Malcolm and Gemma will have to do those things. Stephen, you can sing as well, and you could even do a few of those tricks Papa taught you."

Stephen nodded. "We can take along one or two men, those who are best in close fighting."

"Dress them as pilgrims, not jongleurs," Harald stuck in. "I will take the garb of a monk, with hood up to hide my visage. You need me, because I can find my way around the hall. I went over every inch of the place, I think, looking for a way out of there."

"And were there any?"

He shook his head regretfully. "None except the main gate and the small postern door."

"We will rescue him in the night," Aline planned. "Just before dawn. And we shall bring clothes for him to wear—another monk's garb with hood. If he wears it forward, the guard will not recognize him. We can go out when the gates open, with the rest of the people."

Stephen's eyes flashed. "That's it! I will take my man Humphrey. He's much the height of James. He will wear a monk's robe. Then he can take it off and put it on James, so that it appears that the same monk is leaving."

"Yes!" Excitement built in Aline. Perhaps it was actually possible to rescue James. "You are right. It would not do to have an extra monk appear overnight. Humphrey can bring some other clothes and change into them, something not as noticeable, and leave with us."

"It will work!" Stephen's eyes glowed with enthusiasm. "I shall send a message to Richard to meet us as we leave." He began to happily make plans, but then he stopped and turned toward Aline. "But *you* are not coming."

"Not coming! Don't be absurd. I most certainly am."

"You cannot," Stephen said bluntly. "You cannot ride. It might harm the baby, and you will only slow us down."

"I will not slow you down. And the babe will do fine. 'Tis a Norwen, after all. You have to have me. Gemma and Malcolm are not enough to pass for a troupe. You can only sing a little and do a few tricks, whereas I sing and play the lute." Her eyes lit up. "Besides, Gemma and I can do this routine she used to do with Marigold. Do you remember that, Gemma?"

Gemma laughed. "Of course. Marigold was enormously fat, and Beorn and I would scamper around her and do all sorts of thing—pull at her skirts and even slide right under her—and she would scold and waddle after us. Malcolm and I could easily do it."

"And I can easily do Marigold's part. It was nothing agile or strenuous. Once I have padded my chest and shoulders to match my stomach, I shall look the part."

"No! James would slaughter me if I let you put yourself in such danger."

"And if you do not, James may not be here to get furious with you," Aline shot back. "He is *my* husband, and I am going to make sure he is safe."

"Aline, think of the babe, if not of yourself."

"I *am* thinking of it. I will not have my child grow up without a father. He will not have a mother who can do nothing but weep or who was such a coward that she let her husband die rather than lift a finger to save him!"

"This is quite a bit more than lifting a finger. You could lose the babe."

"I could lose James! He needs me, and I will go to him. If *you* choose not to go, then stay here."

Stephen's face turned red with rage, and he began to sputter. Aline turned on her heel. "I am going now to prepare for the trip. I suggest you do the same. We will leave tomorrow before dawn."

They left before daybreak the next morning and rode hard and fast to Tanford Hall. Aline gritted her teeth and made no complaint, even though their pace jarred her body. At least it did not make her go into labor, as she had feared it might. They left their horses hidden in the trees down the road from Tanford's keep, with one of Stephen's men to watch over them. Then they circled Tanford Hall and approached it from the other direction, Harald and Humphrey, dressed as friars, going on several minutes before the others.

Aline looked up at the keep as they drew near. What if James was already dead? Or what if he was so badly hurt that he could not walk? As if sensing her thoughts, Stephen took her arm and pressed his fingers into it, communicating strength without words. She cast him a small smile and continued walking. Whatever happened, at least she and Stephen would face it together.

"Don't get much of your kind anymore," one of the guards remarked jovially as she and the others passed by.

"Why not?" Stephen asked, doing a commendable job of looking young and nervous. In the tattered, brightly colored jongleur garments he had borrowed from Harald and with that expression of anxiety on his face, no one would have imagined that this was

the same young man who had led their fast ride to
Tanford Hall, as well as organized the movement of
his men and the Earl of Norwen's to rescue them,
should the need arise, after they left Tanford Hall. He
had, Aline thought, a good bit of the actor in him.

The guards chuckled. "There are those who say the
devil walks here," one said, and the two of them
laughed uproariously.

"But don't worry, lad," he said with mocking reassurance. "His Grace is partial to jongleurs and fools."

Aline kept her eyes on her feet as they walked
through the courtyard and up the steps into the great
hall. She must remember, she told herself, to walk
and act once again as a common person. She must not
raise her head and look others boldly in the eye, as
she had grown used to doing the past year.

The hall was a vast, cold place, and Aline hurried
instinctively to the huge fireplace, where other travelers were already gathered. To her relief, she glimpsed
the brown robes of two monks. Humphrey, well
padded around the middle with his extra set of
clothes, was jovial and talkative. Her father, on the
other hand, sat in quiet contemplation. He looked
very different, she thought, with the dark stain on his
hair and skin, and she was hopeful that if he stayed by
the hearth, the Duke would never give him a second
glance.

She knew that she looked even more different,
with her hair and skin stained brown with walnut oil.
As a further precaution, she wore a *sayon*, the short
shoulder cape and hood worn by the lower classes, to
cover her head. Working furiously through the night,
her mother, Gwendolyn, and the maids had sewn a
large tunic in bright blue and yellow, of the sort worn
by jongleurs. Aline wore it over a good deal of

padding, so that her pregnancy was hidden beneath layers of supposed fat. Aline hoped that her very size would draw the eye away from her face, which was far too thin to match the rest of her body. As a final touch, she had rubbed charcoal on two of her teeth to give herself an even more unattractive appearance. Gemma, Stephen, and Malcolm were similarly dressed in garish clothes, Stephen's and Malcolm's garments ending in carefully cut tatters over hose of equally outlandish and contrasting colors.

Stephen nudged Aline's arm and bent his head to hers to murmur, "In a moment, look up and to the right of the dais." He added fiercely, "But don't cry out or change expression."

Aline tensed all over. She dreaded what she would see. She fixed a pleasant expression on her face and glanced around, looking with what she hoped appeared an entirely normal curiosity toward the head table at the far end of the large room. Her gaze swept to the right. It was all she could do to suppress a cry, and she hoped that her anguish did not show.

A cage made of wide woven strips of metal hung from the high ceiling. A man crouched in it, unable to either stand up or stretch out fully. His clothes were torn, his chest almost completely bare, and wide, angry red blotches dotted his chest and arms. His face was distorted with livid bruises, and it was very swollen. One eye was almost completely shut.

It was James.

Nausea roiled in Aline's stomach. It was all she could do to turn calmly away and sit down on the hearth, fighting all the while to keep down her last meal. She wanted to burst into tears at James's pitiful condition. She wanted to run screaming to the front of the room and beg someone to let him out. She pressed her lips together and prayed fervently to the Virgin.

Then a saving anger rose up in her, clearing her head and turning her deadly calm. She would free James; she would get back at that low, inhuman man who had harmed him. And in order to do that, she would act her part with a vengeance.

Food was served to the main table, and the players were called upon to perform. As Aline walked past her father toward the front of the room, he winked at her, keeping his face turned away from the head table.

Aline glanced up and saw Tanford seated on the dais. His wife was by his side and farther down the table were Lady Agnes and her husband. Aline swallowed. Lady Agnes had been with her for a much longer time than Tanford had and would be more likely to recognize her. It was also possible she might recognize Gemma, for she had often been around while Lady Agnes was teaching Aline. But the lady was not the sort to pay attention to lowly servants, and Aline knew that most people saw little difference between one dwarf and another.

Stephen performed better than Aline had ever imagined he could. He mimicked a lower-class accent to perfection, using it to introduce his company. Aline pretended shyness, looking down and grinding her toe into the floor, sticking a finger in her mouth like a little girl. Gemma jumped and bounced and twirled, as did Malcolm, and the audience chuckled. Then Stephen and Aline sang a bawdy song that soon had everyone holding their sides with laughter. After that Gemma and Malcolm performed their tumbling tricks while Aline retreated to the side. Next Stephen sang two songs, sweetly, and then so did Aline. They finished with the routine in which Aline played the part of the fat Marigold, mugging and shrieking and starting with surprise at each new antic the dwarf and child did.

They bowed and retired to the hearth, but the whistles and clapping were so vociferous that Gemma returned for a few tricks and Stephen sang another song. They returned again to the hearth, and Aline sank down gratefully. She tired much more easily these days, and the padding added extra weight. Their fast and furious ride to Tanford Hall had exhausted her. Added to that was the fact that she'd slept little since learning that James had been taken. She was running on sheer nerves and willpower now. She knew that she would be able to get little sleep this night, not with James right there before her, and all their lives hanging in the balance.

She turned away and began to eat. Now that the Duke's family and the knights had eaten, the food was being doled out among the lesser beings, the servants and visitors. The bread tasted like sawdust in her mouth, but Aline forced herself to eat it. She had to keep up her strength for the ride home tomorrow. She forced down a few cold turnips and a hunk of meat that Stephen seized for her, but the rest of it she tied in a kerchief and stuck in her capacious pocket to give to James later. He would need it far more than she.

The Duke's voice boomed out at the other end of the room. "But what about my friend? I do not think he has received any entertainment this evening." He turned and looked up toward the cage where James crouched. "I did not hear his voice lifted in song."

He chuckled, and several of his knights laughed, too. Lady Agnes and her husband shifted uneasily in their seats, glancing toward the Duke and away.

"Perhaps it will take another taste of that poker to make him give voice. Do you think so, Wilfrid?"

Aline's stomach turned and she bit her lower lip so hard that it bled. Beside her Stephen was ashen beneath the walnut tinting of his skin. His fingers dug into his legs. Aline looked down at her lap.

"We cannot give ourselves away," Stephen whispered warningly, and she nodded. She knew that. James would have no hope if they did. But how could she sit idly by while they tortured her husband?

"Aye, Your Grace, it might at that." A large, ugly man stood up from the table. "Shall I give it to him?"

"Yes, I think I should enjoy that." Aline watched, horrified, as the man lumbered over to the great fireplace, stopping beside Gemma, and plunged a poker into its red-hot embers.

24

"*Your Grace,*" *Lady Agnes's* husband said, leaning forward to look at the Duke. "Do you think this is wise? The king is bound to find out what happened to him, as is Norwen."

"You think I am scared of the Earl of Norwen?" Tanford sneered at his son-in-law. His eyes glittered evilly in the dim light, and Aline was convinced that he had grown quite mad during the last few months.

"It is said that Norwen will not rest until his wrongs are avenged," Lady Agnes's husband, Lord Baldric, reminded him. "You saw what he did to William of York and Godfrey Beaufort."

Beside her, Stephen murmured with grim satisfaction, "Aye, he will tear this keep down stone by stone for what Tanford has done. And Tanford will be a lucky man if he dies a quick death."

"I am not such a coward as you, Baldric," Tanford countered. "If you cannot stomach it, I suggest you retire with the ladies."

Baldric's face set grimly, but he subsided. Lady Agnes glanced uneasily at her mother, and the two women started to get up.

Wilfrid, holding the poker, its tip glowing, turned away from the fireplace. At that moment Gemma jumped up with a shriek, leaping high in the air, and all eyes in the room turned to her.

"You great oaf!" she shrieked in a high voice. "You burned me."

The lumbering Wilfrid stared at her, his mouth open. "I did not."

"Most surely you did." Gemma skipped forward almost to the tip of the poker, then jumped back and executed three neat backward flips.

Stephen, seizing on her cue, jumped up from the hearth and shouted, "Come back here, you little wench! How dare you disrupt His Grace's entertainment?"

He grabbed the poker from the surprised Wilfrid's hand and proceeded to chase Gemma about the great hall. She jumped and rolled and flipped, all the while uttering wild shrieks of mock terror, rolling her eyes, and flapping her arms. Stephen whipped the poker about, dropped it, retrieved it, and stumbled at appropriate moments.

The entire hall roared with laughter. Aline ventured out with a rolling gait, swinging her wide padded hips so that Stephen bumped into them. He sprang back exaggeratedly, as if he had bounced off her. Then Malcolm got into the act, and for the next few minutes, the room was wild with mirth.

The Duke, who continued to drink all through this second performance, staggered to his feet when the show finally died down and tossed Gemma and Stephen a handful of coins, then collapsed into his chair again, lolling back drunkenly. Stephen almost

ruined his performance by simply looking down at
the coins, but then he recovered and made them all
laugh by pretending to wrestle for the money with
Malcolm and Gemma.

Lady Agnes made a gesture toward the Duke's
squires, and they came forward to lift him from his
chair. He lurched from side to side as they supported
him out of the room. Lady Agnes sighed and stood
up, motioning for everyone else to retire as well.
Gradually the crowd trickled away. Aline sat down
heavily on the hearth, holding her head in her hands,
weak with relief.

Soon the servants had cleaned up and left, having
put a great log in the fireplace to burn through the
winter night. The travelers made their sleeping spots
close to the fire. There were three strangers besides
Aline's "troupe" and the spurious monks.
Unobtrusively, Aline and her group tried to settle as
far away from the strangers as they could.

Aline lay on her pallet, unsleeping, waiting for
quiet to settle over the keep. To her surprise, she
must have dozed, for she awakened with a start when
Stephen tapped her shoulder. Her eyes flew open, but
she made no sound.

Stephen bent close to her ear and whispered, "I've
been keeping watch. They have no guards on him,
and no one seems to patrol the hall."

"Do you think we could get him out early?" They
had not planned to free James until right before
dawn, so that no one would discover him gone before
they could get away from the castle.

"I think we must try it. I fear he will be unable to
walk after days in that cage." Stephen's voice pulsed
with a quiet rage. "We should free him and help him
stretch out. If a guard comes in, then . . ." Stephen

meaningfully slipped a dagger out of his tall, soft boot. Aline swallowed. Stephen had always seemed a mild and friendly young man, but at this moment she had no doubt that he would kill anyone who got in their way.

"All right. Let's do it," Stephen said.

Aline could do nothing to help them, so she, Gemma, and Malcolm stood guard, watching for signs of anyone approaching or one of the other travelers awakening. Stephen's man Humphrey, the tall "monk," stood beside the cage, and Aline's father climbed up on his shoulders. Despite his age, Harald was still lithe, and his fingers were equally nimble. He worked at the lock on the cage with a long metal instrument, and finally the lock released. Harald pulled open the door and leaned in, speaking softly to James.

The figure in the cage hesitated, then began to move forward. The chains holding the cage to the ceiling creaked loudly as James crawled to the door and cautiously stuck his head out. Harald clambered down from Humphrey's shoulders, and Stephen, Harald, and Humphrey picked up a blanket, spreading it out and gripping it firmly among them. It had been the only way they could think of to get James down from the cage; it seemed unlikely that after days spent in that cramped place he would be able to climb out onto Humphrey's shoulders. James stared down at them for a moment, then turned around with painful slowness and began to wriggle out the door of the cage, feet first.

Aline glanced around anxiously. The three other travelers had not been awakened by the noise. No guard came striding down a corridor toward them. She looked back toward James. The lower half of his body was out. The cage was tipped wildly and swaying with his movements. He gripped the doorframe and swung out. He held onto the frame for an instant, then released it, falling backward.

He hit the blanket, bouncing a little, but the three men held it steady and lowered him to the ground. Aline drew a shaky breath of relief and hurried over to the group huddled around James on the floor. He was trying to stand up, but could not; his muscles had been too long bent. Aline could see the agony contorting his features as he tried to straighten out his legs.

"Take him to my blanket," she ordered crisply. "I shall try to work out the cramps." Sore and tight muscles were something she was familiar with, although his, she knew, would be far worse than anything she had ever experienced.

Humphrey picked James up as if he weighed no more than a child and carried him to Aline's blanket, close to the fire. He laid him down, and Aline dropped to her knees beside James and began to knead his thigh muscles. James winced and clamped his lips tightly together to stifle a groan. Aline knew that her fingers were probably pure torture to his abused muscles, but she continued doggedly.

"Aline?"

She glanced up at James's face. He was staring at her intently in the dim light, his eyes so swollen he was looking through slits. "Yes," she whispered, bending down closer to his ear. "I am here. I am sorry to hurt you, but you have to walk in an hour or two."

He nodded, and his tongue came out to wet his lips. "Water?"

"Yes, oh, yes, I am sorry." Tears sprang into Aline's eyes as she realized how thirsty he must be. There was a bucket of water near the hearth that Stephen had brought in earlier for their use, and she lugged it over to the blanket. She dipped a cup into the water and held it out to James, putting a hand under his neck to support his head. James struggled up onto his elbows and gulped greedily.

Aline pulled the cup back. "Nay, wait, go slowly, or you will make yourself sick."

He nodded, took two breaths, then drank another sip. Aline brought out the kerchief filled with bread and meat that she had saved from her meal and tore off a piece of bread, which she held to his lips. He took it greedily, too, but she could tell from the cautious way he chewed that his mouth was horribly sore. It was only to be expected, for his face was so bruised that he was hardly recognizable.

"I am sorry," she whispered, her throat clogged with tears. She tore off another piece of bread, this time soaking it in water before she slipped it into his mouth. That piece went down more easily, and she repeated the process with several more bits of bread. Then she tore the meat into the tiniest strips she could.

"I thought I heard you singing," James mumbled. "I thought—I thought they had driven me mad."

"No." Aline gave him a trembling smile. "I did sing."

"I fear I dream *this.*"

"'Tis quite real," Aline assured him as she fed a bit of meat into his mouth.

She fed him a few more strips of meat, then wrapped up the kerchief and set it aside. "You can eat more later. You should take it slowly. I must work on your legs again."

She went to work on his other leg, kneading and rubbing, then returned to the first one. Her father came over and spelled her for a time. Aline stood up, stretching; her back ached ferociously. She glanced at the cage. The men had stuffed some rags inside it in something resembling the shape of a crouched man, and they had locked the door again. It was a crude effort to disguise James's escape, but it might at least suffice for a casual glance in the dim light of dawn, and that would give them a few more minutes of precious time to escape.

Aline turned back. Her father had James up and walking a little, though in a bent position. Aline bit her lower lip, watching them, as they walked out into the hall and back. Then James lay down on the blanket and Harald once again began to rub his muscles. Aline dipped a rag in the water bucket and knelt by James's head. With her gentlest touch she began to wipe away the encrusted blood and dirt on James's face. He winced and flinched away, shooting her a look that should have dropped her on the spot.

"God's bones, woman, are you trying to finish me off?" he whispered.

"Obviously you are feeling better," Aline whispered back. "You sound just as ill-tempered as ever." She could not allow herself to give in to pity for James. If she let herself think about how awful he felt and what had been done to him, she was likely to burst into sobs right there and be useless to everyone. Besides, pity would not stiffen James's spine for the ordeal that lay ahead.

She was pleased to see his eyes flash in the old, familiar way, and she turned away with a little smile to rinse out the rag and return to washing him. There was little that could be done for his looks; no guard would think he was a simple monk if they caught a glimpse of his battered face. He would simply have to keep his head down piously, with the hood pulled far forward to hide his face.

Aline almost lost control when she reached his

chest and had a good look at the ugly burn marks. She was certain that this evening was not the first time Wilfrid or some other had decided to take the red-hot poker to James's skin. It made Aline's flesh crawl to think of it, and she wished that she had the Duke in her power for just a few minutes. On James's back, she found a deeper wound, a cut or an arrow wound. There was nothing she could do here and now except clean it, however. When—and if—they got back to Beaufort Place, she would put a poultice and bandage on it. Fortunately, it had already started to heal.

Humphrey, who had changed into serf's clothes, brought Aline the monk's robe he had worn, and Aline and Stephen helped James into it, first wrapping padding around his stomach so that he would appear to be the same potbellied friar. Aline tossed the bloody rags into the fire.

It was still not yet quite dawn, and they had to wait it out until the gates opened. Aline lay next to James, facing him. It would look strange her lying this close to a monk, but she knew that she would not go to sleep and so she could quickly move if she heard someone approaching or one of the other travelers awakening. Right now she had to be close to James, to reassure herself that he was alive and there with her.

His eyes were closed, but when she took his hand in both of hers, they fluttered open. Weakly, he squeezed one of her hands.

"You came to rescue me," he murmured.

"Of course. What else would I do?"

"You risked your life."

Aline nodded. "I love you. I could not leave you to die at Tanford's hands."

He stretched out his hand and ran his thumb over her lips. "You look different," he commented.

"Aye, I am as wide as a cart," Aline joked. Then she held up a hank of her hair. "And my hair is brown."

"Brown!" He looked so horrified that Aline almost laughed out loud. How could he care about such a thing at a time like this?

"Don't worry. 'Twill not remain so forever."

James took her hand and raised it to his lips, wincing a little as they touched. "Thank you." He smiled at her. "How could I have doubted that you loved me?"

Aline drew in an anxious breath. "Then you believe me? You know I did not lie when I told you I loved you?"

He nodded. "I believe you. No woman would risk her life—and that of her child—to save a man she did not love, especially when she would be an heiress if he died. When I heard your voice . . ." Tears glittered in his eyes. "I felt calm all at once. Peaceful. I thought I was dreaming, but it was such a wonderful dream. I thought then that I could die in peace."

"Nay. You cannot. You must live, for me and our child."

"I will." There was something of the old iron in his voice. His lids fluttered closed, and he slept.

Dawn came not long after that. At the first pale lighting of the room, Aline sat up and began to shake her companions awake. James stirred and sat up gingerly, and Aline gave him the remainder of the food to eat while she rolled up her blanket. Stephen and her father walked James up and down a little to loosen his legs again. Then they gathered their things and started out the door. They walked across the courtyard, Aline and the rest of the "troupe" in front, and the supposed monks following them at some distance. Humphrey walked along with the entertainers.

The guard nodded toward them, barely sparing them a glance. He was little interested in people leaving the castle, only in those trying to force their way in. As Aline passed through the gate, she glanced over her shoulder at James and her father. James was walking slowly, but normally. Aline wondered how much pain it was costing him to hold himself straight.

They started down the road, walking as briskly as James could. Aline's neck prickled, and as they walked they waited tensely for some cry as James's identity was discovered. None came. But they dared not look back, for fear it would seem suspicious. On and on they walked, fervently hoping that Harald and James were following them, until finally the road took a turn and they were out of sight of Tanford Hall.

Stephen left the others there and ran on ahead to fetch their horses and bring them back. Aline crouched behind a stone wall for modesty and stripped away her excess padding; there was no point in carrying its extra weight. She wadded up the padding and stuffed it down behind the wall, then joined the others in waiting for James and Harald. Soon Harald and James appeared. James was moving less stiffly now, his healthy, powerful body responding quickly to exercise. They all set out walking to meet Stephen.

James glanced over at Aline. He had pushed back his hood to see better, and his face looked even more lurid in the morning light. His gaze traveled over her, lingering on her swollen abdomen. He smiled.

"You look better this morning," he said.

Aline smiled back at him, her heart swelling with joy. "I am sorry I cannot say the same about you," she rejoined, combating her pity with humor. James chuckled and took her hand.

No one said much; their nerves were stretched too tightly. At any moment they expected to hear the pounding of horses and hooves and the cries of Tanford's men pursuing them. They knew that they could not hope it would take long for James's absence to be noticed, and that then Tanford's men, mounted, would have little trouble running down this group on foot. They hurried as fast as they could. Aline's side began to hurt, and she was soon breathless and sweating. The pace was too fast for her in her condition, but she dared not slow down. She would be risking not only her own life but that of all the others as well.

At last Stephen came thundering down the road with their horses. They hurriedly mounted and turned, nudging their steeds into a run. They came to a crossroads and took the north road, knowing that Tanford would expect them to go the other way, toward Beaufort. They rode steadily. Little by little, Aline dropped back. Now and then a pain sliced through her abdomen. She tried to ignore it. She saw both Stephen and James glance back at her worriedly, and she knew that they realized she could not keep up the pace.

A sound began to impinge on her consciousness. At first she thought it was distant thunder, and she glanced up at the gray November sky, wondering if it was about to rain. Then she looked behind her. There, in the distance, rode a company of men, shields flashing in the sunlight. Tanford's men were after them!

Stephen shouted, and they all spurred their horses faster. A great pain ripped through Aline's abdomen. She dropped the reins, crying out, and doubled over. James dropped back and reached down to scoop up her reins. Aline grabbed her saddle and held on for dear life as James led her horse. They thundered along the road. Behind them, ever closer, came the sound of the horsemen following them.

Norwen was waiting for them ahead somewhere, Aline knew. Stephen had sent him word of their plan and arranged for him to meet them with his troops. Stephen's own men had been sent to augment the Earl's forces. But the problem would be whether they could reach the Earl before Tanford's troops swooped down on them.

Another pain gripped Aline, and she held on tightly, her face beaded in sweat. Suddenly she felt a gush of warmth between her legs, wetting her skirts, and she knew that her water had broken. She was in labor. She let out a cry of despair and pain. It would be impossible for her to make it. She could not hold on long.

Then James's arm was around her, lifting her from her horse and onto his, settling her in front of him as he had done so long ago. Aline cried out in protest, knowing that, carrying a double weight, they would fall behind the others. They were, in fact, already a good distance behind them. Stephen looked back, and James waved him ahead.

"Go on! Lead them off!"

Before Stephen could protest, James turned his horse's head, and they sailed over a low stone wall and into the field beyond. Aline cried out in pain as they came down jarringly, and James clutched her more tightly. "I am sorry, love," he said in a low voice. "But we cannot stop just yet."

They cut across the field, heading toward a group of huts in the distance. Aline clung to James's monk's robe, struggling not to scream as stab after stab of pain racked her body. The contractions had been growing in strength and number all through the ride, but now, since her water had broken, it seemed as if they no longer stopped, only lessened for a moment, then rose again in a storm of pain. The horse bounced her unmercifully; she sobbed into James's robe, praying only that she might die quickly.

Behind them she heard a rising ululation, as some of Tanford's men took out across the fields after her and James. In the distance she heard Stephen shouting, "Á moi! Á moi! For God and Beaufort!"

Then, miraculously, there came an answering bellow: "For Norwen."

Aline glanced up, so startled that she did not feel the pain for a moment. Across the crest of the hill came a wave of horsemen. They charged, pennants flying, the sun glinting off their armor. And in the center rode a huge man, arm upraised, brandishing a long sword that glittered in the sunlight. He rode like a madman, outdistancing all those around him, and as he rode, he bellowed, "Á Norwen!"

James thrust his arm up in the air, fist clenched, shouting, "Á Norwen!"

Straight toward the approaching soldiers, James spurred his horse forward. Aline wrapped her arms tightly around his waist and held on, praying that they would reach the men in time. James laughed as they rode, the cool air caressing his injured face. Behind them the voices of their followers stilled. Then Aline heard the sound of hooves running madly in the opposite direction. Aline raised her head and peeked over James's shoulder. Tanford's forces were in full flight.

"James! They're running!"

James pulled to a stop and turned to look back. He

laughed. "They'll never make it. Richard will cut them down like wheat." Despite the pain in his cheeks, he grinned hugely.

The line of Norwen's men thundered down upon the two of them, parting and sweeping around them like water around a rock. Aline thrilled to the power and majesty of their charge. Then a ferocious pain split her abdomen, and she doubled up, forgetting about Norwen and the battle, about everything except the babe inside her that was suddenly desperate to get out.

She groaned. James looked down at her, and the elation of their escape drained out of him as terror rushed in to take its place. Aline was going to give birth, and he was alone in this field with her.

"Oh, God."

"James, help me," Aline whispered. "Please help me."

His worst nightmares flooded in on him. He knew with a cold certainty that Aline would die in his arms, that the babe his lust had planted in her would kill her. He had faced Tanford and his tortures with courage, but now he was weak with fear.

Aline groaned as another stab of pain slashed through her, spurring James out of his momentary paralysis. He could not sit here like a fool and do nothing while his wife suffered! He swung off his horse and lifted Aline down. Picking her up in his arms, he strode toward the shelter of the huts in the field.

There was no one inside the huts; their occupants had all wisely fled at the approach of the two armies. James laid Aline down on a pile of blankets next to the wall. The place was filthy; it was the one thing he knew Aunt Marguerite despised in a birthing place, but there was little he could do about it. At least

Aline was out of the wind and cold. There was even a banked fire in the center of the hut, its smoke curling up to the hole in the thatched roof.

He took Aline's hands, and her fingers dug into his so fiercely that her nails cut his skin. He didn't even notice. His entire attention was fixed on Aline's pale, sweating face, contorted with pain. Finally, her contraction subsided, and she lay panting.

"What should I do? I know not."

"Nor do I," Aline gasped. "But I think it matters not. This babe will come, no matter what is done or not done."

She groaned as another contraction seized her, and her hands clenched around his. He waited, while in the distance came the sounds of swords clashing, horses screaming, men shouting.

"If this," said a panting Aline during the brief respite between contractions, "is not just like your child, to be born in the midst of a battle!"

James smiled. He was still anxious, but the terror was gone. He was here, and he would help Aline, and she would not die. He would not let her die.

"And if it is not just like my wife," he shot back, "to decide to give birth with men fighting all around."

There was a sound of footsteps outside, and James whirled, his hand going to his only weapon, the long dagger Stephen had given him and which he had secured to his arm inside the friar's long sleeve. Gemma's face appeared at the low doorway, sweating and anxious.

"Is she all right? What has happened?"

"She gives birth!" James snapped. "What do you think is happening?"

Gemma quickly crossed herself and moved uneasily into the hut.

"Here, come help her," James went on, but Gemma shook her head, staring at Aline with big eyes.

"I don't know how. I never had any babies myself. And no one ever wanted me around at a birth. They were afraid I would taint the baby."

James swore and turned back to Aline. "Hold on, dearling, hold on. It will come."

Aline nodded, reassured by his voice even in the midst of her pain.

"Where are the others? Do any of them know anything?" James asked desperately.

"Them?" Gemma sneered. "What would they know? They are all men. Anyway, Stephen and Humphrey donned their armor and rode out to join in the fight. Harald's outside, but he knows not, I'll warrant."

"Then run and find a woman who has had children," James ordered. "There must be women who live here. They have but gone into hiding. Get them back."

"James!" Aline cried out, and he whirled around.

"What? What is it?"

"I think it's coming. James, I can't—I have to—" Her face contorted, and she jackknifed her knees, digging her heels into the blankets. She groaned, pushing.

And so it was that while the battle raged beyond them, James delivered his own son into the world. The boy was a purple thing, slick with blood and curled up tightly and for a terrifying moment, as still as death. But James hooked his forefinger into the babe's mouth and cleared it, and then the little purple scrap of flesh began to squall loudly, arms and legs pumping.

James wiped the rest of the blood from him, tearing a strip of cloth from Aline's bliaut, which seemed cleaner than anything else around. He wrapped him up in another strip and carried him to Aline's arms.

She reached for him, pale, but smiling and eager. James bent down and kissed Aline on the forehead, then knelt beside her, gazing down at his wife and son. He had never felt such pride and joy.

"I love you," he told her tenderly. "Stephen was right. It was pride that held me back. I didn't listen to you, only to my own hurt. When you came into that keep to rescue me, risking your own life to get me away from Tanford, I knew what a fool I had been. I want no wife but you, no children but yours."

Aline reached up and smoothed her hand over his cheek. "But what about the wife you wanted? The noble wife who would give you fine heirs?"

"I could have no finer heirs than this one right here," he started, his voice undeniably rich with pride. "And I was simply too foolish before to know the wife I *needed*."

"But what about the gossip? The rumors? It will shame you to have one such as me for a wife."

"I am proud to have you for a wife," he retorted fiercely. "There was never any lady nobly born who was braver or more clever or more beautiful than you. You are all I want, all I will ever want. Let them talk. What does it matter? I am a bastard, but that is not the sum of me. Nor is your birth the sum of you. I have spent far too long brooding over the harm of my birth. And why? I have a family—a brother who comes to fight for me, a wife who loves me, and now a son. What more could I want from life?" He shook his head. "There is nothing more. You are all in all to me."

"James!" Aline sat up and curled an arm around his neck. His arms went around her, holding her and the baby close to him. "I love you. I love you!"

"And I love you." He smoothed his hand up and

down her back. "And as soon as you are well, we will go home. To Chaswyck Keep."

"Yes," Aline agreed. "I would like that."

"Good." He laid her gently back down upon the blankets. "Then sleep, my love. I will be here beside you."

Aline's eyes fluttered closed wearily. "Do you promise?" she murmured.

"I promise," he replied, settling down beside her. "Always. I will be with you always."

Epilogue

James leaned back contentedly in his chair, waiting for his wife. It was spring now, and all around Chaswyck Keep life was springing up: the trees were budding and the first few hardy flowers beginning to bloom; the ewes were lambing, and foals tottered around the field on their spindly legs, looking both foolish and somehow graceful. It was a pleasant time, and he was most content.

His wounds were long since healed. However, he was not quite as handsome a man as he had once been. There were scars on his body where Tanford had burned him and a thick scar across his forehead that cut down through an eyebrow. His nose had been broken as well, and had not healed perfectly straight. But James rather preferred not carrying the burden of being perfectly handsome, and Aline seemed not to mind the changes. She told him quite seriously that she thought he looked even better now, like a mature, handsome man instead of a pretty boy. James simply laughed and told her he hadn't been a boy for years, but somehow her words warmed him, whether they were true or not. The important truth lay in the fact that Aline thought so.

The day James's son was born, Richard had beaten Tanford's men soundly in a battle in which Stephen had won his knight's spurs. Norwen had chased them all the way back to Tanford Hall. They had closed the gates against him—and their own men—and Richard had been furious that he had not been able to drag the Duke out and kill him. He had laid siege to the castle, but it was well defended and had held out for several months before King Henry, who hated fighting among his nobles, intervened. The king had censured Tanford, ordering him never to return to Court, and had taken several of Tanford's properties as forfeit for his unlawful actions; one of them he gave to James. His defeat had driven the Duke utterly mad. His daughter and her husband now ruled in his stead, and it was said that the Duke was locked up in one of the towers of Tanford Hall, where he alternately raged and whimpered, his mind completely gone. James thought it an even more fitting retribution, perhaps, than if Richard had slaughtered him.

James and Aline's babe, though he had been early and small, had had a lusty will to live, and had survived the winter, growing daily bigger and stronger. They had named him Henry, after both the king and James and Richard's father, and he was the delight of his grandmothers'—and everyone else's—eye. He was sleeping soundly down the hall right now, his nurse on a pallet by his side.

And James was looking forward to a night with his wife.

He wasn't sure why Aline had hidden herself behind the screen to change into her nightclothes, but he was sure he would find out—and equally sure it would be a delightful discovery. Aline was an eager and inventive lover, and motherhood had not diminished her passion. Certainly, James's desire for Aline had not lessened a bit. If anything, he thought it grew with each passing day.

"What are you doing back there?" he asked, smiling.

"Just be patient," Aline answered. "You shall find out. I have sewn a garment which I think you will like to see."

"I would rather see you without any garment at all."

Aline chuckled throatily, and James's loins stirred at the sound. He thought about lying in bed with her, her hair, once more red, spilling over him. He shifted restlessly in his chair.

Then Aline came out from behind the screen. She stopped for effect, posing. James's mouth dropped open, and his eyes traveled slowly down her body, from head to toe.

She was dressed as a Saracen dancing girl, with bright tattered scarves for a skirt, all sewn to a belt of chains and bells that jingled with her every movement. A thin veil lay over her hair, and another was drawn across the lower part of her face, revealing her great, alluring, golden eyes. More veils were wrapped around her torso, cleverly concealing her breasts, yet revealing the rosy hint of her nipples beneath them. Her stomach was bare, and an emerald winked in her navel.

James was immediately, compellingly hard. He remembered the night he had covered her with jewels, placing the emerald in her navel like that, and his veins turned to rivers of fire. He remembered, too, the first time he had seen Aline, and though the memory was a little hazy, he could recall quite well the flash of her tanned legs and the sweet jiggle of her hips.

He started to stand, but Aline motioned him back down. "No. Sit. I am going to dance for you."

James did as she said, the air rasping through his lips. Aline began to move her hips, slowly, seductively. She moved forward, her arms swaying gracefully, her feet shuffling in slow rhythm. He watched the play of her muscles beneath the bare skin of her stomach; the jewel glittered.

She danced only for James, her eyes locked on his, every movement subtly seducing him. Slowly, one by one, she began to remove her veils, until finally she was down to only one thin veil wrapped around her breasts, her nipples pointed and dark against it, and a few still sewn to her belt. Her hips churned faster. She swirled, her skirt whipping out around her and revealing her slim legs.

Aline dropped at his feet, panting, her dance ended. She raised her head and looked up at him. James's eyes glittered ferally.

"Did you like my present?" she asked, smiling.

He smiled back, standing and reaching down to pull her up. "Yes." His hands slid possessively down her lithe body.

"And shall I dance for you again?"

"Yes. Only for me."

"But of course." Passion shimmered in her golden eyes. "Everything I have is only for you. I love you."

"And I love you." James gazed down into her eyes, caught by her spell. Then he bent and swooped her up in his arms and carried her to their bed.

Evensong by Candace Camp

A tale of love and deception in medieval England from the incomparable Candace Camp. When Aline was offered a fortune to impersonate a noble lady, the beautiful dancing girl thought it worth the risk. Then, in the arms of the handsome knight she was to deceive, she realized she chanced not just her life, but her heart.

Once Upon a Pirate by Nancy Block

When Zoe Dunham inadvertently plunged into the past, landing on the deck of a pirate ship, she thought her ex-husband had finally gone insane and kidnapped her under the persona of his infamous pirate ancestor, to whom she bore a strong resemblance. But sexy Black Jack Alexander was all too real, and Zoe would have to come to terms with the heartbreak of her divorce *and* her curious romp through time.

Angel's Aura by Brenda Jernigan

In the sleepy town of Martinsboro, North Carolina, local health club hunk Manly Richards turns up dead, and all fingers point to Angel Larue, the married muscleman's latest love-on-the-side. Of course, housewife and part-time reporter Barbara Upchurch knows her sister is no killer, but she must convince the police of Angel's innocence while the real culprit is out there making sure Barbara's snooping days are numbered!

The Lost Goddess by Patricia Simpson

Cursed by an ancient Egyptian cult, Asheris was doomed to immortal torment until Karissa's fiery desire freed him. Now they must put their love to the ultimate test and challenge dark forces to save the life of their young daughter Julia. A spellbinding novel from "one of the premier writers of supernatural romance." —*Romantic Times*

Fire and Water by Mary Spencer

On the run in the Sierra Nevadas, Mariette Call tried to figure out why her murdered husband's journals were so important to a politician back East. Along the way she and dashing Federal Marshal Matthew Kagan, sent to protect her, managed to elude their pursuers and also discovered a deep passion for each other.

Hearts of the Storm by Pamela Willis

Josie Campbell could put a bullet through a man's hat at a hundred yards with as much skill as she could nurse a fugitive slave baby back to health. She vowed never to belong to any man—until magnetic Clint McCarter rode into town. But the black clouds of the Civil War were gathering, and there was little time for love unless Clint and Josie could find happiness at the heart of the storm.

Glory in the Splendor of Summer with
101 Days of Romance

BUY 3 BOOKS —
GET 1 FREE!

Take a book to the beach, relax by the pool, or read in the most quiet and romantic spot in your home. You can live through love all summer long when you redeem this exciting offer from HarperMonogram.

Buy any three HarperMonogram romances in June, July, or August, and get a fourth book sent to you FREE!

Look for details of this exciting promotion in the back of each HarperMonogram published from June through August—and fall in love again and again this summer!